T0354539

HEAD ON

Books by Jerry Banks

—ᴀ—

Barry O'Shea Fiction

The Lukarilla Affair
Secret Agenda
Second District
Vital to the Defense
Head On

Non Fiction

Five Decades in Court
The UC

HEAD ON

JERRY BANKS

ISBN: 978-1-4669-4071-0 (sc)
ISBN: 978-1-4669-4072-7 (e)

Trafford rev. 06/07/2012

 www.trafford.com

North America & international
toll-free: 1 888 232 4444 (USA & Canada)
phone: 250 383 6864 ♦ fax: 812 355 4082

ACKNOWLEDGEMENT

Many thank you's to Lisa Keller for editing and rewriting this novel. It was edited several times before, but she put the finishing touches on the story that made it what it is. Thanks again, Lisa.

1

ON TUESDAY, MAY twenty-ninth, 1973 the Oregon Coast was experiencing an unusual heat-wave. The dry sand on the beach in front of the Ocean House sizzled. The sun shown down on it as it had on Memorial Day, the day before. It had been a wonderful holiday weekend; for once the weather cooperated. At three o'clock a boy and a girl waded in the shallow water, the waves of the ocean climbing up their legs as they came to rest on the shore. A younger boy dug playfully in the wet sand. A small thin woman stood close by in a red swimming suit that highlighted her cute figure. She smiled, as the wind blew her long brown hair, and her green eyes kept close track of the children playing in the water.

A lean tan man closed on them, walking through the dry sand in loafers, the wind blowing his heavy black hair. He wore a loose, green-striped sport shirt and tan shorts. As he reached the wet sand, he approached the woman. "Amy," he shouted, "its time to gather up the kids."

At the sound of his voice, the woman turned to greet him. Her green eyes glistened when she took his hand. "Oh, Michael, this weekend has been so much fun. I hate to go."

He looked into her eyes. "I know darling, but I've got to get back to work tomorrow, and the kids have school."

Amy turned and looked at the boy and girl. Michelle, the girl at ten, mirrored her father, tall for her age, thin and thick black

1

hair. The seven year old boy, Bruce, on the other hand, favored his mother's looks with cute features, green eyes and brown hair. "Come on you two. You heard your father. It's time to go back to the hotel and get ready to go home." She reached down, took the five year old, Dustin's, hand and pulled him up.

"Can't we stay a little longer?" Michelle pleaded.

"Yeah, just one more wave," Bruce chimed in.

Michael looked at them sternly and held out his hand. "No. Come on right now."

Bruce lowered his head. "Oh, all right," he said as he waded toward his father.

Michelle, seeing the determination on her father face, followed her brother, put on her flip-flops when she reached the shore, grasped her father's outstretched hand and began walking with him back through the hot dry sand toward the hotel. Amy still holding Dustin's hand walked beside Michael. Bruce also donned his flip-flops and followed behind, still with his head down.

The family was the Ralston's. They lived in Portland and had driven down to Gearhart by the Sea on Friday to spend the Memorial Day holiday at the beach. Michael Ralston at thirty-seven had been an accountant at one of the national firms for fifteen years and had just reached junior partner status. Amy Ralston turned thirty-three earlier in the month and took care of the home and children. The children attended Chapman Grade School, Michelle in the fifth grade, Bruce in the second grade, and Dustin in kindergarten.

The hotel stood on a hill where the sand of the beach began and overlooked the ocean. A four-story wooden structure, it had a large veranda off the first floor on the ocean side with a central stairway leading down to the sand.

When the Ralston's reached the hotel, they went up the stairway onto the veranda. Inside the hotel they took the stairway to the second floor, where they entered their two-bedroom suite on the ocean side of the hotel. They had packed their suitcases after lunch before going down on the beach. All that was left to do were showers for Amy and the children. While they showered and got dressed, Michael began taking the suitcases down the stairs and out to the parking lot where he packed them into their vehicle.

Their vehicle was an early van called a Caravan. It had a rectangular body with the front seats located over the front axle, facing a vertical windshield, installed above and directly behind the front bumper. Michael had purchased it new six years ago when its German manufacture, Warner Carriage International (WCI), introduced it into the American market. Now several American manufacturers had produced similar vehicles to keep pace.

As he loaded the last of the suitcases, Michael noticed Amy and the children emerge from the hotel onto the small porch. All dressed in bright colored shirts and shorts, they made him proud, so proud that he decided to take their picture. Before they could proceed down the stairs, he grabbed his camera from the front seat on the van and held his hand up at them. "Hold it there. I want one final picture."

Amy gathered the children around her on the stairs.

Michael pointed the camera at them. "That's perfect. Give me a great big smile." He clicked the camera.

"Michael, you come up with the kids and let me take one," Amy said. He passed her on the stairs, gave her the camera and gathered the children around him.

Amy lifted the camera. "Everyone smile." And she took the picture.

Michael took Bruce and Dustin's hands and led them down the stairs. Michelle followed behind. Amy got into the front seat of the Caravan. Michael opened the back door, and Dustin got in and climbed back to one of the third row seats. Michelle and Bruce sat in the second row seats, Bruce behind his father and Michelle behind her mother. Michael sat in the driver's seat, started the Caravan and at ten minutes after four the Ralston's left for Portland.

—m—

At a cattle yard just off I5 in North Portland, a heavy set, middle age man, dressed in faded-denim coveralls and a blue striped cap, loaded two Holstein cows in a small cattle trailer attached to a black pickup. His name was Lyle Bentwood, and he worked for a dairy just south of Seaside on US 101. He had come to Portland earlier that Tuesday to pick up the cows. His employer purchased the vehicle, a used 1970 Monarch pickup, a month earlier form Jorgensen Motors in Seaside.

The yardman helping Bentwood stared one more time at the animals. "You got yourself a couple of fine Holsteins there."

Bentwood smiled. "Yep, my boss is going to be real pleased."

"Can I pour you a cup of coffee before you get on the way?" the yardman asked.

"No thanks, I better get going. It's nearly four, and I've got a couple of hours of driving to do."

Bentwood closed the gate on the trailer and secured it firmly. Then he got into the pickup, started it and drove out of the stockyard onto I5 heading for Portland. The sun shown brightly, so he had his dark glasses on, and he drove with the driver's window open and his left arm resting on the sill. When he reached Portland, he took the Sunset Highway (US 26) turn off and proceeded to the coast.

As Bentwood drove west through the valley lands west of Portland, he had the sun visor down as the sun was low in the sky. As he approached the foothills of the Coast Range, the sun fell behind the mountains, although there remained several hours before actual sunset. Just before heading up into the mountains, he stopped for gas at a small service station on the right side of the road.

The attendant started filling the tank. While the tank was filling, the attendant came to the driver's side window. "You want the water and oil checked?" he asked.

Bentwood had just changed his glasses from the dark ones he had been using to his normal distance glasses. He turned and looked at the attendant. "Yeah, that's a good idea and would you wash the windshield too?"

The attendant raised the hood, checked the water and oil. "Their fine," he said, closing the hood. By the time that the attendant had washed the windshield, the gas pump clicked signaling a full tank. The attendant took the nozzle out of the filler pipe, returned it to the pump and came back to the driver's window.

Bentwood handed him a credit card. The attendant took it and went inside the office. A few moments later the attendant returned with the credit card attached to a clip board. He gave the board to Bentwood. "Could I have your John Henry?" he asked.

Bentwood retrieved his credit card, signed the receipt on the clip board, and left.

Driving through the mountains, Bentwood admired the scenery. With Memorial Day past he encountered little traffic. At about five-fifteen he reached the summit before Jewell Junction and drove downhill easing his speed to about fifty mph. As he proceeded down the straight stretch east of the Junction, he saw a small piece of wood in the road ahead. He said to himself, *I better not swerve to miss it with the cattle trailer behind.* He drove over the wood, and the front of the pickup came down with a jar. Suddenly, he heard something smash into the windshield, blinding him and spraying him with small pieces of glass. With no vision ahead, he quickly jammed on the brakes, and the pickup began weaving from side to side.

The Ralston's headed south down US 101 to the Cannon Beach Junction and then headed east on the Sunset Highway across the flat coastal lands just west of the Coast Range. It was about five o'clock when they began climbing the mountains.

With the sun low in the sky behind them, Amy admired the scenery. "I just love the mountains and the trees this time of the evening."

Michael looked at her briefly and smiled. "I only hope they appreciate the lovely lady that's admiring them."

Amy smiled at him and poked his shoulder lightly. "Darling, I never tire of your compliments."

Further up the road, Bruce pointed out at the several businesses on the right side of the road. "Daddy, what's this place called?"

"Elsie's its name, but there's not much to it, just that restaurant and a couple of other buildings," Michael replied.

Michelle eyed a car parked, faced in to the restaurant. "There's Montana. I don't think we have that one, do we Mommy?"

Amy took a list of states out of the glove compartment and studied it. "No, we don't. I'll add it."

In a few minutes the Caravan rounded a corner going about fifty-five miles per hour, crossed the bridge at Jewell Junction and started up the hill on the long straight stretch.

Suddenly Amy screamed. "Michael, look out that pickup's . . . !"

A terrible explosion interrupted her.

The front of the pickup collided with the left front of the Caravan. The pickup drove into the Caravan, through the driver's seat and into the second row of seats. The Caravan turned right slightly before impact, and the force of the pickup pushed it further to the right toward the shoulder. The trailer jack-knifed to the right, pulled violently at the rear of the pickup and finally broke loose, traveling backward until it went off the north side of the road, down an embankment and crashed into a tree, coming to rest on its left side. The trailer's action pulled the pickup back from the Caravan and over onto its right side where it slid some feet before coming to rest on the highway.

Horrible sounds continued until the vehicles came to rest. A large cloud of dust followed, along with the sound of metal parts settling on the pavement and the shoulder of the road. Then silence. Very soon several other vehicles, approaching from the east and west, stopped, and people got out and rushed to the accident vehicles. Someone at the Elderberry Inn just east of the accident scene called for help and before long a state police car and a forest service fire truck arrived.

The police car came from the west and parked on the shoulder west of the scene. Two patrolmen emerged from the car and ran to the vehicles. One, a sergeant, appeared tall and muscular and had a thin brown mustache under his wide-brimmed hat. The other, also wearing a wide-brimmed hat, was shorter, stockier and square-jawed.

Two firemen also ran to the vehicles and searched for accident victims. They found them trapped inside the vehicles. They used their tools attempting to pry open the doors of the van. One of the policemen, the shorter one, reached through the side window of the pickup and tried to arouse the driver without success.

The sergeant talked to the people at the scene. "Did any of you witness what happened?"

"I was just coming out of the corner up east of here," one man said, "when I heard the crash and saw what looked like one vehicle climbing over the other."

"I was coming east and was the first vehicle on the scene," another man said. "The collision had already occurred; the vehicles had come to rest and the dust was settling."

"Has anyone checked the vehicles for survivors?"

"We did," said a man, pointing to another man. "We went to the driver's side of the pickup, what left of it. We saw the driver, bleeding and pinned inside, unconscious, I think. I tried the door but couldn't budge it. The hood was against the windshield. Those guys went to the other vehicle." He pointed at two men and a woman, crying.

One of the men spoke up. "When we got to what looked like a van, we tried to look inside." He shook his head, his eyes watered. "It appeared, it appeared that the pickup just drove through the driver's side and into the back seat behind the driver," he stammered. He paused, obviously shaken. Then he regained some composure. "We saw a woman on the passenger's side and two children in the back on the right side. One of the children, a small boy, was crying. I tried the doors, but I couldn't move them. The woman and the other girl weren't moving. They were covered with blood. About then, the firemen arrived and started working to open the doors."

The sergeant looked at the van and saw the fireman prying at the doors on the right side. He went quickly back to the patrol car and grabbed the radio. "We're going to need back-up and ambulances as soon as possible."

"Two patrol cars are already on the way," the dispatch answered. "A rescue truck left the fire station near Elsie minutes ago. They should be arriving at the scene now. Two more have just been dispatched from the station in Vernonia as we speak."

Just as the sergeant put the radio receiver back, the patrol cars and the rescue vehicle arrived, and two paramedics emerged with cases in their hands. The sergeant and the medics ran to the vehicles. The fireman had just freed the back door of the van, and the medics went to work try to get the little boy and the girl out.

The boy cried uncontrollably.

One of the removed the unconscious girl, laid her on a stretcher, and covered her with a blanket. He then pulled her seat forward. The other medic then removed the little boy, seeing a huge cut in his leg.

The boy sobbed. "Mommy, mommy!" he cried.

The medic put him on a blanket outside the vehicle and worked to stop the bleeding. Once the bleeding was under control, he noticed a usual position of one of his arms. He examined it. "It looks like his arm is broken." While the boy continued to cry, the medic neutralized it.

Meanwhile, the medic who had removed the girl attended to her on the stretcher. She bled from a gash on her forehead, and more blood came from somewhere under her shirt. A patrolman helped him with the stretcher. They put her in one of the rescue vehicles. The medic stayed in the rescue vehicle attending to the girl.

The rescue vehicles from Vernonia had now arrived, adding four more medics to the rescue workers. Two of them ran to the van, where a fireman was trying to free the door to the front passenger. One of the medics relieved the medic who attended the boy. The door finally opened, and the new medic and the one that had been with the boy removed the unconscious woman and laid her on a stretcher. They carried the stretcher to the same rescue vehicle holding the girl and placed it inside.

The medic, who was first on the scene, stayed the woman, attending to her, joining his partner with the girl. The driver of the rescue vehicle called a helicopter. "Tell the chopper to land at the Timber and Vernonia Junction east of here. We'll make the transfer there."

The driver started the vehicle and sped away from the accident scene.

One of the firemen had been examining what was left of the left front of the van where the pickup had encroached. "Come here quick," he shouted. "I found the driver of the van."

The police officer and a medic rushed to the fireman's side and looked. "Oh my God," the police officer exclaimed. "He's nearly decapitated."

The fireman pointed to the indentation made by the front wheel of the pickup. "Look what's under there."

The police officer and medic looked. The medic put his hand on his forehead, closed his eyes, and shook his head. "Good Lord, the poor kid was literally run over."

"Is he still alive?" the police officer asked.

The medic leaned in and placed his hand on the boy. "No, and I don't think he knew a thing after the collision."

While all this was going on, two of the Vernonia medics tried unsuccessfully to reach the unconscious driver of the pickup who was pinned under the steering wheel by crushed metal. The vehicle rested on its right side, and the medics couldn't open the right door. They got one of the other firemen to help. The fireman, with the assistance of one of the two tow-trucks that were now on the scene, got the pickup righted. When they had it back on its wheel the fireman, went to work on the driver's door. It was frozen shut. The fireman got the jaw-of-life and, with the help of medics, ripped the door off.

One of the medics jumped in the vehicle and examined the unconscious driver. He yelled out at his partner. "He's alive, but barely, and his left leg is pinned under the dash. We'll need another helicopter when we get him out. Have the chopper meet us at the Vernonia-Timber Junction."

They worked for some time before they finally freed the leg. One of the medics looked at it. "God, it's a mess. I don't know if we can save it."

They removed the driver, got him in one of the remaining rescue vehicles and took off to the east.

Another rescue vehicle took the little boy to the hospital in Portland where the helicopter had taken the mother and sister.

The police officers from Vernonia directed the stalled traffic around the accident scene one direction at a time using the west bound lane and its shoulder.

The sergeant and his partner now busily inspected the scene. They noticed the skid marks left when the jack-knifed trailer pulled the pickup away from the van and the mark left when the trailer left the highway. Following the marks, they discovered the trailer north of the highway heavily damaged on its side down the embankment.

They climbed down the embankment and examined the trailer. The sergeant went to the rear, worked at the latch, and finally pulled the door open. "Look what we have here," he said. "Two dead cows."

The officers climbed back up on the road and continued examining the marks on the road. The sergeant pointed to several short black skid marks crossing the road at an angle. "Here's where the pickup driver set his brakes."

The other officer pointed to the pavement in the east bound lane. "That's right and you can see the point of impact here where the severe gouging of the pavement in the east bound lane meets the end of the skid marks."

"That must be where the trailer jack-knifed," the sergeant said, "because these marks going west take off here, indicating the trailer pulled the pickup away from the van before it broke away and went over the embankment to the north."

They measured the skid marks and photograph them and the gouge marks in the pavement.

Then they examined the vehicles. The sergeant looked at the hood of the pickup back against the broken windshield. "It looked like the hood flew open and back against the windshield, blinding the driver. I'll bet that's why he crossed the centerline."

They measured the vehicles as best they could front to back and side to side. They took extensive photographs of the van in its position when they got to the scene. They also photographed the pickup on its side before the tow-truck right it and photographed the pickup after being righted.

About this time a television crew from Portland came on the scene. The reporter interviewed the sergeant in front of the camera.

While this was going on, the other patrolman from the first patrol car on the scene walked back to the east about a quarter of a mile, inspecting the road. He noticed a small log in the westbound lane. He came back as the reporter finished interviewing the sergeant. He took the sergeant aside. "I found a small log up there on the road. If the pickup ran over it, it might be just what jostled the hood loose. I know the log may have been move by other vehicles after the pickup ran over it, but let's measure from the log to the start of the skid marks anyway." They did, and they took the log with them.

While the scene was being investigated, a medical examiner from Portland arrived. He got out of his hearse and walked up to the two patrolmen inspecting the scene. "I'm told there are fatalities. Where will I find them?"

The sergeant pointed. "Over there in that vehicle partially on the shoulder. They're on the left side."

The medical examiner and his assistant went over to the van. The medical examiner spoke to a tow-truck driver standing by the van. The tow-truck driver pointed to the body of the van's driver.

The medical examiner saw the partially severed head, but knelt down and felt the driver's pulse anyway. He turned his head and looked up at the tow-truck driver. "How did this happen, do you know?"

The tow-truck driver pointed to the pickup. "I think that pickup crashed into him and through him."

"That would explain what I'm seeing."

The medical examiner still on his knees next examined the body of the boy back of and partially under the driver's badly crushed body. He saw the imprint of a wheel across the body. He looked up at the tow-truck driver. "And that would explain what I see here as well. They're both dead. Could you give us a hand in removing the bodies?"

When the officers finished their investigation and the medical examiner had the bodies of the deceased loaded into the hearse, the tow-truck drivers began loading the vehicles on low-boys. They took the vehicles to a police wrecking yard near Aloha west of Portland and secured them to be examined again later.

At ten o'clock that same night, the state police sergeant knocked at the front door of a small two-story red frame farmhouse on a hill east of US 101 south of Seaside. The farmhouse was one of several buildings on the hill, including a large red barn with white letters on its side reading: Towson Dairy.

The house was dark except for a light somewhere in the rear. After a second knock, a light came on inside the front of the house followed by another light outside on the porch. The door opened, revealing a large man in his sixties with wiry grey hair and sunken blue eyes, dressed in an old faded blue bathrobe and slippers. The man looked at the sergeant. "Yes," he said.

The sergeant took off his wide-brimmed hat. "Are you Elmer Towson?"

"Yes, I am. What's the trouble?"

"There's been a bad accident on US 26 east of Elsie, involving a truck registered to you pulling a cattle trailer." The sergeant went on to tell Towson the details of the accident, including the two deaths in the van. "Your driver was unconscious, badly injured and airlifted to a hospital in Portland. Do you know if he had family in the area?"

"No, he doesn't," Towson said. "He's single. He's been with us for four years and lives with two other employees in our bunkhouse."

"How old is he?"

"Forty-five, I think. Had he been drinking?"

"We saw no evidence of it. Does he have a drinking problem?"

"No, not that I know of, although he does have a drink now and then when he's not working."

The sergeant reached inside a pocket of his uniform and pulled out a pad and a pencil. He wrote something on the pad, tore a page from it and gave it to Towson. "Here's the name, address and phone number of the hospital where the helicopter took him. I don't know if he'd regained consciousness when he got there."

"Thank you, I'll call right away.

The sergeant stepped back, put on his hat, turned around and walked back to his car. Towson closed the door.

Inside the house as he walked through the living room, his wife called out from somewhere in the rear of the house. "Elmer, who was at the front door?"

"A state patrolman. Lyle's been in a terrible accident. I'm calling the hospital right now."

At a table at the far end of the living room he picked up a telephone, looked at the note the sergeant gave him, and dialed.

"Emanuel Hospital," an operator answered. "How may I direct your call?"

Towson told her what he knew about Bentwood being airlifted to the hospital. "I'm calling to check on his condition."

"Would you please hold and I'll check?"

After what seemed a long wait, a man came on the line. "I'm Doctor Shirley. I understand you are calling about Lyle Bentwood?"

Towson explained who he was and that Bentwood was an employee.

"Well, he's regained consciousness, but he's in the operating room now. He has serious internal injuries, and we don't know if we can save his leg. I suggest you call back in the morning. We'll know more then."

Towson hung up and immediately dialed his insurance agent at the agent's home.

2

THE NEXT DAY in Portland at six-thirty in the morning Barry O'Shea sat at the breakfast table in his kitchen drinking a small glass of orange juice and watching the news on a small portable TV. His usual breakfast, a bowl of Rice Krispies rested on the table.

The morning anchor reported on a bad fatal accident that happened the evening before on the Sunset Highway west of Portland. The news report grabbed Barry's attention because the accident involved a Monarch pickup and a WCI van, both vehicles manufactured by clients represented by Barry and his law firm.

Barry looked away from the TV and toward his wife, Sarah, who stood in front of the sink, washing a melon. "Sarah, honey, come look at the TV. They're reporting on a fatal accident between a Monarch pickup and a WCI van last night on the road to the beach."

Sarah came over to the table just as the camera panned the vehicles at rest at the accident scene. "Wow, what a mess. Was anyone killed?"

"Apparently two people, a father and his son."

"How horrible."

"When we get to the office, put in a call for Steve Hinkley at Monarch. When I'm done talking with him, get me Verner Schultz at WCI."

Sarah gave him a wry smile. "Always true to the American client first."

Barry shook his head. "You know that's not the case. I've done Monarch's work for almost ten years, and WCI has only been a client two years. I owe it to Monarch to talk to them first. If it turns out there's no conflict, WCI's entitled to our representation too."

Barry and Sarah lived in a two-story English Tudor house in an area know as Portland Heights. They bought the house because it was close to downtown where they both worked, Barry as a lawyer and Sarah as his legal secretary, at the law firm of *Swift, Wyman & Wiggens*.

Barry joined the firm in the late fifties and had practice trial law ever since. Now in his early forties, he headed the firm's trial department. His tall thin frame, sandy short hair and fair complexion made quite an impression on juries, in spite of the fact that he always wore steel rimmed glasses.

Sarah had been with the firm two years longer, as the secretary for the senior partner, Elmer Wiggens. When Barry joined the firm, he worked closely with Wiggens, and Wiggens made Sarah Barry's secretary as well. Freckle-faced and tall with a trim figure and brown hair, Sarah was bright and enthusiastic. In spite of her parent's wishes, she quite college, went to a local business school and became a legal secretary. She loved the law and the challenges it offered.

After two years of working together, Barry began to realize that there was more to his relationship with Sarah than business. She had the same feeling, and soon they became lovers. They married in 1963.

Swift, Wyman & Wiggens occupied the fifteenth floor of a new downtown office building. Barry and Sarah arrived there at seven-thirty. Barry had the northwest corner office, and Sarah's desk sat right outside his door. They walked down the hall together, Barry going directly into his office and Sarah sitting at her desk and placing a call to Detroit.

Barry sat down at his large maple desk in his tan leather chair. He leaned back, looked out the windows and contemplated the accident. The windows of his office looked north at another modern office building across the street and east over the Willamette River, several blocks away, toward the residential east side of Portland and the Cascade Mountains in the distance. His desk faced east and in front of the east facing windows sat a tan leather couch with a butler table in front of it. Small conference table occupied the space in front of the north windows with four cushioned and straight-back chairs gathered around it. The white walls were adorned with a Japanese screen behind his desk and gold framed diplomas and certificates of admission of the practice of law and the courts on the south wall. A tan carpet covered the floor.

Sarah interrupted his thought. "I've got Mr. Hinkley on the phone."

Barry reached for the telephone on his desk. "Hi, Steve. I'm calling to report a bad accident involving one of your vehicles." Monarch had the firm on retainer to report any accident involving Monarch vehicles as soon as the firm became aware of the accident. Barry described what he had heard on the morning broadcast including the fact that someone suspected that the hood flew up on the pickup, blinding the driver and the fact that two deaths were involved. The pickup then crossed the highway and hit the van head-on. "We'll order the report from the state police. The news broadcast said the vehicles had been towed and secured at a police lot west of Portland. I'm sure the police will tell us where it's located and let us examine the vehicles."

"Good work," Hinkley said. "I'll alert our product investigation group, and, when we get the report from you, they'll be in touch to come out for an inspection. We'll try to keep a low profile, but it won't make a difference. A suit most assuredly will follow sometime."

After ending this conversation, Barry dialed the number of WCI in Aurora, Illinois.

An operator answered the telephone.

"May I speak to Verner Schultz?" Barry asked.

Schultz had been the head of WCI's litigation department for some time. He had recently received the title of Vice President.

"May I tell Mr. Schultz who is calling?"

"Tell him it's Barry O'Shea from Portland, Oregon."

"Just a moment, please."

A moment later the telephone rang and Schultz answered.

"Verner, this is Barry O'Shea in Portland."

"Oh yes, Barry. How are you?"

"Fine, but I want to report a bad accident involving one of your original Caravans." He went on to give Schultz a brief description of what he'd heard on the news broadcast. "I've already talked to Monarch. I'm getting the police report and will send you a copy. Monarch will be sending out their engineers once they've receive the report."

"Thank you for the notice. And I appreciate your prompt action in seeking the police report. After I've read it, we may be contacting you, if you see no conflict with Monarch."

The call ended.

Later that morning Monica Richards typed a report at her desk on the third floor of the Builders Exchange Building in downtown Portland. The building dated back to the twenties and occupied a half of block between Southwest Fourth Avenue on the west, Third Avenue on the east and Stark Street on the north. It had been the home of Western Indemnity Company's Portland office for more than twenty years. Western had the whole third floor with offices on the east and west sides and a long counter off the elevator lobby on the south. The rest of the floor contained desks where insurance adjusters, secretaries and support personal worked.

A secretary nearby put down her telephone and turned to Richards. "Monica, Mr. Grassley wants you in his office."

Richards finished a paragraph, got up and walked toward the office in the northwest corner. Glass windows and a door enclosed the east side of the office. A brass plaque on the door announced Clayton Grassley as the office occupant. When Richards got the office, she knocked on the open door.

The man inside turned to the open door. "Monica, come on in. Thanks for coming so promptly." He motioned to a chair next to his desk. "Have a seat. I've got an assignment you'll like, a rough one with two deaths. Our insured is the Towson Dairy in Seaside."

Richards sat and took the file Grassley passed her.

"As you can see, the file's thin. We just got the assignment, and nothings been done. All you'll see in there is the letter faxed earlier today from the agent."

Richards opened the file on Grassley's desk and confirmed what he said. The letter said that the accident was a head-on on US 26 up in the Coast Range between the insured's pickup and a WCI Caravan. The pickup crossed the centerline, and there's a suggestion that its hood flew up. The pickup driver is in Emanuel Hospital.

Richards finished reading the letter and looked up at Grassley. "As least the hospital is a place to start. I'll call them and get right out there." She got up and headed back to her desk.

At thirty-six Richards was a tall and striking looking. She'd been married for several years. The marriage ended in divorce with no children when she was thirty-two. She's remained single since then. She had long brown hair, an ample but physical figure, and when she caught you in the gaze of her hazel eyes, she had your attention. She wore a white blouse, open just enough to draw a stare, dark brown slacks and black pumps.

She called the hospital and was told that Bentwood was recovering from surgery. He had lost his leg, but she could see him for a limited time.

—◊◊◊—

Richard entered the lobby of a hospital floor and approached a woman dressed in a nurse's uniform behind a counter. "I'm looking for a patient. Lyle Bentwood's his name." She identified herself and told the nurse why she as there.

Before the nurse responded, a doctor holding a chart came to the counter and talked with the nurse to whom Richard had spoken. The doctor pointed to the chart and seemed to be giving orders. The nursed nodded and spoke briefly to the doctor, looking in the direction where Richards stood.

The doctor turned and looked at Richards. He nodded, left the station and approached Richards. "I'm told you want to talk to Mr. Bentwood. He's resting well and is alert. You may see him only for a few minutes, but I must caution you. He's lost his left leg just above the knee. I know you'll want to ask him what happened. You can do that, but be careful not to press him. He's in a very delicate mental situation, as you can imagine. He remembers some things and not others. Take what he tells you but don't examine him. It that understood?"

Richards nodded. "I understand fully. I won't ask any unnecessary questions, just what happened."

The doctor led her to Bentwood's room, and they went inside. Bentwood lay in bed, the covers midway up his chest, staring at the ceiling. His head and part of his face were bandaged. Richards could tell from his shape in bed that he had a large frame. His face looked pale, and, as they came up to his bed, he turned his head and stared at Richards. She noticed he had blue eyes.

"Lyle," the doctor said, "this lady is from the dairy's insurance company. She is investigating the accident for the dairy, and she'd like to ask you a few questions."

Bentwood continued to look at Richards. He spoke slowly. "I'll tell you what I can." Richards pulled up the only chair in the room and sat. "I understand you were hauling some cows from Portland to the dairy when the accident happened."

"Yes, yes ma'am I was. And I understood they didn't survive."

"I think that's right. I understand the accident happened on the downhill straight stretch just beyond the Elderberry Inn."

"Yes ma'am. I had just come out of a left corner and was headed down the hill, when suddenly something hit the windshield. That's all I remember."

"Do you have any idea what hit the windshield?"

"No I don't. I don't remember anything being in my way. I just remember a smashing noise and small particles of glass coming at me."

"Do you know whether the pickup's hood had been opened recently?"

"I don't think so." Bentwood looked up at the ceiling for a moment. Then he looked back at Richards. "Wait a minute. I just remembered. I got gas before I went up the hill into the mountains. It seemed like the service station attendant checked the water and oil."

"Are you sure?"

"Yes, I remember him asking if I want the water and oil checked, and I said yes."

"Do you remember how he put the hood down when he was finished?"

"Not really. I assumed he just slammed it down."

"But you don't know that?"

"No, I guess I don't."

"One more thing before I go, if anyone else tries to talk to you about the accident, other than the medical staff, don't do it. Refer them to me." She gave Bentwood her card.

Richard left the hospital and drove back the insurance company's office. At her desk she called the state police office in Salem and was told a report would not be released for several weeks. She ordered it. "Where are the vehicles now?" she asked.

"Wait a minute," the woman on the line said. "I'll see if I can find out." The woman came back on the line. "There at a police lot on the north side of the Bertha-Beaverton Highway in Aloha west of Portland. There's a small state police office in front of the lot. Call before you go out there to make sure someone will be there when you want to look at the vehicles." She gave Richards the number.

Richards immediately called the number. A man answered. She explained what she wanted.

"Sure," the man said, "you can look at the vehicles. You can photograph them, but don't move them or disturb them in any way."

"Can I come out now? It'll take me about a half-hour to get there."

"Yeah."

Richards left the office, got her car from the lot across Stark Street, drove out of Portland on the Berth-Beaverton Highway through Beaverton and, when she got to Aloha, she quickly spotted a police car parked in front of a small police office. She parked next to the patrol car, got out and went into the building. Inside she approached a counter and saw a patrolman sitting at a desk behind it.

He looked up. "You must be the insurance lady I talked to."

Richard smiled. "The one and only."

The patrolman smiled back. "Well, you're Johnny, or sorry Lucy-on-the-spot. You're the first investigator who's come to see the vehicles."

Richard grinned at him. "Actually, I'm Monica."

The patrolman got up and held open a swinging door. "Come on through and follow me. We'll go out the back door. The vehicles are out back."

She followed him. The door led to a large graveled empty lot, except for what appeared like the remains of vehicles off to the left and back a ways.

The patrolman pointed. "That's them."

As they walked closer, Richard gasped. She looked in disbelief at what had been the Caravan. "My god, what happened to that one?"

"I'm told the pickup ran over the left front and side of it. At least the investigating officers said they found evidence where the pickup had gone clear into the back seat."

She looked closer at the van. Two-thirds of the left front and side of the van were flattened. On the left side you could see tire indents on the flattened metal. The right side and roof slanted inward as did the roof over the right side back seat area.

The pickup sat to the left. Richards immediately notice the hood, elevated and back against the shattered windshield. She walked around the pickup. The box and rear end were twisted. The left front had nearly disappeared, crushed and displaced to the back of the cabin. The displacement looked angular, involving the right front wheel as well.

The cattle trailer appeared intact except for the flattened left side and rear end.

Richards photographed all three vehicles from every angle. When she finished, she turned to the patrolman. "How long will the vehicles be here?"

"I don't know for sure, but I assume for some time. I know they'll remain until the police investigation is done, and there's no more interest in them from the parties involved."

Richards handed him her card. "Would you give me a call before anyone disturbs the vehicle?"

"I'll put your card in the file with a note to do that."

Richards left the lot. It was warm so she had her window open. She drove west a short distance and turned right on a road that connected to the Sunset Highway. When she reached the highway, she turned west in search of the service station where Bentwood had gotten gas. As she drove down a straight stretch toward the hill heading up into the mountains, she saw a Legion Oil station ahead to the right. She pulled in and stopped adjacent to the one of the gas pumps. Soon an attendant came up to the left side of her car.

She leaned out the window. "Fill it up with Ethel."

The attendant went to the left rear of her car, took off the filler cap, pulled down the Ethel nozzle and began filling the car.

Richards got out and addressed the attendant. "Where are your restrooms?"

"Go into the office. There around back near the cigarette machine."

Richards went into the office and found the restrooms. She reappeared as the attendant replaced the gas nozzle. She approached him. "You didn't happen to hear about the bad accident down near the Elderberry Inn yesterday, did you?"

The attendant wrote up a ticket and handed the board on which it rested to Richards. "I sure did. I understand two people died. The pickup involved stopped here for gas just an hour or so before. I remember it because he was hauling some cattle."

Richard went back to the car and got her purse from the front seat. She reached into the purse and pulled out a credit card. She gave it to the attendant. "Did you check his water and oil?" she asked.

"Yeah. He didn't need either. What do you ask?"

"I wondered if you noticed any problem closing the hood."

"No, it seemed to close all right, as best I recall."

"Do you really remember closing the hood?"

"Well, not really, but I'm sure I did."

"I'm investigating the accident for an insurance company. There's a suggestion that the pickup's hood flew up and blinded the driver. I wondered if you noticed a problem closing he hood."

The attended acted surprised. "I didn't hear that. Ah, ah, I'm sure it was down when he left the station. That's about all I can say."

Richards showed the attendant a recorder she had been using. "I've recorded our conversations. Is that all right with you?"

"Sure, I ain't got nothing to hide."

After Richards left, the attendant thought some about her visit. Suddenly, he felt a sting of concern about the pickup's hood. He wondered if someone would blame him. He went back into the office and flipped open his telephone directory to the letter S. He saw the name he wanted, Bill Smiley, his insurance agent in Hillsboro. He dialed the number.

"Smiley insurance," a woman answered.

"This is Pete Wilkerson out in Manning, can I speak with Bill?"

"One moment, please."

A man came on the line. "Hi, Pete. What can I do for you?"

"I just had a visit from an insurance lady." He explained the visit.

"You did right," Smiley said. "It's probably nothing, but I'll let your insurance company know there might be a problem. In the meantime don't discuss this with anyone else until your insurance company contacts you."

"Thanks, Bill. I feel better already."

3

HARRY SUGERMAN AND his wife Lydia lived on SE Twenty-Ninth Street in a district know as Eastmoreland a couple of blocks from a golf course with the same name. Their house, a white two-story colonial built in the twenties, sat on the northwest corner lot of the intersection with Lambert Street. The Sugerman's, now in their late fifties, had lived alone since the marriage of their only child, a son.

On Saturday afternoon on June second, Harry Sugerman arrived home after his early morning golf game. When he came into the kitchen from the garage, he walked up to his wife, empting the dishwasher. "How'd the visit to the hospital go?"

"Not too well," his wife answered. "Amy's still in intensive care and can't see visitors. She's got a spinal cord injury among other things. The doctors fear paralysis. Michelle's recovering. They stitched the cut on her forehead, but she won't be released of at least another day because of internal bleeding. I brought Dustin home. He's in a cast and upstairs sleeping."

"How's he handling all this?"

"The poor kid doesn't really grasp the horror of it all. He knows that his father and brother didn't make it, but I'm not sure he truly understands it yet. He cried some on the way home, but not a lot."

"When you drove up to our house, did he want to go home?"

"No, and I didn't even mention it."

"Are you going back to the hospital tomorrow?"

"Yes. I don't expect to see Amy, but if Michelle is stable I can bring her back with me. Why don't you go with me?"

The Ralston's house was on the north side of the Sugerman's house. Michael's mother died when he was three and his father passed away five years ago from cancer. Amy's mother also had cancer and died the year after Amy's and Michael's wedding. Amy's father disserted the family when she was four and hasn't been heard from since. The Sugerman's have been the Ralston's neighbors for the past seven years and have been almost grandparents to their children.

That evening, the door bell rang. Sugerman went to the front door and looked out the small window to the right of the door. He saw a man standing on the doormat. He wore tailored brown slacks and a green long-sleeved shirt open at the collar. He had a baseball cap on his head and a thin mustache.

Sugerman opened the door slightly. "What can I do for you?" he asked.

The man handed Sugerman a card. "I'm an investigator for *Rubin & Watts*. They're Portland's leading automobile accident lawyers. I understand your handling the legal matters for the Ralston's while Mrs. Ralston is recovering. I thought you might be seeking legal representation for her and her family. I am here to introduce my firm and to offer any help you feel you need."

He stepped to one side so he could see Sugerman better. "We know how hard it is to deal with the recovery of accident victims. My firm can take the matter of handling the medical bills, the insurance companies and the accident details off your mind at the critical time."

Sugerman opened the door fully. "Thank you, but I don't have time to get into that now, and I certainly can't obligate Mrs. Ralston to lawyers' fees."

The man motioned with his hand. "Don't worry if you retain our firm there will be no charge. Any fee for the lawyers comes out of any recovery that they make for the Ralston's. Why don't you think about it and use the card to call the firm?"

"Mrs. Ralston's in intensive care and is incommunicado. She can't make that decision now."

"I know, but you can authorize us to get involved now, and, if she decides otherwise later, we'll abide by her wishes with no charge." Then his voice took an urgent tone. "But I must advise you that the accident needs to be investigated as soon as possible, and our firm has all of the tools to do that."

Sugerman retained the card and thanked the man, closing the door. He went back to the living room where his wife read. He explained what the man wanted. Then he examined the card. "He seemed insistent about the need to investigate the accident soon. I think I should call Michael's friend, Miles O'Doul. He's an accountant and may know what we should do."

Sugerman walked into a small den. A telephone sat on a desk against one wall. He pulled out the chair at the desk, sat down, opened the top right drawer and pulled out a telephone book. He opened the book and searched for O'Doul's home number. When he found it, he dialed the number. The phone rang several times and finally a male voice answered.

"May I speak to Miles?" Sugerman asked.

"Speaking."

"Miles, this is Harry Sugerman." Sugerman told O'Doul about the visitor he had just had. "I don't know what to do. He sounded like time was the essence."

O'Doul laughed half-heartedly. "I'm sorry for the sarcastic laugh. Your caller isn't funny, more like disgusting. I'm sure you've heard the term 'ambulance chasers.' Well, you were visited by their runner. *Rubin & Watts* have that kind of reputation. Deep six the card. One of Michael's buddies is a lawyer in Beaverton. I don't think he does trial work, but he should know when Amy needs a lawyer and who to call. I'll try to reach him and get back to you."

The following Monday morning Denny Wilson sat with his back to his desk, leaning back in his chair looking out the window at the wheat field behind the office building and the grove of fir trees in the distance. Wilson practiced law in Beaverton with an older partner, Sam Witchhaxel. They're office was on the south side of the Bertha-Beaverton Highway just west of Beaverton, occupying half of a one-story building set back from the highway with a small parking lot in front. At thirty-nine Wilson had a full head of red hair, was somewhat over weight, and when he didn't have a cigar in his mouth, he normally had a smile on his face.

The telephone rang and interrupted his reverie. He picked it up and answered.

"Denny, this is Miles."

"Hi, Miles. How's your golf game."

"Just like normal, awful. But I'm calling about Mike's accident."

Wilson turned around, facing his desk and sat upright. "God, I heard about it. Sounds like Mike never knew what hit him. What can I do to help?"

O'Doul told him about the telephone call he received Saturday evening from Harry Sugerman. "You know they live next door to Mike and Amy. They're taking care of the kids while Amy's in the hospital."

"I hope you told him to tell the runner to bug off."

"Yeah, but I also told them you're the guy they should talk to."

Wilson pulled a pad up close and picked up a pencil. "Sure, what's his phone number?"

O'Doul gave it to him.

He wrote it down on the pad. "You know I don't normally do this kind of work, but I'll talk to him and see if I can calm him down."

"That's what I thought. Give him a call as soon as you can. He needs some advice."

After O'Doul hung up, Wilson dialed the number O'Doul gave him.

"Hello," Laura Sugerman answered.

"I'm Denny Wilson, a lawyer in Beaverton," Wilson said. "Miles O'Doul called me and asked me to call about the Ralston's. Michael was an also friend of mine."

"Oh, yes, Mr. Wilson. But it's my husband you should talk to. He's at the office. Let me give you his number." She gave it to him.

"Thank you, Mrs. Sugerman. I'll call him right away."

Wilson dialed again.

"Sugerman Investments," a woman answered.

"May I speak to Harry Sugerman?"

"Who should I say is calling?"

"Denny Wilson. I'm a lawyer and a friend of Michael Ralston. Miles O'Doul asked me to call Mr. Sugerman."

A moment later Sugerman came on the line. "Thank you for calling, Mr. Wilson. Did Miles explain the problem?"

Wilson smiled. "You mean the confrontation with *Rubin & Watts'* runner?"

Sugerman spoke with a voice of concern. "That's right. The man said it was urgent that we get legal advice for the Ralston's. With Amy isolated in intensive care, I didn't know what to do."

"Do you know how long it will be before she can talk and make decisions?"

"I have no idea. But I think she may have some paralysis, so even when she can talk, I don't know if she will be in shape to handle this matter."

30

Wilson tried to calm Sugerman. "I'm sorry to hear that, but there is really no rush. Pay no attention to what the runner said. There is no urgency for her to get legal advice. If the truth be known, the only urgency involved is *Rubin & Watts'* desire to beat some other ambulance chaser."

"Oh I'm glad to hear that," Sugerman said.

Wilson said, "Tell the hospital that she's not to be disturbed by any lawyers or their representatives. She's in the hands of doctors. Let them take care of her without any legal worries. When she's stable and hopefully home, you can talk to her about legal representation. I'll be glad to see her then. If after several months, she's still incapacitated, you might give me a call, and we'll discuss it further."

"Thank you so much, Mr. Wilson. I'll mark my calendar, say in September, to call you if she hasn't."

"Call me Denny. Just call when you're ready."

The sun shown through the windows of the Merchants Exchange Building at an angle from the east. It was Monday morning, August sixth, and the beginning of the week had typewriters humming on the third floor. Richards sat at her desk, opening her mail. The mail girl had left more than usual this morning, but Richard's eye quickly caught and envelope from the state police. She reached for it, slipped a letter opener into the envelope and slit it open. Inside she saw the report for the May twenty-ninth accident on the Sunset Highway.

She read the report. It listed the pickup crossing the centerline as the cause of the accident. It found an unexplained release of the hood of the pickup as a contributing cause. She turned her chair around to face a small filing cabinet. She opened the top drawer, thumbed through the files and pulled one out. She returned her chair to face the desk and opened the file. The label read: Insured—Towson Dairy, Accident—May 29, 1973. She looked in the file, found the telephone number of the police office in Aloha and picked up the telephone and dialed.

"State police," a man answered.

"This is Monica Richard. You may remember me. I visited your office in early June and looked at the vehicles involved in a collision on the Sunset Highway on May twenty-ninth."

A looker like you—how could I forget, thought the officer. "Yeah, I remember. You're the gal from the insurance company."

"Has anyone else inspected the vehicles?"

"Yeah, one guy from the van's insurance company. I got his card here somewhere. Hold on a minute."

He left the phone for a moment and then came back on. "I found it. His name's Chip McLaughlin of Major Casualty."

Richards paused. "I know him. He sent the dairy a letter, making a claim for the collision insurance they paid. Why I called is I got the police report in the mail today, so I suppose that means their investigation is over. Does that mean you ready to release the pickup?"

"Yeah. Do you think the dairy wants it?"

"No, but we do. We're going to pay the dairy a total loss under our policy."

"Okay, Miss. Bring me the paperwork and the vehicle's yours. Better bring a low-boy. You're not going to drive it away. By the way, do you know if the other people want the van?"

Richards thought. "I'll talk to them. Better hold on to it, will you?"

"Yeah, but tell them we won't hold it more than two months. If they don't claim it, we'll sell it for salvage."

After she hung up, Richards left her desk and walked to Grassley's office. Again the door was open, and Richards knocked.

Grassley sat behind his desk, talking on the telephone. When he heard the knock and saw Richard's head peering in, he motioned her to come in.

Richards entered and sat at in a chair beside Grassley's desk as Grassley continued his telephone conversation. A few moments later, Grassley said, "Okay, Mike. You take it from there and call me when you've got something to report." The person on the other end of the call spoke briefly, and Grassley said, "Good bye."

He hung up the telephone and turned to face Richards. "What's up, Monica?"

"I want to talk about the Towson Dairy accident." She told him about the police report and her call to the police lot. "I told him we'd take possession of the pickup. If the hood flew up and blinded the driver, I thought we should have someone take a look at it to see if we can determine why. If it's someone else's fault, we may have a subrogation claim."

"That's good thinking. And in addition to having to pay Monarch for the vehicle, we've got a hundred thousand of liability insurance exposure in this matter. We can afford to hire some help. What about Wayland Chang? He's with Rutledge Engineers, and he's resourceful. He can find something wrong with about anything."

Richards nodded. "I'll call him right away. He will have somewhere we can store the vehicle. Another thing. Towson Dairy forwarded me a demand letter they received from Major Casualty the insurer of the Caravan. They have collision coverage for the Caravan. Obviously we owe it, even if someone else is responsible to us. Shouldn't we pay the insurer and get the Caravan too? I think Chang will want to see it."

"Sure. If we have a subrogation claim, we can include that also."

Richard got up. "All right. I'll pay it and get the title. Then assuming Chang is on board, I'll have him arrange to pick up the vehicles and store them."

She left Grassley's office and went back to her desk, where the Towson Dairy file still lay open. She found the demand letter signed by Chip McLaughlin. Major Casualty's office was just one block north on Fourth Avenue in the Board of Trade Building. She dialed the number.

"Major Casualty," a woman answered.

"May I speak to Chip?" Richards said.

"Let me see if he's in?"

The woman came back on the line. "He's out. Can I leave him a message?"

"Yeah, tell him Monica Richards called. I'm stopping by the Embassy after work, if he'd like to drop in and buy me a drink."

Richard hung up the telephone and pulled out her telephone directory. She looked under Consulting Engineers and found Chang's firm. She dialed the number.

The telephone rang. "Rutledge Engineers," a woman answered. "How may I direct you call?"

"Wayland Chang, please."

"One moment, please." She heard the phone ringing.

"Wayland Chang here."

Chang was thirty-seven and had been with Rutledge Engineers for fifteen years. A Chinese-American, he spoke slowly and had a slim build and blue oval eyes. He had a mechanical engineering degree from Oregon State University.

"Wayland, this is Monica Richards from Western Indemnity. We insure Towson Dairy in Seaside. One of Towson's pickups was involved in a serious accident on the Sunset Highway near Elderberry Inn in late May. It appears the hood flew up, blinding the driver and resulting in a head-on collision. We need someone to look at the pickup for us to see why the hood flew up. Was there a manufacturing defect? Was the hood not latched properly? In other words, we want to know if we have a case against someone else in this matter. Are you available to help us?"

"I think so. Who are the other parties and the vehicle makers?"

"The other vehicle was a 1967 Caravan manufactured by WCI, the driver, who died in the accident, was Michael Ralston, the passengers were his wife and three kids, and the pickup is a 1970 Monarch."

"Then I have no conflict. I'd be glad to look at the vehicles for you. Where are they?"

"Out on a state police lot near Aloha." She gave him the address and the contact. "I'll get the title to both vehicles. I'll have them in a couple of days. We want you to arrange to pick up the vehicles and move to wherever you can store them for inspection. As soon as you've made the arrangements, call me and I'll meet you at the lot with the vehicle titles."

"Fine, Monica. I'll take it from here and give you a call."

At four-thirty Richards' phone rang.

She picked up the receiver. "This is Monica."

"Hi, beautiful," a man said. How about if I meet you at the Embassy in fifteen minutes?"

"See you there, Chip."

Richards got to the Embassy at five. It was located behind the Board of Trade Building on Third Avenue. It was a regular hang out after work for adjusters in the area. When she entered she looked down the long bar at the left and didn't see McLaughlin. She thought, *I knew he' be late. He wanted me to sit and wait.* She pulled out a stool and sat about mid-way down the bar. The bartender came over. "What can I get you, Monica?"

"Nothing right now, Ernie. I'm waiting for Chip."

In about ten minutes, McLaughlin came in. About thirty, he had blonde combed-back hair and a thin sharp face, but because of his tall frame, he was almost handsome. He wore a gray plaid jacket, dark trousers and his tie hung loosely from his neck.

McLaughlin immediately spotted Richards at the bar. *I think every time I see her what's a great looking broad like that doing adjusting insurance claims,* he said to himself. She wore a tight blue sweater close around her neck and a short dark brown skirt. Her sweater hugged her ample breasts, and the skirt revealed long well-shaped legs with her feet resting in brown satin pumps. He walked down the bar, pulled out the stool next to her. "Ernie, let me buy this gorgeous babe a drink."

The bartender looked at Richards. "What'll it be?"

"A gin and tonic with a lime, Beefeaters if you got it."

"One Beefeaters gin and tonic with a lime." The bartender looked at McLaughlin. "Your usual, Chip?"

"You got it, Ernie." He turned and looked Richards. "Well, don't you look sexy tonight? I'd like to think you're coming on to me, but I sense your invite is more involved with business."

Richards batted her hazel eyes at McLaughlin. "If you're free later tonight, we can get something to eat and see if anything develops, but for now keep you pants buttoned, your right I've got a business proposition for you."

McLaughlin blushed slightly and then laughed. "Then why don't we adjourn to one of the booths with our drinks. We can talk more privately there."

Richard nodded. She gave him her hand, and they got off the stools, walked over to a booth nearby and sat opposite each other.

Richard leaned forward, putting her forearms on the table, and gazed at McLaughlin with her hazel eyes. "You remember that letter you sent Western about the dairy pickup that struck a WCI van on the Sunset Highway in May?"

"Sure. You got the file?"

The bartender brought their drinks to the table.

"I do, and I'm going to make you a hero by paying your claim, if you'll assign the title to the van to us."

"Boy, you're easy. You can have the title. Might I ask why you want it?"

Richards took a sip of her drink and laid the glass back on the table. She looked at McLaughlin. "We expect to get sued by your insureds. We've hired an engineer to look into a possible claim against Monarch. He wants your vehicle, as well as ours, or an examination."

McLaughlin moved across to Richards's side of the booth. "Is that the business you wanted to discuss?"

"That's it."

"Well, now that it's over, let's enjoy our drinks. What have you been up to lately?"

She smiled at him and moved closer. "Lots of work, but a little play now and then. How about you? Didn't I hear you were mixed up with a wedding now long ago?"

He shook his head. "That's old news. She got cold feet, walked away and left me a bachelor."

She picked up the paper coaster and dabbed her eye, pretending to wipe a tear away. "Poor boy. I feel so sorry for you."

He laughed. "I can see you're so sad."

They continued to talk while they finished the drinks.

"You want another?" McLaughlin asked.

"Sure, why not."

He waved at the bartender. "Ernie, two more." He put his arm on top of the booth and over her shoulder as he looked into her eyes. "Monica, I think this is the first time we've talked when it didn't involve business. When you relax, you're actually quite a gal."

She stared at him and put her elbow on the table with her arm upright. "When I'm off work, I like to play hard. Give me your hand and let me see how good you are at arm wrestling?"

He took his arm off the banquet and held his hands out open in front of him. "Whoa there. I'm not arm wrestling a girl."

"Afraid I'll beat you?"

"Maybe, but I'm not going to find out."

"Why don't we have a little wager? If you win, I'll buy the dinner. If I win, you buy and take me home with you." And she laid her hand on his crotch and squeezed what she found there."

He put his arm on the table and raised his hand. "With an offer like that, I'll let you win."

She put her arm down and snickered. "I thought so. I just remember I can't join you for dinner. I have another date." Just then the bartender brought the second drink.

Richards got up, took the glass from the bartender, and drank it down in one gulp. She looked down at McLaughlin. "I'll have your draft tomorrow. Call me when you have the title and maybe we can meet again to exchange them. Thanks for the drinks." She turned and left.

4

O N WEDNESDAY, JANUARY seventh three years before, Gunter Sweigert, at thirty-four years of age, sat at his desk in his office, which was actually a large cubical on the second story of the engineering department. He wore a white shirt and a blue floral tie under a white shop coat. He started in the engineering department in Germany of German vehicle manufacturer, Warner Carriage International (WCI) at twenty-one. After the company built a new plant in the Aurora, Illinois in 1966, he was transferred there to become project manager for its newly designed vehicle called the Caravan, which it planned to market in the Untied States.

WCI built the plant just off Butterfield road. The architecture of the several buildings that made up the plant was unique, and their location gave rise to the campus style manufacturing facility that became popular in the seventies. The assembly building sat at the hub of the campus with other buildings, administration, engineering, advance design, and control and testing, located outside as spokes of the hub. A large oval test tract surrounded the plant. The arrangement from the air resembled a giant wheel.

The Caravan design featured a snub nose with the front axel under and slightly behind the driver. It resembled a rectangular box on wheels, but despite its commercial look it became instantly popular with the middle class.

The engineering building had two stories and a basement. The cubicles of engineering design occupied about a third of the second story.

Sweigert had a brown crew cut, a sharp-lined face, a thin physique and a brusque personality. He seldom smiled, but when he did, his deep green eyes glistened through his glasses, and a charming appeal emerged. He pickup up his telephone and dialed.

"This is Tracy," answered a woman.

"Tracy, Gunter here. Could you come in?" I want you to see something."

Tracy O'Grady joined WCI when plans for the Aurora plant became public. At the time she had recently graduated as a mechanical engineer from Virginia Tech, and she began as an intern in the then small engineering department. Her energy and quick understanding of the tasks at hand soon became noticed, and she began to advance. Four years later she found herself as the assistant project engineer for the Caravan.

Still single at twenty-six, O'Grady's Irish background and Southern upbringing contributed to a personality that assisted her advancement. Her appearance helped as well, blue eyes, freckle faced, straight blonde hair, cute figure and an ever-present smile.

O'Grady had the cubicle down the aisle and three away from Sweigert. She put down the telephone, picked up a long white pad and headed for Sweigert's office. She entered Sweigert's cubicle. "What's up?" She sat in a chair beside Sweigert's desk.

Sweigert eyed her. "I've been intrigued with the van United just put on the market. You know the one with a short snout rather than the stub-nose."

"Yeah, I've seen it and wondered about its stability and visibility."

Sweigert shifted in his chair, picked up a drawing in front of him and turned it toward O'Grady. "I've done some preliminary design work with out Caravan. Take a look at the drawing and see what you think."

She stood, bent over his desk and studied the drawing. "What yawl've done is interesting. Why d'yawl move the front axel and engine up in front of the diver's compartment?"

"To improve the stability, but I don't know what the design does to the visibility. I'm trying to decide whether it warrants building a prototype and doing some testing."

She looked at the drawing again and thought. "D'yawl have that marketing report we got earlier this month? That might have a bearing."

He turned to a filing cabinet behind his desk. He opened a drawer and leafed through some files. Finding the right one, he took it out and opened it on his desk. He took the top sheet off and gave it to O'Grady who had sat I see that it finds that we continue to lead all competition with the present Caravan. From a marketing standpoint it doesn't make much sense to change the design unless there is another reason to do it."

She looked at the report briefly. "That's what I thought. D'yawl know of another reason?"

He lowered his eyebrows. The lines of his forehead grew apart, and he glared at her through his glasses. "I do, and I think you do too. With the engine and axel out front in the short snout, there's added crush to protect the driver in a head-on collision."

O'Grady winced. "Of course."

His expression changed. He broke into a smile, his eyes glistening. "Take it easy, Tracy. I didn't mean to be so hard on you." He got up and went to her, took her hands and raised her up. "It's been a long day. Let's go down to Charlie's Place, have a drink and talk some more about this in a more comfortable atmosphere."

She leaned slightly toward him, looked in his eyes and smiled. "I don't know how I stand yawl, Gunter. One moment yawl frightens me, and the next yawl's a lamb. How can I say no? Yawl go down to

Charlie's, and I'll be there shortly. I've got some matters to clean up here. It won't take me long."

About twenty minutes later O'Grady parked in the lot in front of Charlie's Place, a tavern located a mile north of the WCI plant. As she approached the front door, she looked up and smiled at the neon sign over the door depicting the name of the tavern and the grinning face of Charlie smoking his ever present cigar. The front door entered into a horseshoe shaped building with a bar extending all the way around the U of the horseshoe. Customers gathered on stools at the bar and at tables that filled out the room in the center of the room. Two fireplaces were located to the right and left of the front entrance and at the ends of the horseshoe.

O'Grady searched the room and finally spotted Sweigert in one of the upholstered chairs arranged around the fireplace to her left, reading a paper. A drink rested on the table in front of him. She went over and sat in the chair next to his.

When she sat, it got Sweigert's attention. He put down the newspaper and turned toward her. "Well, look who's here. I thought you forgot."

O'Grady had a coy smile on her face. "Then yawl must have missed me."

He frowned. "Not really, but I'm nearly finished with my drink. On the other hand, now that you're here, I suppose I could order another."

"I suggest that yawl do, since yawl offered me a drink in a comfortable atmosphere."

A waitress came over, took a drink order and left.

Sweigert settled back in the chair and downed the rest of his drink. He turned to O'Grady. "What do you think about my design. Do you think further testing is in order?"

"I thought about it on the drive over. I think yawl should go forward with a prototype and testing."

"Then it's settled. I'll make a proposal and submit it to Dalripple."

Gordon Dalripple was the chief engineer.

Their drinks came, and they continued to talk about the testing they would do if management went for the idea.

As they finished their drinks, Sweigert leaned over towards O'Grady and put his hand on top of hers. "Charlie serves a tender steak, do you want to stay for dinner?"

O'Grady pulled her hand away. "Not tonight. I don't think yawl's wife would understand."

"Does that mean you might like to do it some other time?"

O'Grady lowered her eyebrows. "Would she understand some other time?"

Sweigert laughed. "That's what I like about you. You answer a question with another question. Okay, let's give up." They both got up and left.

On Monday March ninth the first prototype came off the assembly line. The plant took a production Caravan and modified it by moving the engine and front axel forward and adding four feet of sheet metal around the engine and wheels.

Sweigert stopped by O'Grady's cubicle and saw her sitting at her desk working. "The Caravan prototype is finished," he said. "I'm taking her out for a test drive in tomorrow. Would you like to join me?"

O'Grady looked up. "Is that wise? The forecast is for snow."

"That's no problem. Snow this time of year isn't a big deal. In fact seeing how it maneuvers in a few inches of snow will be a plus. Come on; I need your input."

O'Grady pondered. "All right," she finally said. "I'll go. When are you leaving?"

"In the afternoon around two from control and testing."

"I'll be there.

The next afternoon it had turned cold and gray. O'Grady stood outside the control and testing building wearing a wool coat, a scarf, gloves and boots, when Sweigert pulled up in the modified Caravan. He also wore warm clothing.

He rolled down the driver's window and called out. "Hey, Tracy. Come on. Let's get going before the snow starts falling."

O'Grady opened the passenger's door, climbed in, fastened her seatbelt and off they went.

Sweigert headed west on Butterfield road, across the Fox River and then north along Mill Creek. When they were just south of Mill Creek it started to snow. The vehicle handled well in the light snow. Soon, however, the snow fall became heavier.

O'Grady pulled up her collar and folded her arms on her chest, rubbing her hands together. "It makes me cold seeing the snow fall even though yawl has the heater running."

As they approached Keslinger Road visibility worsened and the snow began piling up. Sweigert attempted to turn right on Keslinger Road, but the vehicle started to skid. Although he tried to control it, the vehicle slid off the left side of the road into a small ditch. When he attempted to drive out of the ditch, the slick snow caused the rear wheels to spin. They were stuck, and it continued to snow, harder now. Although only a little after three-thirty, dusk began to fall.

Sweigert raised his collar. "We wait until the snow stops. Then I'll see if I can get us out of here."

The snow continued, covering the van, except for the windshield, where the wipers worked hard. The road disappeared under a blanket of snow.

O'Grady now leaned against Sweigert. "I know the heater's working, but I'm freezing."

He put his arm around her and held her close. "Does that help?"

"Yes, but what are we going to do?"

"I don't know. Even if the snow lets up, it's gotten too damn dark to make any examination of our situation. I think we're probably better to stay put as long as the engine's running."

Soon they heard something some distance away coming toward them. They saw blinking lights and then a snow plow down the road. They were in the ditch on the wrong side of the road and the snow plow approached heading west. When the snow plow had come to within several feet of them, it stopped, and the driver got out. He came to the passenger's door.

Sweigert reached over O'Grady, rolled down the passenger's window. "Thank God you arrived," he said to the snow plow driver. "We slipped trying to make a right turn and went off the road to the left."

"I'll go by you," the driver said, "attach a chain to your rear axle and see if I can pull you out."

He got back in his truck, plowed by the van and got out with a chain. After several minutes, he had the chain attached to the van, and he pulled the van out of the ditch onto the road, facing the wrong way.

The driver stopped his truck, got out and walked back to the van. He went up to the driver's window and spoke to Sweigert. "I think you can turn around in the lane I've plowed. Then follow me east. There's a motel and restaurant about two miles down the road. You can pull in there and wait out the storm."

They followed the plow down the road and saw the motel and restaurant. The plow pulled to the right pushing the snow away from the entrance to the motel. Sweigert followed, and, when the plow had gone down the road, he pulled in front of the motel and stopped. A neon light shown from above the door with a sign reading: Office. Sweigert got out of the van and shuffled to the office door. He went in.

Several minutes later he returned to the van. He opened his door and put his head in the van. "Tracy, I got us a room for the night. We'll stay here until the storm breaks."

O'Grady got out of the van and followed Sweigert to a room a couple of doors from the office. Sweigert took a key and opened the door, standing aside for Tracy to enter.

O'Grady looked at the stark room. It smelled stale. It had a double bed, a chair, a low long table with a TV on it, a floor lamp and a small table beside the bed with a table lamp and a telephone. In the rear was a small bathroom. As she entered, she looked back at Sweigert. "Who gets the bad?" she asked sarcastically.

Sweigert went for the telephone. "I'm calling my wife and telling her where we are." He dialed. When the call was answered, he said, "Honey, we were out testing the new prototype vehicle when the snow hit." He explained how they gotten to the motel and told her they staying here until the storm breaks. He sat on the bed and listened for a few moments. Then he said, "All right, honey. I'll call when we can come home."

O'Grady had taken the chair. She grinned at Sweigert. "I notice yawl didn't tell her who you we holed up with. Chicken."

Sweigert blushed. "I know, but I thought I'd leave well enough alone when she didn't ask."

O'Grady chuckled. "Yawl's sure smooth, ain't yawl?"

Sweigert took off his coat, hung it up on a cloths rack on the wall and took off his boots. He went to the TV and turned it on. He looked back at O'Grady. "Well, we might as well make the best of it. How about some TV?"

O'Grady got up took off her coat and scarf, hung them up on the same rack and took off her boots. She stacked two pillows on the head board, laid down on the bed and put her head on the pillows. "I guess I'll watch. What about some food? This engineer's hungry."

Sweigert put on his boots. "I'll see what I can find. The snow plow driver said there was a restaurant here too." He went out the door.

About fifteen minutes later he returned with two sacks.

O'Grady pointed to the sacks. "What yawl got in there?"

Sweigert opened one sack. "Just what the doctor ordered." He took out two cups and a couple of sandwiches and placed them on the long table. "There's soup in the cups." Then he opened the other sack, removed four bottles of beer and handed one to O'Grady. "They got these from the refrigerator, so they should be cold. But we should have some ice also." He picked up a small container from the long table. "I saw an ice machine two doors down. I'll get some." He left the room again.

Shortly, he came back. He saw that O'Grady had gotten one of the cups of soup and was drinking it as she sat on the bed.

"I couldn't wait for yawl." she said. "But I did stack the other pillows so you could sit on the bed and eat."

Sweigert opened a beer and took it with a cup of soup and a sandwich over to the bed. "Thanks, I'll join you." He sat down on the other side of the bed and leaned against the pillows.

When they finished with the soup and sandwiches, O'Grady took the cups and the wrappers from the sandwiches and put them in a waste basket. Then she got another beer, sat back on the bed, leaned against the pillows, and watched the TV.

Sweigert watched her and smiled. "You're a very tidy lady, Tracy."

"Oh, I'm not much, but its all yawl got."

He leaned over and kissed her lightly on the lips.

She pulled back and stared at him, her green eyes glistening. "That was sort of sneaky, if yawl ask me"

He put his hand behind her head, pulled towards him and kissed her fully.

She rose up and pushed him back against his pillows. Then she crawled over on top of him, took his head in both hands and engaged his lips, slipping her tongue inside his mouth. After several moments, she lifted her head and looked down at him. "If it's kissing yawl want, that's the way it's done."

He turned her on her side, placed his hand on her breast and started rubbing it.

She unbuttoned her blouse. "That'll make it easier for yawl," she whispered.

He slid his hand in and found a bare breast. *She's not wearing a bra*, he said to himself. He caressed it.

After a few moments she rose to her knees and looked down at him. "Don't you think it would be easier if I got rid of these cloths?" She stood and began disrobing in front of him. When she finished, she just stood there, staring down at him.

He stared back, taking in her bare body. "My, my, Tracy. You're an attractive lady, but naked you're gorgeous."

She smiled and bent down, taking a hold of his belt and loosening it. "Let's take a look at yawl."

He sat up, draped his legs over the side of the bed and together they stripped him of his clothes. He sat there naked.

She looked him up and down. "Wow, that's quiet a big fella yawl got between your legs. Don't you think it's time we put him to work?"

He pulled her down on top of him, and they had sex.

Later they lay naked side-by-side. He looked up at the ceiling. "You know I shouldn't have done that," he said. "I'm a happily married man."

She turned and glared at him. "What was that suppose to mean?"

"I wasn't chiding you. You were great. It's just the situation."

She put her hand on his stomach and began rubbing it. "Oh let's just chalk it up to being stranded together on a snowy night." She continued to caress him. After a while she moved down and found him getting hard again.

He turned over, got on top of her, and they had sex again.

Several hours later the snow had stopped. As soon as the road cleared, Sweigert called his wife and told her he was on the way home. They left the motel and drove back to the plant.

The following year on Monday February first, a presentation took place before a small gathering of employees seated inside the large room of the first floor of the engineering building. A large object loomed in the center of the room covered with a gray tarp. The chief engineer, Gordon Dalripple, addressed the group from a lectern set in front of the draped object. He wore the standard engineer's white shop coat. Although of Bavarian heritage, he spoke near perfect English.

"Ladies and gentlemen, after months of design, redesign and testing, it is my pleasure to introduce you to the newly 1972 WCI Caravan." Several employees pulled the tarp off, revealing a shinny gray vehicle similar to the original Caravan but modified in the front end. This model had lost its snub nose, which had been replaced by an angled nose around the engine and front axle ahead of the driver's compartment. "I'll turn the presentation over to Gunter Sweigert, the project engineer, to describe the new features."

Sweigert rose and went to the lectern. He also wore a white shop coat. "As you can see, we moved the front axel and engine forward and provided an angled nose. This increases the safety by adding strength and crush space ahead of the driver's compartment. In earlier models there was little protection from head-on impacts."

He went forward to the vehicle and highlighted these features with his hands. "The design further provides a much more pleasing presentation of the vehicle. It smoothes the severe edges of the original box shape to a sleek angular design of a projectile. We studied these changes for about a year, designing and redesigning, and tested each design in the field. We did crash testing to prove the added safety of the design. We are satisfied with the improvements, and the new Caravan will go into production later this year."

An employee raised his hand. Sweigert acknowledged him.

"Did the redesign have anything to do with complaints about the safety of the occupants of the driver's compartment?"

"No," Sweigert answered. "We had no complaints, but we are constantly reviewing the features of our vehicles and comparing them with the competition. We saw a competitor had moved the front axel forward and immediately realized the safety enhancement of the design. But before we actually produced such a vehicle, we wanted to field test the overall handling and visibility from the driver's perspective. The test proved that moving the front axel and engine together with the changing of the slop of the front end actually improved the handling and did not affect the visibility to a significant degree."

The newly designed Caravan came on the market in October 1971.

5

A COOL WIND blew from the north over the bay into San Francisco. The sun shown from low in the sky. It was Saturday morning, January tenth, and the year was 1970. Rich Lewis parked his car on the east side of Van Ness just beyond the intersection with Bush in front of the Monarch dealership, Hamlin Motors. Inside the high windows flanked by shinny granite walls, Hamlin displayed a number of its cars on highly polished floors. Lewis entered the double glass doors and began examining the cars.

A salesman in a white shirt with a blue striped tie came over to Lewis. "She's a beauty, isn't she? And there're 275 horsed under her hood."

Lewis turned to face the salesman. "Yes, she is, but I'm not interested in a sedan. I have a place in the Sierras north of Tahoe, and I need a pickup. I saw your ad in the Chronicle, and thought I'd come in and take a look."

The salesman pointed. "I see. Well, we have only that one over there, but we have more in the back."

Lewis walked over to the pickup.

The salesman followed close behind while Lewis examined it. "This one is our ton and a half version," the salesman said. "What were you looking for?"

Lewis walked around the vehicle, studying it from all sides. "A ton and a half will work fine for my needs. The most I'll be pulling is a boat with an outboard motor. It like the color, dark green is sort of unique for a pickup. Does it have four-wheel drive?"

"Actually, this one doesn't, but I can show you one that has and, coincidently, its forest green as well."

"Let me see it."

Lewis followed the salesman through a door, down a hall and out to a small lot in back. Among the vehicles there, a green pickup sat at the far end. They went over to it.

The salesman pointed and looked at Lewis. "This retails for twelve thousand four hundred ninety-nine dollars because it has four-wheel drive, but I think we can take a little off that and keep the payments low. Do you have a trade-in?"

Lewis answered, "No." He opened the driver's door and got inside. He turned in the seat and faced the salesman. "And I'm not interested in payments. If I see what I like, I'll offer cash. Can I drive it?"

"Sure. The keys are in it. I'll climb in, and you can drive it out on Polk for a few blocks."

Lewis drove the pickup off the lot and out onto Polk for several blocks. When he returned, both he and the salesman got out of the vehicle. Lewis looked at the salesman. "I'll give you eleven thousand for it."

The salesman looked dejected. "I said a little off. Eleven thousand is more than a little. I can't go that low."

"Well, what will you sell it for? No fooling around. What's your bottom line?"

That salesman blushed. "I don't deal with people like you very often. Give me a minute to talk to my boss."

The salesman went inside, leaving Lewis with the vehicle. Lewis went around the back of the vehicle and examined the bed and the towing mechanism.

In a few minutes the salesman returned. "We'll sell it for twelve thousand two hundred fifty."

Lewis looked him in the eye. "Make it eleven thousand seven hundred fifty cash, and you've got a deal."

The salesman looked down at the ground. Then he looked up at Lewis. "You drive a hard bargain."

"Do we have a deal?"

"Yes."

A year later on a Friday evening in February, Rich Lewis drove his pickup east on I 80. His family had been at their cabin north of Tahoe since the beginning of the month. He left work earlier in the day and was rejoining them for the weekend. He had built the cabin several years earlier in the Hobart Mills area off the two-lane highway 89 just north of Truckee and near Donner Ski Bowl. When he turned north on highway 89 darkness had set in.

As he proceeded north, he encountered light traffic. He rounded a left hand turn and saw the headlights of an approaching vehicle. As the vehicle got nearer, he suddenly realized that it was gradually heading into his lane of travel. He immediately braked and turned sharply to the right. At the last moment the driver of the other car seemed to realize the problem. He also swerved right, but his vehicle side-swiped the pickup, causing it to veer even further to the right and eventually to leave the road, careen down a small hill and smash head-on into a large pine tree.

Fortunately, Lewis had his seatbelt attached. When the pickup hit the tree, it stopped abruptly forcing him forward into the steering wheel. His neck bent forward, and his head struck the windshield. He lost consciousness for a moment. When he became aware of his surroundings, he sat behind the damaged steering wheel bleeding from his forehead. He quickly loosened his seatbelt and tried his door. It opened. He fell out of the door onto the ground. Slowly he rose and stood leaning into the tree for support. His pants were torn at both knees and one knee was bleeding. When he got his bearings, he slowly climbed up the hill to the side of the road, where he collapsed on one knee.

The other vehicle had proceeded up the road and stopped on the opposite shoulder. The driver ran back down to where the pickup had left the road and arrived just as Lewis went down to one knee. The driver stopped at Lewis's side and looked down at him. "I fell asleep. I awoke just before we collided and couldn't turn right fast enough. Thank God you're alive."

Before long several vehicles stopped at the scene, and their passengers gave assistance until the police arrived. One of the patrolmen grabbed a first aid kit and bandaged Lewis' forehead and knee to stop the bleeding. Soon an ambulance came on the scene, and eventually took Lewis to a small hospital in Truckee.

A tow truck pulled the pickup back on the road and towed it to a wrecking yard in Truckee.

The following Wednesday, an adjuster for Lewis' insurance company came to the wrecking yard to examine the pickup. Lewis met him at the lot. They walked out to where the pickup sat. Lewis walked with a limp and had his head bandaged.

The adjuster had a damage form on a clipboard. He went around the vehicle and marked on the form with a ballpoint pen. He recorded severe damage to the front end, where the tree and the pickup met. The impact crushed the grill, the headlights, and the radiator, unseated the engine and basically left the front end and engine compartment of the pickup in a mess. One the driver's side the windshield was cracked and the driver's compartment and the bed were crushed by the side-swipe collision.

When the adjuster completed the inspection, he totaled the figures he had written on the form. He turned to Lewis. "Looks like it's gonna cost somewhere between seven thousand and seventy five hundred to repair it, assuming the frame isn't damaged. But I'll bet it is." He opened a small book he carried in his briefcase and turned the pages. "The blue book on this vehicle lists its resale value at six thousand two hundred fifty dollars, so we're looking at a total loss. By that I mean it'll cost more to repair the vehicle that its value."

Lewis nodded. "What's the process?"

"Simple. I write you a check of six thousand two hundred fifty dollars."

"What happens to the savage?"

"We take care of it. We'll probably sell it for scrap, or, if there is any interest, we might put it out for bids at a salvage auction."

Lewis took the check and left.

The adjuster had the vehicle taken to a salvage lot near Sacramento where an auction was being held. On Monday, March thirteenth, Roger Winchester drove a truck with a lowboy trailer into the lot and parked near a barn-like building. On the side of the truck was a sign advertising Roger's Reck & Rebuild, a wrecking yard and auto rebuild facility outside of Kelso, Washington. Winchester traveled up and down the coast buying wrecks at salvage auctions, and he was at the Sacramento lot answering an ad announcing the March thirteenth auction.

He walked into an office in the building, up to a counter and picked up a list of the vehicles to be auctioned. He examined it. The Lewis pickup appeared as the fourth item. He addressed the man behind the counter. "Where are the vehicles? I'd like to look at a couple of them."

"There out back," the man answered. "Each one has a number on the windshield corresponding to the number on the list."

Winchester went out into the lot and examined the vehicles. Once satisfied, he went back to the building and followed a sign designating the location of the auction. He arrived at a large room containing seven rows of chairs and a podium in front. He observed his competition. He counted nine potential bidders spread out in the chairs. He sat on the aisle of the third row.

About 20 minutes later, several men appeared. One went to the podium and announced that the action would begin. Winchester decided that he wanted the Lewis pickup. Since it was fourth, he wanted to see how the bidding would go. Two people bid on the first vehicle. The first bidder made an offering bid, the second bidder increased the offer, the first bidder also increased the bid and the second bidder let him have it. Winchester upped the bid on the second vehicle. Another man raised the bid and got the vehicle. It took only three bids to purchase the third vehicle.

"The fourth item on the list is a green 1970 Monarch pickup," the auctioneer said. "Do I have a bid for $1,500?"

No one spoke up.

"Come on, it's cheap at that price. Won't someone bid $1,500?"

Again no one bid.

"Well, will anyone . . ."

"One thousand four hundred fifty," Winchester interrupted him.

No one bid higher. He bought the pickup. A tow truck placed the pickup on his lowboy. He secured it, drove off the lot and back up I 5 to Kelso.

He arrived at his facility outside of Kelso on Wednesday afternoon, March fifteenth. He parked the truck on the lot and went inside the shop. He found his rebuild foreman and brought him outside to look at the pickup.

The two men stopped at the lowboy, and the foreman walked around it, examining the pickup.

When the foreman returned to Winchester, Winchester looked at him. "What d'ya think?"

"It's got possibilities."

"I'd like to get around $6,000 for it. It cost me $1,450, and with the expenses, I got maybe $2,000 in it. Can you rebuild it so we can sell it for around that figure and still make a profit?"

The foreman looked at Winchester and grinned. "You know I can. What color do you want?"

Winchester thought. "I don't know. How about black?"

"Black it is."

In June one of Winchester's employee applied for a new title, not disclosing the previous wreck, and the vehicle received a new license plate.

In September that employee and his wife went to Seaside for a weekend at the beach. She drove the family car, and he drove the pickup, which he sold while there to Jorgensen Motors in Seaside for $5,900.

6

TUESDAY MORNING, AUGUST seventh back in 1973, Laura Sugerman exited the elevator on the second floor of Emanuel Hospital. The second floor contained the orthopedic unit. She turned left and went down the hall to room 211. A slip in card on the door sign read Amy Ralston. Mrs. Sugerman entered and saw Amy sitting in her wheelchair reading a book.

Amy heard someone entering and looked up. "Oh, hi Laura, I didn't think you were coming until after lunch.

"I finished my chores early, so I decided to drop by this morning."

"Come in and have a seat."

Mrs. Sugerman sat in the chair facing Amy. "You're looking good. Any word on when you'll be coming home?"

Amy's blue eyes glistened. "Funny you should ask that. The doctor came in this morning and said I could go home first thing tomorrow after his visit."

Mrs. Sugerman smiled. "That's great, and it will work out fine with me. I'm free all day. If I come by at nine, will that be all right?"

"Laura you're so kind. The doctor usually is here about then, so that will be fine. By the way I got a call first thing this morning from Chip McLaughlin, the adjuster for our insurance company. He said Monica Richards, the adjuster for the dairy's insurance company had paid the full amount for the damage to our car. He wants the title to the Caravan because they want the salvage. I think it's in the bottom right drawer of Michael's desk in the den. Could you look, and, if its there, call Chip McLaughlin at Major Casualty. Tell him to come by tomorrow afternoon, and I'll sign it over to them."

"I'll check as soon as I get home."

Amy and Mrs. Sugerman chatted for about an hour before Mrs. Sugerman rose and started for the door. "I'd better get going. Don't you go to therapy pretty soon?"

Amy wheeled the chair after her. "Actually, they're due in any time. It's great of you to come by, and I can't tell how much I appreciate all you and Harry have done. You're like parents to me."

"And you're like a daughter we never had. Is there anything else you'd like me to do to get the house ready for you?"

"No, just make sure Dustin and Michelle know I'm coming home."

Mrs. Sugerman chided her. "You can tell them yourself when they call this afternoon. I'll be bringing them with me tomorrow."

The next morning Dustin, his right arm still in a cast, ran into his mother's arms in room 211 of the hospital. She sat just inside the door in her wheelchair. She hugged him with both arms. Michelle came to the side of the wheelchair, and Amy freed one arm, put it around her daughter and kissed her cheek.

Mrs. Sugerman stood in the doorway smiling. "It looks like your ready to go home."

Dustin backed up and stood on the other side of his mom.

Amy looked at Mrs. Sugerman and then pointed at a small table beside the bed. "Yep, I've been waiting for you. The doctor came early this morning. That stuff on the table goes home with me."

She reached for a cord on the bed. "I'll push the nurses' button, and she'll send the orderly to wheel me out."

Soon an orderly came, the party left 2ll following Amy in the wheelchair and got into the elevator.

When they got to the lobby, Mrs. Sugerman left them and went for her car, a four door sedan. She drove it up the front of the hospital where Amy, the orderly and the children waited. The orderly lifted Amy out of the wheelchair and placed her in the backseat. Then he collapsed the wheelchair and put it in the trunk. Dustin got in the other side of the car and sat next to his mom. Michelle rode in the passenger's seat in front. They left for the Ralston home.

Amy was quiet during the ride. When they turned onto SE Twenty-ninth, she trembled. "I must tell you that I've dreaded this day. As much as I have wanted to come home, I'm frightened by the prospect of getting around, doing housework and caring for Dustin and Michelle from a wheelchair."

Mrs. Sugerman turned slightly while concentrating on the road. "Don't fret. We're here to help you. You'll see the children are also ready to pitch in. Just give yourself time to adjust, and things will work out."

The Ralston house sat back from SE Twenty-ninth with a sloping yard to the sidewalk. A cement walk bisected the yard and led to a front porch and the front door. Fortunately, Amy didn't have to negotiate those three stairs to the porch, because a driveway ran up the side of the house to a garage and a side entrance. During her hospitalization, Harry Sugerman hired a contractor to make the house ready for its wheelchair-bound mistress. One of the things that had been down was the installation of a ramp to the side entrance.

The house, a two-story colonial, nearly matched the Sugerman's, with all of the bedrooms originally on the second floor. The contractor had converted the large formal dining room into a sizeable bedroom and a bathroom designed to accommodate a disabled person who could not walk. At various places on the first floor bars were conveniently attached to the wall to make living easier for a person confined to a wheel chair. There was a contraption next to the bed, which Amy could use to get out of the wheelchair and into bed. Her therapist had been working with Amy on this maneuver at the hospital.

When they arrived at the house, Mrs. Sugerman drove the sedan up the driveway. A husky young man in a white uniform with a dark crew cut and hairy muscular arms waited for them at the bottom of the ramp to the side door. He opened the trunk and retrieved the wheel chair. Then he lifted Amy out of the car and sat her in the wheel chair.

The man looked down at Amy. "This chair's only temporary. You're getting a new one that you'll love. It's waiting for you inside. It's motorized and has a lifting device to help you get into and out of bed and chairs."

"I can hardly wait," Amy said. "Let's go into my house. I've been away way too long."

Before he began pushing the wheelchair, Mrs. Sugerman interjected. "Amy you need to meet Willie Sorrento. He's going to be you're legs during your therapy and for as long after as you need him."

Amy turned and smiled at Willie. "Hi, Willie, I guess I'm at you disposal." She laughed as he pushed her inside.

They entered into the kitchen where a small attractive young woman with short black hair and brown eyes met them. She wore a white short-sleeved blouse, a black skirt, white nylon stockings and black low work shoes.

Mrs. Sugerman smiled and introduced the woman. "Amy, this is Mina Sorrento, Willie's wife and your new cook and housekeeper."

Mina came forward and shook Amy's hand. "I'm pleased to meet you ma'am."

Tears fell from Amy's green eyes onto her cheeks. She looked up at Mina as Mina shook her hand. She started to cry. "The feeling is mutual, I can assure you. I can't tell you what it means to me to have you and your husband here." She put her hands to her face and sobbed.

Mina reached for Amy's head and pulled in toward her chest, patting it softly. "There, there ma'am. We'll help you get settled. Don't you worry?"

Amy gathered herself and looked up at Mina, her green eyes glistening. "Oh, thank you so much. My tears aren't tears of sorrow, but tears expressing the relief I feel knowing I won't have to face being home alone."

Mrs. Sugerman interceded. "Amy, come see what we've done to your dining room."

Willie pushed the wheelchair through the kitchen and entered what used to be the dining room.

Amy put her hands to her face in shock. "Oh, my Lord, what a beautiful sight. I kept asking myself how I could get up to my bedroom. But I see you thought of that." She turned to Mrs. Sugerman and reached for her. "You're such a wonderful friend. You've anticipated everything. I'm so grateful." Mrs. Sugerman came to her, and they hugged.

They went into the living room. Mina had brought in the new wheel chair, and Willie pushed Amy over to it. "Now, you're going to learn how to handle this," he said, assisting her into the new wheelchair." Then he explained the mechanism and showed Amy how to work it. He also had her practice with the lifting device getting out and back into the wheelchair. Meanwhile Mrs. Sugerman had sat down on the sofa and observed Willie's teaching.

Once Willie satisfied himself that Amy could operate the new wheelchair, he smiled at Amy. "Now show me how you can go over and sit next to Mrs. Sugerman."

Amy turned the wheelchair and moved it over in front of the couch where Mrs. Sugerman sat. When she stopped a wide smile appeared on her face. "I did it, I did it," she exclaimed, turning back to Willie.

Amy and Mrs. Sugerman talked for sometime, until Mrs. Sugerman rose. "I've got to get back home. I've got a new gardener coming by at 11." She reached into her purse, drew out a document and handed it to Amy. "I almost forgot this. This is the title you asked me to retrieve from Michael's desk."

Amy said, "Thank you, again."

Later that day, Amy sat in her new wheel chair in the living room facing the sofa. Mrs. Sugerman sat on the sofa. The doorbell rang.

Amy looked toward the kitchen. "Mina would you get that?"

Shortly Mina came into the living room. "It's a Mr. McLaughlin. He says you have a title for him."

Amy picked a paper off the table next to the sofa and held it to Mina. "Here it is. I've signed it on the back."

Mina took the title and left the living room.

Amy turned to Mrs. Sugerman. "Speaking of the accident, Harry told me about Denny Wilson and that I should call him when I was ready. I think the time has come to discuss the financial ramifications of the accident."

"Are you sure, Amy," Mrs. Sugerman asked. "There's no rush."

Amy operated the wheel chair toward the telephone on a table to the right of the sofa. "I'm sure. Do you know what his telephone number is?"

Mrs. Sugerman reached into her purse that was resting on the sofa beside her. She searched for a moment, then pulled out a slip of paper and handed it to Amy. "Here it is."

Amy picked up the telephone, looking at the slip of paper and dialed.

"Witchhazel & Wilson," a woman answered.

"May I please speak to Mr. Wilson?"

"May I tell him who is calling?"

"Amy Ralston."

"One moment please."

After a brief wait, Wilson came on the telephone. "Amy, it's so good of you to call. How are you doing?"

"Just fine, Denny. I just got home and found the wonderful scene our neighbors, the Sugerman, had provided for me. For the first time since the accident, I feel relieved and comfortable with my situation. I want to talk about the financial ramifications of the accident."

Wilson coughed. "Sure, but we don't want to do it on the telephone. Why don't I come by your house? When is a good time for you?"

"Could you come by this afternoon?"

Wilson looked at his calendar. "Yes I could. Say about three-thirty?"

"That would be fine. See you then."

The doorbell rang.

Amy was reading in the living room. She turned toward the kitchen. "Mina would you get that. It's probably the lawyer, Mr. Wilson."

Mina went to the door and peered out the peephole. A medium height red-headed man in a brown suit stood on the porch. He had a cigar in his mouth and a small briefcase in his hand.

Mina opened the door. "Are you Mr. Wilson, the lawyer?"

"Yes, I'm here to see Mrs. Ralston."

"Come in." Mina led Wilson into the living room where Amy sat in her new wheelchair."

As they entered the living room, Amy powered the chair to meet them and held out her hand to Wilson. "Denny, it's good of you to come."

Wilson took the cigar out of his mouth with his left hand and took her hand in his right hand. "It's good to see you Amy. You look good for someone who has gone through what you have."

Amy looked up at him. "Actually, I'm feeling fine in spite of my handicap. My spinal cord was damaged leaving me a paraplegic, but the motorized wheelchair makes my life easier. Come sit down. Why don't you take the sofa? I'll move my wheelchair over there so we can talk."

Wilson put the cigar back in his mouth and sat at the end of the sofa away from the fireplace, and Amy brought up the wheelchair so that she faced him. Immediately Wilson took the cigar out of his mouth. "My God, I put the cigar in my mouth without thinking. Do you have an ashtray where I can get rid of this thing?"

Amy laughed. "I wouldn't know you without the cigar. Don't get rid of it. There's an ashtray on the table over there by that chair." She pointed. "Get it and lay your cigar on it, if you'll be more comfortable that way."

Wilson got up and walked over to the table. He took the ash tray back to the coffee table in front of the sofa, laid it on the table and rested his cigar in it. He sat back on the sofa and opened his briefcase, taking out a legal pad and laying it on his lap. He also took a ball point pen from his shirt pocket and looked up at Amy. "Where do you want to start?"

Her green eyes sparkled as she looked at him. "I can't tell you much about the accident. The last thing I remember is going through Elsie. Michelle and Dustin don't have a memory of it either."

"Don't worry about it. I've got the police report in here." He reached into his briefcase and withdrew a seven page document. "I've also have photographs taken by the investigation officers of the scene and of the vehicles. The sergeant says in the report that he suspects that the hood of the pickup released, hitting the windshield and blinding the driver and that the pickup crossed the center line and hit your Caravan head-on. I don't think it's wise to show you the photographs of the van. Let's talk about your condition and the condition of the children."

She shook her head. "I don't want to see the photographs." She paused and looked in Wilson's eyes. "Well, my condition is obvious. I'm a paraplegic, and the doctor says it's permanent. The children are better off, but the accident has left them with lots of residuals. They miss their dad and brother terribly, as do I. They have trouble sleeping and periodically suffer from terrible nightmares."

Wilson took notes. He looked up. "Has anyone representing the dairy contacted you?"

"Not yet."

"Then I think the first order of business is for me to write them a demand letter. That'll get us a contact from their insurer. I don't expect that'll resolve the matter though. I know you don't want to punish anyone, but we have to be realistic. Although the damage done by this accident to you, your children and family can't be measured, there is only one way it can be dealt with, and that's with money. And it's going to take a lot of money, more I suspect than the dairy's insurance policy. We'll see when the insurance company contacts me, but I suspect you're probably going to have to file a lawsuit."

Amy shook her head again. "I don't want to do that. Isn't there some other way?"

Wilson placed his hand on hers. "I know you don't. But I'm just trying to be realistic. You and the children are entitled to compensation not only for your own injuries, but for the loss of a husband, a father, a son and a brother. The financial loss for the death of Michael can be measured by his life expectancy and the future loss of income during that time, and that's a very sizable amount. And it's an amount you're not only entitled to, but is necessary to care for you and your family in the future. That amount alone is probably going to be much larger than the insurance policy, so you have to prepare yourself to look to someone else for the excess amount, the dairy, the last person to have closed the hood or maybe Monarch Motors."

"How do we figure out what we need?"

"We can hire an economist or maybe an actuary. But first, you need a lawyer with lots of experience in these matters. I don't do much trial work and wouldn't qualify. You need a real pro; not an ambulance chaser, like the one who had a runner contact Mr. Sugerman right after the accident."

Amy looked puzzled. "How do I find such a person?"

"Let me give it some thought. I write the letter to the dairy to get things started. We'll find out how much insurance is involved and what the insurance company intends doing. And while this is going on, I'll make some inquiries to see who's available."

Monday morning, August twentieth Grassley stood by Richard's desk with a letter in his hand. "We finally got a demand from a lawyer in the Towson Dairy matter." He handed the letter to her.

She read the letter and looked up. "It's written by Denny Wilson out in Beaverton. I know him slightly. He's no personal injury lawyer, but he's smart and will know something about the value of his client's case. I doubt if we can settle this for our policy limits of two hundred thousand, but maybe we can work with him."

Grassley cast a doubting eye at her. "Maybe I'm missing something. Can't we simply tender our full policy limits and get out of this?"

Richards chuckled. "Yes, but that'll leave the dairy out there uninsured, and we'll still have to provide them a defense under out contract when he sues them. When I said maybe we can work with him, I had in mind a deal where we give up the two hundred thousand and work with him prosecuting a case against the service station and Monarch Motors. Remember we hired Wayland Chang to inspect the vehicles. I suspect he'll have a theory by now against the manufacturer. I'll propose that one, we give Wayland to Wilson in return for his leaving the dairy out of a suit and two, we'll also hire whoever Wilson gets to file suit to get back the two hundred thousand we paid out. That might interest him, especially since we would help to finance the suit."

Grassley smiled. "I like the way you think. You've got my okay to give it a try."

Grassley started to leave, but turned back when Richards said, "Before I approach Wilson, I think I'll check with Wayland and see if he's made an appointment to get the vehicles."

Grassley nodded and left.

Richards picked up the telephone and dial Wayland Chang's direct number. Chang answered.

"Wayland, this is Monica Richards. I have the vehicle titles. Have you set up an appointment to pick the vehicles up?"

"Yes, I just did yesterday. We can go out anytime, if we call first."

"Call the patrolman in charge at the lot and tell him we'll be there at nine tomorrow morning. I'll meet you there."

7

THE FOLLOWING MORNING, when Richards arrived at the police lot in Aloha, she saw that Chang's pickup was parked in front, and he sat in the driver's seat waiting. She parked next to the pickup, got out and walked around the back of the pickup, just as Chang exited the door.

She walked up to Chang. "How long have you been waiting?"

"I got here about five minutes ago. Shall we go in?"

She started up the two stairs that led to the doorway, and Chang followed. She opened the door. They walked up to the counter, where the patrolman she had met before rose from his desk.

The patrolman walked to the other side of the counter and smiled at Richards. "I thought I'd be seeing you again fairly soon."

Richards introduced Chang and handed the patrolman the titles for the two vehicles. "Here are the titles signed by the owners. We're here to pick them up."

The patrolman examined the titles and then looked out the front window. He looked back at Richards and Chang. "You'll need more that that pickup out there to haul them away."

"I've got a tow-truck and a lowboy trailer on the way," Chang said. They should be here any minute. May we see the vehicles?"

"Sure follow me out the back door." He held open a swinging door in the counter. He led the way out back and to the three vehicles to the left and towards the back of the lot.

Chang immediately began examining the pickup and particularly the hood latching mechanism. He looked up at Richards. "Although the front end is badly damaged on the driver's side, the latching mechanism behind the radiator appears to be intact."

He looked up at the mating mechanism on the hood and pulled the hood down. It didn't mate because of the damage, but he stooped down and looked at the two mechanisms when they got as close at they could. "Hum, that pointed mechanism attached to the underside of the hood goes into the hole in front of the radiator and latches in the notch here," he said to no one in particular. "But there doesn't seem to be any device to secure it if it isn't fully in the notch. There should be a double catch, one you have to release with your hand before the hood will come fully up."

Then he turned to Richards. "I want to examine this closer when we get the vehicles to the garage I've secured, but it looks like the way this vehicle is made, unless the last person who opened the hood made sure it was pushed down square, it could fly open if jostled."

Richards eyed Chang. "Are you sure of that?"

"Almost positive. I'll bet the driver drove over something on the road just before the hood flew back against the windshield."

"My God, the police report says that one of the officers at the scene found a small log or board up the road in the lane Bentwood came down just before the accident."

About then the tow truck arrived, and the driver began placing the remains of the pickup and van on the lowboy with Chang directing so no further damage occurred to either vehicle. They left the cow trailer on the lot for now.

The next morning, when Richards returned to her desk, she looked down at the letter Grassley had given her on Monday, picked up the telephone and dialed Wilson's number.

"Witchhazel & Wilson," a woman answered.

"May I speak to Mr. Wilson?"

"I'm sorry he's with a client."

"Will you ask him to call Monica Richards at Western Indemnity Company?"

She gave the woman her number.

Thursday morning Monica Richards' telephone rang. She picked it up and answered.

"This is Denny Wilson returning your call."

"Hi, Denny. We met some time ago. I have you letter to Towson Dairy. We insure them."

"I remember, Monica. It was a collision loss one of my clients had, I think about three years ago. This time the matter's far more serious. Actually, I'm just helping the Ralstons temporarily. If the matter gets into litigation, I'm going to refer Mrs. Ralston to a more experienced trial attorney."

"I assumed that," Richard said, "but maybe we can work something out short of litigation. Rather than talking about it on the telephone, why don't I come by your office this week?"

"Would nine tomorrow work out for you?"

"Fine, I'll see you then."

On Friday morning, Richards sat in a client's chair in Wilson's office and eyed Wilson with her hazel eyes. Wilson sat at his desk, a cigar hanging from his lips.

Richards released her stare and glanced around his office. The window at her back looked out at the stubble of harvested wheat and in the distance the grove of fir trees. Below it sat a brown leather sofa and a small coffee table, and paneled walls of fir painted brown lined the room. The chair she occupied and a companion chair to her left had a wooden back and arms and a leather cushion that matched the sofa. "I like you office," she said.

Wilson smiled and brushed back his red hair. "It isn't much but I like it too."

On a table also to Richard's left she noticed framed pictures of a boy and a girl. She pointed at them. "Are those your children?"

"Yes."

She smiled. "There quite attractive. I don't see a picture of your wife, but they must take after her?" He smiled back. "Actually, they live with her. We're divorced."

"I'm sorry."

He continued smiling. "No harm done. We just weren't compatible, but we've remained friends. But that's not what you called about."

She glanced at him. She could tell her hazel eyes had his attention. "Actually, I called about your letter. I'll be frank with you, the dairy only has two hundred thousand of insurance, but I'd like to protect them if I can." She told him what she had in mind. "I was present when Wayland made his initial inspection of the vehicles. He thinks the pickup should have had a second feature to hold the hood down, most vehicles do. He also thinks the hood wasn't latched fully the last time it was opened. My investigation found that last time was at a service station several miles back toward Portland on the trip down to the accident. An attendant checked the oil and water in the pickup and must have been negligent in latching the hood."

She shifted in the chair, but didn't lose eye contact with Wilson. "What I'm proposing is that we pay your clients the two hundred thousand dollars and give you access to Chang so you can sue the service station and Monarch Motors in return for your promise to leave the dairy out of the suit. We'll also hire you to prosecute our subrogation claim for property damage we paid and the two hundred thousand against the same two defendants, and, of course, we'll pay our share of the costs to prosecute the cases against Monarch."

Wilson's eyes showed his interest. He cast his glance at an ashtray on his desk as he put his cigar in it. Then he looked back at Richards. "That's an interesting proposal. Of course, I think you owe the full two hundred thousand dollars without any strings attached, but I hadn't give any thought to taking you on as a client and you're helping finance a case against the manufacture. I doubt that the dairy has much in the way of free assets, so, if there's a reasonable case against the manufacturer that might be the way to go."

He picked up his letter opener and spun it his fingers, thinking. He looked again at Richards. "As I told you on the telephone, I'm just helping Mrs. Ralston out until she can retain an experience personal injury lawyer. In fact, she asked me to help her get such a lawyer, and I'm in the process of doing just that. I'll continue that task, and, when I get someone, I tell him and Mrs. Richard about your proposal. I may even recommend it for whatever my opinion counts. Either I or the other counsel will get back to you. Can I buy you a cup of coffee at the restaurant across the street?"

Richards got up and held out her hand. "No, I've got to get going, but it has been nice to meet you again, and I truly hope we can work something out."

Wilson rose and shook her hand. "Thanks, Monica. We'll be in touch."

After Richards left, Wilson mused as he sat back in his desk chair. *Now I must get Amy a first class personal injury lawyer. What was the name of that guy from Nevada who spoke to the Oregon Trial Lawyers a year or so ago?*

He turned his chair to the credenza behind him and below the window. He opened the bottom filing drawer, picked out a folder labeled OTLA and brought it to his desk. He opened it and stared flipping trough the documents in the file. After a moment he stopped and said to himself, *here it is, Wayne Merriman out of Carson City.* He picked up a pen and wrote the telephone number on a pad as he dialed the number.

"Good morning, Merriman & Savage," a woman answered.

"May I speak to Mr. Merriman?"

"May I say whose calling?"

"This is Denny Wilson, a lawyer in Beaverton, Oregon. He won't know me. I was at a presentation he made two years ago here in Oregon, and I have a case I'd like to refer to him."

"One moment please?"

Several moments later a gruff voice came on the telephone. "Wilson, you're right I don't remember you. What's your case about?"

Wilson leaned back in his chair. "It's an auto accident involving the death of a father and son and serious injuries to the wife, a daughter and another son." He went on to describe the accident, the occupation of the deceased, the injuries to the wife and children. He told Merriman that he had the police report and pictures. "Western Indemnity insures the dairy, and I understand that they have the vehicles and have had any engineer look at the pickup. The adjuster tells me that the engineer has found a manufacturing defect in the vehicle."

"How much insurance is there?" Merriman asked, abruptly.

"Not anywhere near enough. The dairy has a two hundred thousand policy."

"Your right again. That's not enough. Has the dairy got any free assets?"

"I doubt it, but I haven't checked. But in addition to the pickup manufacture, there's also a service station whose employee opened the hood about an hour before the accident."

Merriman cleared his throat. "What about the manufacture of the van? Who is it?"

Wilson acted surprised. "The van? What's it got to do with it? It didn't do anything to cause the accident."

"Oh, come now Wilson. Where's your imagination? You ever heard of second collision injuries?"

"No, what's that?"

Merriman clear his throat again. "That's where the vehicle wasn't made safe enough for the passenger, so they got injured worse than they should have. What kind of a van was it?"

Wilson nodded. "Oh, I see what you're getting at. It was one of the original Caravan's manufactured by WCI."

Merriman chuckled. "I see. Well, there may be someone else out there. Those original Caravans didn't have much protection for the passengers in a head-on collision. Anyway, you've peaked my interest. I might just take you case. Why don't you fly down here, and we'll talk about it more."

"Is there an airport in Carson City?"

"Not a commercial one, but you can fly to Reno and rent a car. It's not a bad drive from there down here. How about you see if you can make arrangement to be here next Wednesday, say in the afternoon?"

"I put my secretary to work with the arrangements," Wilson said. "If the air schedule works out, I'll be there. I'll call as soon as the arrangements have been made."

"Meanwhile, send me a copy of the police report so I have it when we meet."

The following Wednesday, Wilson sat, smoking a cigar, in the reception area, just inside the front doors of the offices of Merriman & Savage. Although there were only two lawyers in the firm, the firm occupied all of a small two-story building on North Curry Street, a block from the state capital complex. Its front resembled an old western house set back about twenty feet from a wooden side walk. A cobble stone path led to four wooden stairs up to a narrow front porch. A shinny brass plaque rested on the front wall beside two double front doors adorned with shinny brass hardware that announced *Merriman & Savage*. Two large sash windows were on either side of the front door surrounded by lace curtains.

Wilson perused a recent copy of Life Magazine, when he became aware of someone approaching him. He looked up and saw a tall well-build middle aged man walking into the reception area and towards him. The man had blonde wavy hair that fell just above his shoulders. He wore brown worn cowboy boots, faded jeans, and a single-breasted leather jacket over a white shirt with lapels over the pockets and a string tie, clearly western attire. He had a tan complexion on a large square-jaw face, but his eyes dominated his appearance, heavy blonde eyebrows over deep blue glistening eyeballs.

The man gave Wilson a broad smile and stuck out his hand. "Mr. Wilson I presume. I'm Wayne Merriman."

Wilson took the cigar out of his mouth, stood and put out his hand. Merriman grasped it with a vice grip, causing Wilson the gasp slightly.

"Glad, glad to meet you, Mr. Merriman," Wilson stammered.

"It's Wayne. Out here we go by first name. Yours is Denny, isn't it?"

"Yeah."

Merriman turned to his right and put his large hand behind Wilson's shoulder. "Come this way, Denny. We'll go into my office where we can talk."

Wilson followed Merriman down a hall to the right. At the end Merriman turned into a front room which looked out to the street. An average size room, its walls were adorned with western scenes and a mounted elks head on the back wall over a large desk formed by a polished piece of wood from a huge fire tree. Two chairs with leather upholstered seats and wooden backs and arms sat beside the desk, and a leather sofa and wooden table were under the windows at the street.

Merriman offered one of the chairs to Wilson and sat himself behind his desk. Wilson sat and glanced around the room, particularly noticing the elk.

Merriman leaned back in his chair, lit a cigarette and noticed Wilson staring at the elk. "I shot that in fifty-eight down near Walker Lake. I'd never seen antlers that big, so I had the head mounted."

"It sure is dramatic," Wilson said.

Merriman laid his cigarette in an ashtray on his desk and looked at Wilson. "So is your accident. I was fascinated by the accident scene description in the police report, particularly with the way the pickup drove through the Caravan. It's a perfect example of the lack of protection that vehicle gave to its passengers."

Wilson pulled out a cigar from his shirt pocket and lit it. "I saw that, but didn't realize its significance in so far as the van was concerned."

"Well, hopefully you do now. Tell me, has the insurance company for the dairy been in contact with you or your client?"

Wilson puffed his cigar. "Yes, and that's part of the reason I called you. The adjuster, Monica Richards, made a very interesting proposal to us." Then he explained Richards' proposal. "What do you think?"

Merriman's eyes lit up. "That is interesting, and I like it. Of course, the Ralstons are entitled to the policy limit and much more, but what I like about the proposal is the financial help that is being offered. I doubt that the dairy is a very viable source of money so giving up suing it is really meaningless. Monarch Motors and WCI will put up a good fight, but the backing of the insurance company levels the playing field."

"Then do I gather that you want the case?"

Merriman laughed. "Don't be so anxious. As I said, I'm intrigued. But there are several things I need before getting involved. First, I don't like to go into another state without local counsel. I gather you don't do much personal injury work, but that doesn't matter because I've got that expertise. Would you be the local counsel?"

"Sure, but the client wants you to do all the heavy work."

"Understood. Then there's the matter of the courts. I've never tried a case in Oregon. Tell me about the courts up there."

Wilson put his cigar in the stand-up ash tray next to his chair. "Well, of course, we have the state and federal courts. Oregon has limited discovery in state courts, so if you need discovery, the federal court is the place to get it."

Merriman's blue eyes lit up. "What do you mean limited discovery? Can't you take depositions in the state court?"

"Oh you can take depositions if you know the persons you want to depose, but there is no procedure, such as interrogatories, to find out names of witnesses or experts. Sometimes parties voluntarily agree to share that information, but, if not, you're often in the dark about those matters until trial."

Merriman picked up his cigarette, took a drag and put his head back and let the smoke drift out of his mouth. "That's interesting. Can you get production of documents and things?"

"Yes, if you know what it is you want, but again the procedure is limited by the fact that there is no procedure to find out what's available."

Merriman still had his head back and seemed to be looking at the ceiling. A moment later he brought his head down and looked at Wilson. "I can see where that could be an advantage to an aggressive plaintiff. Can you designate areas of depositions for corporate defendants? In other words, can you make corporate defendants produce people for depositions if you designate the areas about which you want information even though you don't know the names of those people?"

"Yes."

Merriman turned his chair around so he was facing the wall. He sat there for several moments. Then he turn back to face Wilson, his eyes glistened and he smiled. "I'll represent your client."

Wilson eyed him. "What are your terms?"

"The usual, one third of any settlement before trial, 40% of any recovery or settlement on trial and 50% of a recovery on appeal. Of, course the client bears the responsibility for the costs, although in this case since the insurance company is a client, the Mrs. Ralston would only be responsible for the costs incurred that the insurance company doesn't pay for."

"She'll agree to that."

Merriman rose and motioned to Wilson. "Now that that is settled, let me show you my shop."

He headed out his door with Wilson following. They went straight ahead down the hall to another room, this time facing the capital grounds.

Merriman stopped when he entered the room and turned back to Wilson as he entered. "I want you to meet my partner, Alex Savage. Alex this is the man I was telling you about, Denny Wilson."

A short, rather heavy man stood at his desk. He was likewise dressed in western garb and wore a string tie. He had short dark hair parted on the left side and sported a long dark mustache that curled at the ends. He smoked a thin cigar.

Savage held his hand out to Wilson. "Nice to meet you, Denny."

"Alex's my brains," Merriman said. "He handles our clients' business matters, heads up our investigators and paralegals and supervises any research projects. I rely on him for all trial briefs and jury instructions." He turned to Savage. "Alex we've taken on Denny's clients. Denny will be our local counsel."

"It looks like a very interesting case," Alex said, "one that I can't wait to sink my teeth into. I've read the police report and seen their pictures, do you have any other investigation?"

"No, but we will be working with the client's insurance carrier, and I know they've done some. They've hired a consulting engineer who I'm told has found a manufacturing defect in the pickup."

Savage beamed. "That's great. When do we get to consult with him?"

Merriman interrupted. "We haven't gotten that far. I'm just showing Denny around our shop. When we get done, we'll come back and discuss that and other things."

Savage sat back down at his desk. "I'll be waiting."

Merriman led Wilson back out to the hall. He stopped and turned to Wilson. "You may have noticed two secretaries off the hall, one down by my office and one here by Alex's." He looked toward the secretary outside of Savage's office. "This is Alex's secretary, Millie. Millie, this is Denny Wilson. We will be working with him in Oregon."

The secretary said, "Nice to meet you Mr. Wilson."

"Call him Denny, Millie. Like always this will be a first name case."

The secretary smiled at Wilson. "All right, its Denny then."

They walked back down the hall and stopped at Merriman's secretary's desk. He looked at Wilson. "Denny meet my secretary Lou Miles." Then he looked at his secretary. "Lou this is Denny Wilson. You know about his case. We've agree to be associated with him."

Lou Miles was a divorcee, in her early 40s and a knockout, long blonde hair, a stunning figure and long narrow legs that were apparent due to her skirt at her knees. She wore a loose open blouse that showed just enough cleavage. She smiled. "I'll enjoy working with you. Anytime you need anything from down here, just call and ask."

"I appreciate that," Wilson said. "It will be a pleasure working with you."

Next Merriman took Wilson upstairs and introduced him to the firm's two paralegals and their investigator. "This was a perfect day for you visit, since all of our staff was on site," he said, as they were returning to the first floor. "That doesn't often happen. Let's go back to Alex's office and do some planning."

They returned to Savage's office and sat around his small conference table. Merriman sat at the head of the table. He turned to Wilson. "We should schedule a visit to Portland as soon as possible. We want to meet Mrs. Ralston and the two kids, and we want to have a meeting arranged with the insurance adjuster and her consultant."

Wilson lit a cigar and puffed it several times. He looked up at Merriman. "My client is available anytime as are the children. Why don't you pick several dates, and I'll try to arrange the meeting with the insurance adjuster and the engineer as soon as I get back. I'll give you a call to confirm the times."

Merriman looked at Savage. "What about next Wednesday? Alex how are you fixed for September fourth?"

Savage said, "That's fine."

Merriman looked at Wilson. "Then its set, pending the availability of the adjuster and the engineer. Why don't we plan to meet with them on Thursday? We have a plane, so we'll fly up from here Tuesday evening. Any special place you would recommend we stay?"

Wilson rested the cigar in the corner of his mouth. "Since you'll be in a private plane, land it in Hillsboro and let me know when you'll be here. I'll pick you up and make arrangement for you at the one good motel here in Beaverton."

Wilson returned to Portland that evening.

8

THE SUN SHOWN brightly as Merriman's Beechcraft Bonanza landed at the Hillsboro airport at eleven-thirty in the morning on Wednesday, September fourth. The warm temperature greeted Merriman and Savage as they deplaned. They walked to the airport building each carrying a small bag and a brief case. Wilson met them at the arrival gate.

"Welcome to Portland," Wilson said extending his hand.

Merriman put his bag down, grabbed Wilson's hand, gripping it strongly, and shook it. "Thus begins a successful venture. Where do we start?" He picked up his bag.

Wilson turned toward Merriman as they began walking to the parking lot. "At the Ralston's house. I said we'd be there around noon."

True to his word, Wilson pulled up in front of the Ralston's house at five of twelve. The three men walked up the front walk, onto the porch and Wilson rang the doorbell.

Mina Serrento answered the door. "Come in Mr. Wilson," she said. As they entered, she looked at Merriman. "You must be Mr. Merriman."

"Yes, maam," Merriman said, "and this is my partner Alex Savage."

"It's nice to meet you, Mr. Savage."

Mina led the three into the living room where Amy sat near the sofa. "Mrs. Ralston, you know Mr. Wilson. These two men are Mr. Merriman and Mr. Savage."

Merriman went forward and stood before Amy. He looked down at her and held out his hand. "Maam, it is a true pleasure to meet you. My partner, Alex, and I are deeply sorry for you loss and suffering. We are at your disposal, and, while we can't begin to repair or replace what you've loss, I assure you we will do everything in our power to see that you and your children are protected."

Amy took his hand which he gave her without his usual grip. "Thank you Mr. Merriman. I'm glad you're here and have agreed to take my case. Won't you sit?"

Merriman said, "That would be fine." And he sat in an arm chair facing Amy. Savage and Wilson sat on the sofa.

"How was your flight up?" Amy asked.

Merriman leaned forward, resting his large forearms on his legs. "It couldn't have been better. What a beautiful late summer day you have."

"September's usually like this here. Portland's known for its rain, but the summers are wonderful."

"I suppose Denny's explained our arrangement?" Merriman asked.

"Yes, he has, Mr. Merriman, and it's very satisfactory with me. He prepared an agreement making you and him my attorneys for recovering for the accident, and I have signed it."

Merriman smiled at her. "I don't want you to think I'm forward, but we're going to be working closely together for some time now, and I think it would work out better if we used our first names. Mine is Wayne and my partner's is Alex. I believe yours is Amy."

"That's fine with me, Wayne. I'm not one who likes to stand on formality."

Merriman continued to smile at her. "That's great, Amy. I think you know that Denny here has had contact with the dairy's insurance company, and they've made a proposal. Are you aware of that?"

"I'm aware that Denny talked to them. I'm not fully aware of what they are proposing."

Merriman reached into his brief case and pulled out a document which he handed to Amy. "That document contains the proposal. Let me explain it because for once I think an insurance company's on the right tract."

He explained Richard's proposal. "What they'll do is give you the two hundred thousand dollars that they'll call a loan, but you don't have to pay it back. The reason they'll call it a loan is so that we can include that amount in your lawsuit. When we get a settlement either by agreement or from a trial, they'll get their two hundred thousand dollars out to the recovery. But the nice thing is that they'll pay most of the costs of the suit for you. It's a proposal that Denny and I think you should accept."

Amy looked at the document then at Merriman. "Thank you for explaining it. I don't like to read legal documents. If you and Denny think I should accept the proposal, then I will. It sounds fine to me." She handed the document back to Merriman.

Merriman took the document and placed it back in his brief case. He looked at Amy. "Then I want you to leave the legal matters to us lawyers and the insurance company. We'll take it from here. We'll keep you fully apprised of things as we proceed, but anytime you have a question feel free to call." He reached in his back pocket for his wallet, took a card from it and handed it to her. "Here's my card with my address and telephone number. Call anytime you want."

Amy took the card. "Thank you. If we've completed our business for now, Mina's made lunch. I hope you'll stay and join me. It'll be served at the table over there," she said pointing. "We eat in the living room now, because the old dining rooms been converted to my bedroom, since I can't climb stairs anymore."

They got up and Amy led the way in her motorized wheelchair to the table, where they sat, ate and chatted about nonlegal matters.

At three o'clock Wilson, Merriman and Savage said good bye and left for Nendells, a motor hotel in Beaverton where Wilson made reservations for Merriman and Savage. On the trip Wilson turned briefly to Merriman who sat in the front seat. "I've got some other business to take care of the rest of the day, so I'll drop you off at Nendells where you'll be staying. I'll pick you up at eight tomorrow morning, and we can go to my office to plan for Monica Richards' visit at ten. Then hopefully, she's arranged for us to meet the engineer later in the day."

The next morning Merriman wore the same outfit as when Wilson visited Carson City. He sat on the couch in Wilson's office, and Savage occupied one of the wooden chairs.

Wilson, sitting behind his desk, puffed on his cigar and looked at Merriman. "She should be here any time now. You'll like what you see. She's not your typical adjuster, more like a model."

Merriman gave a crafty smile. "Sounds like someone I'd like to meet. How old is she anyway? Her proposal didn't come from some dumb blonde?"

Wilson laughed. "She's somewhere in her mid-thirties, and she has brown hair."

Just then Wilson's secretary stuck her head in the doorway. "Monica Richards is here to see you."

"Tell her I'll be right out." He turned to Merriman. "I'll go get her and bring her in." He got up and left the room.

He returned in a few minutes accompanied by Monica Richards. She carried a small case. Again she wore her white blouse open in the front to catch your attention. Her ensemble also included brown slacks and black pumps.

Merriman and Savage stood as they entered the office. Merriman looked her up and down and thought *you weren't kidding, Denny.*

Wilson introduced Richards. "Wayne and Alex, I'd like you to meet Monica Richards." He turned to Richards. "Monica, this is Wayne Merriman and Alex Savage. They're from Carson City, Nevada and will be associated with me representing the Ralstons."

Merriman smiled pleasantly and held out his hand. "It's a pleasure to meet you, maam. I should warn you that my grip is strong, but I won't harm your dainty hands."

Richards looked Merriman straight in the eyes, engaged his strong grip and shook his hand. "Don't worry about my hands," she chuckled. "As you can see I work out at least an hour every morning and that includes lifting weights." Then she turned, shook hands with Savage, sat on the couch near where Merriman had been sitting and laid her case on the floor in front of her.

Merriman and Savage sat back down, and Wilson pulled up the other chair opposite the table in front of the couch.

Merriman turned to face Richards. "Denny has explained your interesting proposal. I like it, and I've recommended that we accept it. The client had agreed. Do you have it in writing?"

Richards reached down and brought her case into her lap. She opened it and took out a single sheet of paper which she handed to Merriman. "Yes, here it is."

Merriman took a pair of glasses from inside his jacket, held them in his hand and looked at Richards. "You know I like a gal who's prepared. Let me look at it for a moment." He put on his glasses at the end of his nose, dipped his head, and read the document. When he had finished, he looked up and smiled. "There's not a thing I would change." He put the document on the table, took a pen from his shirt pocket, signed the document, and looked up again. "I see that you've already signed it." He turned to Wilson. "Denny give this to your secretary and have her get us enough copies so we all have one."

Wilson got up, took the document from Merriman and left the room.

As Wilson was leaving, Merriman turned to Richards, caught her hazel eyes with his deep blue ones. "Well, that's settled. Monica, our team is on a first name basis. I hope you're comfortable with that?"

Richards nodded. "I wouldn't have it any other way, Wayne."

"I don't know what you have in mind next, but I'd like to meet your engineer. We've been told he's found a defect in the design of the pickup."

"I thought that would be your first move. He's available today, in fact this morning. Do we want him to come here or should we go there? Since he has the vehicles, maybe we should meet him where he has the vehicles stored."

Merriman took a pack of Marlboros from his shirt pocket and offered one to Richards. "Do you care for a cigarette?"

She took one. "I'd like one, thank you."

Merriman struck a match on his jeans, leaned forward toward Richards and lit her cigarette. Then he lit his. He inhaled deeply and said as he released the smoke, "We'll go where he has the vehicles. Why don't you give him a call and arrange to meet him there?"

"Okay." She got up, went to Wilson's desk and dialed the telephone. After a short wait, spoke into the telephone. "May I speak to Wayland Chang?" Another short wait. "Wayland, this is Monica Richards. The Nevada lawyers are here and want to meet you at the garage where you're storing the vehicles. When will you be there?" Another short wait. "One-thirty, fine."

She hung up the telephone and turned to Merriman. "I think you heard. We're to meet him at one-thirty at the garage where he's storing the vehicles. It's close to his office on Portland's east side. It'll take us about thirty minutes to get there. There's a good place to have lunch on the way just west of Beaverton. Why don't we stop off there?"

Merriman stuffed out his cigarette in an ash tray on the table. "That's great. We'll leave as soon as Denny returns."

When Wilson returned with copies of the agreement, he gave one to Merriman and returned the original back to Richards.

Merriman gave his copy to Savage, who placed it in a brief case. "Monica's contacted the engineer," Merriman said to Wilson. "We're to meet him after lunch in the garage where he's storing the vehicles."

"I suggested we stop at McCormick's for lunch, since it's on the way," Richards said.

"Okay, then let's go," Wilson said. He turned to Richards who stood by his desk. "I'll take Wayne and Alex in my car, and we'll follow you."

By this time Merriman and Savage had gotten up, and Merriman said to Wilson. "Why don't I ride with Monica?" He smiled at her. "I'll bet she doesn't want to drive alone, and it'll give us time to get better acquainted."

Richards eyed Merriman. "Actually, I don't mind driving alone, but I'll take you anyway," she said, giving him a wry smile.

They left Wilson's office and drove, Richard in the lead, to McCormick's where they had lunch. After lunch, just before Richard got into her vehicle, she handed Wilson a piece of paper. "That's got the address where we're meeting Chang in case we get separated. I'm sure you can find it."

As they were driving east on the Bertha-Beaverton highway, Merriman turned toward Richards. "Monica, you fascinate me. I've met a lot of insurance adjusters, but rarely a woman and certainly never a woman as attractive as you."

Richard smiled but looked ahead as she drove. "That's not a very clever lead in. But if you must know, I wasn't always an adjuster. When I graduated from college, I got married and became a housewife. The marriage lasted only six years, the last two very rocky. My ex liked to play around, and I finally got tired of it and got a divorce. There I was, single again, twenty-eight and needing a job. I majored in history which didn't exactly lend itself to the job market, except maybe teaching, and I wasn't cut out to be a teacher. I wanted something with more action, and, although there weren't many women adjusting for insurance companies, I liked the action the job offered, so I decided to give it a try. Eight years later I'm still doing it and having a ball. I've found my sex and looks to be an advantage." She turned briefly and gave Merriman a sly smile. "People seem to open up to a good looking woman."

Merriman laughed. "I suppose they would."

"I'm sure you know that I've heard of you and your reputation," Richards said, still looking ahead. "I followed your case in Boulder several years ago, because our company was peripherally involved. That was one hell of a verdict you got for that gal in a tough complicated case. What was her name, Marion Winter something?"

"Marion Wintersmyth. And you're right the case was a tough one. But it takes something dramatic or out-of-the-ordinary to attract me."

"What attracted you to this case?"

Merriman turned and looked at her. "Several things. The usual nature of the accident, a hood flying up blinding the driver of one vehicle, the van's lack of passenger protection from head-on collisions, the death of a promising young accountant, the severe injuries to the wife, and frankly your proposal. I wanted to meet the female who came up with that idea. Now that I have, I'm even more intrigued with the case."

Richard turned and met his eyes again. Then she turned ahead and smiled. "More sweet talk again. I know you'd already taken the case when you met me, but I'll take what you said as a compliment. Do you really think you can make a case against WCI because the style of the Caravan affords less protection against head-on collisions?"

"Yes, I do. I know there isn't a lot of precedent for this kind of a claim, but later models of those styles of vehicles are now built with more protection. The manufacturer will rely on the state-of-art at the time of manufacture as a defense, but I have a feeling that with a little discovery we'll find that they had knowledge that they could improve the vehicle's safety at the time this vehicle was built. I like the challenge of finding out and establishing a precedent. And should we fail, we still have the pickup."

"That's what I've heard about you. I'm glad I'm on your side in this one." She glanced briefly at him. "You've heard from me. Tell me a little about yourself."

Merriman looked at her and smiled. "You obviously don't know much about me, or you'd know that my ego is caressed by that request. Before I regale you with my life story, do you mind if I light up in the car?"

"No, as a matter of fact you can light one for me too."

He lifted the lapel of his shirt pocket and pulled out the pack of Marlboros. He took two cigarettes out of the pack, struck a match on his jeans, put one in his mouth, lit it and extended it to Richards.

Richards turned toward him briefly, opened her lips and pointed to them.

He placed the cigarette between her lips.

She put two fingers over it and inhaled deeply.

He placed the other cigarette between his lips, lit it and also inhaled deeply. When he exhaled, he took the cigarette out of his mouth, rested his left elbow on the armrest and held the cigarette between two fingers of that hand. "I grew up in LA, graduated from UCLA law school in '55 and went directly to work for a firm in Reno that specialized in insurance defense work. I worked there for about ten years, gaining a reputation as the guy to hire to defend the tough cases. But I developed a problem. I liked to gamble, and Reno had gambling. I gambled a lot, so much so that it became compulsive. I became very choosey out the cases I would take because I wouldn't let them interfere with my gambling."

He raised his arm, placed the cigarette in his mouth and inhaled. He exhaled, took the cigarette out of his mouth and returned his arm to the armrest. "When the seniors at the firm realized my problem, they counseled me, but I couldn't stop gambling so they fired me. I was married then and out of work, except for my gambling. Eventually my wife divorced me, the debts piled up, and I frankly was a mess. Still I gambled until several friends intervened and sent me to a rehabilitation institute. It took most of the money I had left. I was isolated from society for two months, but when I came out I had an entirely different prospective on life."

He again took several puffs of the cigarette and returned his arm to the armrest. "Although I was cured of gambling, the experience at the institute made me conscious of the problems of the little people. I wanted to do something for them. I still had my license to practice law, but I decided to change the nature of my practice. Rather than defend the big guys, I would represent the oppressed and injured against them."

He coughed, took a handkerchief from a pocket in his jacket and spat into it. "That was near the start of '67. In my first case I represented a woman in one of the first discrimination cases in Nevada. It got a lot of local publicity, and we got a sizable verdict. After several more verdicts against the establishment, in '69 Alex joined me, and we moved to Carson City. We rented for two years, then bought a house on Stewart Street and remodeled it. When we first moved to Carson City, I took on the Wintersmyth case you talked about. It was a hard tough fight against a large mining company and its high priced lawyers. I won and got Marion a lot of money and a lot of publicity. I guess I've found my way into the elite of plaintiff's lawyers. Most of my cases are now referrals, which I like."

He paused and inhaled his cigarette one more time. Then he reached ahead toward the vehicle's dash and mashed the cigarette out in the ashtray. He turned towards Richard. "For a short synopsis, that's about it."

By now they had passed over the Morrison Street Bridge, preceded northeast on Sandy Boulevard and turned right on Burnside Street to Fifteenth Avenue. Richards turned the vehicle to the right on Fifteenth and looked briefly at Merriman. "The garage we're after is in this block on the right. There, I see it in the middle of the block."

Wilson's car was the only vehicle parked on the right so she pulled in and parked behind it. She and Merriman got out, went to a door to the side of the garage door and entered a small office. Wilson and Savage stood inside talking to a Chinese-American. They turned to the door as Richards and Merriman entered.

Wilson introduced Merriman to Wayland Chang. Chang came forward and offered his hand to Merriman.

Wilson thought *Oh, oh Wayland, you're in for a surprise.*

Merriman grasped his hand with his vice grip and shook it. "Nice to meet you, Wayland."

Chang showed no emotion, to Wilson's surprise. "The pleasure is mine, Mr. Merriman."

"Wayne to you, Wayland, except when we are in court. There you can call me Mr. Merriman."

A small smile appeared on Chang's face. "That will be fine, Wayne." Then he addressed the group. "Will you all follow me through this door into the garage? We'll conduct our discussion with the vehicles present."

Chang opened a door to the side of the room and walked into a large room. The others followed. In the middle of the room sat the remains of the Caravan and the Monarch pickup with its hood back against the broken windshield. Chang went over to a long table located just ahead of the pickup. Seven chairs surrounded the table.

Chang motioned to the chairs. "Will you please be seated? You can see the vehicles from here."

Merriman pulled out the chair at the far end of the table for Richards, who sat. He sat next to her, and Savage sat next to him. Wilson took the chair at the other end of the table.

Chang stood on the side of the table nearest the vehicles, facing the others. He placed his hands on the table and looked directly at Merriman, Richards and Savage. "The first thing I did was to measure the crush on both vehicles to see if I could determine the approximate speed at impact. My calculations indicated that both vehicles traveled at about fifty miles per hour at impact. I reviewed the police report, and this appeared consistent with their findings."

He walked over to the pickup. The front end faced the table. "You can see here on the front of the pickup that its left front to almost the middle of the front end was involved in the collision." Then he went over to the Caravan which sat along side the pickup also facing the table. "You can see from the front of the Caravan that the front of the pickup literally drove through and over the left front of the Caravan back to the second row of seats. That clearly caused the death of the driver and boy seated behind him."

Then he went over to the hood of the pickup and pointed to the mating parts. He explained his theory how the vehicle was deficient in not having a second latch.

Merriman watched and listened intently. After Chang finished explaining his theory, Merriman addressed Chang. "What was out in front of the Caravan to protect against an intrusion such as you have described?"

Chang look puzzled. "I don't understand what you're asking?"

"Well, did the design of the Caravan incorporate any passenger protection in its front end? In other words, was the front axle in front of the driver, was the engine out there and was there metal out there to soften the crush, things like that?"

Chang still appeared dumbfounded. "Of course, the Caravan had a snub nose, so the front axel was either directly under or behind the driver. The engine compartment was also under the driver. The front windshield was effectively the front of the vehicle."

Merriman's blue eyes stared at Chang. "Doesn't that seem unsafe to you?"

"Well, that's the way the vehicle is built. The customer knows that when he buy the vehicle."

Merriman's stare became angry. "Shit, Wayland, the customer doesn't know shit about the safety alternatives. He relies on the manufacture for that. Aren't you aware that most models of vans now have the front axel and the engine compartment out in front of the driver?"

"Yes, but the state-of-the-art at the time was like this Caravan."

Merriman shook his head. "Chang, you need some educating."

Chang sat at the table and talked to Merriman for about an hour.

Suddenly Merriman stood. "It's been a pleasure meeting you, Wayland," he said, "but we must be on our way." As he headed out of the office, he turned again to Chang. "I'll be in touch."

When Merriman arrived at Richard's car, he turned to Wilson. "We'll meet you back at your office."

Wilson nodded as he was getting into his car. "See you there."

Richard drove south on Fifteenth to Belmont Street, turned left and drove to the Morrison Street Bridge. She crossed the bridge, drove around and under it to Front Street, and south on Front to Jefferson. Jefferson led to the road back to Beaverton.

Merriman had been quiet, but, as they proceeded west on Jefferson, he turned to Richards. "I guess we can live with Chang and his theory of a design flaw in the pickup, but he needs back-up, and we need a smarter guy to go after the van. I've got some guys in mind. But I think we're ready to prepare a complaint."

Richard stared straight ahead. "That's fine with me. You're in charge. Work with Wilson on the legal matters."

Merriman laughed. "Thanks for letting me know that I'm in charge. Monica, you should know from your research on me that I don't work on any case where I'm not in charge."

Monica blushed and looked at him briefly. "I didn't mean it that way. I was just telling you that the timing of the complaint was your decision, not mine."

"Oh I know," he said. "I was just seeing if I could make you blush. I found out I can." As they approached Wilson's office, Merriman turned to face Richards. "Say, what's there to do in this town after dark? I'm not going back until tomorrow. Why don't you show me the sights, and I'll buy the dinner?"

Richards stared at the road. "Is that your way of asking me out for a date?" she said. "We just met a few hours ago."

"What difference does that make? You're an attractive gal who must get around, and I'm a lonesome stranger with time on his hands. Don't call it a date, if you don't want. Call it a dinner among new friends."

Richard slowly shook her head while still looking straight ahead. "I don't know. I planned to take a run in the Park Blocks tonight followed by a quiet dinner at home."

"You're a runner too?" Merriman exclaimed. "Why don't I join you? I planned to take a run in the morning anyway."

"Well, I suppose," said Richard reluctantly, "and I guess we can get a bite somewhere afterwards. After we finish at Denny's office, I'll drive you back to Nendell's where you can pick up your running gear. You can change at my apartment."

"Sounds great."

"Will we have to drive back to Beaverton after the run to pick up Alex for dinner?"

Merriman laughed. "You gotta be kidding. Do you think I want him around when I'm courting a good looking dame?"

95

Monica frowned. "A minute ago we were just friends. Now you're going to court me?"

Merriman winked at her. "Come on Monica, I was just testing you. We are just friends, but it's just you and me tonight. Alex likes to stay home and read."

Richards turned her head and gave him a sly look. Then she turned back to the driving.

When they arrived at Wilson's office, Richards parked the car, and they went inside.

Inside Wilson's office, Richards sat on the couch and Merriman joined her. Savage took in one of the chairs, and Wilson reclined in his chair behind the desk with a cigar dangling from his mouth.

Merriman looked at Wilson. "I'll draft a complaint when we get back home. What court should I use?"

Wilson chewed on his cigar. "Do you mean in what county or state or federal court?"

Merriman offered Richards a cigarette, lit it and then lit his own. "Let's talk about state or federal court. You've told us about the differences in discovery, but I think we can get everything we need in state court, where I'm impressed that we can keep the names of our experts to ourselves if we want to. Tell me about the judges."

"In federal court the judges are stronger and keep control of their courtroom. And you know they can comment on the evidence and select the jury. In state court the judges don't comment on the evidence and let the lawyers select the jury."

Merriman took the cigarette out of his mouth and nodded. "Then we want the state court, but which county. Mrs. Ralston lives in Portland. The accident happened down near the coast. Is that a different county?"

Wilson explained that Portland is in Multnomah County and where the accident happened is Clatsop County. He told Merriman that Astoria at the mouth of the Columbia River is the county seat and that it's much more rural than Portland.

"I like a rural court," Merriman said. "Will Mrs. Ralston mind relocating for a few weeks?"

"She could stay with friends at Gearhart. That's just a few miles south and is a beach town. Actually, there are a couple of quaint hotels there where we could make our headquarters."

Merriman smiled at Wilson. "Then it's settled. We file in Clatsop County. When I send you the draft, you put in proper form, and file and serve it. They'll be just three defendants, Monarch, WCI and the service station. I assume you can find the name of the owner of the service station."

"Yes, I can do that."

Merriman looked down at the ashtray, tapped his cigarette over it to free the ashes, and looked back up at Wilson. "I'll take the responsibility to get some more engineering experts to back up Chang. You keep in touch with the medical people. Later we'll work together on an economist and any other professional witnesses that we'll need."

9

RICHARDS LOOKED TO her left and then pulled out of the Nendell's driveway with Merriman. She proceeded west on the Bertha-Beaverton highway. Shortly she turned briefly towards Merriman. "How long have you been running?" she asked.

Merriman turned towards her. "Off and on since college, but more seriously the last six years. How about you?"

"Also since college, and again more seriously since my divorce." She smiled. "Actually, I've had a personal trainer for five years, so you see I'm kind of a fitness freak."

Merriman smiled at her. "A very attractive one, I might add."

She glanced at him briefly and gave him that sly look.

They drove in silence the rest of the way. When Richards got to the Ione Plaza, an apartment building in the Park Blocks of Portland's Westside, she drove into the garage and parked. They took the elevator up to the tenth floor and exited into a hallway.

Richards faced Merriman. "There are only six apartments on this floor. Mine's just around the corner on the east side."

They walked down the hall and entered the apartment. Decorated in a modern mode, the door entered into the living room. Widows overlooking the city adorned the far side of the room, broken in the center by glass doors to a terrace.

Richards pointed down a hallway to the right. "The first door down that way is the second bedroom. You can change in there."

She followed him down the hall, and, after he turned into the bedroom, she continued down the hall to the master bedroom, went in, closed the door and began changing into her running blue halter and shorts. She sat on the bed and put on white short socks with a white ball tassel in the rear and her Nike shoes. She tied her hair in the rear with a rubber band. When she came out and walked back to the living room, she saw Merriman sitting in an upholstered chair, dressed only in red shorts with a white strip on each side, short white socks and Nu Balance running shoes. She took particular notice of his hairy tan chest and muscular physique. *What a body for a middle-aged man* she thought.

When Merriman noticed her, he stood and looked her up and down.

"Are you getting a good look?" she asked, aware of his ogling.

Merriman laughed. "Lady, you must know how you look and appreciate a man who notices." Her tall body made a striking appearance with her long legs and a bust that could not be hidden with the halter.

She shook her head. "Let's stop the admiring and get on with the run," she said heading for the front door.

They went down the elevator to the first floor and out the front door of the apartment building. From there she started running at a brisk pace, with Merriman following, east along Montgomery Street until she came to the Park Block. She turned south and ran several blocks to the end of the South Park Blocks, then turned around and ran north. Her steady pace surprised him, and he labored a bit as they went slightly uphill to the end of the South Park Blocks. But when she turned around and started back toward the north, he began to match her stride.

They continued to run down across Burnside Street to the end of the North Park Blocks. Then they came back uphill to Montgomery Street where, leading, Richards walked a block, stopped and bent down stretching.

When Richards stopped running, Merriman came up beside her and walked panting. "I hope this signals the end of the run."

As she finished her stretch, Richard rose up and gazed at him with her hazel eyes, smiling. "You look a little red. Maybe it was too much for you. You should have said something."

"Lady, you're not too much for me," he said, still panting. "I'm just used to a more flat and gentle run."

"Well, come on back to the apartment. I've got a few more exercises to do."

They walked back to the building, went into the lobby and took the elevator up to ten, Merriman still panting a little.

When they entered the apartment, Richard headed for her bedroom. Halfway down the hall, she turned back toward Merriman. "Come on. I need a sparing mate."

"You what?" Merriman asked, following her.

"My trainer likes me to box when I can. Whenever someone is here during my exercises, I enlist them to be my sparing mate."

The entered her bedroom. It was large with a raised king sized bed, an attractive headboard and skirt, two bedside tables, a narrow table at the foot of the bed, a chaise and an upholstered chair arrangement, and large windows with glass double door to the same terrace shared by the living room. At one end of the room was a small exercise area with a treadmill and weights.

She went to a closet near the treadmill and retrieved two small boxing gloves and two large mitts. The gloves were about a quarter the size of the gloves used by boxers. She put on the gloves and handed the mitts to Merriman.

She laughed. "Put on the mitts and prepare to defend yourself."

Merriman held the mitts. "You've gotta be kidding."

She laughed again. "I won't hurt you. It's just good conditioning for my arms."

He put on the mitts and held them in front of himself. She crouched low and suddenly sprang upward and ahead hitting the mitts with both fists in rapid fashion.

He backed up staggering; he held up the mitts to keep her from hitting him. "My god, slow down!" he shouted.

"Oh, come on, I'm not that strong." She kept hitting the mitts. "I've got to move fast. You're doing fine."

Soon he got the rhythm of the blows and stood his ground. After what seem like an eternity, but actually was fifteen minutes, she stopped and took off the gloves.

She stood before him, sweating. "Now, that wasn't so bad, was it?"

He panted again. "Not for you. You did all the hitting. And you're wrong. You are too strong, and you pack one hell of a punch."

She stood in front of him beside the bed. "Put down the mists and come toward me with you arms like you're going to hug me."

He put the mitts on the bed. "What are you talking about?"

"Just do as I say."

He stepped towards her with his arms out and started to grab her. Suddenly she stoop down turned slightly, trust her right arm forward, under his crotch and lifted with all her might. At the same time she pushed her left hand hard against his shoulder. She flipped him on his back on the bed. Like a cat she jumped on the bed, straddled him, pushed his head back with the palm of one hand and with her other hand grabbed his throat.

He coughed and stammered. "For, for christsakes, let loose of my throat!' You're chocking me."

She let loose of his throat. "Calm down. I wasn't chocking you, although I certainly could have." Still straddling him, she laughed and looked down at him. "My trainer has been teaching me self-defense, and I've never had a chance to try it on someone as large as you. I guess it works."

Merriman quieted. "I guess it does. How about getting off of me?"

"Not until I kiss and make up." She leaned down and kissed him lightly.

He reached his arms up and around her, pulling her down on top of him. He felt the sweat in his arms, and he kissed her fully.

When they broke, she turned slightly and placed her hand inside the front of his shorts. "I want to see if I did any damage." She felt around inside his shorts. "Everything feels fine."

He moaned slightly and began to rise. "Yes, everything feels fine." He reached for her halter.

She pulled her hand out and jumped up. "Not now. You promise me dinner, and I'm so hungry I could eat a horse. Let's shower and dress. There's a shower in the other room for you." She went to a side door. "I'm going to take mine in here." She went in and closed the door.

Later he sat on the sofa in the living room admiring the view of the city through the windows and the double doors to the terrace. Dusk approached. He heard someone coming and turned facing Richards. She wore a sleeveless red dress, exposing her tan arms and chest, revealing enough of her ample breasts. Her brown hair had been tied back with a red bow. He looked at her with that ogling look. "Hello gorgeous."

Richard dropped her head and turned it to the side, her hazel eyes starting at him. "Am I going to have to put up with that all night? I thought we were just friends."

He smiled. "After today, and the way you're dressed, I'd say you're looking for more than simple friendship."

"That's enough of that," she said. "I'm dressed for a four star restaurant, which is where we're going." She took his hand. He got up, and she led him out of the apartment, into the elevator, down to the garage and opened the passenger's door for him.

She drove out of the garage and headed north on Tenth Avenue to Burnside, west on Burnside through Twenty-first and into the parking log adjacent to the Ringside restaurant. "I'm taking you to our best steakhouse," she said, as they exited the car. She took his hand and led him inside a dark entry room with a lounge to the right.

Richards led the way to the maitre'd's stand. "Reservations for two under the name of Richards," she said to the man dressed in a tuxedo and black tie.

"Yes, Miss Richards. I have a nice booth for two. Please come this way." The man led them to a booth back against the wall. They sat next to each other. The man said, "Your waiter will be here shortly. In the meantime may I start you with a cocktail?"

Richards looked up at him. "Two vodka martinis, very dry."

The man left.

Richards faced Merriman. "I hope you didn't mind my ordering for you."

He smiled. "I loved it. Actually, I getting used to it."

When the waiter in a tuxedo and black tie came, she ordered two Caesar salads, two rib-eye stakes medium rare, two baked potatoes and two more cocktails.

After they finished dinner and the waiter had cleared the plates, he asked, "May I bring you coffee?"

Richards looked at Merriman. "How about Irish coffees?"

Merriman looked at the waiter. "Bring two Irish coffees." He turned and put his arm on the booth behind her. "That was a hell of a dinner. You picked a winner." He examined his watch. "It's only quarter to nine. What's in store for the rest of the evening?"

"After we finish the Irish coffees and you've paid the bill, I thought we might go somewhere where we could sit and enjoy the view of the city. It's such a beautiful September evening."

"Sounds good to me. What's the place?"

Her hazel eyes glistened as she leaned into his arm. "I had in mind the terrace off my apartment."

He placed his hand under her chin and raised her head so he could look into her eyes. "You're an interesting woman. Let's go."

He paid the bill, and they left.

By the time they got back to the apartment, darkness had set in, and Merriman could see the lights of the city in the distance through the windows of her living room. "Wow, I see what you had in mind when you said enjoy the view of the city."

She walked across the living room and opened the double doors. "Come on out and get a better view."

They walked out, and Richard offered Merriman a seat on the settee.

He sat, and she looked down at him. "What can I pour you? My bar is well stocked."

"How about straight bourbon on the rocks?"

"I'll make that two," she said as she left.

After several moments, Richards returned with two old fashion glasses filled with a brown liquid and ice. She handed one to Merriman.

He took the glass, put it to his lips and sipped. "Just what the doctor ordered."

She sat next to him and took a sip of the drink from the glass she held in her hand. "It does taste good, doesn't it?"

He put his arm over the back of the settee, gently touching her shoulder. "Maybe the doctor also ordered the beautiful view and the good-looking babe sitting next to me."

"Maybe he did." She nuzzled his shoulder.

When they finished the drinks, she looked at him. "Want another?"

"We got a saying down in Carson City. Does an elk want water?"

"Then come with me. I'll show you where the bar is, and you can make yourself useful. After you've poured the drinks, bring them into my bedroom, and we'll enjoy the view from the chaise and chair." She left for her bedroom.

When Merriman had the drinks made, he walked down the hall and turned into the master bedroom. As he entered, he stopped cold. She was on the chaise, laying on her side, up on one elbow, looking at him. She had undressed, let her hair down and stared at him completely naked.

"Bring my drink over to the table beside me," she said softly.

He walked into the room and put the drink on the table, all the while staring at her. "Wow, you've done it again. A regular Venus DeMilo, only better. You've got long thin tan arms to go with a knockout body and great tits."

She rose and stood beside him. "I thought you might like me better this way. Let me have your drink." She took it and set it on the table. "Why don't you relax too? Sit on the bed and take your boots and socks off."

He did, and she came over and stood before him. He stared again.

She leaned forward, took his hands and pulled him up. "Stand up. I want to undress you."

As he stood she took off his jacket and laid it neatly on the other side of the bed. She took off his string tie and cast it over by the jacket. She unbuttoned he shirt, and he took it off dropped it on the floor. She reached down and undid his belt, admiring the western buckle. She unbuttoned his jeans, reached inside the opening in his underpants, found him hard and squeezed lightly. Then she pulled down his pants, and he stepped out of them. Finally, she got rid of his underpants. He stood naked before her, his erection standing straight up.

This time she stared him up and down. "Now that I've examined all of you, I like what I see. Come over and sit with me on the chaise and enjoy the view."

He followed.

When they got to the chaise, she laid on one side of the chaise and leaned back. Merriman laid on the other side and looked at her. "There's only one view I enjoy now."

She put her arms around his shoulders and pulled him over on top of her.

"God you're strong," he said.

"Not so strong, but gentle," she said. And they had sex.

Later that night Merriman called Savage. "I won't be coming back to Nendells tonight. See you in the morning at eight."

10

FRIDAY MORNING, MERRIMAN and Richards sat at her dining room table, having finished breakfast and now drinking coffee. At seven a.m. the sun shown at the city from just over the Cascade Range. The day promised to be warm.

Richard rose and began clearing the dishes. She turned and faced Merriman. "We'd better get going if you're meeting Alex at eight."

Merriman looked up at her as she took the dishes into the kitchen. "Yeah, you're right, but you make it hard to leave after you filled me with that great waffle. And before I go, I've got something I want you to do."

She returned from the kitchen. "What that?"

"You know the dairy bought the pickup used from the dealer in Seaside. I think we should know about the vehicle's history before we file the complaint. We'll get it ready, but hold up filing until you can do some investigation."

"I'll get right on it. I should have the history for you by the end of next week."

"Great. Then let's go," he said, picking up his small bag and heading for the front door.

On Monday morning around eleven, Richards sat in a straight back chair in the office of Oleg Jorgenson, the owner of Jorgenson Motors in Seaside. Jorgensen sat at his desk, rummaging through some papers. Richards wore the short sleeved white blouse, buttoned up the front with the top three buttons unbuttoned, revealing the start of her cleavage, faded jeans tucked into black boots and had her hair tied back.

Jorgenson picked up one sheet. "Here it is, the sales receipt I got when I purchase the pickup. It lists the owner as Roger Winchester out of Kelso, Washington. I seem to remember a guy and his wife came in and wanted to sell it. The guy claimed he worked for Winchester. He wanted fifty-nine hundred for it, which seems reasonable for a pickup only three years old, so, after having a mechanic give it a good looking over, I bought it."

"Then I guess you were satisfied it was in good working order," Richard said.

"Sure was."

Richards picked up the sales receipt on Jorgenson's desk. She read it and saw Winchester's address and phone number on it. She looked up at Jorgenson and held out the receipt. "Could you make me a copy of this?"

"Sure." He took the receipt into another room and returned with a copy, which he handed to Richards.

Richards left Seaside at about noon and drove north on US 101. The weather still remained warm, so she had her window rolled down. She turned east on US 30 at Astoria and drove to Rainier, Oregon, where she turned left, crossed the bridge over the Columbia River into Longview, Washington. Once in Longview she found the Oregon Beach Highway, turned left and stopped at a service station as she entered Kelso.

When the attendant came to her side of the car, she held out the sales receipt. "Do you know where I can find this guy," she said pointing to the top of the receipt.

The attendant looked at the receipt and leaned down close to the window. "Yeah, he owns Roger's Reck & Rebuild. See that sign to your left. That's Cowlitz Way. Take that across the railroad tracks to Pacific and turn left. You'll see it on the left about a half mile up."

She followed the attendant's directions and saw the facility as she approached it. It looked like an old repair garage, a rectangular building with tin siding, a single door at one end up several stairs and a large door in about the center where presumably you drove in vehicles to be repaired. She thought *I'll bet our pickup was wrecked and this guy rebuilt it.*

She crossed the road, drove in a dirt driveway and parked up next to the single door at the end of the building. She grabbed the sales receipt, went up the stairs, opened the door and stepped into a dirty room with a pot-belly stove, an old wooden desk and a table with dusty manuals and papers piled on it. There were several metal chairs at various angles around the table.

A man in dirty coveralls sat at the desk with his back to her, leaning down and working on a piece of machinery on the floor behind and to the side of the desk. When the door opened, the man said, "I'll be with you in a minute. Find a chair and rest your ass."

Richards took hold of the back of one of the metal chairs, pulled it over to face the desk and sat.

After a few moments the man sat upright and rotated his chair to face Richards. Nearly bald, overweight and not tall, he had jowls and a pug nose. He started at Richards and then gave her a wry smile. "My, my, what have we here? I don't get lookers in here very often. What can I do fer you maam?"

Richards' hazel eyes glistened as she looked at him. "My names Monica Richards. I'm looking for Roger Winchester."

"You've found him," Winchester said.

Richards handed him the sales receipt. "I'm an insurance adjuster for a dairy down near Seaside, Oregon. They bought the vehicle on that receipt from a dealer down there."

"Yeah, I remember that pickup, a green 1970 model. I picked her up at an auction down near Sacramento in the fall of '72. It needed a little work, but its engine ran fine. One of my employees had it, as I remember, for some time before he sold it to the dealer in Seaside. What's the problem?"

Richards turned slightly in the chair, causing the opening in her blouse to sag just enough to expose part of one breast. When she turned, she noticed Winchester eying it. "It's been a bad accident," she said, "apparently caused by its hood flying up blinding the driver."

Winchester raised his eyes and saw her staring at him. "Oh, I'm sorry to hear that, but I'm sure the hood must not have been latched sometime before the accident, because it was secure when we sold it."

Richards turned her head slightly and cast a doubtful eye toward him. "Are you sure the vehicle hadn't been wrecked before you bought it?"

Winchester shook his head. "It had some dents in it, but it wasn't wrecked."

"The reason I asked is I ran a title search on the vehicle, and it looks like the title was issued to you. I figured that meant either you bought the pickup new or you rebuilt it."

"No, yer wrong there, lady. Yer right that I applied for a new title, but I didn't rebuild it, just repaired some dents and painted it black. We can get a new title in Washington any time we want."

Richards rose and started to walk towards the door, when she turned. "By the way would you still have the paperwork for your purchase and repair of the pickup?"

Winchester remained seated. "Nah, that's over a year ago, but I might have a receipt from the auction yard. Let me see," he said reaching for a filing cabinet to his left.

He opened a file drawer and rustled through some papers. He turned back to Richards. "No, like I said, I don't have anything on the pickup." Then he got up and looked at her. "You went to a lot of trouble coming up here," he said. 'How about I buy you a beer? Schroeder's Tavern is just up the block."

"That's mighty nice of you. I could use a beer before driving back to Portland."

He led the way out of the building, and they walked side-by-side up the street to the tavern.

As they entered the tavern, a man behind a long bar held up his hand and waved. "Hi there, Rog. Who's the cutie with you?"

Winchester pulled out a stool at the bar and offered it to Richards. "Monica, meet Ace Schroeder, the owner of this dive."

Schroeder came over and put out his hand. "Glad to meet you, Monica. Be careful of Rog here. He can be a handful."

Richards shook his hand and smiled. "I can take care of myself." She looked down the bar and saw two men engaged with their arms on the bar. "Are those fellas doing what I think they are? It looks like their arm wrestling."

"Yeah, that's how some of the guys decides who buys."

Richards turned to Winchester and winked at him. "I know you offered to buy me a beer, but why don't we try what their doing." She pointed at the two men arm wrestling.

Winchester blushed. "I couldn't do that with a gal. It wouldn't be fair. Just let me buy."

Richards' hazel eyes glistened as she smiled. "You're not afraid to take me on, are you? Come on. It would be fun."

"Come on Rog, show her you're a man," Schroeder chided.

Winchester relented. "Oh all right." And he put his elbow on the bar.

Richards did likewise and gripped his right hand. She turned to face Schroeder. "You give us the go ahead."

Schroeder lowered his head and said, "All right. Get ready, set, go to it."

Richard immediately pushed hard with her forearm. Winchester resisted and then his arm fell down on the bar top.

Schroeder broke out laughing.

Winchester looked shocked. "God, where did you learn to do that?"

Richards smiled at him. "I had two older brothers who taught me. I don't consider myself a weakling, but it's usually speed that counts in arm wrestling."

Schroeder brought the beers, and Winchester paid.

Winchester held out his beer. "Here's to the winner, and she sure ain't no weakling."

They talked for a while.

When Richards finished her beer, she got up. "I better be on my way. One beers enough when you're driving. Thanks for the beer and the challenge." She shook Winchester's hand and left.

Winchester looked at Schroeder. "That's one hell of a woman. I should have shaken her hand before I got into that competition. She's got a damn good grip."

11

BARRY WALKED DOWN the hall to his office on Monday morning, September twenty-four. As he neared, he heard the telephone ringing. He rushed into his office and picked up the receiver.

"Barry, this is Steve Hinkley," Hinkley said. "We've been served in the Ralston matter. The complaint names three plaintiffs, Mrs. Ralston, Michelle Ralston and Dustin Ralston and lists three defendants, Monarch, WCI and the Legion Oil service station. They want a hundred million general damages and an unspecified amount of punitive damages. It's filed in Clatsop County Oregon. I'll fax you a copy."

"I assume you'll fax with it a copy of your engineers' inspection of the vehicles."

Hinkley coughed. "I've got bad news on that score. I simply forgot to assign an engineer to do the inspection. Can you get an investigator to find out where they are? I'll assign an engineer to make the inspection as soon as we hear from you."

"I'll get Ben Lorenzo on it right away. Who's the plaintiff's lawyer?"

"A guy named Denny Wilson with offices in Beaverton, but you'll never guess who he's associated."

"Probably *Winkler & Brady*. They're the best plaintiffs' injury lawyers in Portland."

"You're not even close. He's got Wayne Merriman out of Carson City."

Barry reacted. "Wow, that's probably why they filed in Astoria. Merriman'll think he can bulldoze the small town judge. Maybe he's right, but Judge Olsen may surprise him."

"Tell me about the judge and the community."

Barry leaned back in his chair. "Well, Astoria's a town of about 9,000. It sits at the mouth of the Columbia River, supported by fishing and lumber. It has a lot of history, but not much economy. A lot of Scandinavians inhabited it in the early days, and their relatives still live in the area. The whole county's very rural, only about 28,000 people in nearly 900 square miles. Judge Eric Olson derives his ancestry from Sweden, and he's a typical Swede, heavy blonde hair and short with large features. He's laid back and not real bright, but gets by using lots of common sense. And, once his mind is made up, he's hard to move. I've tried several cases before him, and I think he likes me. As I said, he may surprise Merriman."

"Well, call Wilson, protect the record and get back to me with the vehicles' location."

"I'll do that," and Barry hung up. He called Sarah. "Sarah, call Ben and have him come up to my office, and check the fax room. Steve Hinkley is faxing me a complaint."

Ben Lorenzo had been with the firm a little over five years. He'd been with the Portland Police Department before that as a detective. At six feet, 200 pounds, he looked like a boxer, broad shoulders, square face and black crew cut hair. He usually wore a broad smile and had penetrating eyes. He officed one floor down where the firm had a half a floor devoted to support.

About 10 minutes later, Lorenzo stuck his face into Barry open door. "You called, boss." He entered a sat in a chair he pulled up to Barry's desk.

"I got a job for you," Barry said. Then he explained the case and the need for an engineer's inspection of the vehicles. He asked Lorenzo to find the vehicles and get a copy of the police report.

Lorenzo smiled. "I'll find them. Shall I call Hinkley directly when I do?"

"Yes, but let me know also."

After Lorenzo left, Sarah came in to Barry's office. She held out a document. "Here's the complaint Steve faxed."

Barry took it and examined it. He saw a simple complaint, product liability claims against Monarch and MCI and a negligent claim against the service station. Monarch was charged with manufacturing and selling a vehicle with a defective hood latching mechanism. The claim against MCI was failing to provide adequate structure in the front end of the van to protect passengers in the event of a front end collision, and the service station was claimed to have been negligent in failing to adequately have closed the hood of the pickup. The prayer asks for a hundred million dollars and unspecified amount for punitive damages. Barry thought about filing a motion against the complaint to make the lawyers tell him just how the hood latching mechanism was claimed to be defective, but he decided to try and to talk them into it first.

That afternoon Lorenzo reported back to Barry. "I went to the police lot out in Aloha. I ordered the police report from the cop there. He told me that he had released the vehicle to Monica Richards. I think you know her, an adjuster for Western Indemnity."

"Yeah, I know her, awfully good looking for an adjuster. I'll give her a call."

Barry looked in his telephone directory and found Western Indemnity. He dialed.

"Western Indemnity," a woman answered.

"May I please speak to Monica Richards?"

"May I say whose calling?"

Barry laughed. "Tell her it's an old admirer, named Barry O'Shea."

In a moment a voice came on the phone. "What can I do for you, handsome?"

Barry chuckled. "You can tell me where and when we can inspect the Monarch pickup you took from the police lot in Aloha."

"So, you're representing Monarch. I can't answer your question, because their lawyer's involved. I suggest you call Denny Wilson. You know him, don't you?"

Barry sighed. "Yeah, I know him. Sorry I can't deal with you. I'll call him."

"I'm sorry too. Good bye, handsome." And she hung up.

He called Wilson.

"Yes, we have both vehicles," Wilson said, "but I have to call Wayne Merriman to get permission for you to inspect them. He calls all the shots on this one."

"Please call him. By the way has anyone else called you to tell you that they're involved?"

"Yeah, Larry Sturgis for the Legion Oil station. I gave him the usual extension of time."

"Can I assume that Monarch likewise had an open extension of time to appear?"

"Yes, within reason. We'll call you if we think you're taking too much time."

"Thanks. And when you call Merriman tell him we need to know how he claims the hood latching mechanism is defective. And tell him that I'll file a motion unless you agree to be more specific." And the call ended.

Berry told Lorenzo about Sturgis. "I think I'll ask him to meet me at the Congress for a drink later this afternoon, if he's in."

116

I was shortly before four o'clock. Barry entered the lounge at the Congress Hotel from the door on Sixth Avenue just a few steps from Madison Street. He stepped directly into the bar and looked around. He spotted Sturgis at the far end of the curved bar, sitting on a bar stool smoking a nonfiltered Camel. At forty-nine Sturgis had been in practice several years longer than Barry, and his practice was predominately insurance defense. His life had been easy going, and he showed it, overweight, round red face and slightly bald. He smoked two packs of Camels a day and enjoyed his cocktails. Barry walked over and pulled out the bar stool next to him.

Sturgis saw Barry coming. He smiled at him. "I got here a few minutes ago and have already ordered an Early Times."

Barry sat. "I thought we ought to talk. What do you know about the case?"

"Frankly, not much. I just got the assignment and haven't yet received the file. All I know is it sounds like a hell of an accident."

"Do you know who is representing WCI?"

"Yeah, Walt Roper of *Michaels & Bruce* called me just after you did. He said he just received the assignment and got my name from Denny Wilson after you called him. I hope you don't mind, but I asked him to join us."

Roper's firm was second in line with WCI. *Michael & Bruce*, Portland largest firm, had about fifty lawyers, most of whom concentrated on business practice. It did have several trial lawyers, however, and Barry had tried several cases with Roper.

After several minutes Roper arrived. He gave the opposite impression from Sturgis. Several years older than Barry but still in his forties, Roper was five feet ten inches in height, and had a thin physique, brown neatly parted hair and a narrow face. He always wore a Stetson, which he hung on the wall as he walked to Sturgis and Barry, a curved pipe hanging from his mouth.

Barry and Sturgis got up from the bar and took a booth against the wall where Roper joined them.

The bartender brought Sturgis' drink over to the booth and looked at Barry and Roper. "What can I bring you two?"

"I'll have an Early Times and water," Barry answered.

"Make that two," Roper said.

Barry looked at Roper, "Glad to have you aboard. I don't suppose you know much more than either Larry or I."

"No, I just got the assignment from WCI this morning."

"With Merriman involved I'd guess we'll have our hands full," Barry said.

Roper put his pipe in an ashtray. "Have either of you ever had any experience with Merriman?"

Sturgis shook his head.

"I had one case," Barry said, "but it settled before trial, however, the experience with Merriman was unforgettable, especially the settlement negotiations. I represented WCI. Sam Ewing down in Medford associated Merriman. A Caravan van rolled and caught fire. It carried a family of five, all of whom died, burned to death because the doors wouldn't open. Verner Schultz will remember Merriman well at the settlement negotiations. Merriman made him the fall guy. Anyway I'll let him tell you about it."

The bartender brought the drinks.

Sturgis raised his glass to the other two. "Well, here's to us and a successful defense." The other two held out their glasses until they touched, and all three took a sip of their drinks.

Barry put down his glass on the table. "I suspect we will have conflicts in our clients' positions, but I hope we'll be able to work together whenever possible. Merriman would love to see us fighting each other."

Roper pulled out a tobacco pouch, filled his pipe and lit it. He faced Barry. "I don't really see a conflict with Monarch or the service station. Who's responsible for the accident isn't my concern. As I see it, MCI position is whether there's any liability for not protecting the occupants from an accident like this."

"Well, Sturgis and I definitely have a conflict, but I still think we should handle it deftly so as not to enhance the plaintiffs' case," Barry said.

Sturgis took the Camel out of his mouth and snuffed out in an ash tray. He looked back up at Barry. "I agree."

"Then let's finish our drink and agree to keep it touch."

The next morning Wilson called Merriman. "I got a call from Barry O'Shea." He told me that he is representing Monarch, wants to know when and where his client can inspect the vehicles, and further wants to know specifically what we claim is the defect in the hood latching mechanism. He told him that O'Shea will file a motion unless we'll voluntarily give him the information."

Merriman gave a little laugh. "O'Shea certainly gets around. The last time I ran into him he represented MCI. It was a Caravan that time also. We'll have to let him see the vehicles, but let's not respond just yet. Also before we give him to information he wants, I want to retain a couple of more engineering experts, and I want them to see the vehicles before he does. I'll get back to you."

Merriman hung up and walked down the hall to Savage's office. Savage sat at his desk, hunched over and writing a brief. Merriman entered and sat in a chair facing Savage. "I want to continue our talk about hiring some experts in the Ralston case."

Savage took his cigar out of his mouth and laid it in an ash tray on his desk. "It seems to me that we left it with needing someone stronger than Chang."

"I've been thinking," said Merriman. "I think we need more that someone. We really need two people, one to either support Chang's theory against Monarch or to come up with a stronger reason why

Monarch's liable and another to support our case against MCI. I don't see one guy doing both."

Savage thought for a moment. "Have you ever heard of Penn Rogaine?" he asked.

"I think so, but I can't remember the circumstances."

"Well, I saw him at an NACCA (NACCA stands for the National Association of Claimants' Compensation Attorneys) meeting in LA a year or so. He spoke to the group about vehicle design. He's about forty, very good-looking, enough to be a movie star, and a design engineer. He makes a smooth presentation and impressed me with his ingenuity. I've got his resume around here somewhere." Savage turned around and pulled out a drawer in his credenza behind him. He fingered through several folders. "Here it is," he said, holding out a several sheets of paper to Merriman. "Take a look at it."

Merriman took the resume and glanced through it. It reported that Rogaine attended Indiana University and UCLA. He got a design engineering degree from UCLA in 1958. It further stated that he is a registered Safety Engineer in California and has worked for several after-market guys in vehicle design for about ten years before setting up his own consulting firm. "It says he's worked for an impressive number of plaintiff's lawyers," Merriman said after he finished reading the resume. "Sounds like the guy we need to come up with a design problem with the pickup."

Merriman got up and walked to the window, staring out at the Capital building. He turned and faced Savage. "Now we need someone who's been involved with passenger safety for the van."

Savage picked his cigar up again, took a puff and nodded. "What about Alistair Masters? He's also an engineer from UCLA, and didn't he work on ambulance design with passenger safety the main concern?"

"Yeah, down in Houston. You've got a good idea there. Get a hold of both of them as soon as you can."

When Merriman had left, Savage found Rogaine's telephone number on his resume and dialed, his cigar dangling from the corner of his mouth.

"Rogaine Engineering," a woman answered.

"May I please speak to Mr. Rogaine?"

"Who shall I say is calling?"

"Alex Savage from Carson City, Nevada."

A short pause ensued, followed by a man's voice. "What can I do for you Mr. Savage?"

Savage took his cigar out of his mouth and laid it in the ash tray. "We've got a case that might just be up you're alley." He explained the accident and the case. "We'd like you to consult on the design of the pickup, see how you'd design it so the hood wouldn't fly up."

A pause ensued, following which Rogaine said, "I'm available, but it seems to me that a more important consideration is a design that would allow the driver to still see ahead when the hood gets loose. It's not as uncommon as you may think for hoods to fly up, so it seems to me that the design of the hood should take that into consideration and allow the driver to still see ahead. I think I can find vehicles that have hoods that when fully up give the driver vision ahead."

"I never thought of that," Savage said. "Then you're on board?"

"Yes. I should see the vehicle if it's available."

"It is. It's in Portland. Tell me when you can go up there, and I'll make the arrangements."

"Fine. I'll get back to you." And the call ended.

Savage looked up Master's telephone number in the NACCA manual he had on his credenza. He dialed and got an answering machine. He left his name and number.

That afternoon Savage's telephone rang, while he worked at his conference table. He got up, walked over to his desk and picked up the receiver.

"Mr. Savage, this is Alistair Masters returning your call," Masters said.

"Mr. Masters, you don't know me," Savage said, still standing. "I work with Wayne Merriman in Carson City, Nevada, and we have a case we thought might interest you." He gave a brief description of the case, covering the accident and how the driver and passenger of the van died. "It seems to us that there must have been a way the van could have been designed to prevent these unfortunate deaths."

Masters sounded excited. "I couldn't agree more. I'd like to work with you to find that way. Can I tell you about my experience that would qualify me in this regard?"

"I know about your work in Houston with ambulances, but please expand."

"Well, first of all, there's my educational background. I got a mechanical engineering degree from UCLA in 1960, but my interest lay in safety. I'm a registered Safety Engineer in California. I worked with an environmental firm for several years. Then I was a design engineer with a firm that was retained to design passenger safety features in ambulances in Houston. I've been in the consulting practice for three years."

Savage paused and lit a cigar. "Mr. Masters, Wayne Merriman would like to talk with you further. Could you come to Carson City?"

"Certainly. Just say when."

"How about Monday morning, October eighth say at 10 a.m. in our offices?"

"That's fine. Just give me your address, and I'll be there."

Savage did so, and the call ended.

On October eighth Masters sat in the reception area of *Merriman & Savage* with a polished brief case in his lap. He had a slight build, medium length black hair, neatly combed, sharp face, soft penetrating blue eyes and dressed in a tight fitting gray suit with a light blue shirt and red and gray Pokka-dotted tie.

After about fifteen minutes Merriman appeared and walked over to where Masters sat. As usual he had on his western attire and a string tie. He held out his hand. "You must be Alistair Masters."

Masters stood and shook Merriman's hand, grimacing slightly. "Yes, and I presume you are Mr. Merriman."

"Let's drop the formal shit. I'm Wayne and your Alistair, right."

"That fine with me."

Merriman chuckled. "Come back into my office, Alistair."

They walked down the hall and into Merriman's office, Masters carrying his brief case. Merriman offered Masters one of the chairs in front of his desk and then sat back on his large leather chair behind his desk. Masters sat in the chair and put his brief case in his lap.

Merriman pulled out a pack of Marlboros and offered a cigarette from it to Masters. "How about a cigarette?"

"Thank you, but I don't smoke."

He pulled the pack back and took a cigarette from it. "Well, I do." And he lit it. "Alex tells me you interested in our case and have idea on how the van should have been designed."

"Yes I am, and I do." Masters opened his brief case and took a model of a van from it. He closed the brief case and held up the model. "Since our call I did a little research and came up with this later model of the Caravan. I believe the Caravan involved in your accident was a 1967 model. This small facsimile that I have in my hand is a 1973 version of the same vehicle. But as you can see it has some dramatic design improvements."

He turned the model to show its side. "As you can see the front axle is now in front of the driver's compartment, and the engine is in this angle portion also ahead of the driver. I don't know exactly the speed of the vehicles at impact, but I feel strongly that, when it is computed, we will be able to say that the pickup would probably not have protruded into and through the drivers' compartment and cause the death of the driver or his son."

Merriman had a wide smile on his face. He got up cigarette in hand, walked over to Masters and slapped him on the back. "You're my kind of man, Alistair. I couldn't have set that up better. You're hired."

Masters coughed and looked up at Merriman. "Thank you, sir."

Merriman laughed and slapped Masters back again. "Alistair, its Wayne damn it!

Masters coughed again. "Oh, that's right, Wayne."

Merriman went back to his leather chair and inhaled his cigarette deeply. "I guess the next step is to get you out to examine the vehicles," he said, as he exhaled. "They're in Portland. We're also working with Penn Rogaine. He's concentrating on the pickup. You know him?"

"I've heard of him, but I've never worked with him."

"Well, I'm sure you like working with him. We should set up the inspection when you can both be there. What's your availability?"

"Anytime. As a matter of fact, if he's available I could go over there now."

Merriman stood and turned toward his door. "Let's go down to Alex's office and have him call Rogaine." He led Masters down the hall to Savage's office. They went in and found Savage working at his conference table.

"Alex, we've got ourselves a new expert. Meet Alistair Masters."

Savage got up and extended his hand. "Nice to meet you in person, Alistair?"

Masters shook his hand and show some relief. "The pleasure is mine, Mr. Savage," he looked at Merriman, saw a scowl and quickly added, "or Alex, excuse me."

Merriman grabbed a chair, sat and looked at Savage, "Can you get a hold of Rogaine now and see if he can get up to Portland tomorrow or the next day to inspect the vehicles?"

"I'll try," Savage said. He got up, went over to his desk, picked up his phone and carried it to the conference table and dialed Rogaine's number.

Rogaine answered the phone. "Penn Rogaine here."

"Alex Savage, Penn. I've got Wayne Merriman with me so I'll put you on speaker." He switched to speaker phone. "Can you hear us?"

"Yeah, hi Mr. Merriman."

"It's Wayne, Penn. Alistair Masters also here. We're discussing an inspection of the vehicles in Portland. Alistair says he can go now. Can you make it up there tomorrow or the next day? I'd like you two to make the inspection together, if possible."

"Yeah, I'm free tomorrow. I'll see about plane reservations."

"Nah, don't do that. According to your resume, you're in Carson, California. I'll fly down and get you. How about we meet at the Long Beach airport at ten tomorrow morning? That'll get us to Hillsboro by mid-afternoon so we'll have that afternoon and the next morning to do the inspection."

"Okay. I'll be at the Long Beach airport waiting for you. See you then." And the call ended.

Merriman turned to Masters. That's settled. Did you get here last night?"

"Yes."

"Well, keep the room for tonight, and we'll pick you up at seven tomorrow morning to go to the airport. I think you and Rogaine can figure out the impact speed when you make the inspection. Then we'll compare that with what you find with the police report."

Masters got up and said, "Fine. I'll get out of your hair."

Merriman rose and started to extend his hand.

Masters stepped back. "No, once a day is enough. See you fellows in the morning." He walked out of the door.

12

THE NEXT AFTERNOON, Merriman entered the office of the garage where Chang stored the vehicles, followed by Rogaine and Masters. Change waited just inside. Merriman introduced Chang to Rogaine and Masters.

Masters shook Chang's hand. "It's a pleasure to meet you in person Mr. Chang."

"Please call me Wayland as per Wayne's order," Chang said with a sly smile. He turned to Rogaine and held out his hand. "You must then be Penn."

"Yes, Wayland. Nice to know you."

Chang motioned toward the door to the garage. "Come this way, gentlemen, and let me introduce you to the vehicles."

They went into the garage and gathered around the pickup.

Rogaine said, "Boy, it took a wallop."

They walked around it. The proceeded to the van and did the same thing.

Masters stared at the left front. "Look how far the pickup invaded the occupant's position. It's disgusting."

Rogaine went over to the table and opened his brief case. He took out a copy of the police report and spread it out on the table. He examined several pages of the report. Then he took a note pad, a pen and a measuring tape from his case. He turned to Masters. "Let's run some measurement."

Masters took hold of the "dumb" end of the tape, and they proceeded to measure the deplacement on the vehicles, with Rogaine jotting down the measurements on his note pad.

When they finished, Rogaine went back to the table with his notes and compared them with the measurements in the police report. He looked up at Masters who stood at his side. "I don't know why I'm surprised, but our measurements compare almost exactly with the measurement in the report."

Masters leaned over the table and used a calculator to do some figuring. "And the closing speed is about the same too, fifty miles per hour."

Merriman sat at the head of the table. "We'll rely on the police for their measurements and impact speed, but I wanted you two to make the measurements yourselves, before looking at the report, because it will make you testimony stronger if you have hands on with the vehicles.

Rogaine sat and looked at Merriman. "After Savage called me, I spoke to Chang on the telephone, and he told me his theory about the inadequacy of the latching mechanism in the pickup. I told him I could live with that, but felt that I felt a basic design defect was needed as well. I said I would study the problem and see what I could develop. I told Savage what I suspected, and it became far easier than I imagined satisfying myself. In a couple of days I had twelve examples of vehicles, including pickups, where the driver could see ahead with the hoods completely elevated. That design existed when this pickup was built."

The engineers talked for about an hour and a half more, before ending the meeting.

On the way back to the Hillsboro airport, Merriman stopped at office of *Witchhazel & Wilson*. He spoke briefly with Wilson. "We've completed our inspection of the vehicles and have our theories against the latching mechanism and the design of the pickup settled. You can arrange to have the defendants make an inspection, but only one. Make them inspect the vehicles together and have Chang present to pickup as much information about their inspection as he can."

"That will expose Chang as out expert, won't it?" Wilson asked.

"Yes, it will, but I don't care if they know about Chang. We still have Rogaine and Masters as secrets."

—m—

Later that same day, Russell Popnick waited in the reception room of the executive offices of the Hillsboro airport. Popnick was a business associate of *Swift, Wyman & Wiggens* and had a meeting scheduled with the airport manager over a personnel matter.

Soon the manager came into the reception room and greeted Popnick. "Russ, glad you could come on such short notice. We had to get some advice on how to handle our head clerk." He held out his hand to Popnick.

Popnick rose and shook his hand. "Glad to be of service."

Popnick followed the manager into his office and sat in a chair facing the manager sitting at his desk and also facing windows overlooking the loading area for the airport. Popnick looked out at a sleek aircraft parked in front. "Wow, that's quiet a plane. Is it local or a visitor?" he asked.

The manager turned his chair around and looked out the window. "Oh, that's a visitor and quit a famous one at that. It belongs to Wayne Merriman, the famous lawyer from Nevada." As he looked, three men started up the steps to board the aircraft. "As a matter of face the lead man there is Merriman."

"Who are the other gentlemen?"

"I saw the flight manifest. It listed them as Penn Rogaine and Alistair Masters. When they got here, Merriman introduced them as engineers."

———w———

About mid-morning the next day, Popnick peered into Barry's office.

Barry noticed him and looked up. "Hi, Russ, come in."

Popnick entered and sat at a chair beside the Barry's desk. "I had a meeting with the airport manager at the Hillsboro airport late yesterday afternoon, and I saw something that might interest you."

"What did you see, Russ?"

"Isn't Wayne Merriman on that case you're handling for Monarch Motors?"

"Yes, why do you ask?"

"Well, I saw his plane out the window of the manager's office, and I also saw him and two other fellas board the plane."

"That's interesting, but what makes you think it has anything to do with my case?"

"According to the airport manager, the two other gentlemen were engineers by the names of Penn Rogaine and Alistair Masters."

Barry's eyes widened. "My God, Penn Rogaine, that charlatan. Was he here on the Ralston case?"

"I remembered your talk at the firm meeting last year when he appeared on one of your cases against you. You thought he lied about his credentials, and you said, 'if I ever hear he's going to appear against me again, I'll check him out ahead of time.' "Sounds like you might have a chance now."

Barry immediately got up and went to Sarah's desk. "Sarah, remember the case of *Benson versus Melody Motors*?"

Sarah looked up. "Sure."

"Call records and have them send up the *Benson* file. It's closed. Actually, I don't need the whole file, just the transcript of Penn Rogaine's testimony."

Back in his office, Barry stood with his back to his windows and looked at Popnick. "I wonder how Merriman plans to use those guys. I would have thought he needed a mechanical engineering against Monarch. Seemed to me that Rogaine passed himself off as a design and safety engineer. Well, we'll see what we can dig up."

Shortly after noon while Berry was out for lunch, a clerk brought a portion of the transcript of the trial in the *Benson* case to Barry's office and laid it on his desk.

When Barry returned to his office, he saw the transcript. He picked it up and took it to the conference table where he sat and began turning the pages. He came to the testimony of Penn Rogaine, and he began to read. He found what he was looking for, the testimony of Rogaine giving his qualification. Rogaine testified that he received an engineering design degree from UCLA in 1960. Barry thought, *when he said that I wondered. I'd never heard of that major, engineering design.* Then he read his cross examination of Rogaine. Rogaine said he started his studies at the University of Indiana in 1955 and transferred after his second year to UCLA where he received his degree. He testified that he took basic engineering courses during his second year at Indiana, and advanced engineering courses during his three years at UCLA, including special course in design engineering. He said he minored in mechanical engineering.

After he concluded reading Rogaine's testimony, he went back to his desk and dialed an internal number on his telephone.

Ben Lorenzo answered.

"Ben, will you come up to my office I have an assignment for you."

Within minutes after Barry hung up his telephone, he heard knuckles rap at his open door. He looked up and greeted Lorenzo. "Come on in, Ben and have a seat at the conference table."

Lorenzo entered and sat at the conference table.

Barry also took a chair at the table and opened the transcript to the Rogaine testimony. He brought Lorenzo up to speed on the *Benson* case and his suspicions about Rogaine's testimony. "Frankly, I suspected he lied about his qualifications, but I didn't have any proof during that trial. However, I told myself, if I ever came up against him again, I'd check him out so I'd be prepared. Well, I've just got some information that he may have been hired by the plaintiff's lawyers in the Ralston case, so I want you to do some research for me." He pointed out where Rogaine testified at to his engineering education at the University of Indiana and UCLA. "What I need you to do is get his transcript from both of the schools. I don't want to take a deposition if you can get them without it. Do you think you can get the transcripts without a subpoena?"

Lorenzo smiled. "You know I can. UCLA should have both transcripts. That's where I'll start anyway. I've got a contact there who owes me one. How soon do you need it?"

"That case is not set for trial, but don't procrastinate. I can use it as soon as you can get it."

The next morning Barry sat on the couch in his office with Sarah, conferring with her about a trial he had starting Monday. His telephone rang. He got up and walked over to his desk, lifted the receiver to his ear and spoke into it. "Barry O'Shea."

"Hi, Denny Wilson here. I talked to Wayne. He's agreed to provide you with the specificity you want, and he said to arrange for your client to inspect the vehicles. But he said there would be conditions. He wants only one inspection for all three defendants, so you'll have to coordinate it with Roper and Sturgis. Also, Wayland Chang, our expert, will be present."

131

Barry, still standing, shrugged his shoulders. "If that's the way he'll produce the vehicles for the first inspection, I'll go along, but without waiving our right to further inspections."

"I'm sure he didn't mean to allow you additional inspections."

"I don't care what you think he meant. I'm just telling you that we'll go along with a joint inspection, but not without keeping our options open for further inspections."

"Well, talk to the other defense counsel and give me a call when you want the inspection set up," Wilson said.

"I'll do that," Barry said, "but how is he going to supply us with the specific defect he's claiming?"

"He'll write you a letter. But he said to tell you he will claim the vehicle was defectively designed because it's design did not allow the driver to see ahead in the event that the hood flew up, and the hood latching mechanism was defective in that it was not designed with a safety catch in the event someone closed the hood and did not properly get it seated."

"I'll wait for the letter." And the call ended.

Barry turned to Sarah. "I assume you know what that call was about. Merriman has agreed to produce the vehicles for inspection, but only if all defendants inspect them together. You heard how I qualified the inspection. Get me Steve Hinkley as soon as you can." He sat behind his desk.

Sarah rose, started out to her desk. "I'll get right on it," she said. After a few moments, she called to Barry, "I've got Mr. Hinkley on the line."

Barry reached for the telephone. "Steve, the plaintiffs' lawyers have agreed to produce the vehicles." He told Hinkley about the conditions. "I agreed to the joint inspection as a starter, but told them that we reserved our right to further inspections. How soon can you engineers be here?"

"I don't know," Hinkley answered. "Let me put you on hold and see if I can reach them."

"All right." Barry then switched the telephone to speaker, laid it on his desk and began reading the monthly bar bulletin.

After about five minutes, Hinkley came back on the telephone. "I've talked to our product investigation group. They can move anytime but give them at least a week notice of the time. Then we'll decide who goes and have them call you to coordinate."

"Okay. I'll get back to you when we've set the time." Barry hung up the receiver and called out, "Sarah, would you please come in here?"

Sarah came to the doorway.

Barry looked at her. "Get in touch with Walt and Larry and find out when their people are available for an inspection. Then check my schedule and set a time, so long as it's at least a week and a half down the road. Then call Steve Hinkley and alert him."

Sarah said, "Sure." And she turned and went back to her desk.

The WCI administration building had four stories, the tallest of the five building in hub-like campus in Aurora, Illinois. The fourth floor contained the executive offices and the small legal department. Shortly before noon on a Friday, Verner Schultz sat at his desk staring out his south-facing windows at the grove of oak trees just over the Fox River. Above the trees patchy cumulous clouds floated in the sky of an Indian summer day. Schultz had a brown crew cut which emphasized he short heavy German stature.

A man stuck his head in the door of Schultz's office. "You wanted me?" he asked.

Schultz rotated his chair toward the man and said, "Yes, come in and grab a chair, Gunther."

Sweigert came in and took one of the two chairs facing Schultz at his desk.

"I just got a call from out lawyer out in Portland," Schultz said. "You know the Ralston case."

"Yeah, what's he want?"

"There's going to be an inspection of the vehicles. Unfortunately, all of the defendants have to make their initial inspection together. I want you to go out there."

Sweigert frowned. "I'm not sure I can. I'm up to my eyeballs with a new design that has to be finished in two week. When is the inspection?"

"Monday morning the October twenty-second."

"That's only ten days away. There's no way I can go, but why not send Tracy O'Grady. The vehicle's the original model of the Caravan, and she was my assistant in the design. She'll know what we're looking for."

Schultz shook his head. "I don't know. I know she's smart, but she's not even thirty yet. Will she be overwhelmed by older male engineers?"

Sweigert gave a little laugh. "Tracy be overwhelmed? You gotta be kidding. She can hold her own with anyone. And I'll bet, if anything, she'll use her feminine charm to gain an advantage."

"All right. Our lawyer is Walt Roper at *Michaels & Bruce*. She's to give him a call and make the arrangements."

The next week on Wednesday morning, October seventeenth, the sun shown brightly through the west facing windows of *Smith, Wyman & Wiggens'* conference room on the west side of the fifteenth floor of their building. Barry sat at the head of the dark maple conference table. Three other partners gathered around the table in a meeting of a firm committee.

Sarah opened the conference room door and looked at Barry. "Brad Matcheck of Monarch is on my phone."

Matcheck was a staff engineer in Monarch's Product Analysis section. That section supported outside lawyers in product cases.

Barry looked at the three partners. "Let's recess for fifteen minutes or so. I have to take this call." He got up and followed Sarah down the hall to his office. As he entered, he told Sarah to switch the call to his phone.

"I already have," she replied. "Pick your's up." And she turned away smiling.

Barry sat at his desk and picked up the receiver. "Brad, it's been a long time. Are you coming out on the Ralston case?"

"Hey, Barry, it's good to hear your voice. Yeah, Sid Notice and I got the assignment. Sid's a Monarch designer. He worked on the 1970 pickups."

"That's great. I haven't met Notice, but we'll need someone with his background. When will you be here?"

"Steve said the inspection's set for Monday morning twenty-second, so we'll arrive about noon on Sunday. You don't mind working on Sunday, do you?" Matcheck asked, snickering.

Barry smiled. "You know better than that. We've spent Sundays before. Grab a cab and come straight to the office. I'll set you up at the Hilton. You can check in after we talk.

On Sunday afternoon, Barry looked up from his desk and saw a man with a narrow face, a hooked nose and wavy blonde hair staring in at him. Barry quickly rose and walked toward the man, smiling with his right hand out. "Brad, it's good to see you."

Matcheck held a suitcase in his right hand and a brief case in his left one. He dropped both cases on the floor, looked at Barry, took his hand, raised his left hand and put it on Barry's shoulder. "You're my favorite lawyer, Barry."

Matcheck stood a head shorter than Barry, had a heavy, but not fat, physique and his appearance matched his second generation Czech ancestry.

Matcheck turned as a second man appeared at the door. "Meet Sid Notice." He turned to Barry. "Sid this is Barry O'Shea, the lawyer I've been telling you about."

Notice also had a suitcase and a brief case. He put them down, extended his hand, his green eyes sparkling. "I've heard a lot of good things about you, Mr. O'Shea."

Barry shook his hand. "The pleasure is mine, but call me Barry."

Notice appeared older than Matcheck or Barry. His black hair had a tint of gray above his ears. He wore glasses, had a round face and stood only about five feet five. "Fine, Barry," he said.

Barry motioned to the couch. "Come on in and make yourself comfortable."

Matcheck and Notice sat on the couch, and Barry pulled up a chair to its side.

Barry leaned forward and placed his forearms on his upper legs. "I've been notified that the inspection is to take place at nine tomorrow morning in a garage located on SE Fifteenth Avenue on the east side. Representatives of MCI and the service station will be there also, as will an engineer retained by the plaintiffs by the name of Wayland Chang. I know Chang; he's been on the other side of a lot of cases I've handled. He bends his opinions to help whoever hires him, assuming just those facts that he needs of support his opinions. But he has an Achilles heal, when pinned into a corner, he tells the truth."

"Do we want to converse with the representatives of the other parties?" Matcheck asked.

"Not in front of Chang. Just examine both vehicles and make private notes. If you want to talk to me or each other, make sure it's done out of Chang's hearing. I've told the other defense lawyer that we won't talk in front of Chang. We can talk about common areas afterwards."

"What if we want to come back for a further inspection?" Notice asked.

"I think we'll have to go to court if we need further inspections. But we should get at least one more."

Barry reached over to his desk, picked up a stack of eight by ten photographs and brought them over to the small table in front of the couch. He held one of the photos out toward Matcheck and Notice. "As you can see from this police photo of the front of the pickup, it sustained a lot of damage." He looked at Notice. "Do you think you'll be able to tell the condition of the latching mechanism before the accident?"

Notice examined the photo. "I've studied this picture before, and it looks like a proper design, but I'll be able to tell better when I see the vehicle." Then he looked at Barry. "I've been told that the dairy bought the vehicle second hand. Do we know anything about its history before?"

"We don't. That's the next thing on my agenda. We'll get the VIN number of the vehicle when we see it. Then can start looking into its history of the usage and maintenance."

They talked further for about an hour and a half about the accident and the inspection.

Then Barry got up. "Unless anyone has anything else to bring up, I suggest we call it a day."

Matcheck and Notice stood and started toward the door.

Barry said, "I'll walk out with you."

When they got down to the building's lobby, Barry pointed to the front door. "That's Sixth Street out there. Your hotel occupies the full block on the other side of the street just a block to the north. I'll pick you up at eight-thirty tomorrow morning in front of the hotel." Then he pointed to a door to his left. "I have to take that elevator over there to the garage to get my car."

Matcheck and Notice with their cases in hand walked out the door.

13

ON MONDAY MORNING Barry drove up to the garage on NE Fifteenth Avenue and parked. He, Matcheck and Notice entered the office area and were met by Chang.

Barry greeted Chang. "Wayland, I want you to meet Brad Matcheck and Sid Notice. They're from Monarch."

Chang extended his right hand. "Glad to meet you. The others haven't arrived yet."

Matcheck and Notice each shook hands with Chang.

"Well, that shouldn't hold us up," Barry said. "Where are the vehicles?"

Chang's eyes raised, and he thought a moment. "I guess it would be all right for you to see them now," he said finally. "The lawyers said you had to examine at the same time; they didn't say one of you couldn't see them when you got here. Come this way." He led the way through the door to the side of the office, out into the garage proper.

Upon seeing the damaged vehicles, Matcheck and Notice quickly went to them. They each carried a brief case. The first vehicle they came upon was the Monarch pickup. They walked slowly around it, carefully making their examination. Then they laid their brief cases on the table ahead of the pickup and opened them. Matcheck took a small camera out of his brief case, and Notice took a tape measure and a legal pad from his. They went back to the pickup, and Matcheck took pictures from all angles, some close-ups and some at a greater distance. Notice measured at various places and jotted notes on the legal pad. Neither said anything. Barry and Chang sat at the table and watched.

Soon Chang heard a bell ring in the office, announcing that someone had entered. He went to the office. He returned with Walt Roper and a stunning freckle-faced, blonde woman.

Roper went directly to Barry. "Barry, I want you to meet Tracy O'Grady. As you can see, WCI sent out a very good looking engineer."

O'Grady laid a briefcase on the table. Then she looked at Barry, her green eyes glistening, and held out her right hand. "It's a pleasure to meet yawl."

Barry smiled as he took her hand. "Not only an attractive engineer, but a southern as well."

The bell in the office rang again, and again Chang left the garage. He returned with Sturgis and a tall, thin, balding middle aged man who wore glasses and coveralls.

By this time O'Grady had taken a camera out of her briefcase, moved over to the side of the pickup, introduced herself to Matcheck and Notice and began examining and photographing the Caravan.

Sturgis greeted Barry and Roper. "I think you guys have met Noah Beauchamp."

Barry smiled. "Oh yes, in court many times. Hello, Noah."

Beauchamp grinned and shook both of their hands. "It always seems I'm on the other side. Why don't you two hire me sometime?"

Roper looked a Barry and smiled. "I guess we're just too used to cross-examining you."

At this point Barry went over to Matcheck and Notice. "Come on over to the end of the garage. I've got something to say to you in private," he said quietly.

Matcheck and Notice followed him some distance from the others.

Barry huddled with them. "Be careful what you say to Beauchamp. While he's working for a co-defendant, you can be sure he's here to find something wrong with the pickup. He has too if he's going to help the service station attendant. Also be wary of O'Grady's eyes. While I don't think she's here to find something wrong with Monarch, you never know."

"We've about finished with the pickup for now," Matcheck said. "We'll spend the rest of our time with the Caravan. We want to make some measurement so we can determine the approximate speed of the vehicles at impact. We also want to check closely the type of crush involved. It seems that at least the two deaths might be the result of the lack of structure of the Caravan."

Barry leaned toward Matcheck. "Good point. I'm not sure we can use it as a defense, but it could provide a good negotiating tool."

Barry looked around and saw Roper also conferring with O'Grady, some distance from the others.

The inspection took most of the morning. Barry, Matcheck and Notice finished first, but they stayed around until a quarter after twelve when all of the people left the garage together.

That afternoon Barry sat in a chair beside Matcheck and Notice who sat on the couch in his office.

Notice examined the notes he'd taken at the inspection. "I got the pickup's VIN number. It reads CV847739241. We can get the vehicle's maintenance history from that."

Matcheck looked at Barry. "Sid and I gave the pickup a close look. We both came away with the impression that it had been in at least one previous accident. We can't say for sure, but the VIN number check should tell us."

Barry's eyes fell on Sid. "Did you see anything wrong with the latching mechanism?"

"It appeared to be all right. The mechanism on the front of the vehicle looked in order, although I saw some deflection probably caused by the impact. The hood was damaged as was the latching mate on its underside, presumably in the accident. That latching mate, however, appeared to be the proper design."

"Did it appear that the latching mechanism would have worked properly, if there had been no damage cause by the accident?"

Notice lowered his eyes at Barry. "I'm not sure I understand what you're getting at? Are you asking if the two parts of the mechanism appeared to have been manufactured per design?"

"Yes."

"They appeared that way."

Barry leaned forward and rested his forearms on his legs. "It appears to me that this mechanism doesn't have two catches like some hoods I'm familiar with. By that I mean when you release the hood, you still have to put you hand under it to release a second catch before the hood can be raised."

"You're right. We don't build our mechanism that way. Some say the second catch is a safety measure. In case something goes wrong with the main catch the second catch is suppose to hold the hood down. We disagree. We think it provides a way that a negligent person can push the hood down only so far as to engage the second catch and think he's closed the hood, when actually it isn't fully closed. Our mechanism is designed so that when the vehicle leaves the factory and the hood is closed, it stays closed. If nothing happens to the vehicle afterwards, if you open the hood and apply enough pressure to close it, it says closed. It cannot come open by itself, so there's no need for a so-called safety catch."

"Then how could a service station attendant be the cause of the hood flying up?"

"He couldn't unless he lowered the hood but didn't engage the mechanism. The hood's weight will keep it down, but it will bob-up-and-down as you're driving down the road. The driver should notice that. And if the vehicle drives over something on the road at a speed that causes an upward thrust, the hood may fly up."

Barry's eyes went to the ceiling. He thought for a moment. "Could a previous accident cause something to go wrong with the latching mechanism? In other words, could the matching members get out of line, so that if someone applied enough force to close the hood, the hood could still release by itself while the vehicle is being operated."

"If the mechanism were damaged in a previous accident and not repaired properly, I think it could happen," Notice replied.

Barry lit a cigarette and took a puff. "Well then, we better find out everything can about this vehicle's history."

Matcheck rose and pointed at the telephone on Barry's desk. "Can I use your phone, Barry? I'll call my office in Detroit. We should have the answer pretty quick."

"Sure, have at it."

Matcheck went to Barry's desk and placed a call. When someone answered, Matcheck gave that person the VIN number and explained what he wanted. He hung up the telephone and turned to Barry. "I talked to a technician in my office. He'll research the VIN number and call us back."

About fifteen minutes later, Barry's telephone rang.

Barry put out his cigarette, answered it and handed the receiver to Matcheck.

"It's the technician in you office. He wants to speak to you."

Matcheck took the receiver and identified himself.

"Hamlin Motors in San Francisco sold the vehicle new to a Richard Lewis of that city," the technician said. "The dealership performed routine maintenance on the vehicle for the next two years. There is no record of any accidents, but there's no record of any maintenance after February 1972."

"Is there any record of any sale of the vehicle by Lewis?" Matcheck asked.

"No, I check the registration in California. Lewis is the last registered owner, but he didn't renew the registration this year."

Matcheck ended the call, turned to the Barry and Notice and relayed what he had been told. "He found nothing telling us that the vehicle was later sold to the dairy. Our next stop is Richard Lewis in San Francisco. Barry do you have someone who can track him down?"

"I'll call in our investigator. He should have a contact down there." He went out to Sarah's desk, asked her to track down Ben Lorenzo, and tell him to come up to Barry's office. A few moments later, Lorenzo stuck his head in Barry's door. "You wanted to see me, boss?"

"Yes, Ben come in. You know Brad Matcheck, and this is Sid Notice a truck designer from Monarch."

Lorenzo entered and greeted Matcheck. "Hi, Brad." He then turned to Notice and shook his hand. "Glad to meet you, Sid."

"We've got some investigation that needs to be done down in the Bay area," Barry said. "Don't you have contact down there?"

"You bet I do. Lilly Mendoza. She's a second generation Hispanic. Her parents emigrated from Mexico to the Bay area before she was born and settled there doing domestic work. I met Lilly when I was a detective with the PPD and was in Frisco at a drug seminar. Lilly attended the same seminar as a patrolwoman for the SFPD. A few years later she sent me an announcement that she had set up shop as a PI. I've used her several times, and she does a Cracker Jack job."

Barry asked Lorenzo to have a seat, and explained their problem and what they needed down.

After Barry had finished, Lorenzo got up. "I'll get Lilly right on it."

143

14

LILLY MENDOZA'S PI office was on the third floor of an older five-story building on Market Street, a few blocks from San Francisco's civic center. The office had two rooms, a reception room and Mendoza's small office with one large window that overlooked Market Street. The office housed a dark maple desk, a small walnut conference table, and four straight back walnut chairs. Several pictures of San Francisco and two framed certificates, a PI license and diploma from police officer's school, adorned the walls. Mendoza's secretary worked three days a week in the reception room.

Out of high school Mendoza started as a masseuse in a San Francisco massage parlor. A couple of years later she entered the San Francisco police academy and worked for the SFPD for seven years after graduating. She went out on her own as a private investigator in 1969. Now at thirty-three she remained single, but one wonders why from her appearance. She had long black hair, a tan complexion and at five-ten a physical but attractive figure. Her hazel eyes highlighted her pleasant face and grabbed the attention of anyone caught in her stare.

Next to her PI office, Mendoza maintained a small massage parlor where she practiced her earlier profession off-and-on whenever her PI business lagged. To keep the business separate the sign on the door read: *Personal Massages*.

On Tuesday morning Mendoza sat at her desk, reviewing a report, wearing a white long-sleeved blouse with the sleeves rolled up a couple of turns, faded jeans and Nike walking shoes. Her telephone rang. She picked up the receiver and identified herself.

"Lillie, this is Ben Lorenzo in Portland."

"Hi, Ben, what can I do for you?"

"I've got a job for you, if you have time?"

Mendoza smiled. "I always have time for you. What the story?"

Ben explained their case and how Monarch came to a dead end tracing the pickup's history with the VIN number. He told her that the vehicle had been sold on January tenth, 1970 by Hamlin Motors in San Francisco to a Richard Lewis, but that it had not been registered to anyone else. Lorenzo wanted her to find out what happened to the vehicle while it was owned by Lewis and afterwards.

Mendoza tapped a pencil on her desk as Lorenzo talked. "That should be easy," she said. "I'll get right on it."

Later that morning Medonza decided to pay Hamlin Motors a visit. She left her office building and grabbed a cab at the corner of Market and Leavenworth. The day was clear, but the temperature had a bite to it, so she wore a brown leather jacket over her blouse. She had her hair tied in back and an old SFPD billed cap on her head.

The cab let her out at the corner of Van Ness and Bush, and she went directly into the show room of Hamlin Motors.

A salesman greeted her. "Can I help you, miss?"

Mendoza smiled. "Yes, please." She batted her eyes at him. "I'm interested in a sale you made on January tenth in 1970. Would you have the records of the sale here?"

She had the salesman's attention, but not yet his cooperation. "I'm sure the record is here, although I'm not sure we can show it to you. I think it's confidential."

Mendoza eyed him with her hazel eyes. "If we had time, I'm sure I could convince you to let me look." She pulled out her PI card and showed it to him. "But let's make it more official. I've been hired by Monarch Motors to trace the vehicle, and they suggested I start here."

"In that case, follow me and we'll take a look."

The salesman led Mendoza up some stairs and to an office on the second floor. They entered an office where a woman sat at a desk.

The salesman addressed the woman. "Rachel, this lady is with Monarch Motors. She wants to know about a sale we made on January tenth in 1970." "What kind of vehicle are you trying to trace?" he asked Mendoza. "And do you have its identification number?"

"Yes, it's a pickup," Mendoza answered. She reached in her purse and brought out a piece of paper which she handed him. "The VIN number is on there."

The salesman handed the piece of paper to the woman, and she got up and walked to some filing cabinets in the rear of the room.

Soon she returned with a file, which she opened on the desk. "It appears that we sold a green pickup to a Richard Lewis on that date." She pointed down at a form in the file. "Here's his address. Do you want me to copy the sales invoice for you?"

"Yes, would you please?"

The woman went over to a copy machine, copied the document, and upon returning she gave it to Mendoza.

The sales invoice listed an address on Jackson Street two doors west of Octavia. That afternoon Mendoza parked her car, walked up several steps to a front porch looking out over the bay, and pushed the doorbell.

Soon the door opened revealing an attractive woman in her mid-forties. "May I help you?" she asked.

"Yes," Mendoza said. "I'm looking for Richard Lewis."

"He no longer lives here. We were divorced earlier this year."

"Oh, I'm sorry to hear that. Could I ask where he now lives?"

"Don't be sorry. We'd been separated for about a year, and the divorce was fairly amicable. He has an apartment on Nob Hill." And she gave Mendoza the address and telephone number.

That evening Mendoza called the number Mrs. Lewis had given her.

A man answered. "This is Rich Lewis."

"Mr. Lewis, I'm Lillie Mendoza. I'm a private investigator hired to track down the history of a 1970 Monarch pickup you bought from Hamlin Motors."

"Yeah, I owned such a pickup. Actually, I was about to leave. I usually have a cocktail or two at about this time at the Big Four in the Huntington Hotel a few blocks from here. Why don't you meet me there, and we'll talk?"

"That sounds swell. How will I know you?"

"I'll spot you, if you'll give me a description."

Mendoza gave a modest description of herself. "People have commented on the unusual nature of my hazel eyes," she added.

Lewis laughed. "Then I'm going to enjoy looking for you."

Mendoza decided to take a cab to the Huntington Hotel. She wore a white blouse with a black sweater and a red short skirt. The cab arrived there about a half hour after her call to Lewis. The Big Four restaurant had an entrance on California at Taylor Street. When she entered, she stood in a lounge where a man played the piano. Several customers sat at a bar ahead of her and to her right. One of the customers stared at her, smiled, got off the bar stool with his drink in hand and headed her way.

The customer had a pleasant appearance, probably in his late forties or early fifties, about six feet with a full head of dark hair beginning to turn gray. He wore a brown plaid jacket, a red and brown striped tie, gray slacks and highly polished brown dress shoes.

He came up to Mendoza, still smiling, and put out his right hand. "I'd have spotted you anywhere after your description of your eyes. I'm Rich Lewis."

Mendoza returned the smile. "I gathered you were when I saw you staring my way as I entered." She shook his hand.

He motioned to a small banquet behind her. "Let's take that banquet. It's a little out of the way where we can talk without too much interruption."

She sat.

He set his drink on the table so he could sit beside her, but before sitting he asked, "What can I get you to drink?"

"Smirnoff on the rocks with a splash of water."

He left and went to the bar where he said something to the bartender. Soon the bartender put a glass on the bar with ice in it and took a bottle of Smirnoff's and poured some in the glass. Lewis then retrieved the glass, brought in the table, and gave it to Mendoza. He sat and raised his glass toward her. "Here's to a pleasurable little talk."

She clanked her glass on his. "I hope so."

They talked for about an hour with Lewis telling Mendoza the story of his accident in the Sierras, the damage to the pickup and the insurance settlement he received. "They considered it a total loss."

"What was the name of the insurance company?" Mendoza asked.

Lewis gave her the name.

"What happened to the pickup after that?"

"I don't know. They gave me a check and took the vehicle as salvage."

They continued chatting until Mendoza finished her drink and started to leave.

"Let me buy you another drink," Lewis said.

"I'd like to but I have other plans." She got up and shook his hand.

The next morning Mendoza began the day trying to get hold of the insurance adjuster who had dealt with Lewis. She finally found him in San Francisco. He agreed to meet her in his office.

"I remember the accident well," he said, sitting behind his desk with a file folder in front of him. "Lewis' vehicle left the road a hit a tree. It was a total loss. I have some picture of it that you might want to see?" He pushed the file across the desk for Mendoza to look at.

She sat in a chair facing the adjuster. She leaned forward and examined the pictures that were stapled to one page. She looked up. "My, the vehicle as certainly totaled. Do you mind if I get copies of these pictures?"

"You can have them. The file is closed."

"And can I have you've evaluation form as well?"

"I'll make a copy of that for you."

He told her that he had sold the vehicle for salvage to a salvage yard in Sacramento that he identified.

Mendoza went back to her office, and after several more calls, she learned that the vehicle had been purchased at auction by Roger Winchester, a rebuilder in Kelso, Washington.

She called Lorenzo and told him where the wrecked vehicle went. "I think Kelso's more in your area than in mine. I'll send you the pictures of the damaged vehicle and the evaluation report."

"You're right," Lorenzo said. "I'll take it from here. Thanks for your help. Send me you bill."

15

A WEEK LATER, Lorenzo drove north on I 5 to Kelso. His lights reflected off the pavement as steady rain fell. It wasn't a downpour, but typical Pacific Northwest rainfall, resulting in a dark and dreary day. When he got to Kelso, he exited the freeway and stopped at the first service station he saw. He pulled up to the office, just as the attendant came out the door.

The attendant came up to Lorenzo's side of the car as Lorenzo lowered the window. "Can I help you?" the attendant asked.

"I don't need gas, just some directions. Do you know where I could find Roger's Reck & Rebuild?"

"Sure. We're on Allen Street. Go west until you get to Pacific, turn right and go about a half mile. You can't miss it; it's on your left."

Lorenzo thanked him and drove off. He followed the attendant's direction and saw the sign on Pacific. He drove in the dirt driveway and parked opposite the single door. The rain still fell, so, when he got out of his car, he ran up the stairs, tried the door and it opened.

As he entered a man at a desk looked up at him. "What can I do fer ya?"

Lorenzo explained who he was. "Are you Roger Winchester?"

"Last time I looked I was."

"Then I'd like to ask you about a wrecked pickup you bought down in Sacramento about three years ago."

Winchester reached into his shirt pocket, pulled out a Camel, struck a match on the desk and lit it. He took a puff and then chuckled. "You know yer the second person in 'bout a month that's asked about that pickup, but the first one was a damn site better looking. But yer wrong when ya say it was wrecked. Sure it'd been in a fender bender and needed a little work, but it wasn't no wreck."

Lorenzo thought about the photos he'd seen. "Can I see your records of the work you did on it?"

"I'd like to show you, but, the lady that was here in September asked too, and I looked and found, as I thought I would, that we didn't keep anything. We're just not that big an operation."

"Who was the lady?" Lorenzo asked.

"She worked for an insurance company, the dairy's I think."

"What did you do with the pickup?"

"I think we painted her black and sold it to a dealer in Seaside, but I don't have no records of that either. But the lady had a receipt that showed that's what we did. I think she said a dairy had bought it from the dealer, and it'd been in a bad accident."

After leaving, Kelso Lorenzo continued driving north on I 5 in a steady light rain. He arrived in the state capital Olympia shortly before noon. He pull into the parking lot for the state police, got out of his car, put up his umbrella and walked quickly to the police headquarters building. Once inside he headed for the office of Captain Headly. He had worked closely with Headly when he was a detective with the Portland Police Department. The case involved an escaped murderer from the Washington Penitentiary, and Lorenzo had been instrumental in his capture in North Portland.

He entered Headly's office and went to a desk occupied by a policewoman.

"I'd like to see Captain Headly," Lorenzo said.

The policewomen looked up. "May I telling him your name?"

"Ben Lorenzo. I'm an old friend."

The policewoman got up and went into an office bearing a name plate: Warren Headly, Captain.

In a moment the office door opened and a large state policeman emerged, smiling and walked toward Lorenzo, holding his hand out. "Benji, you old goat what brings you up this way?"

Lorenzo took his hand and shook it. "I've been doing some investigation in Kelso, Warren. Ran into a stone wall and thought you might have an idea that'd help."

Headly extended his arm toward his door. "Come on in and tell me about it. I'll help if I can."

Lorenzo followed him into his office.

Headly motioned Lorenzo toward a chair. "Have a seat." Headly then sat down behind his desk. "What's the stone wall?"

Lorenzo told him about the vehicle history he was investigating and his interview with the rebuilder. "When he told me there had been only minor damage in the earlier accident, I knew something was wrong because I had pictures taken by the insurance company after that accident." He pulled the pictures out of a file he carried and put them on headly's desk. "You can see in the pictures a very badly damaged pickup that the insurance company considered a total loss."

Headly picked up several of the pictures and examined them. "I see what you mean. No way could he rebuild that without major repairs and parts."

"I know, but he claims he only did minor repairs and painting, and he has no records of the work."

"When was the repair done?"

"Sometime between March and September of 1972."

"I don't suppose you have the names of any employees who worked on it?"

"No, and he not going to cooperate."

Captain Headly swung his chair around and looked out his window, seeing the rain falling. He thought for a moment and then swung back toward Lorenzo. "He's got to be covered by the state for workman's comp and has to make periodic filings of his employees. Why don't you get his filings for 1970? That'll tell you who was working for him."

"That's the kind of information I thought you would give me. Where's the comp office?"

"I can do better than that."

Headly picked up his telephone with one hand and spun his directory with the other. He stopped the directory at W and dialed the telephone. "This is Captain Headly of State Police; I want to talk to someone in your organization who keeps the lists of employees you received from employers."

Headly waited, and another person came on the line. "Are you the person who had to lists of employee filed by employer?" he asked.

Headly listened for a moment. "I'm interested in the filings for 1970," then he looked at Lorenzo and asked, "What was the name of the rebuilder?"

"Roger's Reck and Rebuild."

Headly went back on his telephone. "For Roger's Reck, spelled with an R, and Rebuild in Kelso."

Headly waited for several moments and then listened. "That's great," he said. "I'm sending a Mr. Lorenzo over to pick up a copy of that list. Will you have it ready for him?"

He got the answer, hung up the telephone and looked at Lorenzo. "They'll have it for you. Ask for Loretta Sherwood." Then he gave Lorenzo directions to the State Workman's Compensation Department.

Lorenzo got up and extended his hand to Headly. "Thanks, Warren. This will help a lot."

Headly shook his hand. "For an old friend like you I'd do anything to help, especially when that friend caught an escaped murderer for us."

Lorenzo left the police headquarters, went to the comp department and left Olympia at about three o'clock with the names of Winchesters two mechanics in 1970.

The document he received had a filing date of February twenty-eight and listed the mechanics as Wilson Spelling and Poncho Esperenza, both of Kelso. The document contained the addresses and telephone numbers.

Lorenzo stopped in Kelso on his way back to do some preliminary checking concerning the whereabouts of the mechanics. He drove to Roger Reck & Rebuild and parked across the road. *I can't go back in there and expect any cooperation. Maybe there's a bar or tavern around here where the mechanics go when off work,* he thought. A light rain still fell and fog began to limit visibility, but as dusk settled in a neon sign down the street caught his attention, Schroeder's Tavern. He decided to try there. He drove up and parked in front.

Now around four-thirty, the tavern had a number of customers. Lorenzo walked in and sat at a table at the far end. A waitress in her late forties or early fifties came up to the table, and he ordered an Oly.

When the waitress returned and put the bottle of beer and a glass on the table, Lorenzo smiled. "Do either Wilson Spelling or Poncho Esperenza come in here?" he asked.

The waitress looked at him. "Nah, they haven't been around for at least six months."

"Didn't they work for Winchester down the street?"

"Yeah, they were his mechanics, but they got laid off when Rog's business hit the skids earlier this year."

"That's funny. I thought he was still in business."

"He is, but he's doing the rebuild work himself."

"You don't happen to know what's happened to Spelling or Esperenza, do you."

"Spelling's still in town, as far as I know, but he doesn't come in here anymore. I don't know if he's working. I have no idea where Esperenza is."

Lorenzo finished his beer and started back to Portland. His search for the mechanics would have to wait for another day.

On Saturday morning Lorenzo entered Barry's office, knocking on the open door.

Barry looked up. "Ben, come in. I was thinking about you and the VIN number I asked you to track down in the Ralston case. Have you heard from your San Francisco contact?"

Lorenzo sat in one of the chairs beside Barry's desk and opened a folder on the desk. "I sure have." He took some photos out of the file and handed them to Barry. "The vehicle had a previous accident. These are the photos she got from the insurance adjuster who adjusted the loss of the first owner."

Barry examined the photographs. "Wow, look at the vehicle's front end. It appears to have been totaled."

Lorenzo picked up another set of documents from the folder and gave it to Barry. "It was as you can see from the adjuster's evaluation report."

Barry flipped the pages and examined them. "I see that he suggested that the structural member that the radiator is attached to might have been straighten, and he listed the hood as one of the parts of the vehicle that would have to be replaced. I'm not sure of the significance of that, but I can guess. Send copies of the photos and the report immediately to Steve Hinkley so Brad and Sid can comment."

"I will. My contact traced the vehicle to a salvage yard in Sacramento where it was sold to a rebuilder in Kelso. She thought I could more easily follow up with the rebuilder."

"I agree. Have you done it?"

"I visited Roger's Reck & Rebuild in Kelso, and came to a dead end. He claimed the vehicle only sustained minor rear-end damage. All he had to do was some minor straightening and repaint the vehicle to sell it. He denied and major rebuilding." Then he told Barry of his visit to his police friend in Olympia, and his introduction to the comp department. He told him he got the names of two mechanics that worked for Winchester and tried to track them down in Kelso. "They were both laid off earlier this year. One's reportedly still in Kelso, and the whereabouts of the other is unknown. I'm going to follow up."

That same Saturday in the afternoon Roger Winchester pull out a stool and sat at the bar in Schroeder's Tavern.

Ace Schroeder tended the bar. When he saw Winchester, he came over quickly. "I thought you'd be in here sometime today so I didn't call you. Some fella was in here yesterday afternoon and questioned Gert about Spelling and Esperenza. He wanted to know if they still worked for you. She told him they'd been laid off. He asked if they were still around. She told him that Spelling was, but she didn't know where Esperenza had gone. He didn't identify himself."

Winchester showed no reaction. "I wonder what he wanted. Far as I know, neither of them was in any trouble. I don't know what happened to Poncho either, but I'll give Wils a call and let him know."

Later that day after Winchester left the tavern, he drove south on Pacific past the train station to Alder, turned left and stopped at a one-story house between Third and Fourth. He drove up on the dirt driveway beside the house and parked. He walked up two wooden steps to the front door and rang the doorbell.

In a few moments the door opened slightly revealing an unshaven middle-age man with a head of receding, disheveled hair. He wore a rumpled blue shirt, partially unbuttoned exposing his hairy chest, dirty and baggy blue jeans and thongs covering his bare feet. He narrowed his eyes as he looked out. "I'm not taking callers this afternoon, Rog," he slurred.

Winchester stuck his foot in the door as the man started to close it. "Is that any way to talk to the man who paid for your unemployment insurance," Winchester said as he shoved the door open, causing the man to stumble back against the back of a worn sofa covered with a dirty blanket.

The room appeared that it hadn't been cleaned for days. Dirty dishes were stacked on a table in front of the sofa. A plain TV was on in one corner and a faded upholstered chair occupied the other, beside a straight table holding a lamp covered by a crooked shade. An open bottle of Old Crow and a half filled glass rested on the table.

Winchester stepped into the room and closed the door behind him. He glared at the man. "Sit down, Wils. You and me's having a little talk."

Spelling stumbled into the chair.

Winchester sat leaning forward on the sofa facing Spelling. "Ace tells me that there was a man here Friday asking about you and Esperanza. I suspect he wants to talk to you about the work you did on that pickup I got down near Sacramento in March of '72."

"You mean to one we rebuilt?"

"Yeah, that's the one, but we ain't gona tell nobody that we rebuilt it, is that clear?"

"What'ca mean?"

"The pickup's been in an accident recently. Its hood flew up. I talked to the insurance adjuster for the owner and told her all we had to do was minor repairs and a paint job. I described the previous accident as a fender-bender. There's nothing in writing to say otherwise, as I didn't keep no records of the work we did. So I just want to be sure that you remembered the work we did the same as I. You see what I'm saying?"

Spelling squinted at Winchester. "You mean that's what you want me to say?"

Winchester reached in his back pocket and pulled out an envelope which he placed on the table. "That's what I want you to say because it's the truth."

Spelling picked up the envelope and opened it. He looked inside. His eyes suddenly widened. Then he looked up at Winchester. "Yeah, yeah that's what I'll say."

Winchester said, "Do you know where Poncho is?"

"I'm not sure, but I can find him."

"Find him and tell him about our conversation. Tell him what to say and that he'll get an envelope if he calls me."

16

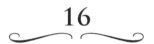

MONDAY MORNING, NOVEMBER fifth the sun shown through the window to Wayne Merriman's right, as he sat at his desk, and brightened a portion of the wall. A cool, crisp morning, the temperature had reached forty-five. Merriman examined a packet of document that arrived by express mail that morning.

Alex Savage arrived at his doorway. "You called me."

Merriman looked up. "Yes, the discovery request we sent WCI with the complaint has been answered. Wilson expressed the documents they sent him. I've just started examining them." He held out half of the stack. "Why don't you take this half, sit down and help me?"

Savage took the documents Merriman gave him, sat in one of the leather chairs beside Merriman's desk, and started examining them. After several minutes, Savage looked up at Merriman. "Look what I've found. A drawing dated December 29, 1969. And look where the engine is on this Caravan." He shoved the document across Merriman's desk.

Merriman picked up the document and reviewed it. "My God, this design is almost identical to the model Masters showed us back in October, and it's dated more than three years before our accident. That makes a report I saw earlier devastating. Look at this." He reached for a document he had laid aside on his desk and gave it to Savage.

Savage read the document and a wide smile appeared on his face. "I see what you mean," he said. "This document bears a date of January 2nd, 1970 and is the marketing department's view of the December design document. They reject the idea of moving the axel and engine ahead of the driver because their present designed vehicle was still leading the competition in sales. We couldn't have prayed for a better production. Who authored the design drawing?"

Merriman looked at it. "It says drawn by Gunter Sweigert, product manager."

"I think we've found our first deponent," Savage said.

Merriman leaned back in his chair, lit a cigarette and thought for a moment. He took the cigarette from his mouth, held it between his fingers, and looked at Savage. "I don't know about that. What was the name of that girl that WCI sent out to examine the vehicles?"

Savage pull open the file he had brought with him. He looked through the correspondence until he got to a recent letter sent to them by Denny Wilson. "Wilson says her name was Tracy O'Grady. According to how she identified her self, she's the assistant project engineer for the Caravan."

Merriman smiled and inhaled his cigarette. "That's what I thought," he said. "I say we depose her first. I know she'll know about those documents, and her answers about them could well sink WCI."

"I'll get right on it," Savage said. "I'll request O'Grady first and then Sweigert."

"No, let's just ask for her deposition. If we ask for both, they'll probably schedule Sweigert first. They can't do that if we haven't asked for his."

"Yes, but do we want to go all the way back there and not get Sweigert's deposition?"

Merriman gave a curious smile. "I'm sure they'll give us Sweigert, if we ask while we're there. If not, and we feel we need it, this case's value can easily support a second trip."

Later that day Savage sent a letter to Roper with a copy to Denny Wilson requesting Tracy O'Grady's deposition.

On Friday, November ninth, rain had been falling all week; normal for Portland this time of year. Walt Roper sat at his desk reviewing the stack of mail his secretary had just put there. Roper came to the letter from Savage requesting Tracy O'Grady's deposition. After reading the letter, he reached for his telephone and dialed.

A woman answered, "WCI, may I help you?"

"Verner Schultz, please."

"May I tell Mr. Schultz whose calling?"

"Walt Roper in Portland, Oregon."

"One moment please,"

Almost instantly, Schultz came on the line. "Walt, it's good to hear your voice. What's up?"

"I just got a letter from the plaintiffs' lawyers in the Ralston case. They want to take the deposition of Tracy O'Grady."

"Just Tracy and no one else? That's odd. They have seen the rough design drawing by Sweigert and the memo from the marketing department. I would have thought they would be asking to depose him and someone in the marketing department."

"Yeah. I thought the request was kind of strange too."

"Let me check her schedule. What's your availability?"

Roper looked at his calendar. "I'm not in court the first two weeks in December. I could do it any time in there. I think we should do it here in Portland if that's possible. I'd rather have the witness here, than back at your plant."

"I agree with that. Someone else's name is likely to come up in her deposition, and it's too easy for the lawyer to ask that that person be made available if your back here. If Tracy's in Portland, the lawyer can still ask, but he can't take the deposition right then.

I'll check Tracy's schedule for the first two weeks in December and get back to you."

"I'll wait to hear from you," Roper said, ending the call.

Walt Roper's office occupied the southwest corner of the thirtieth floor in Portland's tallest building. When it wasn't cloudy, he had a view of the Mt. Hood to the east and of the Willamette River flowing north through Portland. Typical for December, however, clouds and a light rain prevailed. Dark paneling covered the walls under paintings of old courtroom scenes. A small conference table sat directly inside the door to the office, and a leather couch and matching leather upholstered chairs completed the furnishing of the office.

It was Monday afternoon, December tenth, and Tracy O'Grady sat in a chair opposite Walt Roper at the conference table. Roper asked her if WCI had had any reports of accidents with the Caravan prior to May twenty-eighth 1973.

O'Grady looked directly at Roper. "No," she answered. "So we had no reason to change its design."

Her deposition was scheduled to start tomorrow morning in Roper's office. Today he questioned her in preparation for it.

Roper shook his head. He took his pipe from his mouth, laid it in an ash tray and looked at O'Grady. "I'm glad you did that here and not during the deposition. Remember my earlier caution. Never volunteer information. You should have stopped with the answer, no."

O'Grady's face revealed a sheepish grin. "I'm sorry. I misunderstood yawl's question. I thought the question indicated that yawl wanted to know why we didn't change the design."

Roper leaned forward. "Then you shouldn't have answered the question. I didn't ask about a change in design no matter what you thought. The first caution I gave you when we started preparing for your deposition was never guess what the questioner wants. If you aren't sure, you don't understand the question, and you shouldn't answer. Tell him that you don't understand the question. When you guess at what he wants or means by his question, nine times out of ten you either help him with volunteered information or you set yourself up for his reading your deposition back to you at trial. That's bad, because it gives the impression that you weren't truthful in the deposition. So please remember, if you don't understand the question or if you can't tell what the questioner means, do not answer. Tell him you don't understand the question. Is that clear?"

"Yes, but what if he doesn't clear it up?"

"Keep telling him that you don't understand. Don't answer just because he asks the same question over and over. Are you okay with that?"

She nodded her head. "Yes."

Roper continued questioning O'Grady in preparation for her deposition. He asked every question he expected plaintiff's lawyer to ask. He repeated the question every time O'Grady had trouble with it until he got the answer that satisfied him.

All the while Roper studied O'Grady. He watched the way she answered the questions. Even though the deposition would be taken in his office, he wanted O'Grady to be comfortable answering the questions, and he wanted her answers to be convincing. If she seems to be having trouble or if the way she answered did not seem convincing, he worked with her mannerisms and her body language until she improved.

At the start he took note of her appearance and southern accent. He had no doubts that these two characteristics gave her a head start at being believed. Her ever-present smile and those bright green eyes would be hard for the questioner to overcome. But he expected Merriman to overcome them, so preparation for the deposition was a must. The clock on Roper's desk neared four-thirty when he lit his pipe and gave O'Grady a satisfying smile. "You're ready for bear." He laughed. "I don't mean that literally, but the way you're answering now won't please to the great Wayne Merriman. Let's call it a day."

"I hope yawl's right," she said cautiously. "What time do yawl want me back here tomorrow?"

"The deposition's at nine, so come in for any last minute questions you have at eight-thirty."

The next morning Tracy O'Grady sat at the side of one end of a large rectangular conference table beside Wayne Roper. A male court reporter sat at that end of the table with his shorthand note pad resting on the table in front of him. Barry O'Shea sat at the far end of the table, and Larry Sturgis sat at the end of the table on Roper's side. The table occupied most of the room which had windows in place of the wall behind O'Grady, displaying a view of Mt. Hood on a clear day. But today if O'Grady had turned around, she saw only the Willamette River, dark clouds hiding the mountains.

The door opened and a receptionist appeared. "The plaintiffs' lawyers are here," she said.

Roper stood and walked to the open door. He leaned out and greeted them. "Come in Wayne and Denny." He extended his hand.

Merriman and Wilson had been sitting in a chair in the reception area. They got up. Merriman grasped Roper's hand with his strong grip and shook it. Roper winced.

When Merriman and Wilson came into the room, Barry and Sturgis rose and walked toward them.

"Denny, you know Barry and Larry, but I don't think Wayne has met them," Roper said. "Wayne this is Barry O'Shea, Monarch's attorney, and Larry Sturgis who represents the service station."

Merriman extended his hand to Barry and then to Sturgis. "I'm glad to meet you both."

Barry shook Merriman's hand and noticed his strong grip. "Call me Barry."

Merriman smiled. "And my name's Wayne."

"And you can call me Larry," said Sturgis.

Barry and Sturgis went back to the end of the table and sat.

Roper introduced Wilson and Merriman to the reporter and O'Grady. Looking at O'Grady, Roper smiled. "Be careful if you shake his hand. He's got a strong grip."

Merriman sat opposite O'Grady, and Roper retook his seat. Wilson sat several chairs away.

Merriman looked at the court reporter. "Swear the witness."

The court reporter remained seated and asked O'Grady to raise her right hand. "Do you swear that the testimony you will give in this deposition shall be the truth and nothing but the truth, so help you God?" he asked.

O'Grady raised her right hand and remained seated. "I do," she said.

Merriman began his questioning very politely. Smiling, he quietly asked O'Grady about her background, education and work history. He established that she was thirty and had been with WCI from its inception in Aurora in 1966, having recently graduated from Virginia Tech in Mechanical Engineering.

Merriman looked puzzled. "The way I figure it then you must have been about twenty when you graduated from Virginia Tech, is that right?"

"Yes, sir."

"What age were you when you entered college?" he asked with the same expression.

"Sixteen, sir."

"Then you completed an engineering degree in four years?"

"Yes, sir."

Merriman smiled. "If you don't mind my saying so, ma'am, you're not only a very attractive southern lady, but apparently one smart woman as well."

O'Grady stared at him, her green eyes glistening. "I'll take that as a compliment, but what was yawl's question?"

"No question, Ms. O'Grady, just a compliment. But here's one. Are you single?"

"No, I'm married, but I still use my maiden name."

"What is your present title with WCI?

"I am an assistant vice president assigned as the project engineer for the Caravan vehicle."

"When did MCI first market the Caravan in the United States?"

"In 1966 just after I started with them?"

"Was the Caravan sold in 1970 the same basic design since 1966?"

"There were design improvements, but the configuration was the same."

"When did you first learn that the marketing department had issued a report on a proposed design change to the Caravan?" He handed a multi-page document to the reporter and asked him to mark it.

O'Grady looked at him. "Do yawl want me to examine that document before answering?"

After the document had been marked, Merriman took it back from the reporter and looked at O'Grady. "I guess you might as well. It's been marked exhibit 1 to your deposition." He handed it across the table.

O'Grady carefully read each of the four pages. "I learned about it shortly after the date of the report, January second, 1970."

"And what was the design change they were considering?"

"Basically, moving the front axel and the engine forward of the passenger's compartment."

Merriman placed his elbows on the table and rested his chin on his folded hands. "And what did your marketing department conclude as to whether MCI should make that change to its Caravan?"

She picked up the report again and turned to the last page. "They concluded, and I'll read their language: 'We find that we continue to lead all competition with the present Caravan. From a marketing standpoint it doesn't make sense to change the design unless there is another reason to do it.'"

Merriman gave the reporter another document and had him mark it exhibit 2. He handed the document to O'Grady. "Is the design in that drawing the change that the marketing department was referring to?"

"Yes, sir."

"What is the date of that drawing?"

"It says December twenty-nine, 1969 on it."

"It also says that the author of the drawing is Gunter Sweigert. Who is Gunter Sweigert?"

"He was my boss at that time, the Caravan project engineer."

Merriman lit a cigarette, leaned back and inhaled. He placed the cigarette on an ash tray and looked at O'Grady. "Didn't your company market a 1972 model Caravan designed substantially as shown in exhibit 2?"

The smoke from Merriman's cigarette drifted over in front of O'Grady. O'Grady cleared the smoke away with her hand before she answered. "Yes, we did, but I should explain . . ."

Merriman interrupted. "No explanation is called for in the question."

O'Grady's green eyes flashed as she stared at Merriman. "Mr. Merriman, I want yawl's question put in the proper context. The drawing exhibit 2 was an engineering concept for a design change. In exhibit 1 our marketing department commented on that concept and concluded that, since our present design was out selling other competitors vehicles made with that concept, it didn't make sense to change the design, unless there was another reason for the change. Our product engineer thought there was another reason, to wit: putting the engine and front axle out in front of the passenger's compartment added crush protection in the event of a head-on collision."

The cigarette smoke again came towards O'Grady. She again waved her hand to defect it. "Mr. Sweigert thought we should produce a prototype of his concept and test the stability and visibility of the vehicle with the design changes. He submitted his concept to the chief engineer who agreed. A prototype was built and tested. Eventually, that led to the change in the vehicle's design which was introduced in October 1971 as the new 1972 Caravan. So yawl see, Mr. Merriman, exhibit 1 did lead to a change in the design of the Caravan."

"Thank you, Ms. O'Grady. But as I understand it, certain of your competitors already marketed a van with those same design changes in their 1970 models, is that not true?"

"Several of our competitors were marketing their vehicles with a snub nose, yes, sir."

Merriman crushed out his cigarette and looked at O'Grady. "Ms. O'Grady, did you participate in testing of the prototype?"

"Yes, sir."

"Were there any problems with moving the front axel and engine from a stability or visibility standpoint?"

"No, sir. The visibility was not compromised and the stability of the vehicle was actually improved. That's why we changed the design."

Merriman asked about O'Grady's inspection of the vehicles, but was not allowed to question her as to any findings or conclusions she made since she was acting for counsel.

Suddenly, Merriman looked at Barry. "Unless you've got some questions, we're done."

Barry shook his head. "No questions," he said.

Sturgis agreed.

Merriman got up. "Come on Denny let's get out of here." Wilson also got up. They gathered their papers and left.

Stunned, O'Grady looked at Roper. "What was that all about?" Roper smiled. "I've heard Merriman's strange, but don't be misled by his conduct. He's effective. I suppose he just doesn't want you to become chummy with him."

Barry laughed as he rose. "Oh, I don't think he's strange, just full of himself. He wants to run the show." He changed his expression as he approached Roper. "That brings up a point about which I've been meaning to talk to you. We shouldn't let him dictate discovery. We should take the offensive whenever we can. And I think its time that we do it."

He looked at Sturgis. "I know there are issues in the case where we're adverse, but I think there are also issues we have in common. We ought to plan what discovery we need on the common issues and push for it. For one we need the deposition of Bentwood, the driver of the dairy's pickup. We also need Mrs. Ralston's deposition, her medical information and the medical information on the Ralston children. By medical information I mean reports from their doctors and the bills they've compiled. Do either of you think of anything else right now?"

"I think we should wait on the Ralston deposition until we get the medical information," Roper said, "but go ahead with Bentwood. What do you think, Larry?"

"Yeah, that okay with me, but I want to be fair to both of you and tell you that Merriman's made of move to get my cooperation in the case."

Barry nodded. "I'm not surprised. Have you made a deal with him?"

"Not yet. He hasn't made an offer, but I wanted you to know what might happen."

Barry started toward the door and turned as he was leaving. "Well, as to the discovery we all agree we need, I'll draft a letter to Wilson making a formal request for the medical information, and I'll take steps to subpoena Bentwood for a deposition."

In the elevator as they went down to the lobby, Wilson turned to Merriman. "You certainly weren't surprised that Roper wouldn't let her answer about her findings and conclusions from inspecting the vehicles?"

Merriman laughed. "Of course not. But I wanted Ms. O'Grady to think that I was pissed. It'll keep her off-guard for later on."

Wilson said, "Is there anything other discovery we should look into at to MCI?"

"Yes. An idea came during O'Grady's deposition. I didn't want to follow up on it at the time, because I didn't have the information I needed. Let's send them another request for production. I'd like to see if they had any early head-on crash test of the Caravan. Ask them to produce reports and films of any head-on crash tests of the Caravan from 1966 through 1969."

17

ON WEDNESDAY MORNING a wet snow had fallen during the night, causing Barry to drive slowly down the hill from his home to the office, struggling to avoid sliding into the curb. By the time he arrived in his office at seven-thirty several inches covered the streets downtown. From the wet nature of the snow and the temperature at just above freezing Barry knew, however, that the snow would be melting and be slush at the side of the streets by early afternoon.

Sitting at his desk he dictated a letter to Wilson, copies to Roper and Sturgis, requesting the medical information and giving notice that he had scheduled the deposition of Bentwood for Tuesday, January eighth at nine a.m. in his office. He then dictated a letter to Sturgis, copy to Wilson and Roper, requesting the deposition of Pete Wilkerson, the Legion Service Station owner. He suggested the date of January eighth at one-thirty p.m. in Sturgis' office.

After he completed the letters he called Lorenzo. "Ben, how have you been coming on talking to the mechanics in Kelso?" he asked.

"I'm sorry, boss, I've let that slide," Lorenzo apologized. "I've been on the Critchlow case with Elmer and tracking down the mechanics has been on the back burner."

"Well, the trial in that case ended last week, so get on it. I'm expecting to get a trial setting in the Ralston case soon."

"Will do," Lorenzo said.

Rainy Portland often gets a week of clear skies and cool weather in the winter. It came the second week of the new year. The blue sky, the Willamette River and the snow covered Mt. Hood provided a spectacular view out the east—facing picture windows of *Swift, Wyman & Wiggens'* conference room behind the receptionist on the fifteenth floor of their building.

On January eighth the clock on the far wall of the conference room registered eight fifty-five as Barry chatted causally with Walt Roper, Larry Sturgis and the same male court reporter who reported the deposition of Tracy O'Grady. Barry sat at the far end of the conference table with his back to the picture windows. Roper and Sturgis sat along the same side of the conference table. The reporter set up at the end of the table next to Barry with his pad on the table in front of him.

At nine o'clock the receptionist opened the conference door and looked in. "Mr. O'Shea, Denny Wilson's here with a Mr. Bentwood."

Barry turned his head toward her. "Show them in."

As they entered, Barry noticed that Bentwood limped slightly. *He must have a prosthetic leg,* he thought.

Wilson introduced Bentwood to the lawyers and the reporter. He then took a hold of the chair opposite Barry and offered it to Bentwood who sat down.

Wilson pulled out the chair beside Bentwood and laid his brief case on the table. He opened the briefcase and took several stacks of papers out, leaned across the table and gave Barry, Roper and Sturgis one of the stacks each. "That's the medical information you requested." Wilson then sat.

Barry examined the documents briefly, thanked Wilson and stuffed them in his open briefcase on the floor beside him. He shuffled some to the papers on the table before him and then looked at the reporter. "Swear the witness, please."

Still sitting, the reporter raised his right hand, looked at Bentwood. "Do you swear your testimony on this deposition will be the truth, and nothing but the truth, so help you God?"

Bentwood turned toward the reporter and raised his right hand. "I do."

Barry studied Bentwood as he was given the oath. Bentwood was dressed much as he had been at the time of the accident, a denim shirt and coveralls. When he sat, he took off his cap and laid it on the table beside him. He sat erect.

Barry eyed Bentwood and waited until their eyes met. "You're Lyle Bentwood, and you're employed by Towson Dairy of Seaside, is that right?" Barry asked.

Bentwood looked directly at Barry. "Yes, sir."

"Mr. Bentwood, has Mr. Wilson explained the nature of this proceeding to you?"

"Yes, sir."

"Then you know that I'm going to ask you some questions about yourself, your employment, the accident and some related matters. And you also know that before you answer any question you are to make sure you understand the question, so when you answer I can assume you understood the question. Are all of those things true?"

"Yes, sir."

Barry paused for a moment, looking down at his notes. His eyes came up, and again Barry waited until Bentwood looked at him. "The accident that's involved in this litigation happened on May twenty-ninth last year, just a few days more that seven months ago, in the late afternoon in the Coast Range on Highway 26, is that correct?"

Bentwood still looked directly at Barry. "Yes, sir."

"I understand that you were injured in the accident. Are you recovered from those injuries?"

Bentwood stared at Barry until a slight smile appeared on his face. "I guess you could say that my cuts and bruises have basically healed. I lost my leg above the knee. They fit me with an artificial one that works pretty well. I have phantom pains where the leg was, and they tell me I'll always have some of these. My memory of the accident is vague."

"Do you feel able to answer my questions?"

Bentwood nodded. "Oh, sure."

"Okay. As I understand, just before the accident you had picked up two cows at a cattle yard near Portland and you were transporting them back to the dairy outside of Seaside. Is that correct?"

"Yes."

"After leaving Portland, did you stop any place before you arrived at the accident scene?"

"Yes, I did. Do you want me to tell you about it?"

"Please."

Bentwood shifted in his chair. He leaned back and seemed to relax a bit, but his eyes remained on Barry. "As I approached the mountains, I noticed the sun go behind them, and I glance at my fuel gage and saw the needle below the half-way point. There was a service station on the right side of the road so I stopped there for gas."

"I assume an attendant came to your pickup. What happened then?"

"Well, he asked what I wanted. I told him to fill the tank with regular, and he did it."

"Did he do anything else?"

"Yeah, after he started filling the tank, he came back to my window and asked if I wanted the water and oil checked. I said I did and asked if he would also wash the windshield. He raised the hood, checked the water and oil, and said they fine. Then he closed the hood and washed the windshield. By then the gas tank was full. I gave him a credit card, he filled out the slip, and I signed it and left."

"Did you notice anything unusual about the way the attendant closed the hood?"

"No, he just pushed it down, and it slammed closed."

"Did you stop anywhere else?"

"No."

Barry shifted his chair back and crossed his legs, still looking at Bentwood. "Tell us what you remember about the accident."

Bentwood leaned forward, resting his large forearms on the table and his blue eyes still on Barry. "I remember cresting the summit before the Jewell Junction, and I remember coming out of a left hand turn in the road and heading down the hill, when something hit my windshield. That's all I remember."

"What's the next thing you remember?"

"I think I was in an ambulance, but I don't remember where it was or much about it. The next thing that I really remember was being in my hospital room with bandages on my head and face. There was a nurse beside the bed. I asked her where I was and what happened. She said I was in Emanuel Hospital, that I'd been in an accident on the Sunset Highway 26, the road to the beach, and that the doctor had to amputate my left leg because of damage done to it in the accident."

Barry stood, leaned over the table and reached for a pitcher of water that was on a tray with several glasses. He poured a glass of water, looked back at Bentwood. "You want some water too?"

"Sure."

Barry poured another glass and handed it across the table to Bentwood. He sipped from his glass and sat down, putting the glass on a coaster he had taken from the tray on the table. He picked up a document in front of him and examined it. He put the document down and looked at Bentwood. "I'd like to change subject. You've been represented in this deposition by Mr. Wilson. Tell us how that came about."

Bentwood looked briefly at Wilson, sitting on his left, and then back to Barry. "Well, I didn't hire him. I think the dairy's insurance company did. Anyway, Ms. Richards called me and told me about the deposition you wanted and that I was to go to Mr. Wilson's office. That was yesterday. Mr. Wilson said he would represent me at the deposition, and we talked about what would happen."

"That was Monica Richards you talked to?"

"Yes."

Barry looked down at his notes. He examined them for several moments. "That's all the questions I have for now," he said. He turned and looked at Roper and Sturgis. "Do either of you have anything to ask?"

"Not me," Roper said.

"I have a few questions," Sturgis said.

He got up and switched chairs with Barry. He looked at Bentwood. "Mr. Bentwood, we have been introduced, and you know I represent the service station you told Mr. O'Shea about. Do I understand that it's your testimony that after the attendant checked the water and oil levels, he, to use you words, slammed it closed?"

Bentwood eyed him. "That's what I said, but I didn't mean anything by the word 'slammed.' It is just what I think of when I think of a hood being closed."

"But there was nothing unusual about the way it closed? It closed just as you would have expected if the attendant was trying to close it."

"Again, I didn't notice anything unusual. He just closed it."

"And it seemed tight to you, or you would have said something at the time, wouldn't you?"

"I supposed so."

"Thank you, Mr. Bentwood. That's all."

"I have no questions at this time," said Wilson.

Sturgis looked at Barry. "If it's okay with you, I'll come back here with Wilkerson this afternoon?"

"Okay, we'll see you all back here at one-thirty then," Barry said.

Bentwood rose, leaned over and whispered to Wilson. "Am I free to go?"

Wilson got up and guided Bentwood to the door. "I want to talk to you briefly down in the lobby. Then you're free to go."

That afternoon Pete Wilkerson sat in the reception area of *Smith, Wyman & Wilkens* reading a magazine. A small thin man with angular features and long black hair covering his ears and hanging down the back of his neck to his shoulders, he frowned as he read the lead story about the North Vietnamese take over of Vietnam. He served in the army there in the mid-60's as a mechanic. In 1966 he got caught in a Viet Cong attach on his motor pool, was wounded and left the service with a sour taste.

When he returned to Forest Grove, Oregon in 1967, Legion Oil had its service station on Highway 26 in Manning for sale. The last owner defaulted on the Legion contract two years before, and the station had been out-of-operation ever since. Wilkerson saw the for sale sign one day when he traveled from Forest Grove to Vernonia looking for work. Upon his return to his home in Forest Grove, he called the number on the for-sale sign. After several more calls and a visit from a Legion representative, he put up a small down payment, signed a long term contract and became the new owner of the station.

He wore a gray uniform with yellow Legion decals on his shirt and cap. He had a sharp long nose, wore glasses and his upper lip carried a short black mustache.

At about one-fifteen Larry Sturgis exited the elevator on the fifteen floor and entered the reception area. He immediately saw Wilkerson seated there and walked over to him. "Hi, Pete, I see you're on time," he said, extending his right hand.

Wilkerson put down the magazine, got up and gave Sturgis a weak hand shake. "Yes, Mr. Sturgis, I found the office building and parked in the garage. I hope they'll take care of the parking charge." After the handshake Wilkerson sat back down.

Sturgis took a chair next to Wilkerson. "Don't worry about it. I'll take care of it."

About then Barry came out of the door to the conference room, looked around the reception area and saw Sturgis and Wilkerson. He went over to where they sat. "Hi, Larry. I assume this is Mr. Wilkerson."

Sturgis and Wilkerson got up. "Yes, Barry," Sturgis said, "meet Pete Wilkerson."

Barry looked at Wilkerson with a small smile. "It's a pleasure Mr. Wilkerson, although I suppose in one sense we're adversaries here."

Wilkerson gave Barry a wary look.

"Come on in the conference room, the others are inside waiting," said Barry.

Inside Sturgis introduce Roper, Wilson and the reporter to Wilkerson and had him sit at the end of the table next to the reporter and across from Barry.

Barry sat down and asked the reporter to swear the witness, which he did.

Barry watched Wilkerson as he took the oath. He saw a thin man who appeared timid and ill-at-ease. Wilkerson turned and looked at Barry.

Barry noticed Wilkerson's eyes had a hard time fixing on Barry's. Barry stared at him for a moment. Wilkerson's eyes continued to dart from Barry's eyes up and down.

Barry continued to stare as he questioned. "You're the owner of the Legion station in Manning, aren't you?"

Wilkerson hesitated. "I'm buying it under a long term contract with Legion. I am the operator."

"How long have you operated it?"

"I started in operating the station in November 1967, so a little over six years."

"How many people do you have working for you?"

"I've had one over the years who comes in several times a week. The person has changed a lot of time. I'm really the only full time person." He looked at Sturgis. "Can I explain to him?"

"Sure, go ahead," Sturgis said.

"The station doesn't get enough business to support more people. I'm there by myself most of the time, and I do what mechanical work I can get. I usually have a young guy who spells me some of the time waiting on the gas pumps."

Barry paused, staring at Wilkerson. "Do you remember May twenty-ninth, 1973?"

"Yes."

"How do you remember that day?"

"I know that's the day of the accident." Wilkerson looked away. "I remember for several reasons. An insurance lady was at my station the next day talking about it. She said she represented the dairy the owned the pickup that was hauling the cows. I remember that I had sold gas to that fella late in the afternoon."

"Was that lady Monica Richards?"

"Yes, that's the name she gave me."

Barry continued to stare at him, and Wilkerson continued to dart his eyes around. "Were you alone that day?"

"Yes, I was."

"What else did you do for the driver of the pickup?"

Wilkerson had been looking down. He looked up. "I suppose you want to know about my checking his water and oil level. Yes, I did that. I know you want to know how I closed the hood, don't you?"

Barry smiled. "I'm the one that suppose to ask the questions. But now that you've mentioned it, is there something about the hood that you have watch when you close it?"

Barry could see that Wilkerson was sorry that he said what he did. Wilkerson looked briefly at Sturgis, but Sturgis shook him off. He looked back at Barry and again tried to stare away. "I, I'm sure the pickup's hood had a double catch, almost all cars do. You can put the hood down softly, and it'll only grab hold of the first catch. If you push down harder it goes to lock. I pushed the hood down hard, I always do."

Barry caught Wilkerson's eyes on his. "Now, Mr. Wilkerson, are you telling me that you actually remember how hard you pushed down on this particular pickup's hood?"

Wilkerson frowned. "Well, I know I shut the hood. No, I can't remember exactly how hard I did it on this particular occasion, but I know that I always push it hard enough to lock."

"Thank you, Mr. Wilkerson, that's all the questions I have at this time."

No other lawyers had questions.

As the other lawyers were gathering their papers together, Barry looked at Wilson. "While we're together," he said, "I'd like to request a few more depositions. First, are Mrs. Ralston and her children. I don't think it will be necessary to depose the children, but I'd like to see them and ask them some things informally. I'd also like to depose Monica Richards. From what I'm beginning to understand, I believe you have control over her. I suggest you set them up at their convenience, giving plenty of lead time so we'll all be available."

Wilson stood and wrote something on his pad. He turned to Barry. "I've noted your request," he said. "I'll get back to you shortly and set a time for Mrs. Ralston and the children. I think I can get Monica also, but I'll let you know."

18

ON MONDAY, JANUARY tenth, a cold rain had returned. Barry stared out his windows at people below, umbrellas over their heads, hurrying along on the sidewalks to get somewhere dry. His revere broke when the mail girl came into his office.

"Here's your mail," she said, depositing a large bundle on his desk in front of him.

He turned and looked at her. "Thanks, Linda." Then he began sorting through it, getting rid of the solicitations and like junk mail and putting correspondence, legal papers and magazines in separate piles. While doing this, he noticed he had a letter from Wilson and another from the court in Clatsop County.

He opened the letter from the court first. I contained a card giving notice that a meeting had been scheduled between the judge and the lawyers in the *Ralston* case for Tuesday, February twelfth at nine a.m. in Judge Olson's chambers. The card further explained that the matters to be considered at the meeting were the status of the case and a trial setting.

The letter from Wilson contained his response to Barry's request for further depositions. Coincidently, it set Amy Ralston's deposition of ten a.m. on February twelfth in Wilson's office. In the second paragraph, Wilson said, "Your request for the deposition request for Monica Richard raises another matter. As you know, she is an adjuster for Western Indemnity Company, the insurance company for Towson Dairy. Normally, insurance is not a proper matter in injury litigation. We need to talk about why you want the deposition. Give me a call."

Barry smiled and nodded. He took a cigarette from a pack of Phillip Morris resting on his desk, lit it and inhaled. Smoke slowly left his lips as he exhaled and thought, *Okay Denny, let's talk and we'll include the conflict of the court's date and the Ralston deposition.*

He looked up Wilson's telephone number in the bar directory and dialed.

"*Witchhazel & Wilson,*" a woman answered.

Barry knew she'd ask who was calling. "This is Barry O'Shea. May I please speak to Denny Wilson?"

"One moment, please."

A man came on the line. "Hi, Barry, you must have gotten my letter."

"I just read it and also a notice from the court. It seems Judge Olson want us in Astoria on February twelfth, so you'll have to reschedule the Ralston depositions. Can she and the children be available later that week?"

"I think so. I'll check and send another letter. What about the insurance adjuster?"

"You're right that insurance is not normally relevant in this type of case, but I want the deposition for discovery purposes. I think I'm entitled to find out if her employer is involved in this case, and, if so, the details of that involvement."

"Well, I'm not so sure. I'll discuss it with Wayne and get back to you."

"Tell him that if you resist, I'll take it up with the judge when we're down in Astoria on the twelfth."

"I'll tell him." The call ended.

The county seat of Clatsop County was Astoria. Astoria, a picturesque city of about ten thousand, sat on the Oregon side of the mouth of the Columbia River. It got its name from the early fur trader, John Jacob Astor. It's the oldest settlement west of the Rockies, founded in 1811. Its inhabitants have gorgeous views of the Pacific Ocean, the River and of the tall evergreens, Douglas Fir, Hemlock and Spruce trees.

Constructed of stone in 1904, the Clatsop County courthouse occupied a full block on Commercial Street on a hill side overlooking the mouth of the Columbia River. Its style is American Renaissance. Marble extends up the first floor walls to the top of the doorways, and marble tiles cover the floor. The ceilings are framed with decorative local lumber, stained brown. Oak newels flank the grand marble staircase leading to the courtroom and the judge's chamber on the second floor.

The courtroom's decorations made it one of the most elegant in Oregon with pairs of Ionic pilasters, standing above marble wainscot. Pew-like spectator benches made of oak stained dark occupy the rear behind and oak bar. All of the features before the bar, the tables for the plaintiffs and defendants, the judge's bench and the jury box continue the dark-stained oak motif.

The judge's chambers had the much the same design as the courtroom except that dark-stained oak bookcases lined the walls. The furnishings included a desk, a conference table and the chairs, all in dark-stained oak.

On February twelve at nine a.m. Judge Olson sat at the end of his conference table with his clerk-secretary to his right. Merriman, Savage and Wilson occupied the chairs next to the clerk, and Barry, Roper and Sturgis sat on the opposite side of the table with Barry sitting opposite Merriman and next to the judge.

The judge wore red and white stripped bow tie. He had the sleeves of his shirt rolled up just below his elbows, revealing large hairy forearms. At fifty-two heavy blonde hair covered his and head, which he parted on the left. His face featured a pug nose and heavy blonde eyebrows. A Cuban cigar dangled from his mouth.

After introductions and some small chatter, the judge leaned forward, rested his forearms on the tables and quickly glanced at each lawyer, stopping their conversations. "Well, gentlemen, we've had enough chit-chat," he said in a deep gravelly voice. "Let's get down to business. I've looked over the file, such as it is, and can see this involves a very serious accident and some novel, very novel, theories. The case is straight forward as to the service station and Monarch, but I've never heard of a theory like plaintiffs charges against MCI." He looked over at Merriman. "Is the famous Mr. Merriman the one who's going to explain that to me?"

Merriman smiled at the judge. "Certainly, your Honor. I'd be glad to explain it. But the real brains in our group belong to my partner, Alex Savage. When I first heard him talk about this theory, I was a doubter very much like you seem to be. I asked the question: If they didn't cause the accident, how can they be held liable? Alex sat me down and told me how and why. I think we should let him tell you."

The judge squinted at Savage. "All right Mr. Savage, what have you got to say?"

Savage rose and walked to the other end of the table. He pulled up an easel that had rested against the wall. He looked at the judge. "Thank you, your Honor." He wrote with a black grease pencil on the white pad on the easel. He explained that we have here three defendants and a horrific accident. He told the judge that the accident happened when the hood on the pickup, manufactured by the defendant Monarch, flew up, blinding the driver and causing him to lose control of his vehicle; it crossed the centerline and hit plaintiffs' vehicle head-on. He said that the owner of the pickup and the driver settled with the plaintiffs and are no longer involved and that another defendant, the service station, is here because it serviced the vehicle under the hood shortly before the accident."

Savage still wrote on the easel and looked at the judge. "Now if we assume that we prove that Monarch produced a defective vehicle without which this accident wouldn't have happened and if we assume we have evidence that the service station attendant did not secure the hood of the pickup, one or more of those defendants can be held liable for all of the damages plaintiffs seek. So you understandably might question why MCI is here?"

He put down the grease pencil on the table and placed his hands on the table, leaning forward. "The reason is that the way it designed the van caused much of plaintiffs' damages."

He rose and again began writing on the easel. "This case is a perfect example of the grounds for this theory." He explained that in this case the physical facts of the accident are that the pickup hit the van head-on with its left front striking the left front of the van, in other words, driver side to driver side. He said that normally, that kind of an accident can cause injuries to both drivers. "But in this case the facts are that the pickup drove right through and over the van coming to rest in the back seat, killing the driver of the van and the boy seated just behind him. That happened because in this model van had nothing out in front of the driver to absorb the blow except the windshield. There was no engine, front axel, etc. ahead of the driver as there is in most vehicles."

The judge interrupted, as he snuffed out his cigar and put it back between his lips. "When you describe this accident, I can see potential liability of certain defendants because there is the normal cause and effect. But isn't there something more novel about your theory against WCI?"

"Not really, your Honor. Some writers call this a second collision theory. Others call it an enhanced injury theory, but I don't like either name. I like your analysis, cause and effect. The fact of the matter is that the design of this vehicle resulted in the death of two plaintiffs and enhanced injuries to the other plaintiffs. Now, it is true that we have the burden of proving that those deaths and the enhanced injuries suffered were cause by a defective design in the van, but that's no different than the burden that exists in all cases and the fact that other defendants may also be liable for those injuries is of no consequence. There maybe facts where it is harder to explain this theory, but the facts of this case make the liability abundantly clear if proven."

The judge looked up at the ceiling, sucking on his unlit cigar, and muttered, "Hum." He looked back to Savage. "I think I understand, at least under the facts of this case."

"Thank you, your Honor." And Savage retook his seat.

The judge looked out at all the lawyers. "Let's now talk about the trial date." He turned to Merriman. "How close are you to completion of discovery?"

Merriman smiled at the judge. "Judge, we're ready for trial."

The judge looked at Barry. "Same question to you guys?"

"We're taking the plaintiffs' depositions later this week," Barry replied. "And there's one more deposition we've requested. Mr. Wilson raised some questions about whether they would object, but we haven't heard one way of the other."

The judge looked at Wilson. "Who is this witness and what is your objection?"

Wilson looked uncomfortable. "Uh, Monica Richards, your Honor," he answered cautiously. "She's an insurance adjuster for the insurance company that insured the dairy and the driver. We didn't think insurance could be an issue in the case."

The judge cast a stern look at Barry. "Mr. O'Shea?"

"We're not now claiming that insurance is an issue in the case. We're asking for discovery. We believe that Ms. Richard's employer has made some sort of an arrangement to protect the dairy and its driver from this suit, and we want to find if we're right and discover the details of that arrangement."

The judge nodded with a smirk on his face. "I don't blame you. I'd want to know too. I'm not ruling whether any of this is admissible, but you're entitled to inquire."

He looked again at Wilson. "Can you produce Ms. Richards?"

"Yes, I suppose we can."

"Then get together with Mr. O'Shea and produce her for a deposition later this month." He turned the pages of a calendar he had in front of him. "How about starting the trial on Tuesday, May fourteenth? That'll give us Monday to meet and discuss whatever we need to discuss."

"That's fine," Merriman quickly answered.

Barry looked at Roper and Sturgis. They nodded. Barry looked back at the judge. "That's agreeable with the defendants, judge."

"Then it's settled." The judge turned to Merriman. "Mr. Merriman, while no one has said anything about your status, I suppose you and Mr. Savage would like to be specially admitted to this court for the purpose of trying this case. Is that the case?"

"Yes, we would."

"Then you're admitted. I'll see that the clerk makes a journal entry to that effect. Is there anything more?"

Barry and Merriman shook their heads.

"All right. See you in May," the judge said as he got up and started back to his desk. The lawyers got up and left the chambers.

Thursday morning on Valentine's Day began cold and clear. *Michael & Bruce* occupied the twenty-ninth and thirtieth floors of Portland's tallest building located between Fourth and Fifth Streets. Walter Roper's office, located in the southeast corner of the thirtieth floor, looked out at the Willamette River as it flowed north to join the Columbia. On a clear day, which this was not, he had a view of Mt. Hood to the east.

When Roper arrived at his office, his voice mail indicated that Verner Schultz had called. He called Schultz on his direct line.

"This is Verner Schultz," Schultz answered.

"Verner, this is Walt Roper, returning you're call."

Schultz sounded serious. "I'm afraid I've got some bad news. I just got the crash test reports and films plaintiffs requested in the Ralston case. I suspected that the head-on films wouldn't look good, but I didn't think they'd be as bad as they are. In the 1968 test when the vehicle struck the barrier going thirty mph the penetration was clear through the driver's seat. I'll send them on to you, but before you give them to plaintiffs' lawyers, call me again after you looked at them. We need to talk."

Like Wilson's office, the *Witchhazel & Wilson's* conference room faced south. Venetian blinds covered the windows blocking the view of the wheat fields and of the light rain falling outside. The room contained a small dark wooden conference table surrounded by eight matching chairs, one at each end and three on each side.

The depositions of the plaintiffs began the next day in this conference room. The court reporter set up at one end with his pad and pen resting on the table. Barry sat to his left, his back to the windows. Roper and Sturgis occupied the other two chairs on that side of the table.

Barry turned his chair toward the other two lawyers. "How do you think we should handle the children?"

"I don't think we should all question them," Roper answered. "Why don't you just ask them some questions informally to give us an idea of the kind of kids they are?"

"All right. I'll mix in a question or two about the accident, but I won't put them under oath."

Just then the door to the conference room opened, and Denny Wilson entered followed by a short, attractive woman in her mid-thirties in a wheel chair and a girl and a boy. The woman wore a white blouse highlighted by a light blue plaid scarf and a tan skirt. A blanket covered her legs. She had light blue Ferragamos on her feet. Her long brown hair was tied in a bun behind her head.

Wilson faced the defense lawyers. "Let me introduce Amy Ralston, her daughter, Michelle, and her son, Dustin." Barry, Roper and Sturgis rose, Wilson pointed at them and said, "Amy, this is Barry O'Shea, Walt Roper and Larry Sturgis."

Barry extended his right hand down and shook Amy's hand. "It's a pleasure to meet you, Mrs. Ralston." Roper and Sturgis did likewise.

Barry looked at the girl and smiled. "How old are you, Michelle?"

"I'm eleven; my birthday was last week," an embarrassed tall, thin girl answered.

Then Barry looked at the boy and smiled. "And you, Dustin, how old are you?"

The boy's green eyes glistened a proudly said, "I'm six."

Barry walked around the table until he stood in front of Michelle and Bruce. He knelt down on one knee and smiled at them both. "Where do you go to school?"

Michelle answered, more confidently now. "We go to Chapman Grade School. I'm in the sixth grade and Dustin's in the first grade."

"How do you do in school, Michelle?"

Amy interrupted. "She's a little bashful. She's a wonderful student. So is Dustin so far."

Barry looked up at Amy. "Thank you." Then he looked back at Michelle. "What's your favorite class?"

"I like most everything, but arithmetic and music are probably my favorites."

Barry looked at Dustin. "How about you, Dustin? What do you like most about school?"

Dustin's eyes twinkled. "Recess," he said, laughing.

Barry laughed. "That's not so funny. I liked recess the best at you age too."

"Do either of you remember the accident?"

They both shook their heads.

Barry looked at Michelle. "What's the last thing you remember, Michelle?"

Michelle glance down and slowly said, "I remember getting into the van and leaving the beach. The next thing I remember was waking up in the ambulance."

"How are you doing now?"

"I feel fine," she said. "I got a small scar here." She pointed to her forehead.

"What about you, Dustin? What do you remember?"

Bruce's eyes glistened again. "I remember crying and a man putting a bandage on my leg. My arm hurt. It was broke. I had a cast on it."

"How does your arm and leg feel now?"

"Oh, they're okay I think," he said smiling.

Barry rose and looked at Michelle and Dustin. "Thanks a lot. I enjoyed chatting with you. Now we're going to ask you Mommy some questions. Why don't you two wait out in the lobby?"

Wilson escorted the children back out into the reception area and returned.

Amy's wheel chair was positioned directly across from Barry, and Wilson seated himself at her side. The reporter gave her the oath.

Barry looked at her and immediately noticed her lovely blue eyes. "Mrs. Ralston, we've been introduced," Barry said. "I represent Monarch Motors in this law suit you've filed. I'm going to ask you some questions about your background, the accident and things that have followed after the accident. It's important that you not answer any question that you do not understand. If you don't understand my question, tell me, and I'll try to clear it up. If you answer, I'll assume you understood the question. Is that clear?"

"Yes, it is."

Barry then asked a serious of question about Amy Ralston's background, her marriage to Michael, and their life up to the day of the accident.

"As I understand it, you and your family had been at the beach in Gearhart over the Memorial Day holiday, is that right?"

"Yes, we were."

"Why don't you tell us what you remember about the trip back?"

She looked at Barry. Her eyes looked sad. "We left the Ocean House in Gearhart a little after four in the afternoon on Tuesday, the day after Memorial Day. We were going up into the Coast Range, and I remember," she paused and tears began to form in her eyes, "ah, ah, Bruce, he was our older son, seven at the time, was sitting behind his father, and he asked Michael what the name of the place we were passing was. Michael told him it was Elsie. That was all that I remembered for some time, but recently some memory came back. I now remember we continued up the hill and had just crossed over the bridge below Elderberry Inn, when I saw a vehicle coming at us. I yelled at Michael. That the end of my memory until I woke up in the hospital."

"Where was the other vehicle, by that I mean in relation to the road?"

"It all happened so fast, I don't know. I know it was dead ahead, and I had the impression it was going to hit us."

"Could you tell what kind of a vehicle it was?"

"No."

"Could you tell how fast it was coming at you?"

"No."

"Do you know how fast your vehicle was traveling at that time?"

"Not really. Michael wasn't speeding. Just going the normal speed."

Barry looked down at his notes and then back at Amy. "How long were you in the hospital?"

"I got out of there on August eighth, so from May twenty-ninth, I think that was the day after Memorial Day, until then?"

"What injuries did you sustain in the accident?"

Her eyes began to water again. "I had a lot of bruises, some cuts and a severed spinal cord. Because of the severed spinal cord I had no pain in my legs, but I hurt everywhere in my upper body and head for days after I came to in the hospital. I recovered from those injuries in time while in the hospital, but the spinal cord injury is permanent, as you can see."

"How about your children, how long were they in the hospital, and how have they progressed?"

"I think Dustin got out of the hospital in about four days. He went to stay with our neighbors the Sugerman's. I'm told he had a bandage on his forehead and a cast on his arm. By the time I got home the bandage was gone but the cast was still there. He had that for a couple of more weeks. He's gotten along fairly well, although he still has nightmares, and he misses his brother and father terribly."

She took a handkerchief and dabbed her eyes. "Michelle was in the hospital a few more days than Dustin. She also went to live with the Sugerman's. She also had a cut that needed stitches on her forehead and some internal bleeding. She doing fine, although she has a slight scar on her forehead, and she also has had trouble sleeping and misses her brother and father."

Barry asked her about how her house had been modified to accommodate her needs and about the support she had. She told him what Mr. Sugerman had done and about Willie and Mina Sorrento.

Roper inquired about her expenses and her limitations due to the paralysis.

Sturgis asked about Michael's employment with the accounting firm. "How have you been getting buy since his death?"

Again tears began to form in her eyes. "It's been terribly hard, not so much with the expenses, but I miss him so." She began to sob. After a few moments, she composed herself. "We've made a settlement with the dairy, which has helped with the expenses, and it pays for the Sorrento's."

"How much did you receive from the dairy?"

"The dairy's insurance company paid $200,000. I got about $140,000 of it."

"Do you have any other means of income?"

"Yes. Michael had $150,000 in life insurance, and we get social security. That's what we have to live on."

The Ralston deposition ended.

19

FRIDAY AFTERNOON WHEN Barry arrived at Wilson's office, Roper and Sturgis sat talking in the reception area. He walked over to them. "Hi, Walt and Larry, has Richards showed up?"

"She's in the conference room with Wilson," Roper answered. "I got here just as Wilson was ushering her in. Wow, what a looker. I didn't know insurance adjusting attracted her type."

Barry smiled. "I've met her a few times before. She'll take advantage if you get caught up with her looks."

"Wilson told me it'd be about a half hour. That was fifteen minutes ago."

Barry sat put his briefcase on his lap, opened it and pulled out a legal pad. He studied what he had written on it for several moments. Then he looked over at Roper and Sturgis. "Do you want me to lead again?"

"Yeah," Roper said. "It worked well with Mrs. Ralston, and, since you know Richards, you won't let her take advantage." He laughed.

In a few more minutes the receptionist got their attention. "You three can go in now."

All three rose and Barry led the way, opening the door to the conference room and entering. Wilson met them at the door. Monica Richards sat in the chair Barry had occupied the day before, turned slightly toward the reporter at the table's head with her legs crossed. She wore a blue blouse, open just enough in the front to give the viewer a hint of what it covered, and an off-white skirt that exposed her long well-shaped legs. Her hair was styled down the side of her neck, hanging just below her shoulders with a wave across her forehead over her right eye. She wore round glasses that didn't hide the stare of her hazel eyes.

Again the venetian blinds were closed shutting out a fairly heavy rain that fell outside.

Wilson motioned toward Richards. "I think you know Monica, Barry. I'm not sure about Walt and Larry. But anyway this is Monica Richards."

Barry leaned across the table and offered his hand to Richards. "Sure, I know Monica. How have you been?"

She smiled and took his hand. "Fine. It's nice to see you again, counselor." She nodded at the Roper and Sturgis. "And it always a pleasure to meet other members of the bar."

Roper and Sturgis nodded back. Wilson took a seat next to Richards, and she was sworn.

Barry pulled out the chair opposite Richards and sat. He took his legal pad from his briefcase, laid it in front of him and looked up at Richards. "Ms. Richards, you're employed by Western Indemnity Company, are you not?"

She locked eyes with Barry. "Yes, sir, I am."

"As an insurance adjuster, if I am correct?"

She smiled. "You're correct."

"And Western Indemnity insures Towson Dairy, its vehicles and their operators, is that not so?"

"That's true."

"And you were the adjuster assigned to the accident we are dealing with in this lawsuit?"

She eyes glistened, and she smiled again, still looking directly at Barry. "You continue to be right, counselor."

Barry took her through the things she did in adjusting the claim, including the hiring of the consulting engineer Wayland Chang.

"What did Mr. Chang conclude when he examined the pickup?"

Wilson interrupted. "Mr. O'Shea you know that the answer to that is privileged. I'm instruction her not to answer.

Barry looked at Wilson. "She hasn't said any lawyers were involved."

Wilson turned to the witness. "Ms. Richards, did you hire the engineer after consultation with me?"

"Yes, I did."

"All right," Barry said.

Barry looked at Richards. "Have you met Wayne Merriman as a part of your handling of this case?"

She still locked on Barry's eyes. "Yes, I have. He's quite a person."

"The way you answered that, do I take it that your relationship with him is more than lawyer and client?"

She stared hard at his eyes, and then gave a sly smile. "I don't know what you mean, Mr. O'Shea. Mr. Merriman and I have had a close business relationship."

"Have you settled the claims of the Richards?"

"Yes, we have."

"What is the nature of your settlement?"

"We paid our policy limit, $200,000."

"Did you get a release?"

"No."

"I ask again, what is the nature of your settlement?"

"We have a loan receipt. We've hired Merriman and Wilson to represent us in getting back what we've paid."

"As such are you paying part of their expenses in handling this matter?"

"Yes."

Barry paused and looked at his notes. Then he looked back at Richards. "Ms. Richards, as part of you investigation did you take any statements from anyone?"

"Yes, I took a statement from our insured's driver and a statement from the service station owner."

"Do you have them with you today?"

"Yes."

"Will you please produce them?"

Richard turned and reached down and retrieved a small leather satchel which she brought up and laid on the table. She opened and pulled out several sheets of paper. "Here they are," she said offering them to Barry.

Barry took the papers and examined them for a moment. He noticed the statement from Wilkerson where he said he didn't remember how he closed the hood. Then he handed the papers to the reporter. "Would you please mark these exhibits 1 and 2?"

The reporter did that and handed the statements back to Barry.

Barry took them and gave exhibit 1 to Richards. "Whose statement is exhibit 1?"

"That's the statement I took of Mr. Bentwood."

He handed her exhibit 2. "And exhibit 2?"

"That's the statement I took of Mr. Wilkerson."

Barry leaned back and looked at Richards. "Did you have any contact with Monarch Motors or any of their employee and dealers?"

"No."

"That's all I have for now."

"Did you have any contact with MCI, its employees or dealers?" Roper quickly asked.

"No, I did not."

"Did you talk to anyone other that Bentwood connected with Towson Dairy?" Sturgis asked.

"Well, I spoke briefly with Mr. Towson, but he had nothing to add."

"Did you speak to anyone else involved with Legion Oil Company?"

"No I didn't.

Monica Richard's deposition ended.

By Monday morning, February eighteenth normal weather had returned a steady light rain. When Roper entered his office, he saw Schultz's package on his desk. He quickly unwrapped it and found three reports and three films. He read the reports and a frown appeared on his face. He called his secretary in. "Please get me a projector and a screen. I want to look at these films."

Later that morning after he had watched the films, Roper called Schultz. "I see what you meant when we talked last week. That one film, the off-set barrier test, shows just what happened in our accident."

"I know, but what's worse is that the tests were run in 1966, a year before Ralston's vehicle was made." Schultz replied.

"Verner, I think we have to try and settle this case, and do it now."

"I agree. How do you think we should proceed?"

"Well, we've finished the discovery, except our production of these tests. I'll copy the reports, make copies of the films and send them to Wilson. After he shares them with Merriman and they finish their "celebration," I'm sure I'll get a call wanting to know if we'd like to talk. That's the only way I can think of to get talking. If they don't call, then I suppose I'll have to initiate the talks."

"You right. Go ahead and produce the reports and the films. Then let me know when you hear from Merriman."

"One more thing along this line," Roper said. "I know you're self-insured, but is there excess insurance involved in this claim?"

"Yes. We are self-insured for the first million. We have excess insurance above that. They've been notified, because of the prayer in the complaint."

"Then you'd better get together with them now. If we get into settlement talks, they need to be represented."

"I'll get right on it."

—ᴍᴍ—

Around mid-morning on March fourth, Roper sat musing in his office, staring out at pedestrians rushing for cover from a heavy rain being blown south down the canyon formed by the buildings on Fourth Avenue. His meditation was suddenly interrupted by the ringing of his telephone.

He picked up the reached. "Hello," he said.

An abrupt voice spoke to him on the other end. "Roper, this is Wayne Merriman."

"What can I do for you, Wayne?"

Merriman snickered. "Just off-hand, right now I can't think of anything more you can do. I've been up in the Sierra's hunting for the last week and a half. I get back Sunday, walk into my office this morning and find the present you sent me. I just finished watching one of the films and figure it pretty much cooks your client's goose."

Roper spoke coolly. "I assumed your reaction would be somewhat like that."

Merriman laughed loudly. "Somewhat like that, you say? That film sews up liability all by itself! You better open your wallet."

"You're not getting into my wallet, but my client's interested in talking settlement."

"I should hope so. What are you proposing?"

"A settlement conference with the judge."

Merriman shook his head. "Oh, my. I won't make that kind 'a mistake. My kind of settlement talks don't include a judge. If you really want to talk settlement, I'll talk to you and your client. As a matter of fact bring that pretty little thing, Tracy O'Grady, with you along with someone with enough authority."

"Do you want me to get in touch with the other defendants?"

"For god's sakes, no. Why complicate things. You're stuck with liability. I want to hear what you'll pay to get out of the case."

"All right. Where do you want to do it?"

"I'll come up there. Can you get organized in about two weeks?"

Roper looked at his calendar. "I think so. Let's tentatively schedule it for our offices at ten o'clock on March eighteenth. I'll check with my people right away and confirm the date with you later this week."

"You got a date, partner. Have Tracy and your people ready to hear my presentation. I'll give them a recess to mull it over, but I want an offer, one that makes sense given your client's liability, before I leave."

"I'll call them and get back to you."

On the eighteenth at eight-thirty Roper's secretary stood in the doorway to his office. "Mr. Schultz and company have arrived. Shall I show them in?"

Roper studied some figures he had recorded about the Ralston's medical and funeral expenses. He looked up. "Who's with him?"

"Miss O'Grady and another man."

"Show them in."

In a few moments Verner Schultz appeared at Roper's open doorway. He was a short, stocky man with close cropped hair that had just started to turn gray. He wore a brown worsted suit and a paisley tie.

Roper got up and strode toward Schultz with his right hand extended. "Welcome to Portland, Verner. Did you have a pleasant flight?"

Schultz looked up at Roper and shook his hand. "Yes, a smooth one, and the hotel arrangements you made for us were very satisfactory. He turned to his right and motion toward the man and lady behind him. "You know Tracy. Let me introduce Bret Lyons, the Chicago claims manager of Universal Reinsurance Company."

Lyons appeared to be in his middle forties. He was rail thin, about six feet, and had a narrow face with ruffled brown hair combed across his forehead just above his eyes. He wore a light camel's hair sport coat, gray slacks, brown brogues and a plain green tie. He smoked Camels, at least two packs a day.

Tracy waved her hand at Roper. "Hi."

Lyons stepped forwarded and offered his hand. "Nice to meet you."

Roper shook his hand. "Same here." He motioned toward a small conference table to the left of his desk.

"Why don't we sit around that table and talk?"

They sat.

Schultz looked at Roper. "Let me explain the insurance picture. WCI is self-insured up to a million dollars. Thereafter there are several layers of excess insurance, all administered by Universal Reinsurance Company. Bret is here representing the excess carriers."

Roper looked first at Schultz and then to Lyons. "I take it you two have discussed your positions in this case."

"Yes," Schultz said, "I've told Bret that WCI wants to settle this case. I've filled him in on the discovery and what it shows about WCI's liability. We feel that we are exposed and don't want to go to trial. I've told him that we'll pay our one million dollars to get the case settled. So I believe he understands that, if Merriman wants more than one million dollars to settle with WCI, everything above the first million is the excess carriers' responsibility."

Roper looked at Lyons. "Is that about it?"

"Yes, it is," Lyons replied.

Roper looked at Schultz. "Have you put a demand on those carriers to settle?"

"No, because we don't have a demand as yet. If we get a demand over one million, and it seems reasonable, we will insist that they settle or take over cost of our defense and suffer the consequences."

"How about Tracy? I know Merriman requested her presence, but other than as the project engineer, have you assigned her any particular part of this settlement talk?"

"No. She's here because Merriman requested her."

At ten, Roper's secretary opened his door. "Mr. Merriman is here," she said.

Roper turned toward her. "Usher him into the main conference room and tell him we'll be in shortly."

20

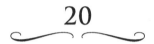

T he *Michael & Bruce* main conference room was located behind the receptionist on the east side of their building with a view of the river and the east side of the city.

When Roper and his group entered they saw the tall, well-built frame of Merriman seated at the north end of the table. He wore his usual leather jacket and string tie. A cigarette, Lucky Strike, rested burning on an ash tray on the table in front of him and to his side.

Merriman rose from his chair and walked slowly toward Roper. "It's good to see you, Walt. I know Tracy, but introduce me to the other gentlemen."

A short stocky man came forward and extended his right hand. "I'm Verner Schultz, vice president of litigation for WCI." He motioned toward the other man. "And this is Bret Lyons, Chicago claims manager for Universal Reinsurance Company."

Merriman shook Schultz's hand noticing that he too had a strong grip. Then when Lyons likewise extended his hand, he shook it as well. Lyons tried to hide his grimace, but Merriman caught it.

Merriman walked back to the north end of the table and sat. Roper, Schultz and O'Grady sat facing the window, and Lyons walked to the other side of the table.

As he was sitting, Merriman looked up at Schultz and Roper. "Why is Lyons here?"

Schultz explained the insurance positions of WCI and the excess carriers.

"That's interesting." He looked at Lyons. "Glad to have you here. By the way, may I call you Bret? I like to deal informally."

Lyons sat. "Sure."

Merriman sat and studied the group for several moments. Then he looked down the table at O'Grady. "Tracy, I got a real shock when I saw the film of the off-set barrier crash test run with the Caravan in 1966. It showed about same penetration into the right side of the Caravan as in our case. The barrier drove right through the driver's seat and into the seat behind it, destroying the dummy driver and the dummy in the seat behind. I immediately thought that's Michael Ralston and his son, Bruce. When did you first see that film, or were you at that crash test?"

Tracy's smile was gone. "As you can see from the report, I was present."

Merriman stared at her. "Then, then you saw the barrier penetrate clear into the second row seat, didn't you?"

"I don't remember back that far. But I must have."

"When you saw it, I'll bet you told them, you can't make the vehicle that way? Is that what you said?"

"No."

Merriman came upright in shock. "What? You saw the dummies destroyed. Why didn't you tell them not to market the vehicle that way?"

"I frankly don't remember."

"Weren't you the assistant project engineer on the Caravan at that time?"

"Yes."

"And you still didn't tell the project engineer not to make the vehicle?"

"He saw the test too."

205

"So you figured you'd just keep you mouth shut and let him and the others do what they wanted to do?"

"I don't remember."

Merriman leaned forward and rested his forearms on his legs. He stared at O'Grady. "But you knew from that day forward that if the Caravan was hit head-on, right front side to right front side, at a closing speed of 50 miles per hour, the driver of the van wouldn't survive and, if there was a passenger behind him, the passenger probably wouldn't survive either, didn't you?"

O'Grady stared back, tears welling up in her eyes. "I didn't think about it."

Merriman straighten up again and stared at her. Then he slowly got out of his chair and stood next to the table, leaning over it. He reached over and snuffed out his cigarette in the ash tray. Then slapped the table loudly with his hand and looked down at O'Grady. "Well, Tracy, you'd better think about it now, because that's what I'm going to talk to you about, the death of Michael and Bruce Ralston, the paralysis of Amy Ralston, the injuries to Micelle and Dustin Ralston and the loss Amy, Michelle and Dustin have sustained loosing their husband, father, son and brother. All of those things that wouldn't have happened if you and the others in authority at WCI had done what you should have after witnessing that crash test."

Merriman straighten up, rested his right foot on his chair and pointed at O'Grady. "And Tracy, just think about the extreme danger that Caravan posed to its driver and passengers, a danger you chose to ignore from 1966 to this very day. How many of those models of Caravan are still on the road? Maybe, Tracy, you can't say exactly, but you do know there a lot of them and that their drivers and passengers are at risk every day of serious injury or death."

Merriman looked at Schultz. "I know why you're here. When I saw those 1966 crash tests and films, I knew before long MCI would want to talk settlement. Anyone with your intelligence would immediately know when he saw those tests that MCI shouldn't have marketed that Caravan. And if MCI shouldn't have marketed it, how could it go to trial in this case? You knew you had to try to settle."

Merriman took his foot off the chair, picked up a black grease pencil and walked to a white pad mounted on the wall. He turned and looked a Schultz and then at Lyons, writing on the pad as he talked. "Let me tell you two what you're facing. I'll just talk in conservative round figures. The ones you'll hear in trial will be more. The medical and funeral expenses to date for Amy, Micelle, and Bruce and the deceased Michael and Dustin come to about one hundred seventy-five thousand dollars."

He wrote that figure on the pad. "Amy's paralysis will require future medical and related expenses for the rest of her life, about at least twenty thousand dollars a year. She's thirty-four and has a life expectancy of seventy-five years. Forty-one years at twenty thousand a year comes to eight hundred twenty thousand dollars."

He wrote that figure on the pad. "Michael Ralston was thirty-seven at the time of his death. He had just made junior partner in a national accounting firm where he could work at least thirty more years. He earned fifty thousand dollars the year before his death and was projected to earn seventy-five thousand the first year of his partnership. Over those thirty years his yearly income would continue to rise to at least the level of two hundred thousand per year. If we assume an average figure of one hundred twenty-five thousand dollars for thirty years, his family lost at least three million seven hundred fifty dollars. Those out-of-pocket damages come to four million seven hundred forty-five thousand dollars."

He wrote those figures on the board. A glass of water rested on the table to the right of Merriman. He paused, took a drink from it. "Those figures don't cover the larger losses of pain and suffering and loss of companionship the three living Ralstons have suffered from this accident. That figure is conservatively more than five million dollars."

He wrote that figure on the pad. "And then there's the matter of punitive damages. No case could better fit the need for punitive damages. WCI's conduct in this case amounts to at least reckless disregard for the life and safety of its customers, if not outright malice. The judge will clearly submit punitive damages to the jury, and it will likely award them, in what amount, I don't know, but I would guess it would take at least fifty-five million to get WCI's attention."

He wrote down that figure, came back to the end of the table and leaned forward with his hand resting on the table. "So you see its going to take a lot of money to settle with the Ralstons. You say, yeah, but the other two defendants should bear some of that. Maybe, but I think the jury will find you alone liable for the punitive damages and for the better share of the general damages. With my conservative figures you're looking at an exposure of at least fifty million dollars."

Merriman took another drink of water, leaned back into the end of the table and looked a Schultz. "Verner, I assume you one million's in the pot, is that right?"

"If you make a demand for more than a million, you're right."

Merriman laughed loudly. "Verner, you know my demand will be way over that million." He looked at Lyons. "So, Bret, I guess I better start talking to you. First thing I'll say to you, Bret, is if you're thinking of getting out of this for some low-ball figure such as five million, forget it. Second, if you going to try to convince me to sell my clients on a structured settlement, forget that also. But, Bret, in spite of the egregious conduct of you insured, I'm not greedy nor are my clients. In fact the figure I'm going to give you should make you look like a hero. Bret, my clients will settle this case with MCI for thirty million dollars."

Merriman sat down and stared at Lyons. No one said a word for several moments.

Lyons stared angrily at Merriman. "I think the demand is outrageous, but I want to call my company," he said abruptly.

Merriman squinted his eyes and spoke softly but firmly. "You think my demand is outrageous, do you, Bret? Well, Bret, before you call your company, let me tell you something about outrageous. If I have to try this case, I'll relish the task of convincing the jury that the conduct of your insured was much more than outrageous. Bret, I'll show the jury the 1966 off-set head-on crash test film, proving that Tracy and her boss saw what happened to the dummies inside the vehicle, and proving, Bret, that the report and the film remained in the hands of WCI until this trial without any action being taken. And after that, Bret, it'll be easy to convince the jury that WCI acted in reckless disregard for the health and safety of its consumer and should be punished with a substantial punitive damage verdict so as to send it the message that this conduct will not be tolerated. The jury won't think thirty million is outrageous, and Bret, they'll prove that with a verdict substantially in excess of that."

The room fell silent as Merriman stared at Lyons. Lyons said nothing, but slowly got up and left the room, followed shortly by Roper, Schultz and O'Grady. Roper took Lyons to a vacant office where he could use the telephone, and Roper, Schultz and O'Grady repaired to Roper's office.

Schultz and O'Grady took two straight back upholstered chairs. Roper went out to visit with his secretary, returned in about five minutes and sat behind his desk.

Schultz broke the silence. "That was quite a show, wasn't it?"

Roper nodded. "Yes it was. Merriman's got a reputation for trying a powerful case, and we just got a taste of what's to come."

O'Grady's asked stoically, "What d'yawl think he'll settle for?"

Roper looked at her. "I was studying him in particular when he was chastising Bret not to give him a low-ball offer. I think he may have had another reason in using the five million dollar figure. It might have been an invitation for an offer somewhere in that neighborhood. Also his speech about forgetting a structured settlement was bullshit. I've talked to O'Shea about Merriman settlement conduct, and he said if we can figure out how much cash Merriman wants for his fee, he thinks the rest could be structured. A structured settlement could fit the Ralston's needs. It would provide Amy Ralston with a steady income and a future amount to provide the kids with college money and some start-up money when they're out on they're own."

"How do we figure out what he wants?" Schultz asked.

"I don't know for sure, but one third of five million is around a million six, so I'd guess somewhere between that figure and two million."

Roper's secretary came and handed Roper a letter she had prepared.

Soon Lyons retuned to Roper's office. He stood next to Schultz's chair and looked at Roper. "My office agrees that his demand is out-of-line."

Roper handed him the letter his secretary had prepared. "That may be, but the demand is above MCI's retention, so this letter is MCI's formal demand that you settle, or it will hold your company responsible for any verdict above one million dollars and for it expense in defending itself further in this matter. If you're not going to accept his demand, I suggest you come up with an offer that'll settle this case." Then he told Lyons of his discussion with Schultz and O'Grady while he was on the telephone.

"Has this O'Shea fella had experience with Merriman in settlement talks?" Lyons asked.

"Yes, on at least two occasions," Roper said, and he looked at Schultz. "In one of those cases he was representing WCI and their Caravan."

"Well, let's see if we can adjourn for lunch and come back about two," Lyons said. "That'll give me time to see if I can make a counter-offer."

"I'll talk to him." And Roper left his office for the conference room.

When he entered the conference room, Merriman sat at the end of the table reading a magazine. He looked up at Roper and smiled. "Walt, I didn't expect to see you. Are you the messenger with my thirty million?"

Roper laughed. "No, and I'm sure you didn't expect that I was. Lyons needs to do more talking with his bosses. Let's recess this until two this afternoon and see then what he comes up with?"

Merriman rose and picked up his magazine. "Okay partner, see you then."

At two all the players gathered again in Roper's conference room. After everyone had taken the seats they previously occupied, Merriman rose slowly and stood at the end of the table looking first at Schultz, Roper and O'Grady and finally at Lyons. "Bert, I'm told you have something to say to me."

Lyons looked up at him. "My company will add two and a half million to MCI's one million, making our offer three and a half million."

Merriman laughed. "Oh come on, Bert. You gotta' be kidding, or, if not, you're telling me you want to try this case. Which is it?"

"I'm not kidding, and we don't want to try the case. The offer is a fair one considering that you don't want a structured settlement."

"Well, I talked the situation over again with Amy Ralston, and she does see some sense in a structured settlement if it's large enough to provide for her for life and for the kids college and for their security for say the next ten years after that. But the settlement has to be partially in cash, as I'm not structuring my portion."

"That puts a different picture on it. Let me make a phone call?"

Merriman smiled at him. "I suggest you do that. I'll be waiting right here." He sat and picked up his magazine.

Schultz, Roper and O'Grady followed Lyons out of the room. They went down the hall to Roper's office.

Standing inside of Roper's office, Lyons looked at Roper. "I know you're position, but what do you think I should offer as a structure?"

"How much would it cost you to structure a twenty million dollar settlement and cash of at least two million?"

Lyons sat at Roper's conference table and did some computation with his adding machine. He mumbled to himself, *three million five hundred thousand at 15% for forty years comes to about twenty-one million.* Then he looked up at Roper. "We could probably offer a twenty million structure for forty years and three million in cash at a cost of a little less that six and a half million."

"Are you prepared to do that?" Roper asked.

"That'd be stretching my authority a bit, but I could do it."

"Then offer it."

He did, and it settled MCI's case.

The following Wednesday, Barry worked at his desk, reviewing a deposition, when the telephone rang. He picked up the receiver. "Barry O'Shea," he said.

"Barry, this is Walt Roper. I have something I need to tell you, but I rather do it in person. Are you free? Can I come over to your office?"

"Sure, come on over."

Ten minutes later Roper sat in Barry's office in a chair in front of Barry's desk. He looked at Barry. "We had a settlement conference with Merriman in my office all day Monday. I experienced what was the classic Merriman you told me about. I had Verner Schultz with me, and he also forewarned me. Also present were Tracy O'Grady and Bret Lyons, a claims manager for WCI's reinsurer. Merriman, of course, picked on Tracy at first, but since WCI only had a million involved, Bret soon became his fall guy. The same pattern you discussed with me."

Roper lit a cigarette and took a puff. "But the bottle line is that we settled."

"I'm not surprised," Barry said. "After I saw that crash test, I knew WCI's had a loser."

"Yeah, after Merriman finally agreed that a structured settlement met the Ralston's needs better than straight cash, so long as there was enough cash involved to meet his, Merriman's, needs, we finally settled. We bought a twenty-one million dollar structure for three and a half million, and paid three million in cash."

"What kind of a structure did the three and half million buy?"

"Twenty-one million over forty years."

"Wow, that much. Lyons must have gotten a good deal somewhere."

"He came with it, although he didn't expect he could use it, even though it offered the best deal for the family."

"I'm glad he came prepared."

Roper took another drag from the cigarette. "I'll give you something in writing confirming this, so you can submit it to the court."

"Thanks. I'll try to get this before the jury, but I don't think the judge will let me. Anyway, at least he'll know of the settlement amount so at a minimum he will reduce any verdict against us by that amount."

21

WEDNESDAY MORNING, APRIL third in Carson City Merriman walked down to Savage's office. The sun shone brightly at the capital as it rose in the sky. Savage sat behind his desk, as usual with a thin cigar in his mouth.

Merriman pulled up a chair and faced his partner. "It's time to get Chang and Rogaine together for some trial preparation. What do you think about the idea of pulling Sturgis and his expert into at least one joint conference?"

"I don't know. Doesn't that seem a little risky to let a co-defendant in on our theories?"

"I guess that would be the conventional wisdom, but you know I'm not much for conventional. I look at it this way. Sure, ordinarily Sturgis' tactic would be to defeat us, but this isn't an ordinary case. Here he should side with us against Monarch. His expert should do that, and once his expert shoots that bullet, his strategy is set. He has to side with us. So I say, let's bring him into the mix and plan together. At least let's let him think he's in the mix. He won't know that we aren't sharing everything."

Savage lowered his eyes. "I should have known you wouldn't have suggested this without a plan. You want me to set up a joint conference?"

"Yeah, how about next week in Denny's office? And we can adjourn to Chang's office if it's appropriate."

"I'll go to work on it right away."

The following Tuesday a steady rain fell outside of *Witchhazel & Wilson's* office in Beaverton. Inside in the firm's conference room Larry Sturgis, Noah Beauchamps, Denny Wilson, Wayne Merriman, Alex Savage, Wayland Chang and Penn Rogaine sat around the conference table, with Merriman at the head. A slight cloud of smoke filled the room. Wilson and Savage smoked their cigars, and Merriman puffed on his Lucky Strike.

Merriman laid his cigarette in the grove of an ashtray and looked out at Chang, Beauchamps and Rogaine. "I've invited you guys here to go over your theories and to prepare for trial. Wayland, it's my understanding that you and Noah pretty much agree on the defect in the pickup. The hood member should have been manufactured with a double catch to prevent the hood from flying up if someone didn't seat the hood properly. Is that right?"

Chang looked at Beauchamps. "That's my theory. Do you agree Noah?"

"Yes, that's my thought also," Beauchamps replied.

Merriman looked at Rogaine. "And Penn, you take a different tack. You think the Monarch pickup should have been designed so that the driver could see ahead in the even the hood flew up. Is that right?"

"Yeah, like I told you before. The pickup should have been designed with a hood that rose up as it goes back. Can I draw you a picture?"

"Sure." Merriman pointed to the other end of the table. "Go to the easel over there with the white pad on it"

Rogaine went over to the easel and picked up a black grease pencil and began drawing. "This is a rough drawing of what the driver sees looking our through the windshield. The hood is down so he had a clear view ahead. In the pickup in question the windshield is flat, and the back of the hood abuts the bottom of the windshield, so if the hood files up it totally blocks the driver's view ahead, like this." He draws another drawing beside the one he first drew with the hood up blocking the windshield.

"But if the windshield's design curves from the sides to a higher point in the center and the hood back is likewise curved, then if you build risers into the raising mechanism of the hood, when the hood is raised in its up as high as it goes, the driver still sees ahead through the opening left by the curvature, like this." He draws another drawing below the other demonstrating.

Merriman studies him. "Is that something you just thought up?"

"Well, as I told you when we first met. I thought it could be done, but I did some investigating and found that there are several manufacturers who design the hood and windshield similar to what I have suggested. When I got in the driver's seat of those vehicles with the hood raised, I could see ahead."

"Were those vehicles in existence when this accident happened?"

"Yes, and some 1970 pickups, particularly the Japanese Shinto and WCI's half ton, had a design like that."

Then Merriman faced Sturgis. "You see why I didn't think you'd be compromised meeting with us. Chang's theory is the same as your engineer, and Rogaine's improved design sort of takes you off the hook as well."

Sturgis nodded.

Merriman looked back at Chang, Beauchamps and Rogaine. "Okay, now let's work with you three to make sure your direct examination goes as planned and give you some help with the cross examine we expect."

Merriman concentrated on Chang's and Rogaine's direct examination, and Sturgis concentrated on Beauchamps. Both Merriman and Sturgis then cross examined all three.

After Sturgis, Beauchamps and Chang had left, Merriman, Wilson, Savage, and Rogaine remained in the conference room, sitting around the table.

Merriman leaned back in his chair, lit another Lucky Strike, took a drag and looked at the ceiling for a moment. He brought his eyes back to Rogaine. "You know the whole time while we worked with you guys I felt something missing. And I think it's the drama that's lacking."

Rogaine's blue eyes sparkled as he looked at Merriman. "I've got an idea that might add a spark. Let me go back to my office and work on it for a few days. I'll call you in a week if what I have in mind pans out."

On Thursday morning, two days later, Barry arrived at his office at seven-thirty. The sun, rising in the east, shown through his windows. Rain fell all night, but the morning arrived crisp and clear. A call from Steve Hinkley, scheduled for eight, arrived ten minutes early.

Barry answered it. "Hi, Steve, are Matcheck and Notice there?"

"Yes, they're on speaker."

"The trial is about a month away," Barry said, "so I felt we should communicate and make plans. But first, Steve, have you told Brad and Sid what our investigators have found out about the pickup's history?"

"They've been brought up-to-date, including the nature of the previous accident, and they've seen the pictures of the damage."

"Then Sid, going back to the questions I asked you in my office after we made the inspections of the vehicles, do you think that the previous accident could have had something to do with the hood flying up in our case?"

"I think it could have, but I'd like to examine the pickup again."

"I'll see what I can do. Can you do it on one trip, that is, can you do it when you come out for the trial?"

"Sure, just tell us when we should be there, and we'll come a day early to make the inspection. It won't take long."

"Well, the trial starts on Tuesday, May fourteenth in Astoria. Maybe you should arrive in Portland on Friday. I'll make arrangements for you to see the vehicle that afternoon. Then we can work in my office over the weekend preparing for trial and go down to Astoria on Monday."

"Unless we hear to the contrary," Matcheck said, "we'll be in your office around noon Friday."

—⁂—

After Barry hung up the phone, he got up and walked out of his office and up to Sarah. "Honey, will you see if you can find Lorenzo and have him come and see me."

Sarah looked up at him and smiled. "Sure."

Later that morning, Lorenzo looked in Barry's open door. "Boss, you wanted to see me?"

"Yes, Ben come in and sit by my desk."

Lorenzo entered and pulled a chair beside Barry's desk and sat.

Barry looked at him. "The trial in the Ralston case starts next month. Have you talked to UCLA about Rogaine's transcripts?"

Lorenzo shook his head and slapped his leg. "Gosh, Boss, I forgot clean about that. I get on it right away."

"Also we need to find those Winchester mechanics and see what they say."

"That's on my list. I'll start on that right after I call my contact at UCLA." And he got up and left.

That afternoon Lorenzo sat in his office looking in his contacts directory. When he found the number, he dialed.

When an operator answered, Lorenzo asked, "May I please speak to Leslie Smart."

"Who shall I tell Mr. Smart is calling?"

"An old friend, Ben Lorenzo."

A moment later, a man came on the line. "Ben, you old fart. How have you been?"

"Fine, Les. Long time since we talked."

"It sure is. What can I do for you?"

Lorenzo explained what he needed.

"I'm sure I can get it," Smart said. "It might take a few days; we're snowed here right now."

"I understand. Can you get it for me say by the first week of May?"

"Oh sure, but remember I'll need a subpoena before I can release it."

"I'll get one. What if I come by on Thursday, May ninth?"

"That'll be fine. Come at one in the afternoon. That'll allow you to fly down in the morning. Our offices are in Murphy Hall. It'll be great to see you."

Late morning, April 15, tax day, Lorenzo was back in Kelso searching for Wilson Spelling at the address he had gotten from the workmen comp department. Rain fell, but he found the address on

Alder. As he departed his car, he raised an umbrella over his head, hurried up the two wooden steps and rang the doorbell.

An unshaved middle-age man with disheveled hair opened the door.

"Are you Wilson Spelling?" Lorenzo asked.

"Who wants to know?" the man sputtered.

Lorenzo identified himself as an investigator for a law firm, checking on a repair of a wrecked pickup at Roger's Reck & Rebuild about three years ago. He showed the man a picture of the wrecked green Monarch.

"I don't know nothing about it."

"In understand that you worked for Winchester at that time, isn't that right?"

"I might of, but I don't remember working on that pickup."

Next, he drove to the address he had for Poncho Esperenza. After introducing himself, he showed Esperenza the picture of the wrecked green pick up. "Have you ever seen that pickup before?"

Esperenza, a heavy man dressed in soiled coveralls, a torn long sleeved faded blue shirt and reeking of alcohol, held picture in his shaking hands and stared at it for moment. "I, I think I worked on it, but I'm not sure."

"Was that while you worked for Winchester at Roger's Reck & Rebuild?"

Suddenly Esperenza looked up, like a light had gone on above him. "No, no I was wrong, I never seen that pickup."

Lorenzo suspected what had happened. "You're sure of that."

"Yeah, yeah, I'm sure."

The next morning Lorenzo reported to Barry about the mechanics.

22

MID-DAY FRIDAY MAY tenth, Matcheck and Notice arrived at Barry's office. Barry greeted them as they appeared at his door.

As they entered, Matcheck gazed out the east-facing windows. "What a view. That mountain is spectacular. Last time we visited, we couldn't see anything but the rain falling."

Barry sat behind his desk. "Yeah, it's a great view whenever it's clear like today."

Matcheck and Notice sat on the couch.

Barry looked at them and lit a Phillip Morris. "How was your flight?"

Matcheck grinned. "Nothing unusual, except it was on time. Are we cleared for another examination of the vehicle?"

"Yes, anytime after two this afternoon." Barry looked at his watch. "Actually, I see it's nearly one-thirty. We might as well go to the garage and get my car."

All three got up, headed out of Barry's office and took the elevator to the garage. Then they drove across the Burnside Bridge and out to Chang's garage on the eastside.

Before they exited the car, Barry got their attention. "When you make your examination, don't explain or talk about you findings. Even if Chang leaves us alone, don't talk as he might have a microphone somewhere in the garage that will pick up what you say."

They entered Chang's office area and were greeted by Chang who took them into the garage area where the vehicles still sat. As Matcheck and Notice went over to the pickup, "I've got some work going on in my office," Chang said to them, "so I'll leave you. When you're done, come into my office and inform me."

"Will do," Barry said. "I don't think we'll be very long."

Chang then left.

Notice examined the hood. He took a pocket knife from his satchel, opened it and scratched the hood lightly near its edge. He also took out a small magnifying glass and examined the area of the scratch. Then he turned to Matcheck. "See here." And he pointed at the scratch area.

Matcheck took the glass and examined the area.

Then Notice made another small scratch on the right front fender. He examined that area, as did Matcheck.

The two engineers made a further examination of other areas of the pickup and looked again at the Caravan, apparently studying the crushed areas.

Then Matcheck turned to Barry. "We're done. Let's go."

They walked into the office, thanked Chang and left out the office door.

They went to Barry's car and boarded, Matcheck in the front passenger's seat and Notice in the rear.

Before Barry started the car, Matcheck looked at him. "I suppose you want to know what we saw."

Barry turned toward Matcheck and grinned. "You damn well know I do."

Notice leaned forward. "When I made the scratches it revealed the number of coats of paint on the surfaces of the scratched areas. The scratch on the hood showed a primer coat at the bottom, and two other costs of paint, a red one over the primer and a black one over that. We know the pickup at the time of the accident was black, but the red coat under the black indicated that the hood was originally red. The scratch area on the fender, however, shows a primer coat on the bottom, then a green coat of paint and finally a black one. The pickup when Lewis bought it was green. Somebody replaced the hood with a red one before Winchester painted the pickup black."

"Would that affect the latching quality of the hood latch mechanism," Barry asked.

"It could," Notice replied, "depending upon the condition of the replaced hood. It appeared to be a Monarch hood, but I can't be positive on that, and, even if it was, we have no way to know whether it had been previously damaged and if it was proper aligned."

"Well, of all the things we know, the service station attendant opening the hood before the accident, the fact that, if the hood is properly latched, it won't come up, the fact that it is not the hood that originally sold with the vehicle and the fact that it did come up in this accident, can you tell me what probably caused the hood to release?"

"Yes. I think that, when the hood was replaced, it probably was not aligned properly with its mating mechanism on the vehicle."

Barry started the car and smiled. "Well, gentlemen, I think the inspection went well."

They returned to Barry's office and worked the rest of the afternoon on trial preparations.

Later that afternoon, Barry worked at this desk, and Matcheck and Notice review papers on his couch. Barry got up and went to Sarah's desk. "Honey, I haven't heard from Ben. He went down to LA yesterday. He should be back."

Sarah looked up at him. "I'll see if I can find him."

At about four-thirty Lorenzo stuck his neck in Barry's door. "Boss, I guess I forgot to tell you. My contact called me Wednesday night at home and told my they have been having trouble finding Rogaine's transcript. Apparently when they moved some years ago, some of the older transcripts were misfiled. They will let me know right away when they find it."

"Damn it. They better find it before he gets on the stand. Come on in Ben. I think you've met Brad Matcheck. This is Sid Notice, another Monarch engineer."

Lorenzo entered and shook Matcheck's and Notice's hand. Then he pulled up a chair and sat beside Barry's desk facing the couch.

Barry explained to him what they had learned from the inspection of the pickup that day.

Lorenzo nodded and smiled. "That gives me an idea. When I interviewed the mechanic, Esperanza, he almost slipped and told me how they repaired the pickup, and then he fell in line with Winchester. I think I'll have another chat with him. And I'll take a subpoena along."

Early Saturday morning the sun began rising over the Cascades and dawn shifted to full daylight. The blue sky above and the slight chill in the air forecast a warm and sunny day in Portland. Merriman and Richard jogged through the Park Blocks. Merriman and Savage had flown to Hillboro on Friday to confer with Wilson and Amy Ralston prior to going to Astoria for the trial. Merriman spent the night with Richards while Savage stayed at Nendels. Merriman and Savage would fly to Astoria Sunday with Wilson, where they would be met by Amy and the Sorrentos who would drive down in Amy's van. They had reservations for the trial at a motel near the waterfront, just east of the bridge that spans the Columbia River and carries the Coast Highway 101 over into Washington.

Merriman turned his head over his left shoulder, as he jogged, and smiled at Richards beside him. "After spending last night with you, Monica, I'm surprised I have the strength to jog like this."

Richards laughed and looked up at Merriman. "Wait a minute big cowboy, don't tell me that you can't keep up with a frail little lass like me."

"Frail little lass, you say," Merriman laughed, panting. "Sex with you is as invigorating as wrestling a steer, only a lot more sensual. After the third time last night, I felt as exhausted as a marathon runner. Although you treated me kinder than the time we put on the gloves, and you beat the shit out of me."

She laughed harder. "Oh come on now. You loved the little boxing match we had, and after your back flip onto the bed, don't tell me you didn't enjoy yourself."

"I came back for more, didn't I," he said still panting and laughing.

After the jog, they went back to Richard's apartment, showered and dressed.

Richard walked to the kitchen. As she entered, she turned toward Merriman. "You go out on the balcony and read the paper. I'll fix breakfast, and we can eat out there."

Merriman stepped out of the living room onto the balcony marveling at the view. On the balcony was a small glass table surrounded by four wrought iron metal chairs with green and white striped cushions. The table contained two place settings and the morning Oregonian. Merriman sat at one place setting and began scanning the sports page of the paper.

Several minutes later, Richards came out on the balcony with a tray carrying glasses of orange juice, plates of pancakes and butter and a pitcher of syrup.

She set a glass of orange juice and a plate of pancakes down at the place settings before Merriman and placed the other glass of juice and plate of pancakes at the other place setting, and she sat.

Merriman dug into the pancakes. "Wow, these are great. The athlete's also a great cook."

"Thank you," Richards said. "What are your plans for the rest of the day?"

Merriman finished the pancakes and put down his fort on the plate. He looked at Richards. "I'm meeting Savage at Denny's office later this morning. We have some last minute matters to deal with before we go down to Astoria on Sunday."

"I'm planning on driving down there on Monday," Richards said.

Merriman drained his orange juice. "I can save you the trip. We're flying my airplane down on Sunday, and we have room for one more."

"Yeah, but I'll need my car."

"I don't know why. We've rented two cars to use down there, and there's an extra room at the motel for you in case you decided to come with us."

Richards thought for a moment. "Well, I guess it would be fun to fly. I haven't anything else planned for Sunday, so I guess you've go another passenger."

Merriman got up, walked over to Richards, leaned down and kissed her. "Welcome aboard."

Early Monday morning, May thirteenth, Barry got up at five a.m., and he and Sarah left their house at six to pickup Matcheck and Notice at their hotel. They were on the road at a little after six. The sun had just risen, starting what appeared to be a gorgeous day. They left Portland on the Sunset Highway for the drive over the Coast Range and down to the coast where it intersected with US 101 and drove north to Astoria. The drive took a little less than two hours. It was a wonderful introduction for Matcheck and Notice to the beautiful scenery of the Northwest mountain ranges, covered with majestic Douglas Firs, Hemlocks and Spruce evergreens and deciduous Laurels and Elms, newly coated with their green leaves.

Barry had rented a Victorian house about a block and a half from the courthouse for his team. While over a hundred years old, it had been remodeled several years before, not to change the exterior, but to bring the interior more up-to-date. They arrived there about eight.

Barry parked the car in front of the house. The house sat on a hill above the street. It had a long front veranda that was accessed by a two section cement stairway.

Matcheck exited the car and stood on the sidewalk, gazing at the house. "My god, this, and its neighbors, make one historic sight!"

Barry and Notice joined him and took the suitcases from the trunk. Then all four climbed the stairs, went onto the veranda and Barry unlocked the front door.

When they entered, Matcheck and Notice stopped in the entry hall and stared at the living room ahead. Someone had totally reconfigured it into an office and conference area.

Barry smiled at them. "You obviously notice that I had the leasing agent make some modification to the house to make it more functional for our purpose. Take your things up the stairs," he said pointing to the right, "and get settled. Let's meet in the living room in half hour."

Notice turned and started up the stairs with his suitcase. Then he turned and looked down at Barry. "I guess I should ask. Is there a particular bedroom assigned to me?"

"I'm sorry. I overlooked that. There are four bedrooms and four baths up there. The one at the top of the stairs is the master bedroom. Sarah and I will take that one. You two take any of the three remaining."

Matcheck joined Notice and went up stairs. Barry and Sarah went into the living room, leaving their suitcases in the entry hall. A large fireplace and mantel occupied the far wall alone with French doors on either side. The French doors had full length glass curtains gathered in the center and tied the door edge. The windows in the doors looked out on a spacious lawn surrounded by a rock garden.

In the room at either side of the fireplace were two identical large stuffed chairs covered in a dull red floral pattern. Some distance back a sofa covered with the same pattern faced the fireplace. Attractive antique appearing tables were beside the chairs and the sofa with table lamps on each. To the right of this setting were two desks, one equipped with a modern typewriter, a copy machine and a telephone. The other desk sat closer to the wall at the far end of the room in front of a window and had a telephone on it. Two captain's chairs sat in front of the desk and a high-back executive chair was behind it. A dictation machine sat next to the telephone. The left side of the room contained a large conference table surrounded by six captain's chairs, one at each end and two each on the sides. In the far corner of the room sat a small table with a telephone and a straight back chair.

Sarah carried two large briefcases into the room and went straight to the desk with the typewriter. Barry carried another large briefcase and placed it on the other desk. The briefcases carried the files for the case and office supplies. Beside Sarah's desk was a long table against the wall to the right of the room. Sarah took the files from the briefcases and placed them on the table. Barry likewise took the files from his briefcase and put on the table in order. Sarah took other supplies, such as typing paper, paperclips, a stapler, a scotch tape holder, a dictation receiver, etc. and arranged them on the desk and in its drawers. Barry also took supplies from his briefcase and placed them in the drawers of his desk. The briefcases were stored beside his desk.

Barry sat in the executive chair and looked at Sarah, standing beside her desk and arranging materials on top of it. "Well, honey, it looks like we're settled in. It didn't take as long as I thought. Are you ready to go to work?"

Sarah smiled and sat in her secretary's chair. "I'm at you beck and call."

"Why don't you start on the requested instructions and our trial brief? When the others come down, you can break and join us at the conference table and take notes. After that you can go back to the court documents."

Shortly, Matcheck and Notice joined Sarah and Barry in the living room-office.

Barry greeted them. "Let's go over to the conference table and sit down."

Barry sat at the head of the table, and Sara sat to his right. Matcheck and Notice sat to his left.

Barry looked at Matcheck and Notice. "We've got a meeting with the judge at three this afternoon. Brad, you will go to the meeting with me. Sid you stay here with Sarah. The trial will start tomorrow morning at eight-thirty a.m. with some opening remarks from the judge and the selection of the jury. Again Brad, you will be the company representative sitting at counsel table with me. Sid, you will sit in the back of the courtroom, unless the judge excludes witnesses. That doesn't happen too often in civil cases. Brad, you can talk to me, but whisper so neither the judge or the jury hear you. Don't do it too often, but do it whenever you have something important to communicate. Unless there is an urgent need for you to get a message to us, Sid, don't come forward. We can talk at recesses. That's all I have for now. Are there any questions?"

There were none, so Barry and Sarah returned to their desks and worked, and Matcheck and Notice went outside to look around.

Merriman, Savage and Wilson met with Monica Richards and Amy Ralston in a small conference room Merriman had rented from the motel. They all had arrived the previous afternoon and had checked in at the motel office. Each was given a ground floor.

They sat around the table with Merriman in command.

He looked out at the others. "We have a meeting with the judge at three this afternoon. "Amy, are you comfortable accompanying us? If you are, I believe you should be there. There may be things that come up that we'll need you input on."

Amy looked at Merriman. "I can be there. Willie can drive me up to the courthouse in the van. Isn't there a disabled person's entrance behind the building up on the hill?"

Wilson spoke up. "Yes, that's the back entry to the first floor. The main entry is on Commercial Street, but to get to the doors entering the first floor you have to climb a number of steps. There are no steps to the back entry door as it's up the hill on Duane Street. Inside the door is an elevator to the second floor where the courtroom is."

"Okay, we'll meet you outside the courtroom at quarter to three," Merriman said.

Merriman looked at Richards. "Monica, tell us the schedule you've worked out with the witnesses."

"On the assumption that Tuesday will be taken up with jury selection and opening statements, I subpoenaed Bentwood and Wilkerson for Wednesday morning." She said that the sergeant, the other state police officers, the two firemen, the medics, the tow truck drivers and the medical examiner are scheduled for Wednesday afternoon. She told them that Wayland Chang, Roger Winchester and Penn Rogaine will be here Thursday morning and that she had subpoenaed the Emanuel Hospital records for all three plaintiffs for Thursday afternoon and scheduled Dr. Marshall also for Thursday afternoon. For Friday morning she arranged for Willie and Mina Sorrento to be here with Michelle and Dustin Ralston followed by the economist. "We'll conclude Friday afternoon with Amy. I don't know if you'll want to call the Monarch engineer as an adverse witness, but presumably he'll be in the court at all times."

"I'll leave it to you, Monica, to keep track of the witness," Merriman said, "to keep them informed as to how were going, and to arrange for alternate times for them if needed."

Richards winked at Merriman. "I'm on top of it."

23

A T THREE P.M. the lawyers and parties gathered in the courtroom of the Clatsop County courthouse. Merriman, Savage and Wilson stood next to the left side of the lawyers' table talking. Merriman wore his western attire, except for his dirty boots. They were polished. Savage wore a brown worsted suit, a yellow and black tie, and cowboy boots. Amy Ralston sat in her wheelchair just behind the bar and talked to Leslie Richards who stood beside her. Willie Sorrento who brought Amy into the courthouse sat in the first row of the spectator benches.

Barry and Larry Sturgis sat at the other end of the lawyers' table, facing each other and talking. Barry wore a pale green summer suit, white shirt and a green paisley tie. Sturgis wore a tan summer suit, a white shirt and a red and black stripped tie. Matcheck sat in a chair behind Barry, and Wilkerson sat behind Sturgis. Both Matcheck and Wilkerson was dressed casually, Matcheck with a green checked sport shirt and Wilkinson with a long sleeved red shirt with a button down collar.

The judge's secretary entered from a side door near the jury box and addressed the group. "The judge will see you in his chambers. If you will please come this way," she said, holding the door open.

Merriman, Savage and Wilson entered first, followed by Barry and Sturgis. Once in the chambers, they saw the judge seated at the far end of the conference table peering at them under his heavy eyebrows and chewing on his cigar.

The judge motioned to the other chairs arranged at the table. "Don't just stand there; have a seat at the table."

Merriman, Savage and Wilson sat on one side, and Barry and Sturgis sat on the other side.

The judge looked first at the plaintiffs' lawyers and then at Barry and Sturgis. "Seems like we're missing someone. Is everybody ready to go to trial?"

"Your right, your Honor," Merriman said. "Walt Roper is missing, because the plaintiffs have settled with his client."

"Has his client been dismissed from the case? I don't remember signing such an order."

Merriman answered, "No, your Honor, not yet. We gave his client a Covenant-Not-To-Sue." He handed the judge a court document. "Here's an order dismissing MCI."

The judge looked at the document and then signed it. "Very well, that company is dismissed. How does the settlement affect the remaining defendants, if it does?"

"It should reduce any recovery to which the plaintiffs may become entitled," Barry replied. "Furthermore, plaintiffs have also settled with the owner and driver of the pickup involved in the collision. You may remember when we were here in February, we asked you for permission to take the deposition of Monica Richards, the adjuster for the insurance company. You gave us that permission. We learned in that deposition that the company paid the plaintiffs two hundred thousand dollars, which was the policy limit, in return for a loan receipt so the company could pursue a right of reimbursement against the other defendants. It is our position that any recovery should be further reduced in that amount."

The judge lit his cigar and sat quietly for a moment. Then he looked at Barry. "Well, you've presented some interesting questions. First of all, I suppose you'd like to tell the jury that MCI settled and give them the amount. And I think you would likewise like to have the jury know that the dairy also settled for two hundred dollars. And I suppose you would request that I tell them that if they find a verdict against one or more the remaining defendants, they must reduce that verdict by the amount of both settlements, is that right?"

Barry smiled. "That's just what I was about to request. It's also one of our requested instructions, which I have here together with our trial brief." He handed the judge some papers and gave copies to Merriman."

"Well, I'm not about to do all that. The jury will not hear of the settlements, either of them, from me or from any lawyers in the case. Is that understood?"

All the lawyers nodded.

"Now, how much did MCI settle for?"

Barry handed the judge another document and gave Merriman a copy. "This document explains the settlement. Mr. Roper gave it to me. I assume Mr. Merriman will agree to it. As it points out, the plaintiffs got three million in cash and twenty-one million to be paid out over forty years."

The judge studied the document. "What is the present value of the twenty-one million over forty years?"

"MCI's excess carrier bought the structure for three million five hundred thousand dollars."

Merriman nodded. "That's right, your Honor."

The judge took the cigar out of his mouth and tapped the ashes from it in an ashtray. He thought for a moment and then said, "Hum." He wrote some figures on a pad. "I guess I understand. Anyway here's how I'll handle it. If the plaintiffs get a verdict in excess of six million seven hundred thousand dollars, I'll reduce that verdict by six million seven hundred thousand dollars. If the plaintiffs get a verdict for six million seven hundred thousand or less, I'll enter it, but grant judgment for the defendants."

Merriman objected. "You can't do that, your Honor. We also represent the dairy's insurance carrier in an attempt to get their money back from Monarch and Legion Oil."

The judge started angrily at Merriman. "I'm not stupid. I know the meaning of a loan receipt. It's a sneaking way of keeping the jury from knowing that you represent an insurance company. I should join them as another plaintiff, but I afraid doing that might get me reversed by the Supreme Court, so I'm leaving this a case just for the Ralstons' claims. What you do with the insurance company's claim is your choice later, but I don't think it will matter, because it'll be bound by a defense verdict as will the defendant or defendants by as verdict for plaintiffs. Do you still object?"

Merriman thought for a moment. "No, your Honor."

He still looked at Merriman. "Do you have any requested instructions and a trial memo?"

"Yes, your Honor," Merriman said, handing some papers to the judge and giving copies to Barry and Sturgis.

The judge chewed his cigar. "Is there anything else to take up at this time?"

The lawyers shook their heads. "No," they said.

"Then we'll take up tomorrow morning. I have some other matters to attend to first, so we'll start at nine-thirty with the selection of the jury. Be on time, as I'll start promptly at nine-thirty with or without any of you. After the jury selection, you'll give your opening statements. That means a statement of the evidence you intend to produce. No, and I emphasize no, arguments."

On Tuesday morning, May fourteenth, a slight beach mist fell outside. At nine-fifteen the judge's clerk took the roll from the approximately fifty prospective jurors sitting in the rows of spectator benches in the left rear of the courthouse. Barry, dressed as he had been the previous afternoon, sat in the chair at the lawyers' table furthest from the jury with his files arranged in front of him. Sturgis, also dressed as he had yesterday, sat beside Barry. Matcheck and Wilkinson sat behind their respective lawyers.

On the other side of the table, Merriman dressed as usual in his western attire sat in the chair closest to the jury. His Stetson hung on a peg on the wall near the jury box. Wilson wore a dark suit conservative red and blue striped tie. He sat next to Merriman. Amy Ralston was in her wheelchair behind the lawyers. Amy wore a bright yellow blouse and a blue chiffon skirt that fell below her knees.

Sid Notice sat next to the center aisle in the last row of benches on the right rear side of the courtroom. He did not know Leslie Richards or Alex Savage, who sat a row in front of him, across the aisle.

True to his promise, promptly at nine-thirty the judge, draped in a long black robe, entered the courtroom from his chambers. "All rise" shouted his secretary, acting as the bailiff, "the Circuit Court of the State of Oregon for the Country of Clatsop is now in session, Judge Eric Olson presiding."

The Judge sat. "Please be seated," he said. "The case before us is Amy Ralston, Michelle Ralston, Dustin Ralston and the estates of Michael Ralston and Bruce Ralston, plaintiffs versus Monarch Motors, an Illinois Corporation, and Legion Oil Co., a California Corporation, defendants. Are the parties ready?"

Merriman stood. "The plaintiffs are ready."

Barry and Sturgis stood. "Monarch Motors is ready, your Honor," Barry said

"As is Legion Oil Co.," said Sturgis.

The judge leaned forward on his heavy forearms and spoke with his deep gravelly voice. "Ladies and gentlemen, and I'm speaking to all the prospective jurors, including you all in the back of the courtroom, this is a civil case arising out of a terrible vehicle accident that happened in the evening on Tuesday, May twenty-eight, a year ago, the day after Memorial Day. A 1970 Monarch half-ton pickup owned by Towson Dairy in Seaside, pulling a animal trailer loaded with two Holstein cows, was proceeding west on US 26, the Sunset Highway, crossing the Coast Range. A man by the name of Lyle Bentwood drove the pickup. It was about five-fifteen, and the pickup had just passed the Elderberry Inn and was heading down the straight stretch toward the Jewell Junction, when the pickup crossed the center line and ran head-on into a Caravan being driven east on that highway by the late Mr. Richards with his wife, Amy Richards, a passenger in the front seat and their three children, Michelle, Bruce and Dustin, riding in the rear seats."

The judge cleared his throat and took a drink of water from the glass on the bench. "As a result of that accident, Michael Ralston and Bruce Ralston died, and Amy Ralston, Michelle Ralston and Dustin Ralston were injured. The defendant Monarch Motors manufactured the pickup, and the defendant Legion Oil Co. serviced the pickup earlier that evening. Plaintiffs claim that Monarch Motors is responsible to them because the vehicle was defectively manufactured and that Legion Oil Co. is responsible to them because it negligently serviced the vehicle. Both defendants deny these charges."

The judge cleared his throat again. "That's a brief statement of what happened. The actual facts will be presented by the parties during the trial. Now, has anyone of you ever heard of this accident or do you know any of the people who I have described?"

Three men and a woman raised their hands. The judge noted where they were seated.

"All right, I deal with you one at a time. First, the man in the third row, tell me your name and what you have heard or who you know."

A middle aged man with a weathered complexion stood. "I'm Henry, Hank, Pigeon, and I live in Seaside. I take milk from Towson

Dairy, and I know of Lyle Bentwood. I've also heard of the accident, a terrible thing. I read about it in the newspaper."

"Is there anything about those things that would influence you in deciding this case? You know the defendants deny any wrong doing and are entitled to have you completely unbiased at the start of this case."

"Well, I don't know Bentwood well. I know he works for the dairy, and I think I've met him a time or two in some capacity. But I don't think that would influence me one way or the other. I feel very sorry for the Russells or whatever their names are, but I don't know that my feelings have anything to do with the two companies involved."

"It's the Ralstons. Thank you, Mr. Pigeon. Now the lady in forth row."

A fairly young lady stood. She had dark complexion, a round face and hair tied in a bun. "I'm Linda Mendez, and I work as a waitress in a café in Elsie. I remember the accident. Lots of our customers talked about it, particularly a state policeman I know. He was at the scene."

"Do you know the policeman's name, as he might be a witness in this case?"

"Yeah, its Ralph Runningshoe, he's an Indian."

The judge looked at plaintiffs' lawyers. "Do know if he's a potential witness?"

"Yes, your Honor, he will be a witness." Merriman said.

The judge looked back at the prospective juror. "With that knowledge do you think you might be influenced in you decision in this case by what you know and who you know?"

"I might be. Ralph is a very good friend."

"Thank you. Is it Miss or Mrs. Mendez?"

"I'm single."

"Then you will be excused, Miss Mendez."

The other two men had read about the accident in the newspaper, but couldn't remember any more about that the judge had just recited.

The judge looked out at the prospective jurors. "All right, the clerk will now call the names of twelve prospective jurors. Come up in the order that you're called and take a seat in the jury box to my left. Start filling the seats in the first row, the seat closest to me first and so on. Likewise, when the first row is full, the next juror called, take the seat in the second row closet to me and so on."

The clerk them pulled twelve slips from a box, and announced the names of the prospective juror each time she pulled a slip out of the box. The prospects were, starting with number one in the first seat to number twelve which as the last juror in the second row: Melba Smith, Sandra Erickson, Willie Overstreet, Diane Atchison, Sam Sousa, Micelle Hoening, Jesus Cruz, Dunstan O'Leary, Jerry Cohen, Silvia Hensgaard, Erick Larson, and Basil Woods.

Now the judge looked at the prospective jurors in the jury box and then out at the rest of the prospective juror in the back of the courtroom. "Would all of the prospective juror stand and be sworn?"

All the prospective jurors stood. "Please raise you right hands," The clerk said. They did. "Do you swear that the answers to all questions asked you will be true, so help you God?"

"I do," they all answered.

The judge then looked at the jurors is the jury box. "The lawyers will now question each of you to test your ability to be fair and impartial jurors. Please don't take offense at any of the questions, as the lawyers must ask them on behalf of their clients. The lawyers have in front of them a copy of the questionnaire you filled out at the beginning of your term so they already know something about you. Therefore, the lawyers should not ask you for information which you've already give them, but they may have additional questions."

Then he looked to the rear of the courtroom. "Those of you who have not yet been called to come forward should listen carefully to the questions asked of the prospective jurors in the jury box. If any of those questions raise any doubt in your mind concerning you ability to be fair and impartial, be sure to tell the lawyers about that if you are called to replace one of the prospective jurors in the box."

The judge looked at the clock on the wall above the jury box. "While it's a little early, we'll take our morning recess before you lawyers begin your questioning of the prospective jurors. Those prospective jurors in the jury box will go with the bailiff to the jury room. The rest of the prospective juror can go outside the courtroom, but remain on this floor of the courthouse and do not talk to any one about the case, including to each other. We will be in recess for twenty minutes."

After the bailiff directed the prospective jurors in the jury box to the jury room, the judge left the bench.

—⁂—

After all of the prospective jurors had left the room, Merriman stood, leaned over and said a few works to Amy Ralston. Then he and Wilson left the courtroom followed by Richards and Savage. Willie Sorrento came forward and sat with Amy Ralston.

Sturgis and Wilkerson also left the courtroom and conferred in the hall away from the others.

Notice came forward and joined Barry and Matcheck, sitting in Sturgis's chair, and the three of them huddled and spoke quietly.

Barry leaned down. "After we finish examining the jurors in the box, we have three challenges per side. That means three for the plaintiffs and three for all of the defendants. Thus Sturgis and I must agree on our challenges, if we take any. Plaintiffs take the first challenge, and then we take one and so forth. When it becomes our turn to challenge, we'll caucus here at the table quietly. This procedure continues until each side is either satisfied with the jury or has used up that side's three challenges."

"Will I be a part of the caucus?" Matcheck said.

"Yes, as will Wilkinson. I'll ask you for your opinion on the prospective juror before I caucus with Sturgis."

24

AFTER THE PARTICIPANTS had returned to the courtroom, the judge entered, and they began to rise. "Remain seated," the judge said. "You only rise at the beginning of each session."

The judge sat and looked down at Merriman and Wilson. "One of you may inquire. First, introduce the people at you table. And then in accordance with the court rules, please sit down and remain seated while questioning the prospective jurors."

Merriman stood and looked back at the Judge. "Yes, your Honor." Then he looked at the prospective jurors. "I am Wayne Merriman. I practice law in Carson City, Nevada, with my partner, Alex Savage." He looked to the rear of the courtroom, where Savage stood and waved to the prospective juror. "One of my clients, Amy Ralston, is seated behind me in a wheelchair." Amy waved to the prospective jurors. "Seated next to me is Denny Wilson, a Beaverton lawyer in the firm of *Witchhazel and Wilson*, who also represents the plaintiffs." Wilson stood.

Merriman sat and looked at Mrs. Smith. "Mrs. Smith, maam, I see from the questionnaire that you and you husband reside in Astoria and that you are employed in an accounting department. Might I ask who your employer is?"

Mrs. Smith said, "Yes, you may. I work for the First National Bank here in Astoria."

"And your husband, what does he do?"

"He's a mechanic in the service department of the local Ford dealer."

"I see. One of the defendants here is Monarch Motors, a competitor of the Ford Motor Company. How do you feel about that company?"

"I don't feel one way or the other about them."

"That's in spite of the fact that your husband is employed by a dealer for one of their competitors?"

"That's right."

"So I suppose your husband has never said anything negative about Monarch Motors or any of the vehicles that it manufactures?"

"That's right."

"Mrs. Smith, maam, it says here in your questionnaire that you have sat on other juries. What kind of cases were those, if I might ask?"

"I sat on a DUIL case, and a Burglary case."

"Well now, you realize that both of those involve criminal law and this case is a civil case. You may not know it, but the plaintiffs' burden of proof is different in civil cases. In a civil case the plaintiffs have the burden to prove the facts they allege by a preponderance of the evidence. That's a lesser degree of proof than required in a criminal case, which is beyond a reasonable doubt. Do you understand that the plaintiffs in this case have that lesser burden of proof?"

"I guess so. I know the burden is beyond any reasonable doubt in a criminal case, and I suppose the judge will tell us what it is in this type of case. I'll follow that the judge says."

"Maam, that's very honorable and the right thing to do. Now, without getting too deep into what we will prove in this case, let me talk to you about some things you need to know to decide whether you can be a fair and impartial juror. First, as you may have surmised, Mrs. Ralston here," and he turned and motioned toward her, "is totally paralyzed from the hips down as a result of this accident, and she will remain that way for the rest of her life. That is why you see her in a wheelchair. I know you sympathize with her, but does that fact cause you to feel that you might lean over, even a little, on her behalf in this case?"

"No, Mr. Merriman, I'll decide this case on all the evidence and what the judge tells me about the law."

"Again, maam, that's all we can ask of you. Now, can we agree that the defendants are large corporations and presumably have many resources at their disposal to defend this case?"

"I suppose that's true."

"Fine, and can we agree also that plaintiffs, on the other hand, are mere individuals?"

"I guess that's true also."

"Fine again. Now, does the fact that the defendants are large corporations cause you to believe at this point, without hearing anything further, that they are in the right?"

"I don't favor either side at this point."

"Thank you, maam. Plaintiffs pass Mrs. Smith for cause."

The judge looked at Barry. "Mr. O'Shea, you may inquire."

Barry stood and looked at the jury box. "Let me introduce the people at our table. First of all, I'm Barry O'Shea, a partner in the firm of *Swift, Wyman and Wiggens*, and I practice law in Portland. Seated behind me is Brad Matcheck, a product engineer for Monarch Motors." Matcheck stood and acknowledged his introduction. "Seated next to me is Larry Sturgis, a Portland lawyer representing Legion Oil Co., and behind him is Legion Oil station manager Pete Wilkerson." Sturgis and Wilkerson stood and looked at the prospective jurors.

Barry, Sturgis, Matcheck and Wilkerson then sat.

Barry looked at Mrs. Smith. "Mrs. Smith, do you know or recognized any of the lawyers or the other people that Mr. Merriman and I just introduced?"

"No, I don't."

"Mrs. Smith, I suspect that there will be some expert witnesses called as witness in this case. One of them is a consulting engineer by the name of Wayland Chang. Do you know of him?"

"No I don't know him either."

"How about a so-called expert from California named Penn Rogaine?"

"No."

"Or a consulting engineer from Portland named Noah Beauchamp?"

"No again.

"I suspect that one or all of those so-called expert witnesses will tell you that there was something wrong with the pickup truck. Will you keep an open mind on that issue until you've heard all of the evidence and heard the judge's instructions about expert witness?"

"Yes, I will."

"That's the case even though what one or more of those witness say seems to make sense at the time?"

"Yes, I'll wait till I hear all of the evidence."

"And wait to hear what the judge says about expert witnesses?"

"Yes."

"If the judge should tell you that you are to evaluate the expert's qualifications in determine whether to accept what he says, can you follow that instruction?"

"If the judge says that, of course I will follow it."

"And you'll decide this case not on whether one side is corporations and one side is individual, but on what the evidence proves, will you not?"

"Yes sir."

Barry looked at Mrs. Smith. "Thank you, Mrs. Smith. Pass the juror for cause."

The judge looked at Sturgis. "Mr. Sturgis?"

Sturgis looked at the judge. "Thank you, your Honor."

Then he looked at Mrs. Smith. "Mrs. Smith and the rest of the jury paned, you will find out that generally I will ask many fewer questions because I'm third in line. But I do have several questions to ask you. First, let me ask you how familiar are with how service stations operate."

"Well, I drive so I'm generally familiar with what service stations sell and what services they offer."

"And of course, your husband is a mechanic?"

"Yes, but I'm not mechanical. I generally know what he does, but not the specifics. I've never seen him in his working environment."

"Have any of the questions asked by the other lawyers caused you to favor one side of the other at this time."

"No, they have not."

"Thank you, Mrs. Smith. Pass the juror for cause."

Merriman looked at Miss Erickson. "Miss Erickson, I see your not yet married and you live and work in Warrenton. How is it that an attractive you lady like you is not married?"

Miss Erickson blushed. "I guess I haven't found the right man yet. But I'm still looking."

The jurors laughed.

Merriman smiled. "That's a good answer to kind of a stupid question. Let me try to do better. What kind of work do you do in Warrenton?"

"I work as a sales girl in a tackle shop. Warrenton has a number of docks where fishing boats moor, offering their services to sport fisherman."

"You drive a car, don't you?"

"Sure."

"And your familiar with what service stations offer, are you not?"

Miss Erickson eyed Merriman. "Of course."

"I mean in Oregon as opposed to California and Nevada, the attendant does all the work. You, the driver, can't pump the gas or wash you windshield, thing like that. The attendant does everything for you. Isn't that what you've experienced?"

"I guess you could say that. I certainly don't pump the gas in my tank, if that is what you mean."

"Yes, that's what I mean. And if you want your oil level or water level check, you have the attendant do that, don't you?"

"Well, yes, but usually they ask me if I want them to check those things."

"Have you from time to time answered the attendant that you want him to check those things?"

"As a matter of fact, I almost always do, because I know what happens when you run a car low on either oil or water."

"Have you had bad experiences with that?"

"Low water I have. We've got lots of hills between here and Portland and some south of here. I have had experiences, particularly in the summer, with my radiator overheating."

"Work with me on this. When you ask the attendant to check the oil and/or water level, what does he do in you experience?"

"He opens the hood of the car, checks the water level by removing the radiator cap and checks the oil level with the dip stick."

"You seem to be fairly knowledgeable about those procedures."

She smiled. "I'm no mechanic, but I no dumb blonde either. I know my way around a car."

Some jurors laughed; others smiled.

"Good. So tell me how in you experience the attendant opens the hood."

"In most cars it's simple. You just reach in over the radiator, release the catch and lift up the hood. To put it down you use its weight to slam shut."

"That's the way you do it with your car?"

"Yeah."

"What do you drive?"

"A 1970 Ford pickup. It's actually my dad's, but I drive it most of the time."

"Miss Erickson, you heard the questions I asked Mrs. Smith about the burden of proof in a civil case, like this, as opposed to the burden of proving beyond a reasonable doubt in a criminal case, didn't you?"

"Yeah, I heard you, but I don't completely understand it. This is my first experience in court."

The judge interrupted. "That's understandable, Miss Erickson. That's what I'm here for to tell you what the law provides. I will do that at the conclusion of the case. So don't worry about it at this time. Go to another matter, counsel."

"Miss Erickson, you also heard what I told Mrs. Smith about what Amy Ralston suffers as a result of this vehicle collision. I want you to listen very carefully to what I now have to say and work with me, if you will. If you are a juror on this case and the evidence tells you that she suffers a terrible disability, both emotionally and physically. She lost her husband and young son. Her other two children suffered less severe injuries, but suffer terribly with the loss of their father and their brother. If that's what the evidence establishes, Miss Erickson, I'm going to ask you to award them a lot of money because that is the only way they can be compensated. Even if the amount I ask for is more than you ever contemplated, will you evaluate the evidence, and if the evidence establishes that they are entitled to that huge amount of money, do you think you can follow the evidence and award that sum?"

Miss Erickson stared at Merriman for a moment. "You're asking me if I could support a large verdict if I thought the evidence supports it? I, I think I could."

"Thank you, Miss Erickson for being so frank. Pass the juror for cause, your Honor."

Barry looked at Miss Erickson. "Miss Erickson, you recognize that at this stage of the proceeding, plaintiffs are asking for millions of dollars in damages from the defendants. But just because someone comes into court seeking damages is no evidence that he or she is entitled to anything. That person must first establish that the defendant, or defendants here, are liable for those damages. And in this case both defendants deny any liability of damages. Mr. Merriman talked about his clients' burden of proof. Well, they have the burden to prove that one or more of the defendants are liable to them by a preponderance of the evidence. I'll leave to the judge the job of telling you what that means, but where this long question is going is that at this stage before you have heard any evidence, you don't think the plaintiffs are or are not entitled to any damages because you haven't heard any evidence. Is that true?"

"Actually, Mr. O'Shea, I follow closely what you said, and I agree with you. I haven't heard any evidence, so I have no idea what I'd do if I'm on the jury."

"Miss Erickson, you heard the questions asked of Mrs. Smith. Is there anything the came up in any of those questions that gives you any concern with helping us decide this dispute?"

"No, there isn't."

Barry smiled at her. "I think I know your answer to my next question, but I'll ask it anyway. If you were seated in my position, and someone with your frame of mind was sitting where you are, would be satisfied with that person on the jury?"

"Yes, I would."

"Thank you, Miss Erickson. Pass the juror for cause."

Sturgis looked at Miss Erickson. "When you get to me, you sometimes get a break. Pass the juror for cause."

Merriman looked at juror number three, Willie Overstreet. "Mr. Overstreet, I see you a logger and live in Jewell with you wife, Selma. Jewell's in the neighborhood of where this accident occurred, but you didn't raise you hand when the judge explained about the accident. Am I right that you've never heard of this accident?"

Mr. Overstreet scratched his bald head. "Yer right, I ain't heard of it."

"Who do you work for?"

"Mostly Crown Zellerback."

"Are you familiar with the stretch of road where this accident happened?"

"Sure, I familiar with it, but I still ain't heard of the accident."

"Mr. Overstreet, will you do me a favor and listen carefully to the evidence we provide, and follow the court's instructions, and, if you find that plaintiffs are entitled to a verdict, will you vote for a substantial amount of money, if you find plaintiffs suffered severe emotional and physical injuries?"

"I don't think I can answer that. I don't like throwing money around. Just 'cause you've sue don't mean you're entitled to nothing. I'll wait and see what comes out, and then decide."

"But, Mr. Overstreet, you'll be willing to award a money verdict if you believe that the plaintiffs are entitled to one, won't you?"

"You're gonna have to prove it, mister. That's all I can say about it."

"We'll do that Mr. Overstreet. Pass Mr. Overstreet for cause, your Honor."

Barry looked at Mr. Overstreet. "Sir, I think I understand what you've told Mr. Merriman. Basically, you don't favor anyone now. You're going to wait and see what the evidence, all of it, shows and hear what the judge instructs you as to the law, before you make up you mind. Is that about right, sir?"

"You said it better than I did."

"Thank you, Mr. Overstreet. Pass the juror for cause."

Sturgis looked Mr. Overstreet and then at the judge. "Pass the juror for cause, your Honor?"

Merriman smiled at Sam Sousa. "Mr. Sousa, you're not related to John Phillip are you?"

Laugher filled the courtroom.

The judge looked sternly at Merriman. "Mr. Merriman, keep to the point, please."

"Not that I know of," Sousa said smiling.

Merriman looked at the judge. "Yes, your Honor. I just thought Sousa was an unusual name, so I thought I'd ask?"

"Asked and answered," the judge said. "Let's get on with the jury examination."

"Mr. Sousa, I see you live here in Astoria, with you wife and children, and you run a hardware store. Have you ever been a plaintiff or a defendant in litigation?"

"Yes, Mr. Merriman I have, twice. Do you want to hear about those cases?"

"If you don't mind. Just the basics."

"I was sued once by a lady who claimed she slipped on a nail and fell in the store. She claimed she was permanently injured and sued me for a lot of money. We went to court, and she lost. Another time a man sued us, claiming he was injured using a small chain saw we sold him. He again sued for lots of money. My insurance company settled the case, and I wasn't very happy about the settlement."

Merriman grinned. "Do I dare ask you why you weren't happy?"

Sousa smiled at him. "I don't think you'd like the answer."

Merriman then looked seriously at Sousa. "Mr. Sousa, let's get serious shall we? I gather you don't have much sympathy for people who bring suits in court. Is that a fair appraisal?"

"I'll be frank with you, Sir. Plaintiffs in suits like this have an uphill battle in my way of thinking."

The judge interrupted. "Thank you for being frank Mr. Sousa. You will be excused. Call another juror?"

Mr. Sousa left the courtroom. The clerk reached into the box and pulled out another slip of paper. She looked at it. "Will Harvey Zell please come forward and take the seat of juror number four," she said.

A short stocky middle age man came forward and sat in juror number four's seat.

Merriman looked at him. "Mr. Zell, you realize that you're under oath?"

"Yes, sir."

"And I take it, sir that you heard all the questions asked of Mrs. Smith, Miss Erickson, Mr. Oversteet and Mr. Sousa?"

"Yes, I did."

"And, sir, would I be correct that nothing came out in any of those questions that would make you feel that you might not be fair and impartial to all sides at this time?"

"That's correct, nothing came out."

Merriman looked down at a stack of papers before him. He read briefly and looked back up at Mr. Zell. "Mr. Zell, I see from your questionnaire that you are married, a family man, and reside with your family here in Astoria. I also see that you own a jewelry store on the corner of Tenth and Commercial. How long have you been in that business?"

"A little over twenty-three years."

"Are you a lifetime resident of Astoria?"

"Almost. I've lived here for thirty-five years. My mother and father moved here when I was twelve. My father started the jewelry business. He's retired now, and I took over three years ago."

Merriman smiled. "I take it you're not of Scandinavian heritage?"

Zell chuckled. "Your right. A name like Zell doesn't come from those countries. Actually, I think it originated somewhere in Germany, but all my ancestors that I'm aware of lived in the United States."

"Mr. Zell, we've had a nice chat. I'd like to see if you're willing to help me with my job here today. I've got an obligation to Amy Ralston and her children to do everything I can to introduce evidence that will result in their receiving a substantial verdict. This is their only chance to recover from Monarch Motors or Legion Oil.

So I better not let them down. If I do offer evidence that warrants a substantial verdict in their favor, would you have any hesitancy in voting for such a verdict?"

"If the evidence indicates that they're entitled to a verdict and a substantial one, I would have no trouble voting for it. Is that what you want to hear?"

"Yes, it is. Thank you, sir. Pass Mr. Zell for cause, your Honor."

"Mr. Zell," Barry said. "I'll be brief. If, on the other hand, the evidence establishes that Mrs. Ralston and her children suffered grievous physical and emotion injuries from the accident, but further establishes that those injuries were not caused by any fault of Monarch Motors, would you have any difficulty finding in favor of Monarch Motors?"

"No, I would not. The fact that someone is injured, no matter how seriously, is not sufficient to make someone liable. There must be proof of fault, in my opinion."

"Thank you, Mr. Zell. Pass the juror for cause."

Sturgis said, "The same is true for Legion Oil, isn't it, Mr. Zell?"

"Yes."

"Thank you, Mr. Zell. Pass the juror for cause, your Honor."

The questioning of the remaining prospective juror in the jury box continued for several hours.

When it concluded, the judge looked down at plaintiff's counsel. "Plaintiffs first challenge."

Merriman and Wilson whispered to each other. The Merriman turned and whisper to Amy Ralston. When he finished, she nodded.

Merriman looked up at the judge. "For the purposes of this case, your Honor, plaintiffs will excuse juror number four, Mr. Zell."

The judge turned to the jury box. "Mr. Zell, you're excused." He looked down at the clerk. "Call another juror."

The clerk pulled another slip from the box. "Beatrice Clark."

An older woman stood and walked forward, passing Mr. Zell as he left the courtroom. She was short and fairly heavy, wearing a long flowered dress. She sat vacated by Mr. Zell.

The judge looked down at plaintiffs' counsel. "You may inquire."

Merriman looked down at the papers in front of him and then back at the prospective juror. "Mrs. Clark, I see by your questionnaire that you're a widow and live in Gearhart. How long since you husband pass on?"

"It's been eleven years now; he died of a heart attack at sixty-nine."

Merriman smiled. "Then Mrs. Clark, if you don't mind, you must be close to eighty?"

She laughed. "I don't mind at all. I'm proud to say I'm seventy-eight."

Merriman laughed also. "What did you husband do for a living."

"Nothing at the time of his death. He'd been retired since sixty-five, but he was a doctor before that. He was as family doctor in Seaside."

Merriman looked down at the paper again. He read and looked up at Mrs. Clark. "I see here, Mrs. Clark that you've served as a juror several times before. Can you tell us about that?"

"Surely. I've served three times before. Last time was three years ago. I sat on a criminal case then. Earlier, I sat on an auto accident case, involving just property damage. The first time was back in the '50s. I don't remember much about that case, except that if was a criminal one."

"Well then, you know there's a difference in the degree of proof required in a civil case as opposed to a criminal case. You have to have proof beyond a reasonable doubt to convict in a criminal case, but in a civil case all that is required is a preponderance of the evidence, isn't that what you remembered?"

"I think so, but I better rely on what the judge says here."

Merriman smiled. "I think you better, also. Mrs. Clark I'm sure you heard all the questions I asked the other jurors, so I'm not going to bore you with repeating them. Just let me ask you this. Will you help me if I prove to you beyond a reasonable doubt that Amy Richards and her children are entitled a substantial verdict against Monarch Motors and Legion Oil by voting for such a verdict?"

"Mr. Merriman, I can assure you that I'll listen and follow the court's instructions, and, if I feel that you've proven your case, I will not hesitate to find in your clients favor. I can't tell you how substantial that verdict will be. That also will be based upon the evidence."

"Thank you, Mrs. Clark. Pass the juror for cause, your Honor."

"Mr. O'Shea?" the judge said.

Barry looked at the judge. "Yes, your Honor." Then he looked up at Mrs. Clark. "Mrs. Clark have we met. You look familiar to me."

"Have you ever stayed in Gearhart?"

"A number of times. My wife's parents have a home there, Henry and Hazel Murdock."

"I know the Murdock's well. I really don't recall you, but you must have seen me at your in-laws a time or two."

"Do you think that might affect your verdict in this case?"

"Certainly not. I like your in-laws very much, but that won't make any difference in this case."

"Thank you, Mrs. Clark. We'll pass the juror, your Honor."

"We'll pass the juror, your Honor," Sturgis said quickly.

The judge looked down at the defendants' counsels' table. "Defendants first challenge."

Barry and Sturgis conferred. The each of them talked quietly to Matcheck and Wilkerson respectively. The conversations took several minutes.

Finally, Barry stood and looked up at the judge. "Defendants are satisfied, your Honor."

The judge looked down at plaintiffs' counsels' table. "Take you next challenge."

Merriman and Wilson talked quietly. Merriman then turned and had a discussion with Amy Ralston. Amy Ralston shook her head. Merriman conferred again with Wilson, and again turned and talked the Amy Ralston. Again she shook her head, sternly this time.

Merriman stood and looked up at the judge. "Plaintiffs are satisfied."

The judge looked down at the clerk. "Swear the jury."

The clerk asked the twelve jurors to stand and gave them the oath. "I will," each juror said.

The judge looked out at the courtroom. "We will take our evening recess now." He turned to the jury. "Let me caution you do not talk to anyone about this case at any time before you retire at the end of the case after I've given you the instructions as to the law. Anyone includes your fellow jurors. Don't discuss the case among yourselves until I've given you the instructions as to the law. Don't read anything about this case in the newspapers, and, if you hear anything about the case on the radio or television, immediately turn it off or leave the room. I don't know if there will be anything about this case in the newspapers or on the radio or television, but there might be. You're to keep an open mind about this case until you've heard all of the evidence and my instructions. Are there any questions?"

There were none.

"Then you're excused. Be back in you're jury room by eight-fifteen tomorrow morning. We'll resume this case promptly at eight-thirty." He looked at counsel. "Counsel, please remain after the jury has left."

The bailiff escorted the jury to the jury room.

"One matter that we have not discussed is plaintiffs claim for punitive damages against Monarch Motors," he said. "It my practice when a charge of punitive damages is made to limit any comments about it until there has been a showing that punitive damages are appropriate. Therefore, Mr. Merriman, I don't want you to say anything about them in you opening statement. Is that understood?"

Merriman stood. "Yes, your Honor."

"We will wait until you have concluded your clients' case to revisit the matter. I'll see you at eight-thirty in the morning."

25

WEDNESDAY MORNING, THE clouds had left, and the sun shown down on a beautiful crisp May day. As ordered, everyone, including the jury, sat quietly in the courtroom at twenty after eight that morning.

Promptly at eight-thirty the judge entered. "Please rise," the bailiff said, and everyone did.

The judge took the bench and sat. He looked out at the courtroom. "Please be seated. We're now ready for the opening statements by the lawyers. In the opening statement each lawyer will tell you what the expect to prove. It is not an argument; but rather a statement of the evidence, so I do not expect any arguments. One of the plaintiffs' lawyers will go first, followed by Monarch's lawyer and then Legion's lawyer. Mr. Merriman will you be giving the statement for the plaintiff?"

Merriman rose. "Yes, your Honor." He then walked behind the counsel table, stood behind Amy, and turned to face the jury. "Ladies and gentlemen, as you know I represent Amy Ralston," and he placed his hand on her shoulder, "and her children, Michelle and Dustin. They will be here later in the trial so that you can see and hear them. Amy Ralston's now thirty-four years old. On May twenty-ninth, 1973, almost a year ago, she was thirty-three. Michelle is eleven years old and in the sixth grade. Dustin is six years old and in the first grade. On May twenty-ninth 1973 Michelle was ten, and Dustin was five."

He walked over in front of the jury, leaned forward slightly and placed his hands on the railing in front of the jury box. "On May twenty-ninth, 1973 at approximately five p.m. Amy's husband, Michael, and her seven year old son, Bruce, lost their lives when their Caravan vehicle, which Michael was driving and in which Bruce was a passenger, traveling toward Portland going about fifty-five mph was hit head-on in their lane of travel by a pickup truck pulling a cattle trailer, going the opposite direction also at around fifty-five mph. The impact of such a collision can't adequately be described, except to say it was horrific! Amy survived, but is now paralyzed for life from the waist down. Both she and Michelle were unconscious at the scene, and Michelle had injuries to her head and internal organs. Dustin was conscious and crying uncontrollably with an injured arm and with a huge cut on one leg."

He paused and eyed the jury. Then somewhat softly he began again. "The pickup truck was driven by a Lyle Bentwood, an employee of Towson Dairy, located just off highway 101 south of Seaside, Oregon. Bentwood had been to a cattle yard just off of I5 north of Portland where he picked up two Holstein dairy cows, and he was driving them back down to the coast at the time of the accident. The accident happened as Bentwood drove down a hill on a straight stretch just west of the Elderberry Inn and as the Ralston's had just exited a left hand turn and were proceeding up the hill toward Portland. Memorial Day fell on May twenty-eighth that year, and the Ralston's had just finished a long weekend visit to the beach in Gearhart. They left the beach to return home Tuesday evening a little after four."

He paused again and spoke in a loud whisper. "Needless to say, what started out as a wonderful weekend ended tragically for the surviving Ralstons."

He stepped back and looked at each of the jurors. "The dairy had a small amount of insurance, and its insurance company quickly stepped forward and paid the full amount of the policy to the Ralstons. But their damage from the accident far exceeds that amount, so Amy Ralston retained Mr. Wilson here." He turned and pointed at Wilson. "And he associated my firm to assist him in advising her. We have investigated the events leading up to the accident and found that a few seconds before it occurred the hood on the pickup flew up blinding the driver and caused him to loose control of the pickup, which crossed the highway's centerline and ran head-on into the Ralston's Caravan. The left front of the pickup collided with the left front of the Caravan, and the force of the impact drove the pickup through the drivers' seat instantly killing Michael Ralston and into and over the rear seat of the Caravan behind Michael where Bruce sat, also killing him instantly. After the collision, the pickup and its trailer separated, and the pickup slide on its right side down the highway some distance. The trailer jack-knifed and broke loose from the pickup and went off the highway on the north side, down an embankment and crashed into a tree. Collision pinned Mr. Bentwood inside the pick-up, and he received multiple serious injuries. The firemen at the scene finally rescued him using the jaws-of-life instrument. We will present you with evidence from the police officers, fire personnel and medics who arrived at the scene, assisted in the removal of the injured persons and conducted an investigation at the scene."

He walked forward again and rested his hands on the railing of the jury box. "We hired several engineers to assist us in studying the vehicles involve and the accident. They advised us of several serious defects in the Monarch pickup that caused the accident. We also discovered that the pickup had been in a previous accident. We will bring to you the person who rebuilt the pickup and sold it to a dealer in Seaside who in turn sold it used to the dairy. That man will tell you that the damage done to the pickup in the previous accident was minor. That he did some body work on the pickup and painted it black. The engineers we retained found that the defects in the pickup were there when it was originally sold and were not affected by the previous accident."

He paused and looked at each juror. "We also learned in our investigation that about an hour before the accident, Mr. Bentwood stopped at a Legion Oil service station just off the highway in the neighborhood of the Vernonia junction for gas. The attendant raised the hood to check the water and oil level. When he was done, there is some question whether he secured the hood properly. Just before the hood flew up, the pickup ran over a piece of wood on the highway, which may have been enough to release the hood."

He rose up and looked at the jury. "Those are the facts that will establish that Monarch Motors, and maybe Legion Oil, is or are liable to the Ralstons for their physical and emotional injuries caused in this accident and for their losses they suffered due to the deaths of their husband and father." He walked over to an easel with a white pad mounted on it. He took a black grease pencil and began writing on the pad. "The evidence of the damages suffered by these people will be presented to you by hospital records, their doctor, their own testimony and the analysis of their situation by an economist. I won't go into all of that now, but let me summarize about what you hear. First of all, past medical and funeral expenses come to about one hundred and seventy-five thousand dollars."

He wrote that figure opposite medical and funeral expenses to date. "Amy's paralysis will require future medical and related expenses of about twenty thousand dollars per year for the rest of her life. She is thirty-four and her life expectancy is at least seventy-five years. That's forty-one years times twenty thousand dollars equaling eight hundred twenty thousand dollars."

He wrote that figure down on the sheet as future medical. "Amy has had to hire Willie and Mina Sorrento as a house-man and cook for two thousand two hundred and fifty dollars a month plus room and board. That expense from August sixth, 1973 to date has amounted to twenty thousand five hundred dollars, and she will incur future charges during her lifetime in the approximate amount of nine hundred thousand dollars.

He wrote that figure that figure down as hired help. "Michael had just been made a junior partner of his accounting firm where he was projected to work at least thirty more years. He earned fifty thousand dollars a year before his death and was projected to earn seventy-five thousand the first year of his partnership. Over the thirty years his yearly income would continue to rise to the level of at least two hundred thousand dollars per year. If we assume an average of one hundred twenty-five thousand dollars per year for those thirty years, the family lost three million seven hundred fifty thousand dollars."

He wrote that figure down as loss of earnings. "Thus just the out-of-pocket damages are about five million, six hundred seventy-five thousand dollars. That figure doesn't allow anything for Amy's pain and suffering to date and the pain and suffering in the future for not having the use of the legs and the other inconveniences she suffered from being paralyzed. That figure doesn't allow for Micelle and Dustin's pain and suffering, and it doesn't allow anything for the emotional loss these people had suffered losing their father and husband. I suggest that ten million dollars would be a conservative figure of those losses. A verdict of at least sixteen million dollars will be called for. He wrote that figure down as pain, suffering and emotional loss.

He let that sink in for a moment. 'Thank you very much." He returned to counsel table and sat.

The judge looked down at Barry. "Mr. O'Shea, do you wish to make an opening statement at this time?"

Barry stood. "Yes, your Honor, a brief one." He walked over and stood in front of the jury. "Ladies and gentlemen, "there's basically no disagreement about how this tragic accident occurred or about the fact that the accident took the lives of Michael and Bruce Ralston. Also there is not dispute that Amy Ralston became paralyzed from the waist down as a result of the accident. The accident and these unfortunate consequences were not, however, caused by Monarch Motor Company."

Barry walked over to the easel Merriman had used. He turned over the paper Merriman had written on and produced a clean white sheet. Then he stood to the side of the easel and began writing as he spoke. "The evidence will show that the pickup vehicle was sold by one of Monarch's dealers in January 1970 and that when the vehicle was sold it was not in a defective condition as alleged by the plaintiffs." He wrote and underlined <u>at the time of sale vehicle NOT defective.</u> "Some of that evidence may occur during the plaintiffs' case, but you'll have to wait for most of it until we present the defendants" case. I believe that plaintiffs' only evidence that there was something wrong with the pickup that caused this accident will be way of opinion testimony from two so-called expert witnesses." He wrote and underlined <u>plaintiffs' evidence only opinion.</u> "At the end of the trial the judge will explain what weight you may give to that type of testimony. You will be given some help in that regard during our cross-examination of those witnesses. We will test their credibility, the credibility of those opinions and their qualifications to give such opinions. The evidence that we will later present will be based upon facts and will show that the vehicle was not defective at the time of its sale and will disprove the plaintiffs' witnesses' opinion testimony." He wrote and underlined <u>monarch's evidence-factual-shows opinions not credible.</u> "Thank you." He walked back to his seat and sat.

The judge looked down toward Sturgis. "Mr. Sturgis, do you desire to make an opening statement at this time?"

Sturgis got up. "Yes, your honor, and I likewise will be brief." He walked over to the jury and placed a hand on the railing of the jury box. "Ladies and gentlemen, the only claim against Legion Oil is that it failed to adequately secure the hood latching mechanism on the pickup prior to the accident. There will be no evidence to support this claim. The only person with knowledge about this charge is the attendant, Pete Wilkerson. He will testify that he always secures the hood and tests it by trying to pull up on the hood. He believes he did this on the occasion when he serviced the vehicle right before the accident. Legion Oil is not responsible for this accident and any of the unfortunate results of it. Thank you." Sturgis sat down.

The judge said, "We'll break for lunch. Be back and be ready to continue the trial at one-thirty."

Promptly at one-thirty the judge took the bench. "Call plaintiffs' first witness."

Merriman stood, turned and looked back. "Plaintiffs call Lyle Bentwood."

A heavy set middle-aged man dressed in a plaid long sleeved shirt and faded denim coveralls, caring a blue striped cap walked forward with a decided limp. When he arrived at the clerk's desk he stopped.

The clerk stood. "Please raise your right hand," she said. "Do you swear that your testimony will be the truth, the whole truth, and nothing but the truth, so help you God?"

"I do," the man replied.

The clerk motioned toward a witness chair to the right of the judge and in front of the jury box. "Please be seated and tell the court and jury your name."

The man sat. "My name is Lyle Bentwood."

The judge looked at Merriman. "You may inquire, Mr. Merriman."

Merriman remained seated. He looked at the witness. "Good Day, Mr. Bentwood."

Bentwood smiled. "Hi."

Merriman looked at the jury and saw several of them smile back at Bentwood. He looked back at Bentwood. "Mr. Bentwood, tell the jury about yourself, where you work, what you do, and why you're here."

Bentwood shifted in his seat; then turned to the jury. "I work for Towson Dairy in Seaside. I'm kind of a jack-of-all-trades. I do lots of jobs including handling the cows, milking them and driving equipment and vehicles. I'm here because you subpoenaed me, probably because I was the driver of the pickup involved in the accident."

"You mean the head-on accident of May twenty-nine, 1973 at about five p.m. on Highway 26 near the Elderberry Inn?"

Bentwood looked down. "Yep, that's the one," he said softly.

"You were going west pulling a cattle trailer, weren't you?"

"Yeah."

"Where were you coming from?"

"The stockyards on the north side of Portland. I'd picked up to Holstein cows and was bringing them back to the dairy."

"Did you stop anywhere on the trip before the accident?"

"Yeah. I stopped at the Legion Oil station just east of the Vernonia junction for gas."

"Tell the jury what happened at that gas station."

"Like I said I stopped for gas. Had the attendant fill'er up. Then the attendant asked if I wanted the water and oil levels checked, and I said, 'yes.' He opened the hood, fiddled around under there, and put the hood back down. He told me the water and oil was fine. I paid him with a credit card and went on my way."

"You said he put the hood down. How did he do that?"

"I don't know. Can't remember exactly. I imagine he just dropped the hood or gave it a push. Anyway it went down."

"Did he say anything about the hood or how it went down or anything about it?"

"No."

"When did you notice something going wrong?"

"I was on the straight stretch just after Elderberry Inn, going down the hill, when suddenly something hit the windshield and blinded me. I tried to control the truck but almost immediately there was a terrible crash and everything went blank. The next thing I remember was waking up in an ambulance with a lot of pain, especially in my right leg."

"Do you remember seeing the Caravan before the accident?"

"No."

"How fast were you traveling when something hit your windshield?"

"About fifty to fifty-five."

Merriman paused, looked down at his notes and then back up at Bentwood. "Do you remember running over something in the road just prior to something hitting your windshield?"

"You know, I kind'a do remember running over something, like a board or small log. I'm not sure, though."

"Thank you. I have no further questions."

The judge frowned and looked a Barry. "Mr. O'Shea?"

Barry remained seated and looked directly at Bentwood. "Mr. Bentwood, did you regularly drive that pickup?"

"Yeah. I normally drove it."

"Were you employed at the dairy in September 1972 when Mr. Towson purchased it from Jorgenson Motors in Seaside?"

"Yeah."

"As I understand it, the pickup was black in color?"

"That's right."

"From September 1972 until late May 1973 did you ever have any trouble with the hood?"

"Not as far as I know."

"Did you ever raise the hood?"

Bentwood paused and thought. "Now that you mention it, I don't think I ever raised it, and I don't think it was ever raised when I was driving it. We did, however, have it serviced at Jorgenson Motors, so they might have raised it, probably did."

"Thank you. Barry looked at the judge. "Nothing further, your Honor."

The judge looked down at Sturgis.

Sturgis remained seated and said, "No questions."

The judge looked at Bentwood. "You may step down, and you're excused." The judge looked back to Merriman. "Call your next witness."

Merriman stood and looked behind the defendants counsel table. "Plaintiffs call Pete Wilkerson."

Wilkerson stood, walked forward, and took the oath from the clerk. He was dressed in a kaki shirt and trousers with a red Legion Oil emblem on one side of the shirt and a red name tag, Pete, on the other. He sat in the witness chair and looked at the jury. "My name is Pete Wilkerson, and I'm employed as a service station manager by Legion Oil Company."

Merriman looked at the witness. "Mr. Wilkerson, I understand that you serviced the Towson Dairy pickup the afternoon of May twenty-ninth, 1973, is that correct?"

"Yes, sir, I filled his tank and checked his water and oil levels."

"You had to raise the hood to do that?"

"Yes, sir."

"How did you close the hood after checking the water and oil levels?"

"The same way I always did it. I closed the hood by lowering it and pushing down solid. Then using my hand I check it by trying to raise it without pressing the lever under where it attaches to the vehicle."

"Did you do that in this instance, on May twenty-ninth, 1973 in the late afternoon?"

"Well, I don't remember exactly, but I'm sure I did."

"Thank you," Merriman said. "I have nothing further."

"No questions, your Honor," Barry quickly said.

Sturgis also followed quickly. "No questions."

The judge said, "We'll take out afternoon recess. Be back in you chairs in twenty minutes." He then left the bench.

—m—

When the court reconvened, the judge looked at the jury. "The next witnesses will be two state police officers, two fireman, two medics, two tow truck drivers and a medical examiner. So we don't have to bring any of them back tomorrow, we may work a little longer this afternoon.

Merriman then called the sergeant and officer Runningshoe, who responded to the scene and investigated the accident. They testified to what was in the police report.

Merriman looked at the sergeant. "Did you find the point of impact?"

"Yes, it was the left front of the pickup and left front of the Caravan in the east bound lane."

"Did you inspect the condition of the pickup?"

He described the damage. "And the hood was lying back against the windshield," he said after he finished describing the damage.

Later Merriman looked at officer Runningshoe. "Did you check the road up the hill in the direction the pickup was traveling?"

"Yes, I walked back about a quarter of a mile and found a small log in his lane of travel. We discussed it and both concluded that if the pickup ran over the log, it might have jarred the hood loose."

"Did you see the driver of the van?"

"Yes. One of the firemen discovered him and called me. I went over and looked. He was nearly decapitated. Then the fireman pointed to the seat just behind him, noting the indentation made by the front wheel of the pickup and pointing down under it. I saw a young boy who had been literally run over. Both individuals were dead."

Next Merriman called two of the fireman, two of the medics who assisted the injured at the scene and transporting them to the hospital, the tow truck drivers and the medical examiner. They testified to their activities at the accident scene and the condition and injuries of the surviving occupants.

After the last medic testified, the judge looked at the jury. "My prediction has proved correct as it is now nearly six-thirty. We appreciate your patience. That'll be all for this evening. We'll reconvene at eight-thirty tomorrow morning.

26

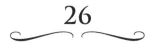

THURSDAY WAS ANOTHER clear crisp Day. Court reconvened at eight-thirty.

Merriman quickly stood. "Plaintiffs call as their next witness Wayland Chang."

A slim man of Chinese ancestry, dressed a tan tropical suit with a white dress shirt, a paisley tie and brown loafers, walked steadily up through the bar and stopped at the clerks table. He had a thin file in his hand. He was given the oath, sat in the witness chair, setting the file on the ledge beside him, and turned to the jury. "My name is Wayland Chang, and I reside in Portland."

Merriman sat down and looked up at Chang. "Mr. Chang, will you tell the jury about yourself, your education, and your occupation?"

"I am thirty-seven years old and practice engineering in Portland as a consulting engineer. I attended Oregon State University where I graduated in 1969 with a BS in mechanical engineering. I worked as a mechanical engineer for Caterpillar Tractor in Dallas for seven years, designing and supervising manufacturing of various Caterpillar products. I've been in the consulting business with Rutledge Engineers for the past eight years."

"As a consultant, have you had occasions consult with lawyers concerning accidents involving motor vehicles?"

"Yes, many times."

"In some of those case did your analysis involve whether the accident was caused by a defect in one of the vehicles?"

"Yes, I've been called upon to do such an analysis on numerous occasions."

"Were you hired in those cases by both plaintiff's lawyers and defense lawyers?"

"Yes, I have been."

"Are you familiar with Mr. O'Shea?

Chang looked at Barry and smiled. "Yes, he's cross examined me on a number of occasions, and he hired me on one occasion."

Merriman paused, looked down at his notes and then back up at Chang. "Mr. Chang, how did you get involved in this case?"

Chang looked at the back of the courtroom where Monica Richards sat. "On August sixth, 1973 I was hired by Monica Richards of Western Indemnity. She told me about the collision on May twenty-ninth and the vehicles involved, a 1967 Caravan manufactured by WCI and a 1970 Monarch pickup. She told me that the hood flew up on the pickup, causing the driver to loose control, and the pickup veered into the oncoming lane and hit the Caravan."

Chang turned and faced the jury. "She hired me to look at the pickup and see if I could find out why its hood flew up. I told her that I had no conflict, and I would look into it for her. I asked her where the vehicles were, and she answered that they were in a state police lot near Aloha. She said she would get the titles to both vehicles in a couple of days, and she wanted me to arrange to pick them up after that and have them towed to wherever I could store them for inspection. I told her I would make those arrangements and call her. She said she would meet me at the lot with the titles so I could take possession of the vehicles. She and I met at the lot on August twentieth."

"Did you inspect the pickup at the lot?"

"Yes."

"Describe your inspection."

"I examined its hood latching mechanism. Although there was substantial damage to the hood, the latching mechanism near the radiator appeared to be intact. I looked at the mating mechanism under the hood, but couldn't pull the hood down and attach it because of the damage. I could see, however, how the pointed mechanism under the hood was supposed to go down into the hole near the radiator and latch in a notch there."

He looked at Merriman. "What I didn't see disturbed me." He looked back at the jury. "There wasn't any device to secure the hood if it wasn't fully in the notch. I felt there should be a double catch. One you have to release with you hand before the hood would come loose and rise. I told Monica I wanted to look at it further when I got it into our garage, but it appeared to me that unless the last person who opened the hood made sure it was fully latched, it could fly up if the front end of the vehicle was jostled."

Merriman sat back in his chair and stared at the ceiling of the courtroom for a moment. Then he looked back at Chang. "Was there a time when we met and I became you client?"

Chang stared at Merriman with his oval blue eyes. "Yes, on Thursday morning, September fifth, Monica introduced you to me at the garage and had me explain my theory to you. We went into the garage, and I showed you at the pickup how the hood could fly up."

"Mr. Chang, do have an opinion whether the pickup was in a defective condition when it was initially sold?"

"Yes, I do."

"What is that opinion?"

Chang looked at the jury. "I believe the vehicle at that time was in a defective condition in that the hood, if not securely fastened, could fly up if the vehicle was jostled. The vehicle should have had a double catch so that could not happen."

"Thank you, Mr. Chang. I have nothing further."

"Mr. O'Shea?" the judge said.

Barry looked at the judge. "May I have permission to approach the witness? I'd like to look at the file he has with him."

"Certainly, and if you need time to examine it, we can take a short recess."

Barry stood and walked up to Chang. Chang gave him the file, and Barry quickly perused it.

"That won't be necessary, your Honor." And Barry returned the file to Chang. He stood in front of Chang.

"Mr. Chang, if I understand your testimony, you were originally hired by the Towson Dairy's insurance carrier to find someone else responsible for this accident, isn't that about right?"

Chang looked at Barry. "Well, I was hired to examine the pickup."

"Yes, but you were hired to find something wrong with it, weren't you? Otherwise, the dairy would be responsible for the accident, since its pickup drove across the centerline into the Ralston vehicle."

"Well, after I made my inspection I could see why the hood flew up and blinded the driver."

"But you don't know that the hood flew up, do you?"

"Not personally, no, but it was up against the windshield when I first saw it, and the police report said it flew up."

"You know, don't you, that if the vehicle is in the condition it was when originally sold, and the hood was properly secured with the pointer mechanism fully down so it latches in the notch, the hood cannot fly up or come up without being properly released, don't you?"

"Yes, that's right."

"So something else had to occur in this instance if the hood flew up? Someone had to pull the hood latch release lever, or someone had to fail to fully latch the hood after opening it, or some other circumstance had to occur that wasn't present when the vehicle was originally sold."

Chang continued to look at Barry. "I think your right, but I don't know what you mean by some other circumstance had to occur."

Barry smiled at Chang. "Well, let's say for example the vehicle was in another accident and the hood wasn't repaired right or was replaced and not aligned properly. Would you feel the manufacturer was responsible if something like that caused the hood to fly up?"

"Of course not."

"Thank you, Mr. Chang. I have no further questions."

"Mr. Sturgis?" the judge said.

"No questions, you Honor."

"Any further questions, Mr. Merriman?"

"Just one, your Honor. Mr. Chang, you don't know that the vehicle had been improperly repaired, do you?"

"No."

The judge turned and looked at Chang. "You may step down, and you're excused." He looked at Merriman. "Call you next witness."

"Plaintiffs call Roger Winchester."

A bald, fairly short, and overweight man, dressed in working clothes, came from the rear of the courtroom, walked slowly forward, and stopped at the clerk's desk.

After the clerk gave him the oath, he stared at her with sagging eyes and said, "Yep." Then he shuffled over the witness chair and sat. "I'm Roger Winchester, the owner of Roger's Reck and Rebuild," he said.

Merriman had been looking down at something on the table. He looked up at Winchester and brushed his long blonde hair back. "How are you, Mr. Winchester?"

Winchester looked down at Merriman. "I'm doing just fine, thank you."

"Where is your place of business?"

"Kelso, Kelso, Washington," he replied.

"We're dealing with a black 1970 Monarch pickup in this case, that I believe you sold to Jorgenson Motors in Seaside in September 1970, do you remember that?"

Winchester continued to look at Merriman. "That's what it said on that receipt that good looking gal showed me last September."

"Where did you get the vehicle?"

"If I remember right I picked it up at an auction yard down in Sacramento in the fall of '70. It'd been in a wreck, but it seemed in pretty good shape so I bought it to fix up and sell."

"Did you do that?"

"Sure, that's my business."

"Do you have any records of what you did to it?"

"Naw, I don't keep things like that, but I remember that pickup and what we did to it."

"Tell the jury what you did to the pickup?"

Winchester turned to the jury. "We knocked out some dents out and repainted it. I checked it real close. There weren't any bends it the frame. The previous accident didn't wreck it. It was more like a fender-bender, but it needed a new coat of paint."

"Was there anything wrong with the hood?"

"You know that lady told me about the accident she was involved with. Said the hood flew up and cause a head-on. The hood wasn't damaged when we worked on the vehicle. It was snug when we sold it. I didn't do anything to the hood."

"You sure of that."

"Yeah, I'm sure."

Merriman smiled at him. "Thank you, Mr. Winchester. I have no further questions."

The judge looked down at Barry. "Mr. O'Shea?"

Barry looked at Winchester trying to make eye contact, but Winchester's eyes were directed downward. "Mr. Winchester?"

Winchester looked up. "Yes."

"A title search of the vehicle shows a new title issued in your name. That usually means that you rebuilt it. Isn't that really what you did?"

"No, here in Washington you can have the title issued in your name for any reason," Winchester said looking at Barry. "I said all I did to the pickup was repair some dents and repaint it, and I say that again."

"But there's no question that the pickup you bought in Sacramento at the auction house is the same one you sold to Jorgenson Motors in Seaside, is that right?"

"Yeah."

"Incidentally, what color was the pickup before you painted it black?" Barry asked.

"Green," Winchester replied.

Barry looked at the judge. "No further questions, your Honor."

"Mr. Sturgis?" the judge said.

Sturgis said, "No questions, your Honor."

"We'll take the morning recess," the judge said. "Be back and ready to resume in twenty minutes."

—m—

In the hall outside of the courtroom Barry and Matcheck conferred away from the others. "That's a bunch of bullshit," Matcheck said quietly. "We know he replaced the hood."

"Unfortunately, we'll probably have to wait until it's our turn to show that," Barry said. "I did all I could to give the jury a hint that something more is coming."

Matcheck shook his head. "Somewhere I've heard that the insurance company settled after the first accident on the basis that the pickup was totaled."

"You're right, but we'll have to wait to prove it."

The court reconvened, and the judge looked down at Merriman. "Call you next witness."

Merriman stood and looked to the rear of the courtroom. "Plaintiffs call Penn Rogaine."

A nattily dressed thin man wearing a tight fitting gray suit with a blue shirt and a red Pokka-dot tie walked smartly forward. He had a sharp face and a full head of black hair neatly parted and combed. He carried a black leather case. After he had been given the oath and sat in the witness chair, he looked straight ahead with his penetrating blue eyes. "My name is Penn Rogaine, and I do business as Rogaine Engineering in Carson, California," he said following the clerks instruction to state his name.

Merriman stood beside the table and smiled at him. "Mr. Rogaine, you are an engineer?"

Rogaine looked at the jury. "Yes, I am."

"Tell the jury about yourself, your schooling and work history."

Again Rogaine looked at the jury. "I started college at Indiana University in Bloomington, Indiana majoring in engineering. I went there for two years and transferred to the University of California in Los Angeles, more commonly referred to as UCLA, where I got a degree in design engineering in 1958. I worked for several after-market firms designing vehicle parts for ten years. I set up my consulting firm in Carson six years ago. I do engineering consulting for many companies and lawyers."

"Are you a licensed engineer?"

"Yes, in the state of California."

Merriman still stood. "Mr. Rogaine, did I hire you to consult with me on aspects of this case?"

Rogaine turned to the jury. "Yes, you did, and specifically you asked me to analyze the design of the pickup's hood in connection with the Ralston accident."

"Did you do that?"

"Yes, sir."

Merriman looked at the jury as Rogaine answered. Then he turned and looked again at Rogaine. "Tell the jury what you did."

Rogaine looked at Merriman. "May I refer to my file?"

"Surely."

Rogaine brought up his case, laid it on a shelf beside him, opened it and brought out a small file. He opened the file and held in his lap. He shuffled through some papers, pulled out one and reviewed it. Then he turned to the jury. "I attended an inspection of the vehicles involved in the accident on October ninth, 1973. They were located in a garage in Portland, Oregon. During the inspection I examined both damaged vehicles, but paid particular attention to the pickup and its hood design. The hood was open and back against the windshield. I studied this and concluded that with the hood in this position the driver could not see ahead."

Merriman again looked at the jury before turning back to Rogaine. "Did you arrive at any conclusions regarding the hood design of the pickup?"

"Yes, I did. One conclusion."

Merriman looked at the jury. "What was that conclusion?"

Rogaine looked at the jury. "It was my opinion that the hood was defectively designed, because when the hood comes up the driver cannot see ahead. There are a number of different designs that allow the driver to see ahead when the hood is raised. In those designs the portion of the hood nearest the windshield is concaved or curved, not straight like on this pickup. Then risers are built into the hinge that raised the hood, so that when the hood is up the curved portion rises, giving the driver a clear view of what's ahead."

He reached again into his case, pulled out a slim round can and held it out toward Merriman. "I took a movie of a driver inside a competitor's 1970 pickup with the hood up to show what I have described. May I show it to the jury?"

Merriman came forward and took the can. He gave it to the clerk and asked that it be marked exhibit 1. He then looked up at the judge. "I offer in evidence exhibit 1, which contains the film of the movie the witness took."

The judge looked at Barry. "Any objection to the exhibit?"

Barry looked at the judge. "I haven't seen what the film shows. Could we have a recess so they can show it to me?"

"Yes, that's what we'll do. Mr. Merriman, after the jury is taken to the jury room, you can set up whatever you need to show the film. Show it to Mr. O'Shea, and when I return before we bring the jury back, he can make whatever objection he wants. The court will be in recess."

The judge left the bench, and the bailiff took the jury out.

While Savage brought a projector forward and set it and a screen up, Barry walked to the back of the courtroom where Sarah sat and sat beside her.

In a soft voice he said, "What'd you think of Mr. Rogaine?"

She spoke with an equally soft voice. "Wow, he is like a movie star. The jury is eating him up, particularly the women."

"Have you heard anything from Ben about the UCLA transcripts?"

"He said this morning that he would check again and let you know when we're back at the house at noon."

Savage looked toward the back of the courtroom. "O'Shea, we're ready to show you the film."

Barry came forward and watched while Savage ran the projector. The screen showed Rogaine raising the hood of a competitor's pickup. The hood was curved and raised when he hood came up.

Next Rogaine was behind the steering wheel and the film showed a perfect view ahead with the hood fully raised.

—m—

The judge came back on the bench. "Counsel, do you have an objection?"

Barry stood. "No, your Honor."

"Then bring back the jury."

The jury returned, and Savage ran the projector, showing the jury the film on the screen in front of them. Barry noticed that Jesus Cruz, juror number 7, nodded to Dunstan O'Leary, juror number 8, when the film showed Rogaine looking through the windshield of the pickup with the hood fully raised.

When the film ended, Merriman stood. "No furthers questions, your Honor."

The judge said, "Mr. O'Shea?"

Barry remained seated. "Mr. Rogaine, you said you're a licensed engineer in the state of California. As a matter of fact you're licensed as a safety engineer, isn't that true?"

Rogaine stared at Barry. His blue eyes seemed to flash with anger. "You know it's true, or you wouldn't have asked it that way."

"Well, I asked you because you didn't tell us that. You just said you were licensed in California. California issues licenses to mechanical engineers, structural engineers, chemical engineers, aerospace engineers and civil engineers. Doesn't it?"

"Yes."

"But you don't have licenses in any of those fields, do you?"

"No."

"And you're not an automotive engineer, are you?"

Rogaine continue to stare at Barry. "No, but there isn't a license issued for that category."

Barry smiled at Rogaine. "But most consultants with that background are licensed mechanical engineers, aren't they?"

"Some are, some are not."

"Actually, a safety engineer is someone who deals with OSHA and workplace rules, isn't he?"

"That's part of it."

"It's a major part of it, isn't it?"

"I said it's a part of it."

"And you're not tested for that license, like you are for licenses in the fields of engineering I mentioned earlier, are you?"

"I believe that's right."

"Have you ever applied for a mechanical engineer license anywhere?"

"No."

Barry stood beside the table. "Mr. Rogaine, you said you worked for after-market firms for ten years designing vehicle parts. What are the names of those firms?"

"Well, there was Acme Ambulance. I worked there for six years. They configure ambulances from standard commercial vehicles?"

"Yes, and I believe you designed or worked on designs of interiors from a safety standpoint, isn't that true?"

"Yes."

"What other firms were there?"

"The other four years I worked for Bristol Chain in Carson."

"The only vehicle parts they make are tire chains. Is that what you helped design?"

Rogaine looked down. "Yes."

Barry stepped forward a few feet. "Mr. Rogaine, are you a member of the Screen Actor's Guild?"

Rogaine stared back at Barry. "Yes," he answered forcefully.

"You didn't give that as a part of your qualification for you expert testimony. That's probably because that membership has nothing to do with vehicle design?"

Rogaine continued to stare at Barry. "That's right, Mr. O'Shea, I'm a member because after I graduated from UCLA, I did some acting."

"Is that right? How long did you do that?"

"Well, I still do some of it."

"So your jobs for the ambulance configurer and the chain company weren't full time?"

"You could say that."

Barry sat down. "Mr. Rogaine, what was your major at Indiana?"

"I only went there a year and a half. I didn't have a major."

"Did you take any engineering courses?"

"Yeah, I took a basic mechanical engineering course and an ethics course."

"And I think you said that you were an engineering major at UCLA?"

"Yes."

"Were all you courses engineering courses?"

"Yes."

"Did you tell us what kind of engineering degree you got from UCLA?"

"Design engineering."

Barry tipped his head and looked confused. "I didn't know the engineering department gave such a degree."

"Is that a question?" Rogaine asked.

"I guess not. Mr. Rogaine, you really didn't do much work on this case, did you?"

Rogaine smiled at him. "I didn't have to. The design flaw stuck out like a sore thumb."

"Oh, come now, Mr. Rogaine. You know that the design of Monarch's hood is very common in the pickup industry, isn't it?"

"There's a lot of similarly designed hoods, but in my opinion its not a safe design as this case proves."

Barry looked at the judge. "No further questions, your Honor."

"Mr. Sturgis?"

"No questions, your Honor."

The judge turned to Rogaine. "You're excused. We'll take our noon recess. Be back and ready to go at one-thirty."

27

WHEN THE O'SHEA group got back to their house, Barry went quickly to his desk at the far end of the living room, sat in his chair and reached for the telephone. He dialed and an operator answered. "Give me Ben Lorenzo, Sheila."

A moment later Lorenzo came on the line. "Barry, glad you called. I talked to Leslie Smart an hour ago. He finally got the UCLA transcript, and it also contains the transcript from Indiana."

"Did you ask him generally what it contained?"

Lorenzo laughed. "Funny you should ask. I didn't have to. He knows what we're looking for. He told me Rogaine had a degree from the Art Department, but none from Engineering. Early on he took some engineering courses but did poorly so he transferred his major. He even flunked a mechanical engineering class. He did very well in acting courses. His degree is in art design. Has Rogaine taken the stand yet?"

"Unfortunately, yes. He's testified and been excused."

"I was afraid of that, that's why I sent a subpoena to him several weeks ago. He says he'll come up here with the transcripts whenever we need him."

"Tell him to fly up to Portland Sunday morning. You pick him up and bring him down here to our house."

"It's done." The phone call ended.

After court reconvened, Merriman put on his medical testimony. He introduced the medical records of Amy as exhibit 2, of Michelle as exhibit 3 and of Dustin as exhibit 4. Dr. Nathan Marshall testified to the injuries suffered by each plaintiff and to their future problems, particularly for Amy. He testified to the reasonableness of the medical bills and funeral expenses in the amount of one hundred seventy-four thousand dollars and seventy-two cents to date, and predicted that Amy's medical and related expenses in the future would be about twenty thousand dollars annually.

The judge recessed the case until Friday morning at eight-thirty.

Friday morning the beach mist returned and remained most of the day. The court session began at eight-thirty.

"Be seated and call you're next witness," said the judge as he sat behind the bench.

Wilson stood and looked back at the courtroom. "Call Willie Sorrento."

A husky young man with a dark crew cut dressed in a white uniform with short sleeves out of which protruded two hairy muscular arms walked steadily forward. He stopped at the clerk's desk, was given the oath, sat in the witness chair, and turned to face the jury. "My names Willie Sorrento and I live on SE Twenty-Ninth Street in Portland."

Wilson remained seated. "Mr. Sorrento, by whom are you employed?"

"Amy, I mean Mrs. Ralston."

"When did you begin your employment?"

"The day before she came home from the hospital, I believe it was August sixth a year ago. I was hired by Harry Sugerman to be

Mrs. Ralston's house man. My wife, Mina, was hired as her cook and housekeeper."

"And have you two acted in that capacity ever since?"

"Yes, sir."

"And I gather from the familiar way you referred to Mrs. Ralston, you have been very close to her?"

"Yes, sir, we sure have. We love that lady like our own. We feel the same way about the kids."

Then by means of Wilson's questions, Sorrento told the jury about Amy's days at home at first and how she progressed. It was a touching story of paralyzed lady's courage and will to live life as normal as possible. Several times Mr. Sorrento had to stop briefly as tears began to form in his eyes as he explained how hard Amy worked to achieve this. He testified that Amy paid them, he and Mina, two thousand two-hundred and fifty dollars per month plus their room and board for their services.

Wilson also handled the next witness, Mina Sorrento. Her testimony was nearly the same as her husband's.

The bailiff placed a second chair next to the witness chair, and Michelle and Dustin Ralston testified together briefly. Wilson did the questioning. They told the jury about what they remembered about the trip home before the accident and about their injuries and their recovery time.

Michelle's eyes teared up when she described how she missed her father and brother. Dustin sobbed when asked about this father and brother.

After Michelle and Dustin left the witness stand and the bailiff had removed the second chair, the judge looked at plaintiffs' counsel. "Call you next witness."

Merriman stood and turned around. "Plaintiffs call Jeffrey Babcock."

A tall man in his sixties walked forward. He wore a tweed suit and had slightly receding gray hair. He took the oath, sat in the witness chair. "My name is Jeffrey Babcock, and I am the resident managing partner of the Portland office of Silverman & Steele. It's a national accounting firm." Babcock said with a strong voice.

Merriman remained seated. "Did Michael Ralston practice accounting with your firm prior to his death?"

Babcock looked at the jury. "Yes, he did for fifteen years. He had just become a partner in the firm a month before."

"Are you familiar with his salary before his death, with what he would earn after becoming a partner and with how that figure would be expected to rise over the years?"

"Generally, yes."

"Did you consult with your head office in that regard?"

"Yes, we have a department that projects future income for our partners based on past experiences."

"Based on those facts can you give us some insight into Michael's future with the firm?"

Babcock looked at the jury. "Yes. Michael earned fifty thousand dollars the year before becoming a partner and was projected to earn seventy-five thousand dollars his first year as a partner. Thereafter, his earning would increase each year until they reached approximately two hundred thousand dollars after fifteen years of partnership. Thereafter, it would remain at least at that figure."

"Does your firm have a retirement account for your accountants?"

"Yes we do. The firm pays twenty-five thousand dollars per year into each accountant's retirement account."

"Thank you, Mr. Babcock," Merriman said.

Neither Barry nor Sturgis had any questions.

"Call your next witness," the judge said.

Merriman stood and looked to the rear of the courtroom. "We call Trevor Montgomery, your Honor."

A man in his middle fifties, who had been seated on the aisle of the last row of spectator benches, rose, walked through the bar an up to the clerk's desk. Medium height, thin and angular, his stride was brisk. He wore a light gray pinstriped suit, a solid red tie and highly polished brown shoes. He had a full head of well groomed brown hair and a pencil thin brown mustache. When the clerk recited the oath, he answered with a straight-forward, "I do."

When the man sat down in the witness chair, Merriman, still standing, looked at him. "Please state your name and occupation."

He looked at the jury. "My name is Trevor David Montgomery, and I am an economist."

"Where is your office?"

"I am partner in the Portland firm of Wheeler and Associates. Our firm consists of seven economists with varying specialties."

"Mr. Montgomery, what is your formal training and you work history?"

Montgomery still looked at the jury. "After getting out of the Navy during the war, I attended the University of Washington where I studied accounting and got a degree in accounting in 1948. I worked for an accounting firm in Portland for six years where I got my CPA. I returned to college at the University of Washington and studied economics for two years and received a master's degree in economics in 1956. I've practice economics ever since at the Wheeler firm."

Merriman looked at Montgomery. "Tell the jury what I hired you to do?"

Montgomery continued to look at the jury. "You hired me to calculate the amount of Mrs. Ralston's obligations for future expenses due to her paralysis, and the family's loss of income due to the death of Michael Ralston. I did that and have prepared a chart to show it." He reached into his case, produced a document and held it out. "Here it is."

Merriman walked up to him, took the document and handed it to the clerk. "Would you please mark this exhibit 5?" She did that. Merriman took the exhibit over to the counsels' table and showed it to Barry who then passed it to Sturgis. "I offer exhibit 5 into evidence."

"Is there any objection?" the judge said.

"I have no objection to the exhibit," Barry said. "But I don't see what Mr. Montgomery adds to the evidence we've already heard, except he's made a chart to reflect that evidence. So I would object to his testifying concerning the chart."

"I see your point," said the judge, "but I'm going to let him testify until it becomes excessively redundant."

Merriman took the exhibit, went forward and handed it to Montgomery. "Mr. Montgomery, will you please go down to the easel, bring it over in front of the jury, and, using the black grease pencil on the tray below the white pad, write the figures on exhibit 5 on the white pad so the jury can see them."

Montgomery got up and placed the easel in front of the jury. Then he stood beside it and held the exhibit out in front of him. "It is my understanding that it has been established that the future cost to Mrs. Ralston for medical and related expenses and for help due to her paralysis is approximately forty thousand per year." He wrote that on the easel. "She is thirty-four and according to the mortality tables has a life expectancy of at least seventy years." He wrote that on the pad. "Therefore she will incur those expenses for forty-one years, making the total expense the sum of one million six hundred forty thousand dollars." He wrote that figure down.

He went over to the other side of the easel, still holding the exhibit it in front of him. He looked at the jury as he wrote on the board. "As the last witness said, Michael would have made seventy-five thousand the first year of partnership had he lived." He wrote that figure on the white pad under a heading of future loss of income. "Over the next fifteen years his income would have steadily rise to the figure of two hundred thousand dollars. That's about an average of one hundred twenty-five thousand dollars per year for those fifteen years, or one million eight hundred seventy thousand dollars." He wrote that figure on the pad.

"Presuming that Michael Ralston retired at sixty-five, he had twenty-eight years of accounting income to look forward to. We have computed what his earning would have been for the first fifteen years of those twenty-eight years, leaving thirteen years at two hundred thousand dollars or two million six hundred thousand dollars. When he retired, he became entitled to the retirement package the firm had established for their members. The firm paid twenty-five thousand dollars a year into an accountant's retirement account. In Michael Ralston's case that would have been forty-three years, making contribution of one million seventy-five thousand dollars. But those contributions conservatively invested over forty-three years would have grown by at least 5% per year to an uncompounded figure of three million three hundred eighty-six thousand two hundred fifty dollars." He wrote that figure on the pad.

"Added all together the family lost at least nine million nine hundred seventy thousand two hundred fifty dollars. We know that the five percent interest per year would have compounded, so the family lost at least ten million dollars as a result of Michael death.

"Thank you, Mr. Montgomery," Merriman said sitting down.

"Mr. O'Shea?" the judge asked.

Barry stood and looked up at the judge. "Thank you, your Honor." Then he looked at the witness. "Mr. Montgomery, you know, of course that Mr. Merriman wants the jury to give his clients that $10 million dollars in one lump sum, where had Mr. Ralston lived out his normal life expectancy of say thirty-eight years, they would have received the money over the next thirty-eight years, isn't that so?"

"I guess your right, but I wasn't asked to do that."

Barry looked at the jury and then back at the witness. "I know that, but you could do that. In other words tell us what it would take to give them a lump sum today which they could conservatively invest to receive $10 million over the next thirty-eight years?"

Montgomery looked at Barry. "You mean you want me to do that now?"

Barry looked at the jury. "Yes, if you will?"

Montgomery reached inside his jacket, pulled out a calculator and began making calculations. After several minutes, he looked at the jury. "That figure is approximately six hundred thousand dollars."

"Thank you, Mr. Montgomery."

Sturgis quickly added, "No questions, your Honor."

The judge looked over at Montgomery. "Your excused. And we'll take our noon recess. Be back and ready to resume at two."

Sturgis quickly went over to Merriman. "I'd like to talk to you during the recess."

Merriman told him to meet him in his motel room in about a half and hour.

Back in the living room of their Victorian rental, Barry sat in one of the large chair beside the fireplace, and Matcheck and Notice occupied either end of the sofa each with an arm resting on the back of the sofa. Matcheck pulled a pack of Winston's from his shirt pocket, offered one to Notice and both lit up.

Barry had his glasses in his hand. He looked at Matcheck and Notice. "Well, how do you think the morning went?"

"Not too bad," Matcheck answered. It was the Ralston's show. It hurt some, but you couldn't have done much more than you did. I suppose this afternoon we'll get Amy, and I expect her to do very well. We knew this part of their case would be strong."

"I think Merriman will rest after Amy." He looked over his shoulder where Sarah sat at her desk. "Honey, has Ben got Lewis and that adjuster from Northern California up here?"

"Yes, they're ready to go this afternoon, if you think you'll need them?"

"Have them in the courtroom by two-thirty. If Merriman rests, I'll put them on. When the jury hears them and sees the photos of the pickup, they'll know that their leg has been pulled."

Matcheck laughed. "They sure will."

Barry said. "Let them stew over Winchester's testimony all weekend."

Barry looked over his shoulder again. "Sarah, honey, what's the story on Leslie Smart? When will he be here?"

"Ben said he'll bring him down Saturday night."

"Then let's plan to meet with him Sunday morning at ten."

—m—

Sturgis arrived at the motel at the scheduled time and Merriman invited him into his room. "What did you want to talk to me about?" Merriman asked smiling. He sat down at a chair next to a table.

Sturgis pull up another chair and sat. "I don't think you've made a case against Legion Oil, and I wanted you to know that I plan to move for a dismissal when you close."

"I expected you would, but I think there is just enough to hold you in," Merriman said. "And if you're in, I think there's a good chance the jury will find against both defendants. On the other hand, I agree our case against your client is weak. What will you pay to get out?"

"That's kind of what I expected from you. My client doesn't owe your client anything, but you've put on a sympatric case, and in the unlikely event that the judge doesn't grant my motion, I suppose there is a risk that you might get a verdict against Legion. We're prepared to give you one hundred thousand for your agreement not to oppose my motion."

Merriman laughed. "You gotta be kidding," he said with a wide smile across his face. "It's going to take a lot more than that."

"What's it going to take?"

"At least a half a million," Merriman said.

"I have to talk to my client, but I'm going to tell you that you're too high. I'll talk to you again after we get back in court."

28

FRIDAY AFTERNOON JUST before one-thirty, Sturgis spoke briefly with Merriman. While they were talking, the judge entered. "Call your next witness," he said.

Sturgis went back to defendants' counsel table and sat.

Merriman stood and looked up at the judge. "We'll call Amy Ralston, your Honor." He turned, walked around Amy's wheelchair and pushed it and Amy forward to the clerk's desk. Amy wore a white short-sleeved blouse with her blue chiffon skirt. Her long brown hair fell down her back and around her shoulders.

"Raise your right hand," the clerk said.

Amy did.

"Do you swear that the testimony you will give will be the truth, and the whole truth, so help you God?"

"I do." Amy said with her blue eyes sparkling.

"Mr. Merriman," the judge said, "please put her wheelchair in front of the witness chair at an angle so Mrs. Ralston can see both you and the jury."

Merriman did that, and then returned and sat down at counsels' table. He looked at Amy. "Mrs. Ralston, state your full name for the record and tell the jury where you live."

Amy looked at the jury, her blue eyes again sparkling. "My name is Amy Blackhurst Ralston, and I live in Portland in the Eastmoreland district."

"Mrs. Ralston, you were a passenger in the front seat of your Caravan vehicle when it was struck head-on by the Towson dairy pickup on May twenty-ninth, 1973, and you received your paraplegia from that accident, is that not true?"

"Yes."

"Do you remember anything about the accident?"

"Nothing. I remember we left Gearhart about four that evening and were driving to Portland on Highway 26, and the next thing I remember I was in an ambulance on some type of stretcher at Emanuel Hospital. As some medical people were lifting the stretcher out of the ambulance, I realized that I had no feeling from the waist down."

"Did you ever regain any feeling in that area?"

"No, never."

"Could you describe for the jury what you day is like, how you get around, how you do things and the like. Do you understand what I am asking?"

"Yes, I understand," she said looking at Merriman. Then she turned her eyes to the jury. "When I first got out of the hospital, I could really do nothing by myself. My house had been reconfigured by the Sugermen to make it wheelchair friendly, but I was almost useless with the wheelchair. But soon with the help of Willie I began to slowly get used to the wheelchair and its controls. They had this electric chair for me when I got home. Willie said he would be my legs, and he was for some time."

She took a drink from a glass of water that was resting on a tray over her lap. "I quickly learned that I could not rely totally on him, however. And slowly I began to take charge of myself and eventually became very self sufficient. By that I don't mean that I don't still rely on Willie and Mina for many things, but I can take care of myself now."

She then proceeded to tell the jury how she does every day tasks around the house, such as going to the bathroom, bathing, getting in and out of the bed, preparing meals, and tending to her children. She told them how she goes shopping with Willie and/or Mina, how she meets her children's teachers and attends school functions, and how she makes a social life for herself.

"How are Michelle and Dustin getting along?" Merriman asked.

"They've recovered from their injuries, but . . . ," she answered, pausing as tears swelled in her blue eyes. She dabbed them with a handkerchief. "I'm sorry, I know I can do this without crying. They still have many emotional problems. They miss their daddy terribly; I do too. They miss their brother, particularly Dustin. He idolized Bruce and can't seem to come to grips with the fact that he's gone for good. Many nights their sleep is interrupted by very bad dreams stemming from the accident and its consequences. Their good children and are growing up normally, but there's something missing and they haven't gotten over it, and, I guess to some extent they may never get over it."

Merriman went over the medical and related expenses the family had incurred. He established what the wheelchair cost and the cost of the reconfiguration of her house.

Merriman looked at Amy. "Tell the jury about Michael and Bruce, what kind of a husband and son they were, and how you got along with them?"

Amy's eyes gathered tears again as she looked the jury. "Michael was the best husband I could ever have asked for. I loved him, and he loved me. The Memorial Day vacation we had in Gearhart was typical of the family togetherness we had. Bruce was a good boy, a wonderful brother to the other two, and a loving son. I miss them both terribly," she sobbed.

"Thank you, Mrs. Ralston. That all I have."

Barry and Sturgis had no questions.

Merriman stood and faced the judge. "The plaintiffs rest, your Honor."

"We'll take our afternoon recess," the judge said. "Be back in your seats in twenty minutes, and we'll begin Monarch's case."

Sturgis looked up at the judge. "Before we do, your Honor I have a motion to make."

"Surely, Mr. Sturgis," the judge said. Then he looked down at the clerk. "Would you please take the jury out?"

The clerk got up, and took the jury to the jury room.

While that was going on Sturgis went over to plaintiffs' counsel table and spoke quietly to Merriman. Merriman nodded.

"Now, Mr. Sturgis, what is your motion?" asked the judge.

Sturgis returned to his table and stood. "Your Honor, I move to have my client dismiss from this case on the basis that plaintiffs have totally failed to establish that my client did anything wrong."

The judge looked a Merriman. "Mr. Merriman I'm inclined to agree. Do you want to be heard?"

"No, your Honor."

"Then the motion is granted. Will you prepare an order, Mr. Sturgis?"

"Thank you, your Honor. Yes, I will."

"Now, the rest of us will be in recess for twenty minutes."

Barry and Matcheck both got up. "I sensed something's been going on between Merriman and Sturgis, and now when Merriman declined to oppose that motion, I'm certain of it. I'll bet Sturgis paid something to get that silence." Then Barry looked at the back of the courtroom and turned back to Matcheck. "You talk to Notice. I see Ben back there with our two witnesses. I'm taking them outside to do a little last minute preparation."

He walked to the back of the courtroom where Lorenzo sat with two men. He walked up to Lorenzo. "Hi, Ben." He motioned to the two men. "I assume one of you is Rich Lewis and the other is this is Oliver Henry."

A man in a plaid jacket and a gray jacket stood. "I'm Rich Lewis," he said extending his hand. He was tall, but not as tall as Barry and had a full head of dark hair beginning to turn gray.

The other man also stood. He wore a green sport shirt and tan slacks. He was short and heavy and sported a goatee. "I'm Oliver Henry," he said also extending his hand.

Barry shook both of their hands. "Let's go out in the hall where we can talk."

The four of them left the courtroom.

In the hall, Sturgis came over to Barry. "Can I interrupt and speak to you, Barry, for a brief moment?"

"Sure, if you make it quick," Barry said. I have to confer with these two before I call them as witnesses."

They went a few feet away, and Sturgis explained about his meetings with Merriman and that this morning they settled with his client for two hundred fifty thousand dollars. He gave Barry a short paper explaining the settlement that he could give the judge if plaintiffs got a verdict.

When court resumed, the judge explained to the jury the reason Legion Oil was not longer involved. Then he looked down at Barry. "Are you ready to precede, Mr. O'Shea?"

Barry stood and faced the judge. "Yes, your Honor." He turned and looked at the rear of the courtroom. "Defendant Monarch Motors calls Rich Lewis."

Lewis came forward, took the oath, and sat in the witness chair. "My name is Rich Lewis," he said.

Barry sat down. "Mr. Lewis, you are here pursuant to a subpoena, aren't you?"

"Yes."

"What is you occupation and where do you live?"

Lewis looks at the jury. "I am a lawyer in California, and I live and practice in San Francisco."

"Mr. Lewis, in January 1970 did you purchase a Monarch ton and a half pickup?"

"Yes, I did a dark green one at the dealership on Van Ness Street."

"Do you happen to know the VIN, that's the vehicle identification number?"

"As a matter of fact I do. I still had the sales documents in a file." He took a small piece of paper out of his inside jacket pocket and looked at it. "I looked it up, and it's XVW4657224."

"Two years later, specifically on February eleventh, 1972 was that vehicle involved in an accident?"

He looked at the jury. "Yes, it was. My family was staying at a cabin we had north of Lake Tahoe. It was a Friday night, and I was driving up to the cabin to join them. I was on a two-lane road, Highway 89, just north of Truckee. I rounded a left turn in the road and saw a vehicle coming into my lane. I tried to brake and turn to the right, but the other vehicle side-swiped my pickup, causing it to veer more to the right, leave the road and smash into a large pine tree. Fortunately, I was wearing a seat belt so, other than some bruises on my knees and a cut on my forehead where I hit the steering wheel, I was not seriously hurt."

"What happened to that vehicle, the pickup?"

"A few days later an adjuster for my insurance company met me at the wrecking yard where it was towed in Truckee. He examined the damage to the pickup and said it was a total loss. He wrote me a check for six thousand two hundred fifty dollars and took possession of the vehicle."

"Do you remember the adjuster's name?"

"I had that in my file as well." He pulled a business card from his jacket pocket. "He was Oliver Henry."

"Thank you, Mr. Lewis." Barry turned to Merriman. "You may inquire."

Merriman stood. "Mr. Lewis, you say you're a lawyer. What kind of law do you practice, sir?"

"Taxation."

"What part of the vehicle was damage in that accident?"

"Well, it's been some time, but the driver's side and the front end."

"You didn't photograph the damage, did you?"

"No, I didn't, but I believe Mr. Henry did."

"Thank you, nothing further."

The judge turned to Lewis. "Then you're excused. Call your next witness."

Barry stood and faced the rear of the courtroom. "Call Mr. Henry."

Henry walked slowly forward. He had a belabored gait. He carried a small file folder. The clerk administered the oath.

After he sat down, Barry also sat and looked up at him. "Mr. Henry, will you state your occupation and you residence."

Henry faced the jury. "I'm an insurance adjuster for National Casualty Company, and I reside in Walnut Creek, California. But in February of '72 I lived and worked in Reno."

"You heard Mr. Lewis' testimony. Were you the adjuster that handled the settlement of his claim in February 1972?"

"Yes, I heard him, and yes, I was that adjuster."

"He said you totaled the pickup. What does that mean?"

"It means it would cost more to repair the vehicle than it was worth at that time. I estimated it would take between seven thousand and seventy-five hundred dollars to repair it. I was worth only six thousand two hundred fifty at the time."

"Did you take pictures of the damage to the pickup?"

"Yes, I did, and I had them blow up at your request."

Barry got up and walked to the witness. "May I have those pictures, one at a time?"

Henry opened the folder he had and passed the pictures to Barry one at a time. "The first one is of the right side of the pickup. The second one is of the front end. The third one is of the hood from the right side."

Barry had the picture marked exhibits 10, 11, and 12. He took them over and showed them to Merriman. Merriman spread them out on the table and examined them. Amy leaned forward and eyed them with disbelief. After Merriman returned them, Barry offered them in evidence. Since Merriman didn't object, the judge received them.

"What is the significance of picture exhibit 12?"

"This is the picture of the hood taken from the right side. As you can see it is completely buckled. It would have to be replaced in any repair or rebuild."

Barry looked up at the judge. "May I have the exhibits passed to the jury?"

"Certainly, Mr. Bailiff, will you pass the pictures to juror number one, who will pass them on."

As the pictures found their way to each juror, it was apparent that each juror looked at them with interest and some with shocked expressions on their faces. Sam Sousa, juror number 5, and Jerry Cohen, juror number 9 looked at Merriman with contempt.

"Do you have anything more, Mr. O'Shea?" the judge said, after the jury had seen all three pictures.

"Yes, your Honor, one more matter. Mr. Henry, after you paid Mr. Lewis, what did you do with the wrecked pickup?"

"I had it towed to a salvage lot near Sacramento where it was sold at auction?"

"Do you know who bought it?

"Yes." He reached into his trousers back pocket and pulled out a small paper." "I have the receipt right here," he said holding up the paper. "I was Roger Winchester of Roger's Reck & Rebuild out of Kelso, Washington."

Barry walked forward, took the receipt from him, and handed it to the clerk. "Please mark this exhibit 13."

She did.

Barry took back the receipt, took it over to Merriman, and handed it to him. "Offer exhibit 13."

"No objection," Merriman said, after examining the exhibit.

Amy again leaned forward and looked at the receipt over Merriman's shoulder. With a look of disgust, she shook her head.

"That's it your, Honor," Barry said.

Merriman had no questions.

"We'll take our evening recess," the judge said. "Please be ready to start promptly at eight-thirty on Monday morning. Have a good weekend."

When the plaintiffs' group gathered back at the motel after court, they met in the small conference room. Wilson, Savage and Richards sat at the conference table, Merriman stood with his back to the window, and Amy sat in her wheel chair with Willie Sorrento standing beside her at the opposite end of the room near the closed door.

Amy's blue eyes glared at Merriman. "That fucking Winchester is a god damn liar," she said in a tone totally our-of-character, "and everyone now knows it. How could you not check him out? Would it have been too much trouble to check the vehicles history?" She turned and glared at Richards. "And you, you smart ass slut, I know what you and Wayne have been doing at night here in the motel. Couldn't you, with all your insurance company muscle, have found this out before making me and my children the laughing stock of Astoria?" Then she lowered her head, put it into her hands and sobbed deeply.

Except for Amy's sobbing, the room was silent for a moment. Then Amy raised her head and dabbed her eyes with a handkerchief. She turned to Sorrento. "Willie, take me back to my room. Call room service for my dinner. I don't want to talk to any of these people further tonight."

Sorrento opened the door and wheeled Amy out and down the hall.

After she left, Richards turned and gazed up at Merriman, her hazel eyes penetrating. "Well, Mr. Hotshot lawyer, where do we go from here?"

"Why in the hell am I the scapegoat?" Merriman angrily said. "You were the one who came up with Winchester? Why didn't you check him out? Go down to the auction yard? Find out who was selling the pickup? If you had, we wouldn't be in this mess."

Savage interceded. "Calm down both of you. Playing the blame game isn't helping. So what that Winchester had to replace the hood. Shouldn't a replacement hood stay down if it's designed right?"

"Your right," Merriman said, "but it would have been a hell of a lot better if Winchester had said he replaced it with a Monarch part and was careful to align it properly. But he can't do that now. We'll just have to argue that."

Wilson and Savage left for their rooms.

Richard got up and headed for the door, still smarting.

Before she left, Merriman took hold of her arm and turned her. "Monica, baby, I'm sorry I was mad. You're a big enough girl to understand that. Let's go have some dinner and whatever comes next."

She glared at him. "Let go of my arm. I'm not buying anymore of your sweet-talk, and you can bet that 'whatever comes next' is not going to be in my bed." She left.

29

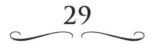

SUNDAY MORNING, BEN Lorenzo entered the Victorian house with Leslie Smart at about quarter to ten.

Smart at forty-six wore suntans and a yellow golf shirt. He had a tan complexion, a muscular build and blonde hair that hung just over his ears and was parted so a shock fell across the right side of his forehead just above his right eye. He carried a small and a large case into the house.

Barry, sitting at his desk reviewing some notes, looked up as they entered.

Lorenzo led Smart over to Barry. "Barry, I'd like you to meet Leslie Smart."

Barry rose and extended his right hand to Smart. "Boy, you don't know how glad I am to see you. The timing of you're arrival couldn't be better."

Smart grabbed Barry's hand and shook it. "I think you'll like what I've got."

"Let's go over to the conference table and lay it out."

They proceeded over to the table. Smart took a several page document from a case he brought with him, put it down on the table and sat with the document in front of him. Barry sat opposite him with Lorenzo at his side.

"What this is," Smart said, "is Rogaine's transcript from UCLA, and it incorporates his transcript from Indiana. You can see from the summary on the first page that he received a degree from the Theater and Art Department in acting and production with a minor in art design." He turned the page. "Most of his studies, particularly, in his last two years related to motion pictures, acting and production. He started out his second year concentrating on engineering with a secondary interest in acting, but as you can see his marks in the engineering course he took were Ds and Cs, while in the courses that related to acting, he did quiet well with As and Bs."

Barry studied the pages of the UCLA transcript.

"You can see that, while at Indiana his freshman year, he took mostly the required general liberal arts courses," Smart said, "but when he got a chance to specialize toward the end of that year, he took a basic engineering course and got a D."

Barry looked at the transcript. "It says basic engineering, is that different that mechanical engineering?"

"Of course. Mechanical engineering is a specialty of engineering, and courses in that are reserved for the junior and senior years. You might take an introduction course earlier, but he didn't at Indiana."

"I don't see any courses in ethics either?"

"No there isn't one."

Barry studied the UCLA transcript. "From this it appears that he was never an engineering major, am it correct?"

"Well, when he started, he initially concentrated on engineering, but as you can see he wasn't a good engineering student. He quickly shifted his course of study to motion pictures, acting and production, and that's what he got a degree in."

"And that was from the Theater and Art Department, not the Engineering Department, right?"

"Yes." He opened the large case and took out several large particle boards. "I took the liberty of making these so we could show the jury blowup what the pages of the transcript contain."

Barry took hold of them and studied them. "This is great. I've had the reporter make me a transcript of Rogaine's testimony. I'll read it to the jury and then show them these."

That same morning Merriman heard a knock on his suite door. He opened it as saw Amy in her wheelchair and Sorrento.

"Can we come in," Amy asked.

"Sure, I'll turn the TV off."

They came in and went into the sitting area of his room. Merriman sat in a stuffed chair opposite the TV. Sorrento wheeled Amy to a position where she was sitting opposite Merriman.

"I wanted to talk about some of my comments to you after court on Friday and to discuss how we proceed from here," she said.

"You were justified is saying those things. I relied to heavily on Richards and her company in the investigation. I should have looked farther into the first accident."

"That's water over the dam," Amy said, "but the truth, as we now know it, makes our case much harder. In fact, as I see it almost impossible."

"Now, hold on," Merriman said sternly. "We still have Rogaine's theory, which, if believed makes Monarch liable even though the vehicle had been in a bad accident. I don't think O'Shea's prepared to deal with the simple fact that the vehicle should have been designed so the driver could see ahead if the hood should fly up."

"You may be right. I just think the jury mistrusts us now."

"Just leave it to me, Amy. I've been in lot tougher situations and pulled out a big one. I'll do it here too."

On Monday the mist had given way to a clear and crisp morning. The weatherman predicted a temperature in the mid-seventies. Inside the courtroom, Barry stood. "Defendant Monarch will call Leslie Smart as its next witness, your Honor." He turned to the back of the courtroom and motioned Smart forward.

Smart now wore a glen plaid suit, a light yellow shirt and a paisley tie. He walked sprightly forward, carrying his small case, with a slight smile on his face. He stopped opposite the clerk and answered her oath with a strong voice. "I do."

After Smart sat in the witness chair, Barry, still seated, looked up at him. "Would you tell the jury your name, your residence and your occupation?"

Smart turned to face the jury. "I am Leslie Smart, and I live in Westwood, California. I'm the Director of Student Affairs for the University of California at Los Angeles, more popularly referred to as UCLA."

"As such are you the custodian of the transcripts of all students who have attended UCLA?"

"Yes, I am."

"Are you here today in response to a subpoena served upon you asking you to bring with you the transcript of the student named Penn Rogaine?"

"Yes, and I have the transcript here," he said, opening his case, pulling the document out of the case and holding it out. Barry rose, walked to the witness and took the document. He looked at it and handed it to the clerk. "Would you please mark this, exhibit 14?"

The clerk did.

Then he held the document up. "Do I understand your testimony that this is a copy of the transcript of Penn Rogaine when he was a student at UCLA?"

"Yes, and it also contains the transcript of Mr. Rogaine at the University of Indiana. When he transferred to UCLA, his Indiana transcript became a part of our records."

Barry took the transcript and placed it on counsel's table in front of Merriman. He waited while Merriman perused it. He noticed that Amy leaned forward and looked at the document over Merriman's shoulder. As she read it and as Merriman turned the pages, a distinct scowl began to form on her face.

When Merriman finished, Barry looked up at the judge. "Offer exhibit 14."

Merriman stood. "I object. Mr. Rogaine's transcript has no relevance. Mr. O'Shea asked him about his studies on cross examination. He can't now attempt to impeach the witness."

Barry started to say something, when the judge interrupted. "Why not? He's your so-called expert witness, and his qualification to give the expert opinion he gave are an issue here. Objection overruled; the exhibit will be received."

"Your Honor, we've taken the liberty of putting the pages of the transcript on some large boards for the benefit of the jury. May we use them?"

"Certainly."

"And I'd like to read the testimony of Penn Rogaine about his qualification to give engineering testimony and compare it to his transcript, if I am permitted."

"Certainly," the judge said again.

Barry took an easel and placed it before the jury. He held several pages of the transcript in his hand. He faced the jury. "On direct examination by Mr. Merriman Mr. Rogaine gave the following testimony: 'I started college at Indiana University in Bloomington, Indiana majoring in engineering. I went there for two years and transferred to the University of California in Los Angeles, more commonly referred to as UCLA, where I got a degree in design engineering in 1958.'"

He placed the board with the blow up of third page of exhibit 14 on the easel. "You can see," Mr. Smart said, "from the transcript the first discrepancy in his testimony is that he only attended one year at Indiana, and he could not major in anything that year."

Barry put the first page of the transcript on the easel. "From the transcript you can plainly see," Mr. Smart said, "that Mr. Rogaine's degree from UCLA wasn't an engineering degree, but a degree from the Theater and Art Department, and it wasn't a degree in engineering design but rather a degree in acting and production with a minor in art, not engineering design. The only thing that is true about what Rogaine told you is that his degree was in 1958."

Barry continued on in this fashion, reading Rogaine's testimony and having Mr. Smart compare it to his actual transcript showing that Rogaine lied when he testified that he took a course in basic mechanical engineer and ethics at Indiana, when he said that he was an engineering major at UCLA, and when he said that all his courses at UCLA were engineering courses. In fact his transcript showed that he only took one engineering course at Indiana. That was basic engineering, and he got a D in it. Whereas at UCLA the transcript shows that at the beginning of his second year he started concentrating on engineering with a secondary interest in acting. When he got Cs and Ds in the engineering courses, he shifted to motion pictures, acting and production courses where he got As and mostly Bs.

When Barry finished with the blowups and Rogaine's transcript, he looked up at the judge. "No further questions, your Honor?"

The judge looked down at Mr. Merriman and saw that he was engaged in what appeared to be a heated conversation with Amy. "Mr. Merriman, it's you turn to examine the witness."

Merriman continued talking to Amy.

"Mr. Merriman, do you wish to examine the witness?" the judge said loudly.

Startled, Merriman looked up at the judge. "Ah, ah, no, your Honor."

The judge turned to Smart. "Thank you Mr. Smart, your excused." He looked down at Barry. "Call your next witness."

Barry stood and addressed the judge. "At this time, your Honor, defendant moves to strike the testimony of Penn Rogaine, as he obviously is not qualified to give opinion testimony in this case."

Merriman started to rise, when the judge motioned him to remain seated. "I'll take your motion under advisement and allow arguments out of the presence of the jury at a later time. Call your next witness."

Barry remained standing and looked back. "Defendant Monarch calls Sidney Notice."

A short heavy-set man with black hair, showing a tint of gray, wearing glasses, and dressed in a blue sports jacket, a white shirt, red and blue tie, and gray slacks walked forward and took the oath. He carried a thin folder. He was sworn and sat in the witness chair.

"Please state you name, residence and occupation," Barry said, still standing.

Notice turned to face the jury. "My name is Sidney Notice. I live in a suburb of Chicago, and I am employed by Monarch Motors."

"What do you do at Monarch?"

"I'm a design engineer. I was the chief designer of the 1970 pickup."

"Where did you take your training?"

"I studied engineering at the University of Detroit. I have a bachelor's degree in mechanical engineering and a master's degree in automotive design."

"What has been you working history?"

"I started after the war at Ford Motor Company as a tool and die worker in their Mercury Plant. Ford offered me the opportunity to go to college at night. After seven years I received my bachelor's degree and was transferred to the vehicle engineering department. I continued my education at night and two years later I got my master's degree. That's when I moved to Chicago and went to work for Monarch."

Barry sat down. "Mr. Notice, did you have anything to do with the design of the 1970 Monarch pickup's hood and particularly the hood locking mechanism?"

"Yes, I was in charge of it."

"We've heard testimony in this case about a locking mechanism that has to two stage lock, do you recall that?"

"Yes, but we didn't design our locking mechanism that way."

"Why not?"

"We design our mechanism to lock tightly when the hood is depressed. If the hood is depressed, the mechanism will lock tightly, and it will not come up unless the operator releases it with the lever in the pickup's cab. We tried a two stage locking device, but found that it had the tendency of misleading the person closing the hood. He could only latch the hood in the first stage, and think he had the hood locked, when in fact he did not. We felt the simple one stage lock was safer and would not allow only a partial engagement."

"Mr. Notice, did you inspect the pickup vehicle that is the subject of this case?"

"Yes, I did twice, the first time on October twenty-second last year and again on May tenth this year. Both inspections were in Mr. Chang's garage."

"What was the VIN number of that vehicle?"

Notice opened the folder he had and looked inside. "The VIN number is XVW4657224."

"What did your second inspection reveal?"

"We scratched the surface at various parts of the vehicle to see how many times that surface had been painted and what colors."

"What did you discover?"

"When we scratched the fender we saw three coats of paint. There was the black on top, and two underneath. The bottom one was the primer coat and the next one was green. We learned that the pickup's color was originally green, so what we found we expected. When we made a scratch on the hood, we got a different result. The bottom coat was still the primer coat, but the coat of paint under the black this time was red. That meant to us that someone had replaced the original hood with a red one. Of course, the hood was very damaged, so damaged that we were not able to tell whether he red one was a Monarch hood or from some other source."

"Mr. Notice, did you check into what it takes to obtain a safety engineering license in California?"

"Yes, all you have to do is fill out an application and pay a fee. There is no education or testing requirement."

"Thank you, Mr. Notice." Barry looked at Merriman and said, "You may examine."

Merriman stood. "Mr. Notice, you've been in the courtroom in the back of the room for this whole trial, is that not a fact?"

"Yes, sir."

"And you heard Mr. Chang's testimony, and I guess you don't agree with him, is that your testimony?"

"I don't think a two stage lock is a safe as a one stage lock."

"But you will agree that Mr. Chang is an independent engineer, won't you?"

"If you mean by that that he's not employed by Monarch, I guess you're right."

"Yes, but you are. As a matter of fact you are being paid by Monarch while your testify here in this court, aren't you?"

"I guess you could say that."

"Well, your on Monarch's payroll and are here at Monarch request, aren't you."

"Yes."

"Nothing further, your Honor."

The judge looked at Notice. "You're excused, Mr. Notice. We'll take the morning recess. Be back and ready to resume in twenty minutes."

After the judge and jury had left the courtroom, Amy grabbed Merriman's shoulder. "I want to talk privately with you," she said sternly.

Merriman turned and faced her. "Let's go down the hall to the lawyer's room."

They left the courtroom, Sorrento pushing Amy in the wheelchair, and entered the lawyer's room.

Merriman closed the door and stood facing Amy with his back to the closed door. "What's on you mind?" he said.

She stared at him angrily. "I'll tell you what's on my mind. I want out of this case. You said we were alright because of Rogaine's theory. Now we know that he's a Charlton and had no business giving engineering testimony. I'm not a lawyer, but it doesn't take a lawyer to see the gaping holes in my case. You relied on a liar and a phony, and they've both been exposed. I've had enough."

"I can't let you quit now," Merriman calmly said.

Her blue eyes riveted at his face. "You can't do anything about it because you're fired." She turned, looked up at Sorrento. "Take me back to the courtroom. I want to tell Denny that I want this case dismissed." Sorrento opened the door and wheeled Amy back to the courtroom. She told Wilson that she had fired Merriman.

"You fired Merriman?" Wilson said in shock.

"Yes, but I don't expect you to continue. I want you to dismiss the case," she said coolly. She explained why.

"I understand, but let me talk to O'Shea," Wilson conceded.

"All right, but I won't allow you to continue."

30

WILSON FOUND BARRY outside talking to Matcheck and Notice. He walked up to Barry. "I need to talk with you."

Barry turned to him. "I'm tied up with these two right now. Won't it wait until the noon break?"

"No, we only have about ten minutes until court reconvenes, and I need to discuss something with you."

Barry turned to Matcheck and Notice. "Why don't you two go inside?" He turned to Wilson. "Let's talk outside."

Matcheck and Notice went inside the courtroom, and Barry and Wilson went down stairs and outside in the back of the courthouse.

"My client is mad as hell, and she wants us to dismiss the case," Wilson said.

"I could tell something was troubling her on Friday afternoon when Lewis and the insurance adjuster testified," Barry said, "and I sensed it got worse when we showed Rogaine to be a phony."

"Well, she wants to quit and won't be talked out of it. In fact she's fired Merriman."

"Does she know that I won't go for it now that we're in out case, unless the dismissal is with prejudice? I also want Richards and her company involved so they are barred from continuing their subrogation claims."

"I told her I wanted to talk to you first because I thought you might want some conditions. Let me talk to her and Richards. But first, we'd better go see the judge, fill him in and see if he'll postpone the case until after lunch."

"Let's go."

Barry and Wilson went back into the courthouse and back upstairs to the courtroom. They went to the clerk and told her that they wanted to see the judge.

The clerk went into the judge's chambers, and then came back out. "The judge will see you now in his chambers. Please come this way."

They entered the judge's chambers.

The judge looked up from behind his desk. "You want to see me?"

Wilson stood before the judge. "Yes, your Honor. My client has a proposal to make to the defendants and she wants to make before the case continues. We request that you recess until this afternoon, so we can have discussions."

"I take it that the discussions could lead to a conclusion of this case?"

"I believe so, your Honor."

"All right. Be back to resume this case, if necessary, at one-thirty."

The lawyers went back into court. Wilson sat down next to Amy. Barry sat with Matcheck and Notice, where Barry explained what Mrs. Ralston wanted to do and what he told Wilson had to happen if she wanted out.

Wilson told Amy what Barry wanted. "Basically, he won't allow you to give up unless you agree to be barred from ever suing his client again on this matter. He further wants the same agreement from Monica Richards on behalf of her employer."

"That's fine with me," said Amy. "What's Miss Richards got to do with it?"

"She's been our silent partner in this case, because she hired Merriman to recover what she paid you."

"I still don't see how she affects my desire to quit."

"Well, before I answer whether she can, let's see what her position is. If you agree with the dismissal and she agrees to drop her right of subrogation, it will be moot."

"Then go talk to her, but I still want out of this case now."

Wilson turned and looked back at the spectator section. He didn't see Richards. He turned back to Amy. "I'll go find her."

"What about the court?" Amy asked.

"That's why we went to see the judge to ask him to recess until this afternoon. We don't have to be back until one-thirty."

"Willie and I will remain here. We'll get some lunch in the courthouse lunch room downstairs."

Wilson finally found Richards in Merriman's suite at the motel.

When he knocked at the door, Merriman answered after several minutes. "I thought you'd be in court," Merriman said tucking his shirt into his pants.

Wilson pushed the door open and saw Richards scrambling with her cloths in his bedroom. "I've been trying to get this case dismissed as Amy demands, but the defendants won't agree to allow it unless Monica also goes along." He looked at the open bedroom door. "And I see I finally found her."

Merriman was pushed back by the front door, despite his size, and staggered into the living room. "What the hell does Monica have to do with it," he said angrily. "Amy fired me, so you're on your own. Richard hired me, not you."

By this time Monica Richards came into the living room with her blouse still hanging down over her short skirt. "I heard you,

Denny. Why am I a part of this? As I heard, Amy wanted out. That's her decision. I'm not a part of it."

Wilson glared at her. "Oh come on now, Monica. You've been in the court and heard the testimony Friday afternoon and this morning. I'm really not a trial lawyer, but even I understand that O'Shea's got us where he wants us. Even the great Merriman can't bail this case out of the problems you two have caused, and Amy's smart enough to see that. Your subrogation case went out the window with Winchester and Rogaine. And O'Shea won't go along with her motion to dismiss at this stage unless your company drops that subrogation claim."

Richards looked at Merriman.

"I have to say he's right," Merriman sheepishly said. "This case's a looser, and your's is even worse. If Amy dismisses and the court makes the dismissal with prejudice, you won't be able to use the loan receipt to bring your case in Amy's name. You'll have to bring in the company's name. Even then you're probably dead, because your right rises no higher that the Ralstons' and they're barred by the dismissal. You better give up as well."

Richards frowned and shook her head. "If that's what the great Merriman says, it looks like I put up a lot of money to finance this case and got fucked. I say the literally, as well as figuratively. And even then what I got was some sex with a wimp who often couldn't get his dick up more than once. Go ahead, Denny, tell Amy I'll go along." She went back in the bedroom and slammed the door.

When the court reconvened at one-thirty, the judge took the bench without the jury in the courtroom. He looked out at the lawyers. "Do you have anything to tell me?"

Wilson stood. "Yes, your Honor. At this time the plaintiffs move the court for an order dismissing this case with prejudice and with costs to the defendants. Furthermore, the Western Indemnity Company, the Ralstons' automobile insurance company, through the representative, Monica Richards, who is now seated at counsel table, agrees to be bound by that dismissal order. Is that not the case, Miss Richards?"

Richards stood beside Wilson. "Yes, your Honor, we agree to be bound by your order," she quietly said.

The judge looked down at the lawyers and parties. "Miss Richards I know you normally must speak louder than that, but I heard you. The motion is granted. Mr. O'Shea will prepare the order." He looked at the clerk. "Now, bring in the jury."

When the jury was seated, the judge looked down at them. "Ladies and gentlemen of the jury, the plaintiffs have voluntarily dismissed this case, so it will not be necessary for you to deliberate and reach a verdict. Therefore, you're excused, and this court is in recess."

On Saturday morning, April fifth, 1975 the meeting room in the basement of the Hilton Hotel in Portland was packed. The Oregon Trial Lawyers held their Annual Meeting, and Wayne Merriman headed a panel of several well-know lawyers. New approaches to product liability headed the list of panel subjects.

After introducing the panel, the moderator turned to Merriman. "Let's start with Wayne Merriman. Wayne, you tried a case out here last year involving a novel and emerging theory. Explain the theory and how you handled it."

Merriman, as usual, presented an imposing appearance, tall, well-built man with his blonde wavy hair, tan complexion, heavy eyebrows and his deep glistening blue eye. He wore his usual single-breasted leather jacket over a white shirt with western lapels over the pockets and a string tie, faded jeans and cowboy boots. He sat with his large arms resting in front of him, looked out at the large audience and spoke in a deep clear voice. "Thank you, Oliver I'd be happy to."

He then explained the Ralston accident with special emphasis on the Caravan van, saying almost nothing about the pickup other than its hood flew up for some unexplained reason, causing the driver to be blinded and to drive on the opposite side of the road. "The left front of the pickup drove into the left front of the Caravan at about fifty miles per hour. The flat design of the Caravan front allowed the pickup to penetrate through the driver's seat and into the rear seat behind him. Mr. Ralston, then a thirty year old accountant, died instantly in this collision as did his seven year old son, who was sitting behind him and found under the left front wheel of the pickup."

He settled his elbows on the table in front of him and joined his large hands under his chin. "My leaned partner, Alex Savage, convinced me that we had a claim against WCI, the maker of the Caravan under a 'second collision' theory. As he explained it to me, while the Caravan didn't cause the collision, its design caused the deaths of Mr. Ralston and his son, as well as injuries to his wife and two other children. It was not designed with protection of the vehicles passenger's in mind. That made the Caravan defective and unreasonable, so we filed suit on behalf of the Ralston family against manufacturer for product liability."

He pulled his arms back. "The viability of this theory received a test before the judge at an early hearing in the case. Alex convinced the learned judge that the theory, while somewhat novel at the time, made sense, and he allowed it to stand. Aggressive discovery followed, where we discovered that the defendant had crash test before the vehicle's date of manufacture that showed that the driver would not survive this type of accident. Engineers at WCI questioned the reasonableness of making the vehicle the way it was made, but their questions went unheeded."

He stood and went to an easel behind him and turned to the audience. "Just before trial we had a settlement conference with the defendant's attorney and representatives of the manufacturer and its excess insurer.

At that conference I explained our position aggressively as follows." Then he replayed his presentation using the white paper mounted on the easel. "In the end the defendant settled, paying three million in cash and a structure over forty years worth twenty-one million more. So you see, the theory, if properly presented and followed by aggressive discovery, proved to be very lucrative."

Following the presentations by the other panel members, the moderator opened the discussion up for questions from the audience.

A woman stood seven rows back and went to a microphone in the aisle. "I have a question for Mr. Merriman. But first let me explain what I've been told about that case. I understand that after that settlement, Mr. Merriman, representing Mrs. Ralston, proceeded to trial in Astoria against the manufacturer of the pickup, Monarch Motors." She explained that his theory against Monarch was that its pickup was defectively in that its hood could fly up and not allow the driver to see ahead. She told the audience that rather than to investigate the history of the pickup, he presented a witness who lied about a previous accident involving the pickup. She explained that he also presented an expert witness, without checking his qualification, to prove a defect, but the expert lied about his qualifications. The so-called expert presented himself as a graduate engineer, when in fact he graduated from the Art Department of UCLA in motion pictures. The so-called expert also lied about his work experience for companies involved in design, when in fact most of his experience involved acting. She told them that an embarrassed Mrs. Ralston demanded that Merriman dismiss the case when these things were exposed. When he didn't, she fired him. "Is that a correct summary of the rest of the case you told the audience about?"

Merriman started at the woman. Then exhibiting a wry smile he spoke in a slow deep voice. "What you heard is an assertion, not necessarily a statement of facts. I didn't come here to engage in a quarrel," he paused. "So I won't."

The End